Fatal Fixer-Upper

"A great whodunit . . . Fans will enjoy this fine cozy."
—*Midwest Book Review*

"Smartly blends investigative drama, sexual tension, and romantic comedy elements, and marks the start of what looks like an outstanding series of Avery Baker cases."
—*The Nashville City Paper*

"Polished writing and well-paced story. I was hooked on *Fatal Fixer-Upper* from page one."   —*Cozy Library*

"An ingeniously plotted murder mystery with several prime suspects and a nail-biting conclusion."   —*The Tennessean*

"A strong debut mystery . . . Do-it-yourselfers will find much to enjoy."
—*The Mystery Reader*

"Extremely entertaining . . . Home-renovation and design tips are skillfully worked into the story, the characters are developed and sympathetic, and the setting is charming. The climax leads to a bang-up ending in which the intelligent heroine has to either save herself or lose all . . . A first-rate mystery and a frightening surprise ending."
—*Romantic Times*

PLASTER
and POISON

JENNIE BENTLEY

BERKLEY PRIME CRIME, NEW YORK

THE BERKLEY PUBLISHING GROUP
Published by the Penguin Group
Penguin Group (USA) Inc.
375 Hudson Street, New York, New York 10014, USA
Penguin Group (Canada), 90 Eglinton Avenue East, Suite 700, Toronto, Ontario M4P 2Y3, Canada
(a division of Pearson Penguin Canada Inc.)
Penguin Books Ltd., 80 Strand, London WC2R 0RL, England
Penguin Group Ireland, 25 St. Stephen's Green, Dublin 2, Ireland (a division of Penguin Books Ltd.)
Penguin Group (Australia), 250 Camberwell Road, Camberwell, Victoria 3124, Australia
(a division of Pearson Australia Group Pty. Ltd.)
Penguin Books India Pvt. Ltd., 11 Community Centre, Panchsheel Park, New Delhi—110 017, India
Penguin Group (NZ), 67 Apollo Drive, Rosedale, North Shore 0632, New Zealand
(a division of Pearson New Zealand Ltd.)
Penguin Books (South Africa) (Pty.) Ltd., 24 Sturdee Avenue, Rosebank, Johannesburg 2196,
South Africa

Penguin Books Ltd., Registered Offices: 80 Strand, London WC2R 0RL, England

This is a work of fiction. Names, characters, places, and incidents either are the product of the author's imagination or are used fictitiously, and any resemblance to actual persons, living or dead, business establishments, events, or locales is entirely coincidental. The publisher does not have any control over and does not assume any responsibility for author or third-party websites or their content.

PUBLISHER'S NOTE: Neither the publisher nor the author is engaged in rendering professional advice or services to the individual reader. The ideas, projects, and suggestions contained in this book are not intended as a substitute for consulting with a professional. Neither the author nor the publisher shall be liable or responsible for any loss or damage allegedly arising from any information or suggestion in this book.

PLASTER AND POISON

A Berkley Prime Crime Book / published by arrangement with the author

PRINTING HISTORY
Berkley Prime Crime mass-market edition / March 2010

Copyright © 2010 by Penguin Group (USA) Inc.
Cover illustration by Jennifer Taylor.
Cover design by Rita Frangie.
Interior text design by Laura K. Corless.

ISBN: 978-0-425-23345-0

BERKLEY® PRIME CRIME
Berkley Prime Crime Books are published by The Berkley Publishing Group,
a division of Penguin Group (USA) Inc.,
375 Hudson Street, New York, New York 10014.
BERKLEY® PRIME CRIME and the PRIME CRIME logo are trademarks of Penguin Group (USA) Inc.

PRINTED IN THE UNITED STATES OF AMERICA

10 9 8 7 6 5 4 3 2 1

— Acknowledgments —

As always, there are lots of people who had a part in bringing this book into the world, and who deserve my eternal thanks, hugs, and kisses:

My editor, Jessica Wade, for letting me continue the journey with Avery and Derek, and my agent, Stephany Evans, for continuing the journey with me.

Artist Jennifer Taylor for another gorgeous cover, and cover designer Rita Frangie and interior designer Laura Corless for another gorgeous book, inside and out.

My publicists, Megan Swartz with the Penguin Group (USA) Inc., and Tom Robinson with Author and Book Media, for getting the word out.

My critique partners, Jamie Livingston-Dierks and Myra McEntire, for help, support, encouragement, friendship, and hot chocolate.

All the other writers it's been my pleasure to know and associate with over the past four years; by now there are too many of you to mention individually, but you know who you are!

Emily Layne Thompson, for donating your name—and money!—for a good cause. I hope you approve of what I've done with it.

Gordon Smith, for help in navigating the ins and outs of the U.S. Navy during World War I.

Everyone who read *Fatal Fixer-Upper* and *Spackled and Spooked* and liked them; especially those of you who said so, to me or someone else!

My friends and family near and far, especially my husband and my two boys. You put up with my crazy schedule, my frequent absences, my weird brand of mothering, and my total lack of the clean gene, and by doing so, you let me be who I am. I love you!

Finally, the late William Avery Ellis of Chandler, Texas, who joined the U.S. Navy on June 3, 1917, and who died of strychnine poisoning—still on the navy base in Dallas—three days later. I took some liberties with your story, since I have no idea what happened to you beyond those few facts, but you inspired the history mystery in *Plaster and Poison*, and for that I am grateful. RIP.

—1—

Wayne's sudden attack of modesty came at a great time, at least where Derek and I were concerned.

It was the first week of November, and we had just finished renovating our latest project, a midcentury ranch on the outskirts of Waterfield. Now we were waiting for someone to buy it so we could find another fixer-upper and do the whole thing over again. Derek had his eye on a run-down 1783 center-chimney Colonial on an island off the coast, accessible only by boat, but until we got our money out of the house on Becklea Drive, another purchase wasn't in the cards for us. It was unfortunate, since Derek was twitching with impatience to get started. I was more sanguine about the matter, since I didn't really want to spend the winter freezing my butt off on an island off the coast of Maine with nothing but 225-year-old walls between me and the elements. I wasn't opposed to buying and renovating the place—in fact, it might be fun—but I wanted to do it four months from now, when the days were longer and the temperatures higher.

"That's fine," Derek said, "but what are we going to do

in the meantime? I don't want your mom to get here in December and find me sitting on the sofa watching TV and scratching my stomach. It wouldn't make a very good first impression."

Considering that the stomach in question was a lovely example of smooth skin and taut muscle, I didn't think my mother would mind too much. However, I shrugged apologetically, knowing that what I was about to suggest would annoy him.

"You could take on some handyman jobs. I know you don't want to do those anymore, but it would keep you busy over the winter, until we could start working on the house on the island, and it would help to pay the bills. People are always asking you to do things for them."

"That's true," Derek said grudgingly, although he obviously felt that after spending the summer and autumn renovating houses of our own, laying tile in other people's bathrooms and painting other people's walls would be a waste of his considerable talent. I had to agree, I just didn't know what else to suggest.

At this point, I had lived in Waterfield for five months, since I inherited my great-aunt Inga's house in June. Derek Ellis was the handyman I'd hired to help me renovate the decrepit Victorian cottage. He'd done so, beautifully, and swept me off my feet at the same time. I was crazy about him—crazy enough to put my New York design career on hold to join Derek in his business, Waterfield Renovation & Restoration—and he seemed to like me well enough, too. I couldn't wait to show him off to my mom and stepfather when they came to Waterfield from California in a month's time.

"And I wouldn't worry too much about what my mom and Noel will think of you," I added. "After Philippe, anyone will be an improvement."

Philippe was my ex-boyfriend, the one I'd left behind in Manhattan when I moved to Maine. Derek had met him once and taken an instant dislike to him. So had my mother, who claimed that he was too good-looking and flirtatious to be trustworthy. She'd hit the nail squarely on the head, as it turned out. He wasn't trustworthy. But since he was history, that was all water under the bridge at this point.

"I'm not sure that's a point in my favor," Derek said.

I rolled my eyes. "Give me a break. You're handsome, you're nice, you're successful, you're a doctor, and you treat me a damned sight better than Philippe ever did. What's not to like?"

"I'm a retired doctor," Derek answered dryly. "I'm not always nice, and at the moment, I have no work. All I've got going for me is my looks, and you said yourself that your mom thought Phil was too good-looking. What if she says the same about me?"

"She won't."

He arched his brows in mock insult. "What? You're saying I'm not as good-looking as Phil?"

I inspected him across the table, with at least an attempt at impartiality. He's thirty-four years old, with sun-streaked hair in need of a cut and blue eyes with long lashes and crinkles at the corners. As I watched, a slow grin curved his cheeks and brought out a latent dimple. A faded denim shirt completed the picture; it matched his eyes and had the sleeves rolled up to the elbows to bare nicely muscled forearms with a dusting of fair hair. As usual, my stomach did a flip-flop, and I had to concentrate to keep my voice steady.

"It's not that you're not cute. But you've seen Philippe. Leather pants, satin shirt, ponytail . . . like he stepped off the cover of some kind of vampire romance. You're not flashy, thank God."

"God forbid," Derek answered piously, but not without a twinkle in his eyes. He leaned forward, causing a strand of sun-streaked hair to fall across his forehead, and gave me a melting smile. "So you think I'm cute, huh?"

I smiled, but before things could develop, there was a knock at the front door.

"Expecting someone?" Derek asked, straightening. I shook my head. "I'll go."

He pushed the chair back and headed for the door. I watched him walk away and thought that while he might not have Philippe's—Phil's—smarmy sex appeal, there was nothing wrong with either his looks or his ability to garner attention from the opposite gender. He'd have no problem charming my mother. He'd had no problem charming me, and I'd been deep into a hating-all-men phase when I met him, courtesy of Philippe Aubert.

Here's the thing: Derek's a genuinely nice guy, in addition to being nice-looking and charming. He's intelligent, funny, caring, capable, and very, very good with his hands. He's also an MD, although he doesn't practice medicine anymore. Mom had harrumphed a little when I mentioned that, but I thought that once she met him and saw how good he was at what he did, and how happy he was doing it—and how happy he made me—she'd agree he'd made the right choice.

I hoped.

Out in the hallway, I heard the front door close. "She's in the kitchen," Derek's voice said. I could hear his footsteps coming closer. A moment later, he ushered Caitlin McGillicutty into my presence.

Kate was my first friend when I came to Waterfield. I met her before I ever moved—she owns the Waterfield Inn, the B&B where I stayed my first night in town. After I learned that Aunt Inga was dead and I had inherited her rundown Second Empire Victorian cottage in need of a truly staggering amount of work. It was Kate who suggested that I renovate the house before selling it, and Kate who recommended that I hire Derek to help me. The two of them had dated a couple of times early on, just after Derek's ex-wife left him, but for whatever reason, the relationship hadn't worked out. No zing, or maybe Derek just wasn't ready to get involved again so soon. Kate started dating Wayne Rasmussen, Waterfield's chief of police, instead, and on New Year's Eve, the two of them would be married. But Derek was still single five years later, and maybe Kate thought it was time for him to move on. Or maybe not. Maybe I was just imagining that she'd thrown us together on purpose.

I wasn't imagining the pout on her face, though, nor the way she flung herself down on the kitchen chair. It creaked, and I gave it a worried glance, concerned that it might be thinking of giving out and dumping her on the floor. Kate is a statuesque woman: a tall Jane Russell type, with an enviably curvaceous figure. She has a mass of copper curls framing her face, which is freckled, open, and friendly, with a wide smile and hazel eyes. The smile was not in evidence at the moment, and the eyes were a flat, muddy brown.

"What's the matter?" I asked, a little diffidently, since I would prefer not to have my head bitten off.

"Wayne," Kate snarled.

Derek grinned. "Cold feet?" he inquired, pulling a third chair around and straddling it.

Kate turned to him. Or maybe *on* him would be more accurate. "Him or me?"

I shook my head at Derek, who grinned unrepentantly.

"What did he do, Kate?" I asked. "You're not serious, are you?"

"About the cold feet?" She scowled at her hands. "No one could blame me if I was, but I guess not. Not really. The timing is just super-inconvenient. Eight weeks before the wedding, seven weeks before Christmas, and with everything that goes into running a business at the best of times—why the hell the idiot couldn't have said something before, when the problem would have been easier to fix . . . !"

She grabbed one of the napkins from lunch and started systematically shredding it all over the enamel surface of the table.

"'The idiot' being Wayne?" Derek inquired.

Kate nodded.

"What problem?" I asked.

Kate looked up. "The problem of where to live."

I wrinkled my brows. I hadn't realized that there was

even a question about it. The chief of police shared a condo with his son Josh, a Barnham College student, on the north side of town. Kate, of course, lived in the B&B. It was a huge house, three thousand square feet or more, with four guestrooms. Kate and her daughter Shannon, also a Barnham College student and Josh's best friend, had two bedrooms on the first floor and took their meals in the B&B kitchen. When Wayne slept over, he did so in Kate's room. Since there was plenty of space, I had assumed that when they got married, Wayne would be moving in. So, obviously, had Kate.

"He's never mentioned it before," she said, "so it never crossed my mind that he might be uncomfortable with so many other people around. And I've been living there for six years, so it doesn't bother me. I'm not sure it ever did."

Derek grinned. "But when you're on your own, you're probably not in the habit of making enough noise to wake the guests."

"It isn't that," Kate said, but she blushed.

"Sure."

Kate insisted. "No, really. A couple of weeks ago he came over to spend the night. Late, after I'd gone to bed. The night when that hit-and-run driver killed Carolyn Tate, remember? The accountant at Clovercroft?"

Clovercroft is a building development. It belongs to Raymond and Randall Stenham, owners of Stenham Construction and relatives of mine on my mother's side of the family. They're Derek's age, and they made his formative years a living hell. More recently, Melissa James, Derek's ex-wife, decided to hook up with Ray Stenham, adding insult to injury.

I abhor Melissa. I don't like the Stenham twins either, having had my own run-ins with them growing up. I hadn't crossed paths with Carolyn Tate during my time in Waterfield, though. Until the accident, I hadn't known she existed. Afterward, I knew her only as a name in the paper.

Apparently, she had been one of the Stenhams' accountants, keeping one of their projects on track financially,

and she had been on her way home from babysitting for
her daughter late one night when she had gotten into a
car accident on a lonely stretch of road on the outskirts
of Waterfield, near Barnham College. It was late and the
roads were slick, and she had been spun off the road and
into a rock wall. The driver of the other car had fled the
scene, leaving Carolyn there, and she had died. Speculation was that maybe the hit-and-run driver had been a college student, possibly someone driving under the influence,
but no charges had ever been filed against anyone, and the
last I heard, Wayne had no idea who was responsible. It
was like the driver had just vanished into thin air. Wayne
and Brandon Thomas, his young deputy, had turned the
college campus inside out looking for damaged vehicles,
and they had talked to all the auto body shops as far away
as Portland in hopes that they could track down the culprit that way, but so far they'd had no luck. Meanwhile, we
were all looking sideways at one another, wondering if our
next-door neighbor or the teenager down the street might
be culpable.

Anyway, the accident had taken place two or three
weeks before this, and from what I understood, it had been
nasty. I focused as Kate continued her story.

"When Wayne arrived at the B&B, he caught a couple
of the guests in the kitchen. They'd snuck down for a post-
midnight snack. Of course, they were frightened out of
their minds when a cop in full uniform—gun, handcuffs,
bloodstains, and all—came through the door at one A.M."

Derek chuckled, and I giggled at the image she
painted.

Kate continued, "He explained the situation, and they
scuttled back to bed, but when they came down to breakfast the next morning and saw that Wayne was still there,
it made him feel uncomfortable that they knew he'd spent
the night."

"*We* know he spends the night," I pointed out.

"But you're not there to see it," Kate answered. "Or
hear it."

"Hah!" Derek crowed. "I told you that's what it was!"

Kate shrugged. "Yeah, well, can you blame him? The chief of police, providing entertainment for all my guests? They're not all from away, you know. Some are local, and Wayne feels it undermines his authority when they see him in his boxer shorts in the middle of the night coming from the bathroom."

"I can see why it might," I admitted, hiding a smile.

Derek didn't even try. "No kidding, Kate."

Kate shrugged, pouting.

"So what does he want you to do about it?" I wanted to know.

The wedding was scheduled for New Year's Eve, and I didn't think either of them wanted to cancel. They seemed totally committed to one another and to getting married. Wayne had his apartment, of course, where he could continue to live after they were married, but Kate needed to be on-site to run the B&B. If she had any plans of getting rid of the business, I sure hadn't heard about it.

"That's just it," Kate said, starting to brush shreds of napkin into a pile on the table in front of her. "There's only one thing I can do, really."

I blinked, disconcerted. "You're not going to sell the B&B, are you? Wayne wouldn't ask that, would he?"

Derek, who knows her better than I do, shook his head at me. "Don't worry, Avery. She's playing us. Enough with the guilt, Kate. What do you need?"

Kate glanced at him from under her lashes. When she saw the look on his face, she must have realized that further prevarication was futile. She grimaced. "I need you to renovate the carriage house for me."

Derek nodded; obviously this didn't surprise him. "Uh-huh."

"What carriage house?" I said.

Kate turned to me. "The one at the back of my property. Tall, pointed roof, double doors, little cupola on top?"

"Right. I remember you telling me you were planning to turn it into an apartment and move out there when Shannon leaves the nest. You want to do it now instead? And be finished by New Year's? Can that even be done?"

I glanced at Derek, who shrugged.

"I know it's a lot to ask," Kate said. "And I won't even be able to help much, with Thanksgiving coming up, and planning the wedding, and guests coming in. . . ."

"Did my mom and Noel call you?" I veered off topic. "They said they would."

"They're booked the second week of December. Two solid weeks of rent for the suite, and they wouldn't even let me give them a discount. Your mom's husband must be loaded."

"He seems to do OK," I said, although I knew that Noel was, in fact, a lot better off than merely OK. "I'm glad you've got it all worked out. And they won't be bothering you much, I don't think. They'll spend most of their time with us."

"They'll spend most of their time with *you*, you mean," Derek corrected.

I turned to him. "What do you mean? Where will you be? Don't you want to meet my mother?"

"I'll be renovating Kate's carriage house," Derek said. "If it has to be finished by the wedding, it's going to be a more than full-time job between now and then. Two months isn't a long time to build a house from scratch, and that's what it's going to be like."

"So you won't be able to spend any time with my mom? But that's the whole reason she's coming."

"Of course he'll be able to spend time with your mother, Avery," Kate said, shooting Derek a look. "This way, you and your mom will have lots of quality time together, just the two of you—shopping in Portland, going through your aunt's attic, sightseeing maybe—while Derek's slaving away, and then at night, you can all get together for dinner and your mom can get to know him."

"But won't you need my help?"

I wasn't entirely sure what disappointed me more, the fact that my mom wouldn't be able to spend as much time with Derek as I'd hoped, or the fact that he was going to be renovating a house without me.

"I'd love to have your help, Tinkerbell," Derek said. "But I don't want to take you away from your mom. You haven't seen her for more than a year. And there'll be plenty of time for you to help me before she gets here. By the time she and Noel show up, you may be so sick of home renovation—and of me—that you'll be glad for a chance to duck out for a while."

"So you'll do it?" Kate asked.

I looked at Derek. He nodded.

"I believe we will," I said.

—2—

I'd never actually been inside Kate's carriage house before.
I'd seen it, of course, squatting at the back of her property, painted a pretty butter yellow like the main house,
but I'd never wandered close. Kate kept her lawn mower
and tiller and aerator and other gardening stuff in it—and
I was quite pleased with myself for knowing the names of
those tools, since before I came to Waterfield, my biggest
exposure to flora had been a potted ficus in my Manhattan
apartment. But since I don't know enough to operate any of
them, there had never been a reason for me to go inside the
carriage house. Now I looked around the dark and chilly
interior with horror.

"You've got to be kidding!"

"Why?" Derek said. It was later that same afternoon,
and he was standing next to me as we had our first look at
our new project. I looked up at him, my eyes wild.

"We can't do this!"

He glanced down. "Why not?"

I waved my hands, indicating the roughly four hundred square feet, story-and-a-half-tall room with cobwebs

dangling from the rafters and a dirt floor. My breath made a cloud in front of me when I spoke; it was several degrees colder in here than outside, and outside wasn't precisely warm. "There's nothing here. No floor, no windows, nothing. I can see daylight through the exterior walls!"

"It's a carriage house," Derek said. "There was no need to insulate it. Cold doesn't bother machinery."

"But Kate and Wayne can't live here!"

"Of course not," Derek agreed. "We'll replace the rotted wood on the exterior and give it a new roof, frame and insulate the walls, run some electrical lines and plumbing before we drywall, put up some interior walls, or maybe it would be better to leave it open, give it more of a loft look. . . ."

He trailed off, looking around, his eyes a soft, dreamy blue.

"It's gonna be awful," I said, stamping my feet and wrapping my arms around myself, imagining driving nails and soldering pipes in this cold. Derek turned to me, his eyes warming.

"It'll be fun. The other houses we've renovated needed mostly cosmetic updating. This"—he glanced around—"this is a blank slate; it needs everything, even walls and floors. The good thing is, we can do anything we want."

He turned back to his vision.

"So long as it's what Kate wants," I reminded him.

"Well, yeah. Sure. But within reason." He put an arm around my shoulders. "You probably took some basic architecture classes in design school, right? How would you set this up? Where do you see the kitchen? Or the bathroom? What sort of style do you see?"

He pulled me into the warmth of his body. I snuggled closer and looked around, doing my best to look past the cobwebs, the cracks in the walls, the dirt floor, and the dirty beams overhead. Picturing gleaming hardwood and sleek furniture, granite counters, and stainless steel appliances.

"It's kind of small," I said after a moment, "and Kate's used to having a lot of space. It's going to be difficult to fit everything in."

Derek nodded. "I see it as being very open," he offered, "with one room flowing into the next."

"But the building's kind of tall—one and a half stories, at least, wouldn't you say?—so maybe we could expand upward? Make the kitchen and living room down here, with maybe a half bath? For guests, you know? And then we could add an upstairs, with a master suite."

"Kate might need some sort of office, too. For the B&B business. Unless she wants to keep that in the main house. Maybe that would make more sense."

"We should ask her," I said.

He let his arm drop from around my shoulders. "You go ahead inside. I'm going to take some measurements while I'm here." He pulled a one-hundred-foot measuring tape off his belt.

"I'll help," I said, reaching for the loose end. Instead of putting it in my hand, Derek grabbed me around the wrist and pulled me to him.

"C'mere, Tink."

"I'm already here," I pointed out, my hands against his chest as I shook my hair out of my face. Often, I keep it piled on top of my head; today, it just happened to be down, warming my ears.

"So you are." He smiled down, both arms wrapping around my waist now. "You're on board with this, right? You think we can do it?"

"Of course we can," I said robustly. When he held me and looked at me with those beautiful blue eyes, and said "we" . . . I believed we could do anything.

"And it'll be fun, don't you think?"

"I'm sure it will."

I wasn't quite as definite this time. This project was a whole lot bigger than any other we'd tackled. I knew my way around a paintbrush and a stud finder—no pun intended—but framing and insulating were as yet foreign concepts to me. The two houses we'd renovated so far, Aunt Inga's Victorian cottage and the midcentury ranch on Becklea Drive, had been in pretty good shape, everything considered. We had torn out carpets (and carpet pads and tacking strips and staples) and Derek had refinished the floors (because he said the sander would run away with me), and we'd painted and tiled and installed new kitchen cabinets and counters and toilets and sinks . . . but most of what we'd had to do had been cosmetic. Surface gloss. We'd never had to do any bona fide construction.

Or I should say that *I* hadn't; obviously the idea didn't bother Derek. He seemed perfectly at ease about the whole thing. I wasn't. That is to say, I was confident in his ability to do it, but I was less confident in my ability to help him.

"Am I going to be able to do anything at all, Derek?" I asked rather pitifully, my cheek against his chest. "You're the one who knows how to frame, and drywall, and install plumbing pipes and electrical wires. . . . I don't know how to do any of those things. I'm just the decorator."

His arms tightened. "You're not just the decorator, Avery. You help with the other things, too. And that's just grunt work, anyway. Anyone can learn how to drive nails and weld pipes. All it takes is practice."

"But I feel useless," I murmured. He shook me and then held me out at arm's length, hands on my shoulders and eyes serious on mine.

"You're not useless. What you do is important. I may be able to install a hell of a p-trap, but if you don't come in after me and make the bathroom look pretty, it's not enough. Don't sell yourself short, Avery."

He let me go with a last squeeze. "I'm going to take measurements now, while you go talk to Kate and discuss what she wants from her new house. Go over what we talked about and make sure it works for her. Wayne's getting older; he may not want to climb stairs to get to his bedroom. Especially if he has to carry Kate. She's no lightweight." He smiled.

"Wayne's forty-six," I said, stepping back. "That's hardly at death's door. But I'll make sure a second-story master suite is OK with her. She'll know what Wayne would say."

Derek nodded. "Then, once we have the measurements and the particulars, you'll design the layout of the new house. Where to put the kitchen, where to put the bathroom, where to put the tub and the sink and the stove and the fridge. I'll figure out where the electrical wiring and the plumbing lines have to go. While I frame and insulate and do all the rest of the boring stuff, you and Kate get to pick out all those pretty things, like tile and countertops and cabinets and light fixtures. The construction won't take more than a few weeks, and then we'll start putting those things in. You'll be helping with that."

Maybe I'd overreacted a little when I thought that Derek wouldn't need me.

"Go on, Avery." He dropped a kiss on my forehead before turning me toward the double doors to the outside. "I don't need help measuring. Go talk to Kate and get us the rest of the information we need to get started. It'll take both of us working almost around the clock to get finished on time."

He swatted me on the butt to send me on my way. I shot him a glare over my shoulder, but when I saw the grin on his face, I refrained from comment.

•   •   •

Kate was in her kitchen, sitting at the computer tucked into a corner of the big room, talking on the phone. To the florist. About the flowers for the wedding. I leaned against the counter and waited for her to finish, listening with half an ear as she discussed baby's breath and sterling silver roses and fronds.

When Derek came on board to help me renovate Aunt Inga's house, he had insisted that I keep the old kitchen cabinets. Over my strenuous objections, I might add. I'd seen Kate's kitchen by then, which Derek had also renovated, and it galled me that she had been able to convince him to let her install brand-new cabinets and a slate floor, while I had to settle for Aunt Inga's existing cabinets and her stained and pitted hardwood flooring.

I understood better now, aside from having come to love my kitchen and to realize that Derek was right. When Kate bought the B&B—long before it was a B&B—the lovely three-story Queen Anne had been used as rental property for years. It had been chopped up into apartments: There had been, as Kate had told me once, three electric meters and three separate kitchens, all of them rinky-dink and ugly, installed sometime in the 1970s with the cheapest materials available at the time. None of the kitchens were salvageable or, indeed, contained anything worth saving. Kate, with Derek's help—or vice versa—had torn all three of them out and built this one from the ground up. The only reason everything here was brand spanking new was because there had been nothing worth saving in the others. Had there been something to save, I had no doubt Derek would have tried to save it.

The end result was lovely. The kitchen was sleek and modern, with dark wood cabinets, granite counters, stainless steel appliances—double ovens, of course, and a warmer, and some other frills suitable for a gourmet cook, or a professional one—and over in the corner by the windows overlooking the backyard, a built-in computer desk and filing cabinets.

"I love your kitchen," I said when she'd hung up the phone.

Kate smiled, swiveling her office chair around to face me. "I do, too."

"Do you want the same kind of kitchen in the carriage house?"

She pondered for a second. "Something lighter, I think. White cabinets. Since it'll be smaller."

I nodded, snagging a piece of copy paper and a pen off the desk to take notes.

"Derek and I were discussing how to set things up." I ran through our various thoughts on the subject and secured Kate's wholehearted approval to the idea of expanding upward.

"Wayne's not so old that he has a problem with stairs,"

she said, "and I'm still on the right side of forty. By a comfortable margin. Stairs are not an issue."

"So a master suite upstairs is OK." I made a note on my borrowed piece of paper. "Tub, shower, or both? Separately or together? Derek wants me to design the place—decide where everything goes—and then he'll figure out how to make it work. Do you have any other requirements or requests? Do you want to keep your office here, or do you want me to leave space for another office out back?"

Kate pursed her lips as she thought. "I think," she said eventually, "that we should leave the office here, in the main house. I'll be here most of the time anyway, during the day. And that way, the carriage house can be more of a retreat. Somewhere we go after the day is over."

I nodded, scribbling madly. This seemed a good thought, one I should make note of, and it also gave me some frame of reference for how to arrange and, more important, decorate the carriage house once we got to the point of adding the pretty touches. Kate lived in a B&B, a gorgeous, gracious place where her job was to make sure that other people had a lovely, relaxing time. But Kate herself was probably not in a position to enjoy it much; she was too busy catering to everyone else's needs. Within the carriage house, maybe she could have the same thing. A retreat for herself, just across the yard, yet private and secluded and romantic. Somewhere she and Wayne could close the door and leave the rest of their lives—Kate's occasionally squabbling guests, the frequently unpleasant aspects of Wayne's job—outside for a few hours.

"Not that there's much in my life I need to get away from, really," Kate continued pensively. "Running a B&B isn't a hardship."

"Sometimes you must wish for some privacy, though. Or wish that you didn't always have people in your space."

"I don't always have people in my space," Kate said. "In the winter, there are fewer guests. And when I don't have guests, I worry about being able to pay the bills."

I glanced at her. She wasn't in financial straits, was

she? Between the wedding and the economy, it wouldn't be surprising if things were pinching a little. None of my business, though. "Well, even if you don't think you need a retreat, maybe Wayne will enjoy having somewhere to go, where he can forget about police work for a few hours."

"It's not like being chief of police for Waterfield is such a high-stress job, you know."

"Hey," I said, "you've had four murders in the five months I've lived here. Five if you count Carolyn Tate's death. Seems like a pretty high incidence to me for a town as small as this one."

"I guess that's true," Kate admitted.

"What's Wayne planning to do with the condo, by the way?"

"I think Josh is planning to stay there," Kate said. "Shannon's talking about moving in."

I blinked. "To the apartment? With Josh? That's . . ." I hesitated, before settling for, "interesting."

Kate's lips crimped. "That's one way to put it. She says that once Wayne and I are married, that will make her and Josh brother and sister—or stepbrother and stepsister— and it'll be OK for them to share an apartment."

"But doesn't she realize that Josh is in love with her?"

"I don't see how she can't realize it," Kate said judiciously, "but who knows?"

"Huh." I thought for a moment. "How is she doing? I haven't seen her for a while."

Kate shrugged, albeit not without a tiny wrinkle between her brows. "She's OK, I guess. I haven't seen her much myself the past couple of weeks. She's been sleeping over with Paige Thompson a lot."

"New boyfriend?"

"She hasn't said anything," Kate said. After a moment she added, "Something's going on, though. Just a couple of weeks ago, she was all excited about the wedding and the honeymoon and everything. Now, I can hardly get her to answer the phone when I call."

I hesitated. "You don't think it has anything to do with

the Carolyn Tate hit-and-run, do you? The accident was a couple of weeks ago, too, and Wayne and Brandon thought that someone from the college might have been involved."

"She wouldn't keep something like that from me," Kate said. "Plus, she doesn't have a car. I guess I'll just have to sit her down and have a talk with her. If I can catch her."

I nodded. "So are you going to let her move in with Josh? If that's what she wants to do?"

"There's not a lot I can do to stop her," Kate answered, albeit grudgingly. "She's an adult; legally she can do whatever she wants."

"That's true."

"And Josh is a big boy. He can take care of himself. If he wants to tell Shannon how he feels, he'll do it. When he's ready."

That was also true.

"And in the meantime, she's probably safer with Josh than she'd be with anyone else. I'd prefer for her to stay here, in her old room, where I can keep an eye on her, but if she moves out, I guess I can turn both the downstairs bedrooms into guestrooms. And Josh'll take care of her, and make sure she doesn't do anything stupid."

Like getting pregnant at eighteen, the way her mother had done, I knew Kate was thinking.

"Shannon's a smart girl," I said, "I don't think you have to worry about her doing anything dumb."

"For a smart girl," Kate countered, "she's being remarkably obtuse about Josh."

I shrugged. Not much I could say to that.

—3—

The month of November went by in a blur. I spent a day or two with pen and paper and a computer program I hunted up, redesigning the carriage house into a romantic retreat for two. It would have a nice, open feeling downstairs, with living room, dining room, and kitchen all flowing into one another, and with a half bath and a laundry closet off in a corner. A second corner would have a staircase to the loft, where there would be a nice, big bedroom and a fabulous master bath. And because the newlyweds would be honeymooning in Paris, I thought making the place look like a Parisian apartment might be fun.

The French city style is very distinct and not too difficult to copy. The floors would be hardwood; it would be no problem to stain them dark. The ceilings would be high, and there was lots of natural light coming in through the big windows Derek would have to cut in the walls. (The tiller and aerator hadn't needed windows. Kate and Wayne did.) We could put a bistro table and two elegant chairs in the dining area; that was all Wayne and Kate would need out here. If they wanted to have a party, they'd set the tables in the B&B instead. The dining room in the main house could seat fifteen or twenty comfortably. This kitchen was for intimate breakfasts and suppers for just the two of them.

The fireplace would be elegant, with a white mantel and maybe some black marble. I could imagine sconces with black silk shades above it, and a matching light fixture above the bistro table. The upstairs bathroom would have a crystal chandelier, I decided, and maybe a black-and-white tiled floor. White fixtures, of course, with maybe some framed silhouettes on the walls.

And the bedroom . . . that would be black and white, too. Maybe some toile on the walls; the kind of black and white wallpaper that looks like old fabric, with scenes of women washing clothes or children playing with small dogs or tending chickens. Or French vanilla paint with love poetry stenciled around the wall. In French. A big white bed with lots of pillows. And—I squinted into space, trying to picture it—a padded headboard? Or why not a whole padded wall? The wall behind the bed. Vinyl or velvet, maybe: something unexpected. That way I could knock myself out on making a cool headboard out of something else. Sheer curtains on the windows, blowing in the breeze. Some kind of funky tiebacks. Black-and-white photographs in black frames, of Wayne and Kate on their Parisian honeymoon. I'd have to tell them to go crazy with the camera . . . give me lots of shots to choose from . . .

Once Kate approved the plans, we got busy. Derek went to work roofing and rewiring, while I drove the truck all over down east Maine, scoping out cabinet fronts and kitchen counters, tiles and carpet colors. I've always loved hardwood floors, but now that I lived in Maine—and was getting my first taste of a Maine winter—I could understand why Kate had requested fluffy carpeting for the loft. Not only would it help to muffle footsteps, but it would be nice for her to curl her toes into when it was freezing outside.

I was having fun, but I couldn't help waiting for the other

shoe to drop. The other two times Derek and I had renovated houses together, bad things had started happening
pretty much right away. In Aunt Inga's house, someone had
broken in and smashed things, as well as tampered with
the cellar stairs so I fell and banged myself up. In the house
on Becklea Drive, there had been unexplained footsteps
and screams, and rumors of ghosts, and then someone had
tampered with the brakes on the car so I'd had an accident.
Here, nothing happened. Work progressed with no snags
or snafus other than the ones that go with the territory.
We came to work every morning to find the place looking exactly like we had left it the night before. The truck
performed magnificently, and no one threatened us with
bodily harm or financial ruin if we didn't stop renovations
immediately. The most exciting thing that happened was
that Derek discovered a heart carved in one of the posts
inside the carriage house, with two sets of initials inside it,
and they didn't belong to anyone we knew.

All this didn't stop worry from gnawing at me, though.
Shannon still spent most of her time away from the B&B,
and I didn't see her at all. When I asked Kate, she said she
hadn't had a chance to talk to her daughter about whatever
might be going on in Shannon's life. And Kate seemed to
have troubles of her own. I felt like I could see her turning
thinner and paler in front of my eyes, but she kept telling
me that everything was fine and that nothing was wrong,
and there wasn't anything I could do but accept it.

For a while I wondered if maybe she and Wayne were
getting cold feet as the wedding drew nearer. He was gone
a lot, too, and I hardly ever saw the two of them together
anymore. But then I realized that he was just pushing himself day and night to try to figure out who might have killed
Carolyn Tate. He and Brandon were both becoming more
and more exasperated and angry as time went by. They
turned Barnham College over a second time, and kept
hounding every auto shop owner between Bar Harbor and
Portland, including Derek's friends the Cortinos, but with
no luck. No car was found, and no arrests were made.

Pretty soon it was Thanksgiving, and Derek was persuaded to stop working to spend the holiday with Dr. Ben and Cora.

Benjamin Ellis is Waterfield's GP as well as Derek's dad, and Cora is his second wife. Derek adores his stepmother—the feeling is mutual—and he loves his dad dearly, although he feels horrible about disappointing his father with his career choice. From where I'm standing, Dr. Ben doesn't seem to be holding a grudge, but Derek still feels that he should have known, before going through four years of medical school and four years of residency, that he wouldn't be happy being a doctor. I don't know how he could have, really, without trying it first, but that's what he says.

Alice and Beatrice, Cora's daughters from her first marriage, had driven up from Boston for the occasion, so the Ellises had a full house. This was the first time I'd met Derek's stepsisters. Alice turned out to be very much like Cora: plump and motherly, with soft, brown hair and dimples, outgoing and friendly. Beatrice was a few years younger, still under thirty, and too thin to have dimples, but she had the same brown hair, grown long and pulled back from her face by a barrette. Her face was pretty enough, if a little plain and pale without makeup, and she struck me as quiet and very intelligent.

Beatrice came alone, while Alice brought her husband Lon, a big teddy bear of a guy with a full beard, and both of their kids. Lon ended up in front of the TV with Derek and Dr. Ben, while I ended up in the kitchen with the other women, helping with preparations for the feast.

It was nice, but kind of different, being part of a family. I'm an only child, and my mother grew up in Maine and my dad in the Boston area, but they settled in New York, so it was usually just the three of us for Christmas and holidays. After dad died, it was just Mom and me. Spending the day with more people was interesting. Especially when they started talking about things I wasn't sure were any of my business.

"Where's Steve?" Alice wanted to know, knife flashing as she chopped pecans for the pie. "Didn't he want to spend Thanksgiving with us?"

"I didn't ask him," Beatrice said.

"Oh, no." Cora looked up from the piecrust to examine her younger daughter. "Did you and Steve have a fight, Bea?"

"Steve doesn't fight," Beatrice said. "Steve isn't around enough to fight."

Cora and Alice exchanged a glance. Beatrice didn't notice; her eyes were fastened on the aluminum foil she was wrapping carefully around the exposed parts of the turkey.

"You did tell him you were driving up here, didn't you?" Cora asked.

"I haven't seen him lately," Beatrice muttered.

"Really? What's he been doing?"

"The same thing he's always doing. Working." She put the bird back in and slammed the oven door with unnecessary force.

"On Thanksgiving?" I blurted. And then I bit my lip when everyone looked at me. "Sorry. But even Derek takes holidays off."

Beatrice shrugged as if it didn't matter, but her eyes gave her away: They were shiny with moisture.

"So you decided to drive up for dinner on your own?" Cora asked gently.

"I've got two suitcases in the car," Beatrice answered, blinking the tears away. Her voice hardened. "If I can't stay here, I'll go to a hotel. And charge it to Steve's American Express card. He can afford it."

She sniffed. Cora, Alice, and I looked at each other.

"Of course you can stay here, Bea," Cora said. "You know that. You don't even have to ask."

Beatrice nodded. After a beat, when I think we all tried to come up with an innocuous subject, we started talking about shopping and Christmas gifts and other things of interest to four women stuck in a kitchen cooking Thanksgiving dinner. A few minutes later, the children came and wanted grandma for something, and then dinner was ready and we joined the men around the dining room table. Nothing more was said about Steve and Beatrice that night. However, as I was walking home with Derek later in the evening, I asked, "Did you ever meet Beatrice's husband Steve?"

The evening was clear and cold, with the smell of snow in the air, but so far we hadn't seen any of the white stuff. I shivered in the open-toed platform wedges I had put on in an attempt to gain a few inches of height. It's only a couple of blocks between the Ellis house and Aunt Inga's, but I wished I'd asked Derek to bring the truck tonight, instead of agreeing blithely that a walk home after dinner would be nice to help offset the sleep-inducing properties of tryptophan.

He glanced down at me. "Once or twice. They've been together for years. Why?"

"Apparently they broke up. Beatrice arrived in Waterfield with a couple of suitcases this afternoon. She'll be staying a while."

"Oh." He thought for a second. "Well, I'm not surprised."

"Is he not a nice person?"

Derek shrugged inside his warm winter coat. "He's nice enough. Or was, when she met him. Law student. Harvard."

"Exalted stuff."

"Beatrice is a wiz, too. Numbers. Frighteningly smart. And they seemed happy the first couple of years they were together, while they were both in school and struggling to get by. Nothing like a little adversity to bring people together. But then he landed this job with a big, important law firm in Boston a couple of years ago, and he's been getting more and more consumed with it. Sometimes he doesn't come home at all. She has everything he thinks she wants: great house in a great location, time, and money enough to go anywhere and do anything . . . but he's never there to share it with her."

"He's not—you know—cheating, is he?" So I'm a little paranoid. Sue me.

Derek shook his head. "Not the type. Just a workaholic."

"And they don't have any kids, either?"

"He's not home enough to make any. And when he's there, he's too tired."

I blinked. "She told you this?" They were honorary siblings, and he had once been a doctor, but still, it didn't seem like something Beatrice would be talking to her step-brother about.

"She mentioned it to Cora," Derek explained. "Six months ago or so. I happened to overhear."

"I see. Well, apparently he decided to work on Thanksgiving, and Beatrice decided she'd had enough. So she came home to Waterfield."

Derek nodded. "Guess we'll wait and see how long it takes him to notice that she's gone. Should be interesting. If I had any money to wager, I'd say at least a week."

"No deal," I answered. "I don't have any money to wager, either; plus, I don't know him."

The road from the Ellises' house to Aunt Inga's went past Kate's B&B.

"Do you think we'll be able to finish the carriage house by New Year's?" I changed the subject. Or would the sky open and dump three feet of snow on us, closing down renovations until spring?

"I don't see why not," Derek answered. "The new roof is on and the framing is done. The plumbing and electric are laid. Tomorrow I'll start insulating and hanging drywall, and after that, we can run the HVAC. It'll be nice and toasty in there by next week." He grinned.

"Sounds good." I grinned back. "Anything interesting turn up lately?"

"In the carriage house? Not since the initials on the post. I showed you those, didn't I?"

I nodded. He had discovered a heart with initials inside

it carved on one of the posts holding up the roof. There were half a dozen of them spread throughout the inside of the carriage house, and we'd been trying to figure out what to do with them when we added the loft. Some would have to be built into a bearing wall holding the floor of the loft up, but some we might be able to remove. Kate had gotten excited about the initials, though, and talked about leaving them, or doing something else with them, rather than chop the post down. Derek, who is always eager to preserve something original, was all for it, and the two of them had been postulating—no pun intended—incorporating the post into a freestanding fireplace or something.

"What were they, again?"

"The initials? W-E plus E-R, and a heart."

"I wonder if Kate ever figured out who WE and ER were."

It could have been anyone at any time in the past hundred years or so since the place was built, or so it seemed to me. But Kate was excited about the find and was probably hoping that it would have some kind of connection to the B&B and the family that used to live there.

"I don't think she's had time," Derek said. "She's been busy with her Thanksgiving dinner stuff and the preparations for the wedding. Maybe you should look into it for her. There's a few days until I need you for anything specific."

"I guess I could do that," I agreed.

"It won't hurt you to stop in at the Historical Society for a few minutes, anyway, to see if they have any information about the family that used to own Kate's house."

"How do you know that it was someone from the family who used to own Kate's house? It could have been anyone in town, couldn't it? A couple of kids looking for a private spot to make out, or something." I waited a second before asking, innocently, "You're sure it was a W and not a D, aren't you?"

DE, for Derek Ellis . . .

Derek grinned down at me. "If I'd carved my initials inside a heart in Kate's carriage house, I think I would remember, Tink. And I don't know any girls with the initials ER, anyway. Back in the days when I was inclined to carve my initials into walls, I was dating Jill Gers."

"Maybe it was a Rasmussen," I said. "You sure it wasn't WR? Wayne Rasmussen? And whatever his first wife's name was?"

"I'm sure," Derek said. "WE and ER. Although it could have been a Rasmussen, I guess. Another Rasmussen, just not Wayne. There have been Rasmussens in Waterfield for eons. Or a Ritter. The family that built Kate's house was the Ritters."

"Really?"

"I believe so. Kate bought the place from someone named Ritter, anyway. Some old lady who went to an old-folk's home afterward."

"What was her name?" We skirted the fence around the B&B and crossed the driveway. "Elizabeth? Erica? Maybe she was ER."

Derek shrugged. "You'd have to ask Kate. Or Miss Barnes at the Historical Society. I can't remember."

"I'll see if the Fraser House is open tomorrow," I promised.

The Fraser House historic home is where the Waterfield Historical Society is located. Miss Barnes is the docent. She's also Derek's old history teacher from high school. Like all women of a certain age—above three and still breathing—she adores him. I added, "Do you want to come?"

"I wish I could," Derek said, "but I think I'd better work on getting the carriage house insulated. They're forecasting snow this weekend."

"Great." I shivered. Derek grinned and put his arm around my shoulders.

Down at the corner, a pair of headlights appeared. A smoky gray car passed us, pulling to the curb across the road from the B&B. The passenger door opened, and a tall young woman in a dark coat and high heels got out. She exchanged a couple of words with the driver before hurrying across the street and up the driveway to the bed and breakfast, coat flapping around her calves. The car idled at the curb for a moment until she was safely around the corner, and then it glided off down the street. I caught a glimpse of the driver's profile, sporting what looked like a self-satisfied smirk, before the tinted glass window cut off my view.

"Who's that guy?" Derek wanted to know, squinting through the dark.

I shrugged. "No idea. Never seen him before in my life."

"That's all we need," Derek said. "Shannon sneaking around with some guy old enough to be her father."

"Those weren't Maine license plates. He's probably just someone's dad, up for the holiday. Maybe one of her friends was in the back seat." Maybe that was why she had been making herself scarce lately. There was a new boyfriend in the picture, and she was keeping him to herself.

"That's possible," Derek admitted, looking a little happier. "So you'll stop by the Historical Society tomorrow? To try to track down those initials?"

"I'll do my best. Anything to make Kate happy. After all, she's paying us." I smiled. Derek smiled back and squeezed my shoulders. We continued our walk toward Aunt Inga's house.

• • •

Miss Barnes is narrow-nosed and gray-haired and as dry as an old mummy, with pinched nostrils and sharp eyes. She's taller than me—the better to look down her nose—and always very properly dressed in a tweed skirt, twin set, and pearls, even in the middle of summer. Today, the mustard-colored sweater under the cardigan had a turtleneck and she had added a pair of thick, brown stockings inside her sensible shoes, but other than that, she looked the same as she had every other time I'd seen her.

"Miss Baker."

And of course she remembered me. The old bat had a mind like a steel trap.

"Hi, Miss Barnes," I said politely. "How are things?"

She smiled tightly, her eyes straying over my shoulder. "Are you alone today?"

"Derek's working on Kate McGillicutty's carriage house," I said.

Kate's B&B was only three or four blocks from the Fraser House, so Miss Barnes knew all about the renovations. The Historical Society had had to approve the changes, since Waterfield Village has one of those preservation overlays that dictate the ways in which one can and cannot modify the properties in the historic area. No one is allowed to tow in a double-wide trailer, for instance, and make it a permanent structure by taking off the wheels, just as no one is allowed to build one of those low-slung brick duplexes, or turn one of the existing houses into a multifamily home. And the Historical Society has final say on things like whether the color you want to paint your house is historically appropriate or the fence you're thinking of putting up is in keeping with the time period. We'd had to jump through hoops during the renovation of Aunt Inga's house.

Derek is on board with the whole preservation thing anyway, but sometimes, the stringent guidelines rub other people the wrong way. Like my cousins, the Stenhams. Before Aunt Inga died and made me her heir, they'd been all set to level her house and build a small community of condos and townhouses on the lot. When I inherited instead of them it all became moot, but I happened to know that they'd had to modify their building plans several times before the Historical Society would give them approval for the project. They may have had to grease some palms, too, to get it pushed through. It's the kind of thing they'd do. The Stenhams don't always play by the rules.

Miss Barnes nodded. "And how is the carriage house progressing?"

I removed my fuzzy, candy-striped gloves and stuck them in the pocket of my puffy, powder blue jacket. "As far as I know, just fine. I haven't been there a lot. Derek's been doing the heavy work while I've been running around

ordering kitchen cabinets and countertops and bathroom
fixtures and such."

"And what brings you here today, Miss Baker?"

"I'm looking for information on the family that used
to own the B&B." I unwound the loopy knit scarf from
around my neck and pulled down the zipper of the jacket.

"The Ritters?"

I nodded. The final step was plucking the warm hat off
my head and squashing it into the other jacket pocket. Winter's a drag.

"The first Lawrence Ritter built the house that belongs
to Miss McGillicutty," Miss Barnes said, rooting through
her old-fashioned file drawer. "He came here from New
York and married Anna Virginia Cabot. The Cabots were
one of the founding families of Waterfield. Anna Virginia
was the daughter of Captain John Cabot and his wife Mary.
She was born in the 1870s, and married Lawrence Ritter
in . . . let's see . . . 1895."

"Did they have any children?"

Miss Barnes nodded. "They had three: Lawrence Junior,
Frederick, and Agnes."

"No one with a name that starts with *e*?" I wanted to
find an ER and a WE.

"Not in that generation," Miss Barnes said. She brought
out a folder, which she placed on the counter. Down the
front of it ran a list of all the Ritters. Miss Barnes put her
finger on a name. "Lawrence Junior was the eldest, born
in 1896. He perished on August 27, 1918, when the *USS
SC-209* was sunk off the coast of Long Island."

"By German warships?"

"By friendly fire," Miss Barnes said. "The *SC-209* was a
submarine chaser. She was mistaken for a German U-boat
and shelled by the *USS Felix Taussig*, manned by the United
States Coast Guard. It was the only time a submarine chaser
was sunk by friendly fire in the Great War."

"Wow." It was quite a story.

"Lawrence Junior left a wife and a son," Miss Barnes
continued. "The boy's name was Lawrence, as well." She

moved her finger to stab another name. "Next we have
Frederick Ritter. Second son. Two years younger than
Lawrence. Enlisted in the army in 1917 and went to France.
Survived the war only to succumb to the influenza pan-
demic in late 1918. No children."

"I guess he didn't have time to have any." People got
married early in those days—Lawrence's wife couldn't
have been more than twenty-one or twenty-two when she
found herself a widow—and Frederick hadn't been more
than twenty-one, either, when he died.

"Likely not," Miss Barnes agreed. "Agnes was the young-
est of the Ritter children. She was born in 1902 and survived the war. She also survived the influenza pandemic
and went on to marry Philip Grant in 1924. They had
four children: Elizabeth, Katherine, Philip Junior, and
Charles."

"Elizabeth?" Here, finally, was an *e*.

"Elizabeth Grant," Miss Barnes nodded. "Born in 1929.
Married Frank Brown in 1952. Died in her bed at sixty-
nine. Cancer."

"Great." So Elizabeth wasn't ER after all; not if her
last name had been Grant and not Ritter. That left only
Lawrence's son carrying on the name. "What happened to
Lawrence Ritter? The third Lawrence. Junior's son. I guess
he was the one who took over the house?"

Miss Barnes nodded. "He was born in January 1919—
several months after his father perished—and he married
Helen Simmons in 1942, just before enlisting in the army
to fight in World War II."

"Did he survive?"

"He did. He came back in 1945 and went to Barnham
College on the GI Bill. He became a CPA, and lived in
what is now Miss McGillicutty's bed and breakfast until he
was killed in an auto accident in the early 1980s. I remember him well."

"Did he and . . . what was her name, Helen? Did they
have any children?"

Miss Barnes shook her head. "They were not so blessed.

Or maybe it was by choice. After Larry died, Helen converted the house into apartments. Back then, the Waterfield Historical Society didn't have regulations in place to prevent such a thing. Helen stayed in one of the apartments herself and rented the other two. That way, she could live for free. After Miss McGillicutty bought the house, Helen Ritter went to a place near Brunswick."

A "place" being a euphemism for an old-folks' home, I assumed. An assisted-living facility.

"Is she still alive?"

"We weren't close," Miss Barnes said, "but I haven't heard that she has passed, so I imagine so. She would be almost ninety years old by now. May I ask why you're inquiring?"

"Oh." I shrugged. "It's a matter of some initials carved in the carriage house wall. A WE and an ER. I'd like to know who they belonged to."

"I'm afraid I can't help you," Miss Barnes said. "None of Anna Virginia and Lawrence's children had a first name that started with an e, and the line died out with Larry and Helen. Although of course we have other families whose surnames begin with r in Waterfield. Rasmussen, Roberts, Rinehart . . ."

"And just as many that begin with e, I guess?"

She nodded. "In addition to the Ellises, there's the Edmonsons, the Elliotts, the Erskines, the Elys . . ."

"I get it. So WE could be almost anyone, and so could ER."

"I'm afraid so," Miss Barnes agreed. "Dr. Ellis's first wife was born Eleanor Roberts, and his father's Christian name was William. So was William's uncle's. William Ellis the elder died during World War I as well."

Another victim of the influenza pandemic, probably. Or someone else who got shot accidentally by his own side. I didn't even want to know.

"You can't think of any kind of combination of the two sets of initials, can you? Like, Derek's granddad, William Ellis, married someone named Elizabeth Rinehart?

Or Wayne's father, Eric Rasmussen, used to date Wendy Edmonson?"

"I'm afraid not, Miss Baker," Miss Barnes said. "Police Chief Rasmussen's father was called John, not Eric, and I don't think the Edmonson family ever had a girl named Wendy. And William Ellis Junior married Charlotte Bohannon. I'm sorry I can't be more help."

"That's OK," I said.

"If you like," Miss Barnes offered, "you can see the census records for the past one hundred years and go through them for combinations of those initials. It won't take more than a few hours."

"Really?" I checked the time. Nowhere near lunch yet. "Sure, I'll do that."

Miss Barnes dug out a stack of paperwork the size of a telephone book and shoved it across the desk toward me with a smile. "Enjoy yourself, Miss Baker."

"Thank you," I said, grabbing it. "I will."

—4—

"How did it go?" Derek wanted to know during dinner at the Waymouth Tavern that night. "Did you find WE and ER?"

I rolled my eyes. "Did I ever! I had no idea there were so many people in this town with names that start or started with those initials. Including your mother—Eleanor Roberts—and your grandfather, William Ellis."

"Paw-Paw Willie." Derek grinned. "You need to meet him sometime. If he ever makes it back up here."

"Back up from where?"

"Florida," Derek said. "He moved to Fort Lauderdale when he retired. Sick of the cold, he said."

"How old is he?"

Derek thought for a moment. "Dad's almost sixty, so I guess Paw-Paw Willie is over eighty-five. Closer to ninety, even. He's healthy as a horse, though. Practiced medicine up until just a few years ago, and plays golf and chess. He'll probably live to be a hundred."

"He must have been born after World War I, right?"

Derek nodded. "Early 1920s. My great-grandfather made it through in one piece, though. Why?"

I shrugged. "No reason. Miss Barnes was talking to me about the Great War earlier today. She knew a lot about it."

"She knows a lot about a lot of things," Derek said. "Retired history teacher, remember? And I think her mother was one of the first Yeomanettes."

"What are they?"

"Yeoman (F)s. Female yeomen. Yeowomen or yeomanettes. Miss Barnes can tell you more about them than I can, but I think I remember the basics."

"Go ahead."

"Well, during World War I, women were admitted to the navy for the first time. Not at the front, but in clerical positions at home. Some of them stayed with the navy for years afterwards. Miss Barnes's mother worked at the Portsmouth navy shipyard at Kittery, I think."

"Interesting."

"It must have been. But you had no luck tracking down WE or ER, huh?"

I grimaced. "Too many people with those initials. If I had some kind of idea when the initials were carved, it'd be easier, but it could have been any time in the past hundred and twenty years or so, since the carriage house was built."

"Actually," Derek said, "the carriage house wasn't built as early as the main house. The B&B is a Queen Anne. The carriage house wasn't built until ten or even twenty years later."

"Really? I wish you would have told me that. Maybe I can cut a half dozen people out of contention. That leaves just . . . oh . . . five hundred or so." I rolled my eyes.

Derek grinned. "Considering that the initials are carved in the side of the post facing the wall, the most logical time for someone to have carved them is when the carriage house was in the process of being built. Hard to get to that side of the post otherwise. If you can track down that date, it'll help you."

"I'll go back to the Historical Society tomorrow morning and see when the carriage house was built. And then maybe I can visit the newspaper archives, just in case."

"You do that," Derek said. "But in the meantime, are you finished?" He glanced at my plate.

"I can be. Why?"

"Got something I want to do."

"Really? What?"

He smiled.

I blushed.

•   •   •

We were on our way out of the restaurant—in a bit of a hurry to get home, I admit, after the exchange we'd just had—when I happened to glance into the corner and caught sight of someone familiar. Shannon McGillicutty is not the kind of girl who'll ever blend in, anywhere. Not only is she tall and gorgeous, but she has a head of long, mahogany hair that's absolutely unmistakable.

"Oh, look," I said impulsively, "there's Shannon . . ."

And then I bit my tongue, but it was too late.

"Where?" Derek stopped abruptly enough that I smacked into him.

I braced myself with a hand against his back, and then used it to give him a gentle push. "Never mind. Let's just go home."

Derek glanced down at me. "I'd love to believe that you're not willing to wait five minutes, but somehow I doubt that's the case. Who is she with?"

"Not sure," I said. It was the truth. I couldn't see the guy. But the mere fact that she was here, at a table for two, tucked away in the far corner of the restaurant behind a privacy screen of fake trees, was reason enough for concern.

"Let's take a look," Derek said, turning. I grabbed the back of his belt.

"You can't just barge up to them. If she's on a date, you'll embarrass her."

"If she's on a date with the geezer from yesterday," Derek said, "she'll thank me later."

He maneuvered us both to a spot where we could see Shannon's dinner companion without being seen. By our quarry, anyway, although some of the other diners were looking at us sideways.

"Same guy," Derek muttered.

I nodded. "Who is he?"

He shook his head. "Don't know him. Nobody local. And too old for her."

The man facing Shannon was Kate's age, seeing forty on the horizon, if not there already. Beyond that, he was a good-looking guy, in an aging rock-star, lived-hard-but-survived-to-tell-about-it sort of way. Dark hair, silvered at the temples, and just a little too long, framing a narrow face with dark eyes, a slightly protuberant nose, and grooved cheeks. Something about him looked familiar, although I didn't think I'd ever seen him before. Maybe it was just that he reminded me of Philippe. The slightly too long, dark hair, the cocky grin, that attitude of being master of the universe . . .

"I don't like him," Derek muttered.

I didn't like him, either. "It's none of our business, though. She's twenty. Technically, she's an adult. She can have dinner with anyone she wants."

Derek thought about that for a moment. "Damn," he said finally.

"I know. I don't like it either. But there's nothing we can do about it. Let's go, before they see us." I tugged on his belt.

But it was too late. Date guy had seen us staring and alerted Shannon, who turned in her chair. If I'd been wondering whether what was going on was innocent, all doubt melted away when I saw her face. Guilt bloomed in the color in her cheeks and in the panic in her eyes. She muttered a few words to her companion before getting up and coming toward us. By tacit agreement, we retreated far enough from the table that he wouldn't be able to overhear.

"What are you doing here?" Shannon wanted to know, her voice low but shrill. She kept shooting glances over her shoulder to her date. Maybe she was afraid he'd sneak out while she wasn't looking, leaving her with the bill. He looked the type.

"Shouldn't that be our question?" Derek retorted.

Shannon turned to him. "Please don't tell my mom."

"We should."

She looked from Derek to me and back, clutching her hands together. "I know what it looks like, but please trust me, OK? I'll tell her myself, I promise. Just . . . not yet."

"When?" Derek folded his arms across his chest and tried to look menacing. Not an easy task since he doesn't have a scary bone in his body. That's not to say that he can't fight, and fight dirty, when the situation demands it, but when it comes to intimidating women, he's woefully out of his element.

"Um . . ." Shannon was clearly casting about for an acceptable compromise.

"Look," I said, putting a hand on her arm and another on Derek's. "It's none of our business what you're doing. Just don't do anything stupid. And if you don't tell your mother about what's going on in the next couple of days, then chances are Derek will tell her for you. Just something to remember."

Shannon nodded, looking grateful. Derek didn't like the agreement I'd unilaterally offered, but he nodded, too. Grudgingly.

I didn't like it much myself, and if Shannon didn't come clean with Kate shortly, I thought I might just beat him to spilling the beans.

•   •   •

The next morning, I was back at the Fraser House, where Miss Barnes confirmed that Derek's assessment had been right: The carriage house had been built more than twenty years after the main house, in the spring of 1918.

"It's probably more of a garage than a carriage house, really," she offered. "By the late teens, the Ritters, being one of the wealthiest families in Waterfield, had probably invested in a car. I'm afraid that's all I can tell you, though. There was no historical overlay back then; the Ritters didn't have to secure permission to build or run the plans by anyone."

"And of course there's no way of knowing who worked on it?"

Miss Barnes shook her head. "My only suggestion is to check the newspaper archives, just in case they made a mention of it."

I nodded, said my thanks, and left.

Waterfield has two newspapers. The *Weekly* is the oldest, established in 1912. Three years later came the *Clarion*, which is a daily. Both are still going strong, but over time, the *Weekly*—being a weekly—has developed more of an emphasis on human interest stories and articles, while the Clarion is more focused on hard news.

Mrs. Graham, the *Clarion* receptionist cum keeper of the microfiche, is a sturdy woman in her middle years, with steel gray hair and glasses, and is extremely efficient. I told her what I wanted and soon found myself at the microfiche machine with a couple of boxes of microfiches. I loaded and started looking.

Since all I was doing was going through a couple of months' time during one particular spring, it didn't take long. The spring of 1918 was taken up with horrible news: Between the war and the influenza pandemic, people were dropping like flies. Speculation was that more than a million Greeks had been killed in the Greco-Turkish war, and the final battle of Flanders or Ypres, Battle of the Lys, was raging throughout the month of April. John Joseph "Black Jack" Pershing was commanding the First American Army in Europe, and in England, the Royal Air Force was formed. Closer to home, the *USS Cyclops* had disappeared without a trace in the Bermuda Triangle, and the 1918 baseball season

was under way. Babe Ruth defeated Philadelphia seven
to one on April fifteenth, making it his third consecutive
opening-day victory.

On the other hand, Lawrence and Anna Virginia Ritter's
new carriage house was a much smaller matter and didn't
rate a mention in the *Clarion*. I kept scrolling through
microfiche, all the way into June, without finding anything
relating to the Ritters or Kate's B&B, and I was just about
to give up and move across the street to the *Waterfield
Weekly* when a name caught my attention.

Local man done to death was the headline. The one-
paragraph article continued, *The United States Navy has
confirmed that a Waterfield man, William A. Ellis, died on
June 6th of this year, just days after joining the war effort.
Mr. Ellis, recently of Chandler Street, joined the Navy at
Elliott on June 3rd, and was accepted as a fireman, third
class. On the evening of June 6th, hours before ship-
ping out for service, Mr. Ellis consumed poison and died
instantly. The Navy is investigating the circumstances. Mr.
Ellis is survived by his mother, Mallessa Ellis of 34 Chandler Street, one brother, and two sisters.*

I sat back on my chair, gnawing on a fingernail. It's not
an attractive habit, and not one I indulge in often, so as
soon as I realized I was doing it, I took the thumb back out
of my mouth. But really, this was shocking.

This, I realized, must be the William Ellis that Miss
Barnes had told me about. The young man who had died in
World War I, whom Derek's Paw-Paw Willie was named
after. The address was the same as Dr. Ben and Cora's.
Derek's—I figured in my head—great-uncle? Or second
cousin twice removed?

Whatever. Miss Barnes had told me that William Ellis
the elder had died during World War I, but she hadn't told
me he'd been poisoned. Why on earth not?

Or maybe she didn't know it, I told myself. Maybe it
wasn't commonly known. Derek hadn't mentioned anything about it. Maybe one poisoning among so many other

casualties—of the war as well as the influenza pandemic—hadn't seemed worth making a fuss over. I wondered if they'd ever caught who did it. The rest of the microfiche I had didn't mention it, if so, and I'd requested another box, just to make sure. As I packed everything up, to give back to Miss Graham behind the counter, I wondered if I'd have better luck at the *Weekly*.

Just like the *Clarion*, the *Weekly* was rife with references to war and atrocity—and baseball—but no information about William Ellis. I did find the information about Kate's carriage house in the April seventeenth issue: a picture of the *Richtfest* or topping-out ceremony.

It was Lawrence Senior who called the ceremony by its German name, and then hastened to assure the reader that he was a proud second-generation American with no German sympathies whatsoever. He may perhaps have protested a little too much, but since that was neither here nor there at the moment, I don't suppose it mattered much.

The topping-out ceremony, or *Richtfest*, took place when the last beam was placed in the roof of the carriage house. The roof itself wasn't on yet, but the structure, or skeleton, of the building was finished. The tradition, the article explained, had long been an important component of timber-frame building in the Old World.

Briefly, what happens is that a small evergreen tree, symbolizing growth and held to bring good luck, is placed on the topmost beam of the new structure. A toast is drunk, and the owner often treats the workers to a meal. For obvious reasons, a topping-out ceremony often takes place at lunch; that way the laborers can get right back to work afterward. Since the ceremony doesn't actually celebrate a finished building, just a finished frame, there's always plenty left to do.

I found the custom fascinating. I'd never heard of it before, but since coming to Maine I had occasionally noticed a small evergreen tree decorated with flags and streamers perched on the top of a building under construction somewhere, where no evergreen tree had any business growing, and I'd wondered what it was doing there. Now I knew.

The picture that accompanied the article was grainy, black and white, and taken from a distance to get the entire building, including the pine tree on top, into the frame. Lined up in front were seven or eight workers in shirt-sleeves and suspenders, bareheaded, and squinting in the bright sun. Their faces were tiny, so it was impossible to see what any of them looked like, but there was a list of names under the picture. I skimmed it. Several men had last names I recognized. There was a Rasmussen; some ancestor of Wayne's, probably. And someone with a last name of Thomas, who might have been related to Brandon. There was a Stenham; certainly an early influence on Ray and Randy and their decision to start Stenham Construction. I didn't pay either of them much attention, though, because there was an Ellis.

Here he was again. William A. Ellis, who had been poisoned a couple months after posing for this picture. Small world.

Or maybe it wasn't that much of a coincidence after all. In a tiny town like Waterfield, smaller still almost a hundred years ago, it wasn't inconceivable—it wasn't even unlikely, really—that I should come across the same person twice. Still, it was interesting.

I counted miniscule heads and matched them to the names in the caption, until I thought I had managed to isolate William. Then I leaned in, until my nose almost touched the microfiche machine.

It was no use. His head was just a speck; I couldn't even tell if his hair had been dark or fair. I'd have to ask Derek if the family might have a picture of great-uncle/second-cousin-twice-removed William sitting around somewhere. There was no way around it; I was now invested in the man and what had happened to him.

There were six other people in the photo, standing at a

distance from the workers and closer to the camera. The
Ritter family: Lawrence Senior and Anna Virginia, their
son Lawrence Junior and his wife Emily, and then Frederick, and finally Agnes, who hadn't graduated to a long dress
yet, but who was wearing a girlish white shift that ended
just below her knees, over black stockings and ankle boots.
Lawrence Senior was portly, and had a big mustache—it
looked like a dark blot on his round face—while Lawrence
Junior and Frederick were taller and thinner, with dark
hair and what looked like pugnacious jaws. Emily was tall
and willowy in a flowery dress and big straw hat that shadowed her face, while Anna Virginia was shorter and stout,
with pale hair, either platinum blonde or white, piled on
top of her head. Agnes's was fastened with a big bow but
otherwise trailed down her back, and she was as dark as
her brothers. Her jaw looked a little stubborn, too.

All in all, they did not appear to be a friendly bunch.
Anna Virginia had the snooty demeanor of someone who
was born with a silver spoon in her mouth and who would
spit at anything less, while her husband looked fat-cat
prosperous and self-satisfied, with a heavy watch chain
bisecting his waistcoat. The young men both had that out-
thrust-jaw thing going, and Agnes just came across looking
spoiled and pouty. Emily was the only one who appeared
semifriendly, but maybe that was just because I couldn't
see her face clearly. She reminded me of someone, I realized. Something in her posture: the slightly rounded shoulders and head drawn in like a turtle's. She seemed to be
shrinking away from her husband's possessive arm around
her middle.

Was it possible, I asked myself, that the initials ER Derek
had found in the carriage house had belonged to Emily?

It hadn't crossed my mind to ask Miss Barnes what
Lawrence's wife's name had been, since I hadn't expected
the initials to belong to someone married, but now that
I'd seen her—and seen her husband—I couldn't help but
wonder. I mean, here was Emily, and here was William

Ellis—WE—and there was the carriage house, under construction, the perfect time to carve two sets of initials in a post, especially if you were one of the crew doing the construction in the first place. . . . It all seemed like too much of a coincidence to be coincidental.

—5—

"I have no idea," Derek said. "I've never heard of Emily Ritter. I didn't know that Paw-Paw Willie's uncle died from strychnine poisoning, either. I'm not sure Dad knows."

He was busy plastering the interior walls of the carriage house and merely glanced at me over his shoulder, as if the news was of no particular importance.

"But don't you think it's interesting?" I pushed.

"I'm sure it is. It doesn't mean that he was murdered, though, Avery. It could have been an accident. Or an overdose. They used small doses of strychnine as medicine back then."

I wrinkled my nose. "Really?"

"I'm afraid so. For heart and respiratory complaints." He smoothed his trowel over the wall and added, dryly, "It works; the only problem is that an effective dose is toxic."

"And that would kind of defeat the purpose."

"Exactly. Or it could have been self-administered, even."

"Suicide, you mean?"

"Right. If—say—he regretted joining the navy and

didn't want to be shipped out. Got scared. Maybe he gave himself a little dose of strychnine to induce vomiting and ensure he was left behind when the others boarded ship, but he took too much and accidentally killed himself instead."

"Or did it on purpose?"

Derek pursed his lips. "Maybe," he allowed after a minute, "but I wouldn't think so. Strychnine poisoning is a nasty way to go. I don't think anyone would choose it as a method of suicide. Not if they had any other options."

I watched him plaster for a moment before I asked, diffidently, "Did you ever see a case of strychnine poisoning while you were doing your medical school residency?"

His face turned grim, and the trowel stopped. "Once. I think it was in my second year. This guy came in, clutching his stomach. He was pale and clammy, sort of twitchy. Couldn't sit still. Incoherent. We did everything we could think of to figure out what was wrong with him. X-rays, ultrasounds, blood and urine tests . . . we were getting ready to slice him open when he went into respiratory failure. Turned out his wife had fed him strychnine."

"Yikes."

He nodded. "It wasn't pretty. Convulsions, muscle spasms, lockjaw . . . eventually the muscles tire and you can't breathe."

"Ugh." I shuddered.

Derek put his tools down and an arm around me. "Why are we talking about this, again?"

"We were discussing your great-uncle William," I said, leaning into him. He smelled like Ivory soap and lemon shampoo, with some paint thinner and sawdust thrown in for good measure.

"Right. Well, maybe death was such a common thing back then, after four years of war and with the influenza pandemic striking people down left and right, that William's death wasn't a big deal."

"Big enough that the newspaper had an article about it," I said. "I wonder who did it? If he was murdered, that is, and didn't do it to himself."

"Poison is a woman's weapon," Derek answered. "Or so they say."

"Right. But why? I mean, why couldn't a man equally well poison another man?"

"He could," Derek said, "and sometimes he does, but men like to hit things. Poison is a safe kind of weapon. You don't have to be there to set it off, you don't have to watch the victim die, and you don't need any particular strength or skill to use it. It's a great leveler. A smaller, weaker person can bring down a big, strong guy. All someone has to do is bake an arsenic cake or pour some cyanide into a bottle of wine, leave it sitting around for the victim to find, and voila, he's dying and they're miles away. Kind of like booby-trapping a basement staircase or puncturing the brake cables on someone's car."

Both of which I had experienced personally over the past six months.

"Right," I said, a little shivery at the thought. "Both of those things were done by men, though."

"That's true," Derek admitted.

"And he died on the navy base. Where there were mostly men."

"Some women, too. Remember the yeomanettes?"

I nodded. "A lot more men than women, though, Derek. And it would depend a little on how quickly the poison works, too. He joined the navy on the third. He died on the sixth. Could he have taken something before the third that didn't kill him until the sixth?"

"Not likely," Derek said. "There are poisons that can build up for a while before they kill you, but with strychnine, it takes a pretty massive dose all at once. It's possible it was given to him before he joined up, and he only consumed it three days later."

"Maybe."

Derek's voice softened as he sensed my disappointment. "I'm sorry, Avery. This may be one of those things we'll never learn the truth about. If he was my ancestor, and I don't know, I don't know who would."

"Can I still ask your dad sometime?"

"Sure. And if he doesn't know anything, we can try to call Paw-Paw Willie. But right now I need your help here, OK?"

"OK," I said, mentally relegating both the initials and the matter of William Ellis's maybe murder/accident/ suicide to the back burner for now.

The last few days of November sped by, and December started. Shannon continued to spend most of her time away from the B&B, although I'm not sure whether she was hanging out with Paige or with the new guy in her life, or whether she was just avoiding all of us.

Derek finished insulating the carriage house and cranked up the new HVAC system. We became toasty warm, even when the skies opened and dumped a foot of snow on Waterfield. Aunt Inga's house looked like a fairy-tale cottage, and Kate took Derek away from work for a half day to help her string lights all up and down the towers and turrets of the B&B.

The Waterfield Inn is a beautiful building. On one end there's a square tower, with a mansard roof topped by a widow's walk, while on the other side, there's a round tower with an onion dome, like the Kremlin. There's a bay window on the first floor, a wraparound porch, intricately carved gingerbread trim, tons of narrow, arched windows, and gables sticking out in every direction. A true Queen Anne, it boasts every Victorian excess imaginable. With Christmas lights strung along all the different angles of the roof, and along the porch, and over both towers, the B&B glittered against the night sky like something out of a Hollywood movie. Noel should be quite impressed when he and Mom showed up.

Speaking of people showing up, Steve didn't. Beatrice's husband, I mean. She settled into the guestroom in Cora and Dr. Ben's house and signed up with a temp agency out of Portland. As it happened, my cousins Ray and Randy Stenham needed someone to fill in for Carolyn Tate temporarily, and that's where Beatrice ended up, in the office at Clovercroft, one of the Stenhams' developments. Bea was seriously overqualified for the work they had her do and must have been bored out of her skull a lot of the time, but maybe she enjoyed having something to do again, after living a life of leisure for the past couple of years. And it was only for a few months, until Ray and Randy could hire someone permanently. Or until Steve got his act together and did something about the situation.

Inside the carriage house, work progressed. I learned how to lay hardwood floors—the real kind; Kate wouldn't stand for anything manufactured, and Derek would probably refuse to install it. After that, we put in the new kitchen cabinets. They were white, with frosted glass fronts, and looked gorgeous. And then we drove to pick up the marble counter Kate had wanted, only available in Portland, and unloaded it, with the help of Wayne, Josh, and Brandon Thomas, Wayne's young deputy, who had been drafted for the occasion.

"Did you ever have a chance to talk to Shannon?" I asked Kate as we stood in the driveway watching the men drag the slab of marble off the truck and through the carriage house door.

I was hoping she'd say yes, so I could avoid being a snitch. I liked Shannon, and didn't want to rat her out to her mother. But I liked Kate, too, and I knew she'd want to know what Shannon was up to. Shannon might be grown, but Kate was still her mother.

Kate shook her head. "She's still spending most of her time at Barnham. And I've been so busy lately that I haven't had time to pin her down." She was watching the men, her face scrunched up against the bright sun and a blue stocking cap on her head.

"Derek and I saw her a couple of times over Thanksgiving weekend," I offered.

"Did you?"

"She was here on Thanksgiving night, right?"

Kate nodded. "Paige had asked her to have dinner with

the Thompsons, and Shannon didn't feel she could say no. Paige and her dad have kind of a strained relationship, and Paige needed the moral support."

"I see," I said. "Paige's dad . . . what does he look like? What kind of car does he drive?"

Kate looked at me like I had lost my mind. "He looks like Paige. Short and fair, around fifty. And he doesn't have a car. Or a license. Wayne took it away after the second or third DUI. Why?"

"Derek and I saw Shannon get out of a gray Lexus on Thanksgiving night. Right across the street." I gestured over my shoulder with a gloved thumb. "It was around seven, I guess."

Kate nodded. "That's about when she got here. She said she'd had dinner with Paige and the Thompsons."

I shrugged. "Maybe the guy was an uncle or something."

"Maybe," Kate said.

"Except . . ."

She squinted at me. "Except what?"

I squirmed. "We saw them again the next night. At the Waymouth Tavern."

"You're kidding."

"Unfortunately not. Shannon begged us not to tell you that we'd seen her, that she'd tell you herself. But I guess she hasn't, has she?"

"Not a word," Kate said between her teeth. I watched as emotions chased one another across her face. Anger, worry, suspicion. "This guy she was with. What did he look like?"

I did my best to describe the man I'd only seen twice, both times at a distance. The dark hair, turning gray at the temples. The dark eyes and swarthy skin. The protuberant nose and thin cheeks. The nice clothes and expensive car with out-of-state license plates. The self-satisfied smirk. As I talked, I watched Kate's expression change from suspicion to dawning certainty, and her eyes turned narrow and flinty.

"Excuse me," she said while I was still in the middle of a sentence.

I stuttered to a stop and watched as she turned on her heel and stalked to the back door of the B&B. It slammed behind her with what was undoubtedly a very satisfying bang.

"What was that all about?" Derek wanted to know when he came up to me a minute later. "I saw you through the window. What were you talking about?"

"I told her about Shannon and the guy at the Waymouth Tavern. She wasn't happy."

"I'd say. She looked ready to chew nails. I've only seen her look like that once before, and that was when her dad called to let her know that her grandmother had died, and they'd had the funeral without inviting her. I don't envy the guy when she catches up with him."

I shook my head. "Me either. Excuse me." My cell phone had gone off. It was my mom, no doubt calling to tell me she and Noel had left for the airport. "Hi. Mom?"

"Hello, darling," my mom's voice answered, far away and staticky. "I just wanted to let you know we're on our way."

"Where are you calling from?"

She was sitting at the airport in Santa Barbara. "The flight out is delayed, of course. They always seem to be. But we'll be in Boston this evening."

"That's great!" I said enthusiastically.

"I don't think we'll be driving up to Waterfield tonight, though, Avery. It's a long flight, with a stopover in San Francisco on the way, and once we touch down, we'll be tired, and we still have to pick up a car."

"OK." It was hard to tell with the static, but her voice sounded strange. Still, it was a reasonable excuse. My mother isn't as young as she used to be, and Noel is older.

"We'll stay in a hotel near the airport tonight and go pay for the car in the morning, and then we'll be in Waterfield around lunchtime."

"OK," I said.

"I'll give Miss McGillicutty a call and tell her to expect us tomorrow instead of today."

"Do you want me to tell her?" I offered. I wouldn't mind an excuse to knock on the door and try to find out what was going on.

"That's OK, darling," Mom said, "I'll do it myself. I'll give you a call when we get in tonight, just so you know we got there all right."

I told her that would be great and hung up, worrying my lower lip.

"What?" Derek said. "Something wrong?"

I shook my head. "Nothing. There was just something weird in the way she talked about spending the night in Boston and picking up the car tomorrow morning instead. Something—I don't know—clandestine, almost. Or secretive."

"Maybe they're looking forward to some hanky-panky in a nice hotel room?" Derek suggested, hiding a smile. "They haven't been married very long, have they?"

"Oh." I flushed. Duh. "Yeah, maybe so."

"You hungry?"

I considered. "I could eat. You?"

"Always."

"You want to go grab some lunch?"

"Actually," Derek said, "I was hoping that you would go grab some lunch and bring it back here. I have a lot of work to do, since we spent most of the morning driving to Portland and back."

"What do you want? Lobster roll?"

Derek nodded. "And a Moxie."

"No problem." I made a face. Moxie soda is the official state beverage of Maine, and it is an acquired taste. Something like what you'd get if you added bitters to root beer or Campari to Coke. It's made from—among other things—wintergreen and gentian root. Incidentally, it was one of the first carbonated soft drinks mass-produced in the United States, all the way back in 1884.

He leaned in for a kiss. "See you later, Tink."
He swatted my butt and sent me on my way.

● ● ●

From Kate's B&B to the little hole-in-the-wall deli that
makes the best lobster rolls in Maine, I had to go down
Main Street, the main drag in Waterfield. It runs from the
harbor to the top of the hill, through the historic district, and
from there north to Augusta. The street is lined with Victorian commercial buildings, with storefronts and offices on
the first floor and storage or lofts above. Derek's apartment
is above the hardware store, and Waterfield Realty, where
Melissa James, his ex, is top producer, is just down the
street. The annual Victorian Christmas Celebration was
due to take place in another week and a half, and many
of the merchants were getting their storefronts ready. As I
passed Nickerson's Antiques, the owner, John, knocked on
the glass and spread his hands to show me his display.

I had met John a couple of months earlier, when Derek
and I were renovating the ranch on Becklea Drive. John's
store focuses mainly on what's called midcentury modern:
1950s, '60s, and '70s stuff. Teak furniture upholstered
with Naugahyde, shaggy wall hangings of giraffes and
zebras, pictures of big-eyed children in rags clutching kittens and puppies, lava lamps, and bucket chairs. He'd gone
with Elvis's "Blue Christmas" as a theme for the window:
There was an old-fashioned turntable on a teak stand, a
white tulip chair, an aluminum Christmas tree with blue
balls and white lights sitting on a fake sheepskin rug, gifts
wrapped in blue and white paper, and a stack of old LPs,
while a 1950s ball gown, with an impossibly tiny waist,
hung from a wall screen.

The display looked great, even if there was absolutely
nothing Victorian about it. I gave him an enthusiastic
thumbs-up and got a grin in return before I continued down
the sidewalk, thinking about the pale blue gown. It was
strapless, with a satin bodice embroidered in swirls and a
plain satin underskirt with a couple of layers of blue tulle

over the top. All it needed was a huge, black flower pinned at the waist, with some seriously sexy, strappy black shoes, black stockings, a black petticoat with a few really stiff layers peeking out from under the skirt, and a half dozen necklaces, and I'd be ready for New Year's Eve.

I was so involved in my plans for the dress—or one like it, in case I couldn't afford John's—that I didn't watch where I was going. As a result I walked right into someone coming in the opposite direction, loaded down with boxes and bags. Several of the bags scattered, and I babbled apologies as I started gathering them up.

"It's no problem," a familiar voice said. "They're Christmas gifts for the kids. Nothing breakable."

I looked up into a pair of blue eyes. "Oh. Hi, Jill. I didn't recognize you."

"You weren't looking at me," Jill Cortino said, with a grin. "You were staring into space and muttering."

I blushed. It's a bad habit, and one I don't seem able to kick. "Sorry. I just saw this really great vintage dress in John Nickerson's window, and I was thinking of how I could jazz it up for New Year's Eve. Of course, I'd probably have to put toilet tissue in the bodice to make it fit. . . ."

"The blue one?" Jill asked. I nodded. "At least you'd be able to get into it. I wasn't that skinny in elementary school."

"You've also had three kids in four years. Cut yourself some slack." I handed her the last of the bags.

Jill Cortino is a native Waterfielder and a contemporary—and old girlfriend—of Derek's. They dated in high school, went to prom together—I'd seen a picture—and then Derek went off to medical school and married Melissa, while Jill studied bookkeeping and stayed single. Everyone assumed she was mourning the loss of Derek, but eventually Peter Cortino moved to town, and things went fast after that. They were married just a few months later. It's been five years now, and they have three children: Peter, Paul, and—no, not Mary—Pamela.

"Where are the kids?" I asked.

"At home, with my mom. Peter's minding the business while I'm taking time out to do a little shopping."

The Cortinos run an auto repair and body shop on the other side of downtown. Peter does the repair and body work, Jill does the books, and they've got another mechanic or two working for them during the busy season. I don't think they're getting rich, any more than Derek and I are, but we're all getting by.

"We should do dinner sometime," I said. "Unless you two are too busy these days."

Jill shook her head. "Business is slow. It always is in the winter. People are driving their beaters."

"Huh?"

She smiled. "Haven't you noticed how some people keep old cars that they drive only during the winter? Beaters."

She pronounced it *beatahs*, like a native down easterner. She added, "People use them instead of their nice cars because of the salt on the roads and the danger of accidents."

"I hadn't noticed," I admitted, "but it's my first winter here. I don't even have one car yet, let alone two."

I do know how to drive, and I have a current driver's license, but I don't enjoy it. Especially after driving Derek's truck off the road and into a ditch a couple of months ago. It wasn't my fault—someone had punctured the brake cables, and things could have turned out a whole lot worse than they did—but it had been scary. I knew I'd have to get a car eventually, but I was putting it off as long as I could.

Jill nodded. "You'll see a lot of accidents as the weather gets colder and the road conditions worsen. Especially involving the out-of-towners. The college kids from places like Florida or Arizona have never had to drive on ice or snow before, and they don't know how to do it. That whole horrible thing with Carolyn Tate last month was only the beginning, I'm afraid."

"I hear the police are still looking for whoever was responsible," I said.

Jill nodded. "They've been back for the third time to

ask whether we've worked on anything suspicious. Like we wouldn't have told them already. They even insisted on going through all our records, as if we'd be lying about it." She rolled her eyes.

"I'm sure it's nothing personal," I said. "They have to ask. And not everyone is as law-abiding as you and Peter."

"Right." Jill looked at me for a second before she smiled. "Anyway, we'd love to get together for dinner sometime. I'll talk to Peter and get in touch, OK?"

I told her I'd look forward to it and went on my way.

—6—

I've never been what you'd call an early bird. Starbucks serves coffee all day, so what's the hurry? Especially this time of year, when the floor is cold and the thought of having to strip to get into the shower is demoralizing, to say the least. And that was before I moved from New York— cold—to the coast of Maine—colder.

Even with all that, I beat Derek to the B&B the next morning. It was the anticipation of seeing my mom later that did it, I guess. I was knocking on Kate's kitchen door before eight o'clock: washed, brushed, and raring to go.

Kate was sitting at the table nursing a cup of steaming brew, looking like she hadn't wanted to get up this morning.

"You OK?" I said sympathetically.

She managed a smile, one that didn't reach her eyes. "Fine. There's coffee in the pot."

"Thanks." I walked over and poured myself a cup. "I looked for you yesterday afternoon, but I couldn't find you."

"I was trying to track down Shannon."

I glanced at her over my shoulder. "And did you?"

"Afraid not. Although I did give her"—her teeth closed with a snap—"*companion* a piece of my mind."

I returned to the table to sit across from her. "That doesn't sound good."

"It wasn't pretty," Kate said.

I wanted to push for details, but aside from the fact that they weren't any of my business, she didn't look like she was in a mood to share. "Well, you look like you didn't sleep much."

Kate shook her head. "Wayne didn't come home 'til around one. He's still asleep."

"I see." Maybe Wayne's arrival was the reason she looked so beat. If he had woken her up and one thing had led to another, say. Some of my worry lifted, and I smiled.

Kate sent me a sour look but didn't comment. "So your mom and stepdad are coming later today, right?"

I nodded. "I can't wait. My mom's great. You'll love her. We lived together until just a couple of years ago, when she moved to California. Weird, I know, for a daughter to live with her mother that long, but we get along really well, and she had a rent-controlled apartment in a really good location, and I wasn't making that much money, and   "

"You don't have to explain," Kate said, looking a little better for the change of subject. "I'm sure your mom is lovely. I'm looking forward to meeting her. And your stepfather works in television, right?"

"Right. Producer or something. Something behind the scenes."

"I guess you don't know him that well, do you? If he's always lived in California and you've always lived in New York?"

I shook my head. "He met my mom three or four years ago. Online, of all places. They hit it off, and whenever he had business in New York, they'd have dinner together. I met him two or three times before he proposed. He actually asked my permission beforehand!"

"Did he really?" Kate smiled. "That's sweet."

"Isn't it? He took me to lunch and showed me the ring and asked me for my mother's hand in marriage. She quit her job the next day and flew to California with him. They got married three months later. On the beach."

"That's wonderful," Kate said warmly.

"I know. What about your family? You never talk about them." I realized, too late, that maybe there was a good reason for that.

Her face closed up. "We had a falling out after Shannon was born. Irish Catholic family, political aspirations, child out of wedlock, all those things. So I don't have much contact with them anymore. My grandmother was the only one who stayed in touch, and she died last spring." She shrugged.

"I'm sorry," I said. I couldn't even imagine having my mother cut me out of her life, and certainly not for something like getting pregnant. Surely these days, and even twenty years ago, that wasn't such a big deal? "Derek mentioned that your grandmother had died recently. Has your family never met Shannon, then?"

"They have. A few times. Not very often since we moved up here, though."

I hesitated. "Do you miss them?"

"It's been twenty years," Kate said with a shrug. "And it's their loss. They're the ones who missed seeing Shannon grow up."

I nodded. She didn't seem upset, but it was still a relief to hear the sound of tires crunching on the snow in the driveway. Kate glanced out the window, her expression wary for a second before it smoothed out. "Here's Derek. Bright and early, as usual."

The truck's engine shut off, and a door opened and closed. After a moment, the kitchen door opened and Derek stuck his head in.

"Kate . . . oh, hi, Avery."

I smiled. After six months, I should be used to Derek, but sometimes, when he shows up unexpectedly—or even when I know he's coming, but it's been a while since I've seen him, like, overnight—I get giddy. Some of it may have been nervousness about having to introduce him to my mom and Noel later on, but some of it was just seeing him, too. Knowing that that melting smile was for me and the way those blue eyes warmed was because he was happy to see me.

The proprieties dispensed with, he glanced at the coffee-maker. "Anything left in there?"

"Help yourself."

He opened the cabinet, found a mug, filled it, and sat down at the table, where he nudged my foot. "You're up early."

"I'm excited."

"Did your mom and dad call last night? Did they get in OK?"

I nodded. "The flight from Santa Barbara was delayed about an hour, and then the flight from San Francisco was delayed some more, but they got to Boston and checked into their hotel. This morning, they'll be having breakfast, and then they'll be picking up their car and hitting the road. She said they'd be here by lunchtime."

"We'd better get busy, then." He drained the coffee in a couple of gulps and reached for my chair. "C'mon, Tink."

"Coming." I gathered my and Derek's mugs and carried them over to the counter.

"We'll see you later, Kate." He guided me toward the door, snagging my coat from the hook on the way. "Here. Put this on. It's nippy today."

"No kidding," I said, the words making a cloud in front of my face as we entered the frigid air.

"It'll get worse before it gets better. Get used to it."

But he put his arm around me again and hugged me closer. I snuggled in, greedily grasping any warmth I could get.

It didn't last long, unfortunately. Upon reaching the carriage house, Derek dropped his arm from around me to fumble for the key under the eave. "Jill called last night," he said over his shoulder. "You two talked about getting together for dinner?"

"We touched on it. But it's probably not the best timing, with Mom and Noel coming. I wasn't thinking about that when I suggested it."

"Your mom and her husband might want some time to themselves one night," Derek said, "and we could try to get with Jill and Peter then. She sounded like she could use some cheering up."

I hugged myself, stomping my feet. This was taking a long time. "She did mention that business was slow. I think this whole thing with Carolyn Tate and the police coming around asking the same questions over and over is bothering her, too."

"I think she knew Carolyn," Derek answered. "She was a lot older than Jill, but I think they went to Barnham together. Carolyn raised her kids first, and then went back to school and got an education." He lowered his arm. "The key isn't there."

"Maybe it fell."

We both crouched and started peering around the stoop. It was Derek who put out a hand to brace himself against the door, and who toppled sideways when the door opened. I giggled, and then tried to stop, unsuccessfully, when he gave me a sour look.

"Someone's been here." He got to his feet.

"Unless you forgot to lock up last night?" I suggested.

"I have two grand worth of marble sitting here, Avery, not to mention a small fortune in tools and copper pipes. I'm not gonna forget to lock up. You watched me, didn't you?"

"Um . . ." I said. The truth was, I had stood there, and I had watched, but as usual when Derek had his back to me, I'd been too busy admiring the fit of his jeans to notice much of anything else.

"You're hopeless," Derek said, but with a grin; he knew

exactly why I hadn't been paying attention. "C'mon. Let's make sure nothing's missing."

He pushed the door open and stepped across the threshold. I followed, fumbling for his hand.

From just inside the door, everything seemed fine, just as it should be. We could see the edge of the marble counter, so at least no one had walked off with that. Derek's tools were where he had left them—an electric drill over in the corner, a bunch of wrenches and screwdrivers strewn about.

I'd never realized it before I started hanging out with Derek, but houses under renovation are like magnets for burglars and thieves. They're empty overnight, usually pretty easy to break into because people don't bother with security systems and dogs when the houses aren't occupied, and often they're chock full of expensive tools and materials. Like the two-thousand-dollar slab of marble Derek and the other guys had hauled inside last night. Also copper pipes, electric drills, nails, screws, drywall, and rolls of electrical wire. All stuff that can be turned into cold, hard cash by someone with an entrepreneurial spirit.

"Can't see anything out of the way," Derek remarked, scanning the room.

I shook my head. "Are you sure you didn't just forget to turn the key last night? Too busy wiggling your tush at me, or something?"

He gave me a look. "I never wiggle my tush. And even if I forgot to turn the key, I know I hung it on the hook. Someone was here."

"Maybe we should drag Wayne out of bed, instead of investigating ourselves. Kate said he was still asleep."

"I'm not afraid," Derek said, squaring his shoulders.

"Well, of course you're not. I'm not afraid, either"—precisely—"but if there was a burglar here, don't you think the best people to investigate are the police? We don't want to mess up any of their evidence."

"I think we need to determine whether there's anything to investigate first," Derek said stubbornly.

I sighed. "Fine. After you."

He glanced at me but led the way farther into the house. I followed, looking around nervously.

Nothing seemed out of place on the first floor, and nothing was there that shouldn't be, either. No sinister footprints across the brown paper that crisscrossed the new hardwood floors, and no conveniently dropped business card with our burglar's name and telephone number. No monogrammed handkerchief or telltale cigarette butt.

"Upstairs," Derek said after we'd made the circuit through living room, dining room, and kitchen, with a peek into the bathroom and laundry closet on our way past.

He started up. I sighed but followed.

The loft was less finished than the downstairs. The drywall was up and the bathroom roughed in, but we hadn't installed Kate's fluffy carpet yet. Kate had requested a light cream, almost white, deep-pile floor covering, and just in case one of us happened to spill a drop of paint or the new toilet overflowed or something, we'd decided it would be safer to leave the installation of the carpet 'til last. So the floors upstairs were lowly plywood. When I got to the top of the stairs, I couldn't help but be grateful that we'd chosen to wait.

"Shit," Derek said softly, stopping on the second-to-top step. "Looks like we need to get Wayne out of bed after all."

"Why?" I peered around him. "Oh, no. Who's that?"

A man's figure was lying on the floor, with an elegant cashmere overcoat covering the still form from calves to shoulders. I could see a dark head and a pair of wool trousers sticking out at their respective ends.

Derek didn't move. "I think it's that guy Shannon's been hanging out with."

"You're kidding. What's he doing here? If she wanted him to sleep over, don't you think she ought to have had him stay in the house and not out here? Are you going to wake him?"

"I think he's beyond waking," Derek said, his voice a little uneven.

"He's dead?"

Derek glanced at me. "Looks that way. Whoa."

He reached out to steady me.

"Sorry," I managed, my voice tinny and far away. "I don't know what's wrong with me. I've seen worse than this before. There's not even any blood."

"It's all right." He half carried, half steadied me down the stairs. "Just sit right here while I go see if there's anything I can do. Just in case I'm wrong and he's just drugged or unconscious. Keep your head down."

He deposited me on the bottom step of the staircase and pushed my head down between my knees before he ran back up the stairs, two or three steps at a time. A minute later, he came back down. "He's beyond anything I can do for him. Are you OK sitting here for another couple of minutes? I need to go get Wayne."

I nodded, concentrating on taking deep, even breaths. "I'll be fine. The sooner you leave, the sooner you'll come back. Go."

Derek gave me another measured look, no doubt checking for signs of shock or incipient breakdown, then nodded and turned on his heel. When he glanced at me over his shoulder before going out the door, I waved a shaky hand. He waved back before ducking out the door and running hell for leather for the B&B.

It was a lonely and scary few minutes before he came back. I made the time pass by telling myself over and over again that this was nothing; that I'd seen much worse before. *Wonder what he's doing here*, my treacherous mind whispered in my inner ear. Had he come to meet Shannon? Or had Kate tracked him down and asked him to come over for a chat? She had mentioned giving Shannon's companion a piece of her mind.

But if so, why hadn't she met him inside the B&B instead of out here? Besides, she was a law-abiding citizen; if he'd had a heart attack or something while they'd been discussing things, Kate wouldn't just have left him here for us to find. She would have called 911 or Wayne or both.

So maybe he'd made his own way into the carriage house and was waiting for Shannon to come home. To tell her that Kate had contacted him, perhaps. Maybe Shannon was avoiding him, and this was his attempt to corner her for a talk. If he'd been waiting a while, maybe he had lain down for a rest; it would explain the neat way the coat was spread over him. And then he had died. Quietly, in his sleep, since I'd seen no sign of a struggle or upheaval. Poor guy.

And the best thing was that he hadn't been murdered like the other dead people I'd come upon since I'd moved to Waterfield. That made it a little easier.

When the front door opened, I jumped and stared at the two men like a rabbit caught in the headlights of an oncoming truck.

"Everything OK?" Derek said, scanning my face.

I nodded, catching my breath. "Fine."

"You look better. Not so much like you're gonna pass out anymore. There's some color in your cheeks again."

"I feel better. Although I don't think I want to talk about it. That would probably make me feel worse."

Wayne nodded. "I don't think you can tell me anything Derek hasn't already said, Avery. Just keep doing what you were doing. I'll go upstairs and take a look."

He stepped toward the staircase. It looked like he had dressed hurriedly; his shirt was untucked and hanging over his uniform pants, and his boots were unlaced. His face looked tired, with heavy eyelids. He didn't look like he had slept well, either, and I don't suppose facing another dead body ever gets easier.

"Did you tell Kate?" I asked Derek, sotto voce, when Wayne was out of sight at the top of the stairs.

He shook his head. "She was in the shower. I figure it's Wayne's responsibility to tell her, anyway. As chief of police, *and* as her fiancé."

I nodded. "I can't imagine she'll be happy that there's a dead guy on her premises, and especially the guy who was going around with her daughter, but at least he died a natural death. That's something to be grateful for."

Derek squinted at me. "What makes you say that?"

I squinted back. "You mean he didn't?" Damn.

"I wouldn't want to go on record," Derek said, "and I didn't examine him closely, but there was some evidence that he may have had a little help."

"What kind of evidence?"

He shrugged. "For one, it looks like he may have eaten something that didn't agree with him."

"Food poisoning?" That didn't sound too bad.

"Or some other type of poisoning. Before someone asphyxiated him. But it's just a guess. The ME will have to say for sure."

"So you're saying someone killed the guy on purpose?" That could complicate things. And implicate a whole lot of people. People who had access to the carriage house and who had had dealings with the guy. Like Kate. And Shannon. And even Josh, who might not have liked the fact that Shannon was going around with a man old enough to be her father.

A stray thought buzzed through my head and out the other side, but before I could try to catch and inspect it, Derek had answered my question.

"No idea," he said cheerfully, "and not my problem, thankfully. We'll just wait until Dudley Do-right gets here, and then we'll tell the police the little bit we know and knock off work for now. They're gonna be busy processing the carriage house as a murder scene for the rest of the day. We'd be in the way, even if they'd let us go to work, and they probably won't. But at least we won't be suspects. We didn't know the guy."

"Thank God. Horrible how he ended up in our work space, though."

He looked down at me. "Seems to follow you around, doesn't it, Tink?"

"Me!" I sputtered, moving away. "Nothing ever happened to me until I moved to Waterfield."

"Nothing ever happened in Waterfield until you came. The last time we had a murder here was in 1999. And then you showed up, and now we've had five in less than a year."

"Four," I said, since one of the bodies had died years before I got here. "No, three." Since Aunt Inga had died while I was still in New York, too.

Derek opened his mouth, probably to argue, but before he could get a word out, Wayne came back down the stairs, his steps heavy. Derek closed his mouth again and watched him. Wayne stopped at the bottom of the staircase and looked at us. We looked back.

"Well?" Derek said eventually.

"He's dead, all right."

Derek snorted. "No kidding."

"Do either of you know who he is?"

Derek and I exchanged a look.

"We've seen him a couple of times," Derek admitted. "With Shannon."

"But other than that, we don't know anything about him," I added. "I don't even know his name."

Wayne looked at me. After a second, he seemed to con-clude that I'd find out soon enough anyway, and he may as well tell me. "The name is easy. What he was doing here and who decided to kill him, if he was killed, may be a little trickier."

"So who is he?" Derek wanted to know. "He looks familiar, although I don't think I've ever seen him before."

"I don't imagine you have, since he's never been to Waterfield before, to my knowledge. But I'm not surprised he looks familiar to you. He looks like his daughter. Or she looks like him."

He looked from one to the other of us, waiting to see if we'd catch on. After a few seconds, he said, "His name is Gerard Labadie. He's Shannon's father."

"Oh, my God!" I said, and I must have reeled, because I felt Derek's hand reach out and steady me. Again.

"Shannon's dad?" he repeated, gripping my elbow. "That prince of a guy who had his fun and then left Kate to raise Shannon on her own, with no help from him?"

"The same." Wayne looked about as disgusted as Derek sounded. "He had his wallet in his pocket, with his driver's license in it, and that's what it said. Gerard Labadie, with an address in Boston, Massachusetts."

"That's where the car's from, too," I nodded.

Wayne turned to me. "Car?"

"The silver gray Lexus I've seen him drive. It has Massachusetts plates."

"Wonder where that is now," Derek muttered.

"If we knew that," Wayne answered, "it might answer a lot of questions." He sighed, and added, scrubbing his hands over his face, "I guess I need to give Kate the news."

He headed for the outside, looking glum.

I lowered my voice. "He'll have to give Shannon the

news, too. And I don't envy him. She'll be devastated, won't she?"

Derek nodded. "Especially if her father's been up here for long enough that she's gotten to know him. You know, I didn't see this coming."

He held the door open for me to pass out into the frigid morning air again.

I shook my head. "I didn't, either. But now that I know, I can kind of see the resemblance."

Shannon had her mother's statuesque height and centerfold figure, but her father's dark eyes and strong nose and chin. And her mahogany or black cherry hair was the sort of thing that might happen if a redheaded Irish girl got together with a swarthy Frenchman to make a baby.

Derek called Wayne to a stop on the snow-covered lawn between the carriage house and the B&B. "Do you want us to come in with you, Wayne? Kate might like to have Avery there when you give her the news. Another woman. But we'll do whatever you want."

"Sure," Wayne said. "When Brandon gets here, I'm gonna have to come back out here anyway, and it's just as well to have someone who can stay with her. In case she takes it hard."

"I'll be happy to stay with Kate until Shannon can get here," I said. "After that, I'm sure they'll prefer to be alone."

"Come along, then." Wayne headed for the back door. Derek and I followed.

Kate was still in the kitchen, cleaning up from breakfast, and she took the news rather well, everything considered. She didn't faint, cry, or have hysterics, although she did turn pale and have to sit down.

"Dead?" she repeated, in a voice that was barely there.

Wayne nodded, eyes narrowed. His own face may as well have been chiseled out of granite for all the emotion it expressed. He might be a cop assessing a potential suspect, but I wondered if he wasn't more of a fiancé assessing his girlfriend's reaction to the news that her ex—and the father of her child—had died, and on her property. Was he searching her face for something more than just normal shock and grief? Some indication that Kate still had feelings for Gerard? Or that she had had a hand in his demise? Did Wayne know that Gerard had been going about with Shannon? Or that Kate had spoken to Gerard the day before?

"When was the last time you saw him?"

Kate blinked. "I haven't seen him for at least six years. Not since Shannon and I moved to Waterfield."

I glanced at her across the table. Her face gave nothing away.

"What about Shannon?" Wayne wanted to know.

"She saw him once in a while growing up. Nothing structured. We didn't have a custody arrangement, since we were never married, and although he's listed as her father on her birth certificate, Gerard never asked for visitation rights. Every once in a while he'd call and want to see her, and I'd let him, but it was never more than once a year or so. He just didn't care enough for any more."

"So you didn't know that he'd had contact with Shannon over the past few weeks?"

It was Kate's turn to glance at me. "I suspected it," she admitted. "Yesterday, when Avery told me she'd seen Shannon with someone. He sounded like Gerard."

"But you hadn't seen him yourself? Or spoken to him?"

Kate flushed. "I called him yesterday, to ask him what the hell he thought he was doing, sneaking around behind my back."

"What did he say?"

"He didn't," Kate said. "I had to leave a message."

"And you didn't hear back from him?"

She shook her head.

"Huh," Wayne said. He had pulled out his tiny notebook and pencil and was taking notes.

"Do you think maybe that's what he was doing here?" I suggested. "He got your message and came to talk to you?"

Kate shrugged.

"Well, were you home last night?" Derek asked.

Kate nodded. "All night. Making place cards for the wedding supper. If he knocked on the door at any time, I would have heard him."

Nobody said anything for a moment.

"Any idea what he was doing in Waterfield?" Wayne asked. "Why he'd suddenly want to get to know Shannon after all this time?"

Kate flushed angrily. I guess she must have forgotten, in the heat of the moment, that one shouldn't speak ill of the dead. "Oh, yeah. He probably found out that my grandmother died and left Shannon enough money to keep her comfortably for the next twenty years, at least."

"Wow," I said. "Really?"

Kate nodded. "I bet you that's why he's here. He was trying to get in good so she'd share it with him."

"Did you speak to her yesterday?"

Kate shook her head. "After I tried to get hold of him, I tried to get hold of her. I had to leave a message there, too. She isn't answering her phone. Not for me, at least."

"I'll call her," Wayne said. "If she won't answer for me, I'll call Josh and make him put her on. She's next of kin; I have to talk to her." He dialed the number and turned away.

"How would Gerard know about your grandmother's death and Shannon's money?" I wanted to know. "If you didn't have any contact with him?"

Kate shrugged. "He may have seen the obituary in the *Globe*. My grandmother was pretty well known in Boston. Or maybe he ran across someone who told him. I do have a few friends left in Boston. And here."

"How many people did you tell?" I wanted to know, a little hurt. She hadn't told us, and I thought we were close. Or at least that she and Derek were close.

"In Waterfield? Just Jill Cortino, in addition to Wayne and Josh. She does some financial planning on the side, when she's not helping Peter run the shop. I thought she might have some ideas for how we could make the money. One can't be too careful about investing these days."

"I doubt Jill has been chummy with your ex-boyfriend," Derek said lightly, resting his hand on my back for a moment. "She has a low tolerance for liars and cheats."

Kate nodded. "I'm well aware of it. I still don't think she's forgiven Melissa for carrying on with Ray while you two were married. She's thrilled you're not together anymore, but she has never stopped despising Melissa for the way it ended."

Derek shrugged. "Water under the bridge," he said.

Before any of us had time to say anything else—and I was biting down on a snide remark about my predecessor, the former love of Derek's life—Wayne turned back to us. "She's on her way. Josh is bringing her."

"How did she take it?" Kate wanted to know, her voice concerned.

"I didn't tell her. Just that she needed to come home because something had happened. Once I told her you were fine, she didn't ask any more questions. We'll tell her about her father when she gets here. I figured you'd want it that way."

"Thank you." Kate leaned into his side, where he was standing next to the chair she was sitting on, and closed her eyes. He ran a hand over her bright curls.

Derek moved his hand from my back to my waist and pulled me closer.

After just a few seconds, Kate lifted her head, some of the strain now gone from her face. "So what happens now?"

"Now we wait for Brandon and the forensic kit," Wayne replied. "After that, we figure out what Gerard was doing in the carriage house, and who'd want to kill him. If someone killed him and he didn't just die of natural causes. And then we get married and go to Paris."

"You make it sound so simple."

"Why shouldn't it be?" Wayne said. "He's only been in

Waterfield a short time, so he couldn't have known more than a few people. All we have to do is figure out which one of them wanted him dead."

It did sound extremely simple. I couldn't help but wonder if he realized as he said it that the two of them, plus Shannon, were likely the only people in Waterfield who knew Gerard well enough to want to get rid of him.

• • •

Brandon arrived first, and he and Wayne disappeared across the grass and into the carriage house. Derek went with them, to have a second, closer look at the body and see if he could narrow down the time of death or see anything that would settle the question of natural versus unnatural death one way or the other. Wayne would get a second opinion from the medical examiner in Portland, of course, who would be doing the autopsy. But he often took Derek's word for things when Derek was on hand. In a small town like Waterfield, procedures are often pretty relaxed, I've noticed.

Kate and I sat down at the kitchen table to wait, silently nursing cups of hot, strong tea. She was probably thinking about Gerard and about how she would break the news of his death to Shannon. I wondered what Shannon's reaction would be. It would depend a lot on how well she knew him, I thought; whether she'd become attached to him during the short time he'd been here, or whether they were still getting to know each other and she had reservations.

"My dad died when I was thirteen," I said, addressing the table. Kate looked up but didn't speak. "He was only thirty-eight. It was an accident. Drunk driver. Kind of like Carolyn Tate. Wrong place at the wrong time."

"I'm sorry," Kate said.

I shrugged. "They caught the people who did it and sent them to prison. Not that that made it any easier at the time. I still miss him sometimes, even though it's almost twenty years ago now. Mom missed him, too, for years. Until she met Noel."

"I'm sure she still misses him," Kate said. "There's nothing wrong with still loving a dead husband even though there's a new love in her life."

"I guess."

We sat in silence a little longer. This time, Kate was the one who broke it.

"I've spent almost twenty years hating Gerard's guts. For seducing me. For not taking responsibility when I got pregnant. For not helping me provide for Shannon."

I nodded.

"But even so, there was a small part of me, somewhere, that still had a soft spot for him. That remembered what it was like, being eighteen and in love. Before it all blew up in my face."

"I'm sorry," I said.

She nodded, and when she looked up, I wasn't surprised to see that her eyes were wet. "I may not have been happy to find out that he was here, cozying up to my daughter without letting me know about it, but I didn't want him dead."

"Of course you didn't," I said.

"I may have felt like I did, yesterday. But I didn't wish him any harm. Not really."

"Of course not."

The sound of a car pulling up outside and stopping in the driveway with a screech of brakes, saved me from having to think up something more to say. I wanted to believe her, really I did, but there was a part of me—a small, treacherous part—that wondered if I could. The expression on her face yesterday, when she realized who Shannon had been spending time with, had been murderous. And I liked Kate, but how well did I know her, really? Well enough to believe she wasn't capable of murder, I supposed, but perhaps not well enough to know, bone deep, that she hadn't killed her ex-boyfriend.

Outside, a car door slammed, and rapid footsteps pounded around the corner. The kitchen door flew open.

"Mom!"

Shannon burst in, hair flying, her face pale and her eyes frightened. I could hear the car engine turn off, and then a set of more measured steps came around the corner and through the open door. Meanwhile, Shannon threw herself at Kate. "Mom! What's wrong? Why are you crying?"

"I'll go get Wayne," I said, getting up.

"I'll do it," Josh offered. He was standing in the door, hands in the pockets of his puffy, blue jacket, a long, striped scarf wound around his neck.

"That's OK," I said. "I'd better." I ducked past him and out before he could ask me why.

When I got back to the kitchen, with Derek and Wayne in tow, Josh had taken his jacket off and gotten himself a cup of tea, which he was sipping from his vantage point by the counter. Shannon had also taken off her coat and had hung it over the back of one of the kitchen chairs. It was clear from the way she was fussing over Kate that she thought whatever was wrong had to do with her mother. Seeing Kate crying probably hadn't helped to alleviate her fears. When Wayne came through the door, she turned to him, dark eyes flashing.

"What did you do to her?"

Wayne rolled his eyes. "I didn't do anything to her. I love your mother."

Kate smiled at him wetly.

"So why is she upset?" Shannon demanded. She straightened, hands on her hips, and tossed her hair back over her shoulder. Josh's eyes turned glassy behind the round frames.

"Have a seat." Wayne waved her to a chair. "We have some bad news."

"What kind of news? Did someone break into the carriage house last night? Is that why Brandon is here?"

She sank down on the chair next to her mother and scooted it a little closer.

"In a manner of speaking," Wayne said. "Yes, someone broke in. And died."

"Oh, no! Who?" She looked around, taking account that none of us were missing.

Kate fumbled for her hand. "Honey, it was your father. Gerard. He's dead."

For a second, Shannon's face was blank, absolutely void of expression. Then—"Daddy?" she asked, her voice cracking. "How?"

Josh swallowed, and I could see his jaw clench and his hand tighten around the mug he was holding until his knuckles showed white.

"It's too soon to know for sure," Wayne said, watching her, "but we believe, on preliminary evidence, that he was poisoned and asphyxiated."

"Oh, my God!" For a second she looked like she might faint. Josh made a movement in her direction, then stopped himself. Hot tea splashed out of the mug and onto his hand, and he turned to the sink, swearing under his breath. The sound of cold water running accompanied Wayne's next statement.

"I have to ask you some questions."

"Sure," Shannon whispered.

She had first heard from her dad a few months ago, she explained. He had contacted her on her Barnham College e-mail account and said he wanted to get to know her.

"That's when he heard about the money," Kate muttered. "Probate was complete in September."

Shannon glanced at her but addressed Wayne. "We went back and forth a couple of times, by e-mail and phone, and then he told me he was coming up to Maine for a while."

"Why?" Wayne had pulled out his notebook and pencil and was taking notes.

Shannon shrugged. "Just to see me. He's been here for a few weeks."

"Staying where?"

"Not sure," Shannon said, biting her lip. "He had the car, so he always picked me up. We never went to his place."

Wayne made a note, presumably to find out where

Gerard had been staying. "Was this the first time he'd been in Waterfield?"

"No idea. If he'd been here before, he didn't try to contact me then."

"Of course not," Kate muttered. "You weren't a rich heiress until this autumn. There was nothing in it for him until then. He always was good at keeping an eye out for Number One."

Wayne looked at her but didn't comment. Instead, he glanced around the table, taking in Derek and me on the way past. "Can any of you think of any reason why he'd be in the carriage house last night? Did you arrange to meet him, Shannon?"

Shannon shook her head. "He always picked me up at Barnham. And I wasn't planning to be here last night. I had studying to do. Midterms. With Paige. He and I were going to get together for dinner on Friday."

A moment passed, and then we could see the realization hit her that there would be no more dinners with her dad, Friday or anytime.

"Did he ever ask you about it?" Wayne asked gently. "The carriage house? What was going on there? Whether anyone lived in it? Anything like that?"

Shannon shook her head. "He mostly talked about him and Mom, when they were young. And me, when I was a baby. About how he always wished they'd been able to work things out between them, but they were just too young when they met. Although to hear him tell it, Mom was the love of his life." She avoided looking at Kate as well as Wayne when she said it.

"Love, my left buttock," Kate spat.

Shannon's pretty face crumpled, her lips quivering, and her mother reached out to her, voice softening. "Honey, I'm sorry. I don't want to upset you any more than the news has already. But the truth is that when I met your dad, I was eighteen and stupid. He was twenty and slick. I thought I loved him. I thought he loved me back. He said he did. But when I got pregnant with you and turned to him for help, he left me to handle it all on my own. So don't talk to me about the love of Gerard's life. If he has one, it's Gerard himself."

"He loved *me*," Shannon whispered.

Kate looked like she wished she could kick herself. Hard. "Of course he did, honey. I didn't mean that he didn't love *you*." She looked up at Wayne, helplessly, as Shannon dissolved into tears. Josh twitched.

It was at this pivotal moment that we heard the sound of another car pulling into the driveway outside. Two doors slammed and two sets of footsteps made their way through the slush and snow to the back door. A light knock heralded the arrival of a small figure in a royal blue coat, who looked around the kitchen for a second until her pair of blue eyes lighted on me.

"Avery!"

My mom had arrived.

—8—

The group broke up after that. Josh escorted Shannon into her room down the hall, where we could hear their voices through the wall, murmuring low. They were best friends in addition to the small matter of him being in love with her, so he might help her more at the moment than even her mother, especially given Kate's conflicted feelings about Gerard.

Kate introduced Wayne to my mom and Noel—as her fiancé, who just happened to be the chief of police, but with no mention of the fact that a suspicious death had taken place on the premises overnight and that was why he was here. After making the appropriate noises, Wayne excused himself. Kate took Mom and me upstairs to the suite while Derek and Noel trotted back outside to unload the car.

The rooms in Kate's B&B are named for the members of the Cabot family. None of the Cabots ever lived in the house, except for Anna Virginia, after she married Lawrence Ritter and ceased to be a Cabot. But as Kate once explained to me, the Cabots were a Waterfield institution and it seemed the appropriate thing to do. There is Captain

Cabot's room; John Cabot was a sea captain back in the day, and so was his father. There is Mrs. Mary's room, Anna Virginia's room, and John Andrew's room, and then there's the Widow's Walk: the suite taking up the entire third floor. That's where Mom and Noel would be staying.

Back in the day, the suite had been the smallest of the three apartments in Helen Ritter's house. Back then, it had consisted of a kitchen, a living room/bedroom, and a tiny bath. Now, most of the walls had been removed, and except for the bathroom—which was the old kitchen—the suite was one big room, with windows on three sides. Because the B&B sits up high, it's possible to see not only most of Waterfield Village from the windows, but also the harbor and the ocean. The view is better in the summer, when the trees are green and the sun shines on the water, but it was still pretty impressive now, in spite of being monochromatically white and gray. The furniture is Victorian and dark, the king-sized bed has corner posts and a canopy, and there's a sitting area with a TV off to one side, as well as a smallish dormer with a desk and chair. That's where the old bathroom used to be. And of course the new bathroom is sublime, with green glass tiles, a double shower, and a jetted whirlpool tub. Everything the honeymooning couple could wish for.

"Oh!" Mom said, looking around, "this is wonderful!"

Kate smiled. It looked strained, but it was a smile.

"Derek did most of the work," I said. It wasn't my intention to denigrate Kate's contribution, but I figured it couldn't hurt to sing Derek's praises to my mom.

"Really?" Mom glanced at Kate, who nodded. "Handsome *and* talented. He does beautiful work."

She looked around appreciatively. Kate looked at me, her eyebrows signaling *You owe me one.*

I turned my back to her to address my mother. "I told you he was cute, didn't I?"

"Gag me," Kate muttered behind my back.

Mom giggled. "Yes, Avery, you did. And you were right. He's definitely cute. And good with his hands."

She winked. Kate rolled her eyes. I blushed.

Luckily I was saved from having to comment by the arrival of the man himself, carrying two suitcases and a duffel bag slung over his shoulder. Behind him came Noel, carrying the other two suitcases. Obviously my mom had packed for every contingency.

Mom's new husband is nothing like what you might expect, considering that he swept her so thoroughly off her feet. I know I was surprised the first time I met him.

My dad was tall, blond, and good-looking: a somewhat similar physical type to Derek. When Mom told me she had met a new man, I figured he'd look kind of like dad did. Maybe not tall and blond exactly, but tallish, handsome, well-dressed . . . all the things I associated with my father, and as a result, with what my mother liked. In addition to that, since I knew Noel was some kind of big shot in television, I pictured someone sort of like George Hamilton: a California high roller, tanned and trim, with blinding white teeth and a face lift.

Noel is short for a man, a mere five feet six or so, and portly. He has no hair left, and his scalp looks like he buffs it with a towel every morning. What hair he used to have seems to have migrated to his eyebrows, which are thick and bushy and snow white. His face looks lived in, with wrinkles at the corners of his eyes and lines bracketing his mouth—from smiling rather than frowning—and although he has his own teeth, and they're perfectly serviceable, they don't cause snow blindness when he smiles.

He was smiling now. "Hello, Avery!"

"Hi, Noel," I smiled back. I'd seen him downstairs, but we hadn't had the opportunity to really greet one another properly. Now I wandered over and pecked him on the cheek, leaving Kate to referee the first meeting between Mom and Derek. Short as my stepfather is, I still had to go up on my toes. "How was the drive?"

"Oh, no problem." He put the suitcases down and shrugged his chubby shoulders. Or maybe he was just circulating them after carrying my mother's bags up two flights of stairs. "The roads were slick, and we took it slow to get a good look around. Your mother hasn't been up to this part of the country for years, and I've never spent much time in rural New England. It looks very different from California."

"I bet. I've never spent much time in California, just that one time I came out for the wedding last year, but I remember thinking it looked like a different world."

"We should get you out there again sometime," Noel said. "You know you're always welcome, Avery. We have plenty of room. And I know Rosie has missed seeing you."

My mother's name is Rosemary. The first time I heard Noel call her Rosie, it was a bit of a fazer, but I've gotten used to it. She doesn't seem to mind, and as long as she doesn't, I guess I can't.

"That'd be nice," I said, with a quick sideways glance at Derek. Just how hard would it be to pry him away from Waterfield for a week or two? Would he want to visit California?

Noel followed my gaze to where Derek was dimpling at my mother. He lowered his voice. "Any wedding bells on the horizon for you two?"

"Lord!" I had to take a breath. "We've only known each other for six months. And he's been burned once before."

"Sugar," Noel said, patting my arm, "I've been burned before, too, more than once. That doesn't mean it can't work out next time." He looked over at my mom, beaming.

"I'm sure," I said.

I wasn't lamenting the fact that Derek hadn't proposed. I'm not one of those women who have to be married to feel validated. We had only known one another a short time, and although I don't have a failed marriage in my past, I've thought I was in love before, and learned the hard way that I wasn't. Usually when they dumped me, or I realized they weren't what I thought they were.

I didn't expect that to happen with Derek. I was pretty sure I had discovered all his bad qualities by now, and I wasn't afraid that he'd cheat on me, either. He's just not the type. People do fall out of love, though, and to be honest, I was a little concerned about Melissa. He'd once told me that she was the prettiest girl he'd ever seen, and if she ever broke up with my cousin Ray and decided she'd like to have Derek back—and who wouldn't?—could I trust that he wouldn't agree to forgive and forget, and give her another chance?

"You want I should tell him?" Noel was looking at Derek. Rather speculatively, I thought.

I shook my head. "Please don't. I don't want him to think I'm fishing."

"I wouldn't be obvious," Noel said. "I'd just hint gently—as a stand-in for your father, you know—that I'd like to know what his intentions are."

I shuddered. "No, thanks. That won't be necessary. If he has intentions, I'm sure he'll get around to telling me. Without any prodding."

"Suit yourself," Noel said with a shrug. "He seems like a nice young man. You could do worse."

"A whole lot worse," I agreed.

By now, Derek and Mom had finished their little talk, and they joined us, while Kate excused herself and went back downstairs. I felt bad that I couldn't stay here to help her, after the shock she'd had, but I knew it would probably help in itself if I got Mom and Noel out of the B&B for a couple hours. No reason for us to sit around waiting for the van from the medical examiner's office to arrive and the body to be removed, after all. I knew I couldn't keep the murder from Mom and Noel indefinitely, or even for very long, but if I removed them for now, at the very least, they might be able to avoid a personal encounter with the late Gerard.

Derek must have done his usual stellar job of charming, because Mom was clutching his arm and beaming up at him. "Derek knows just the place to take the car," she told Noel. "He has a friend who owns a body shop. If we go now, we can probably have everything taken care of by the end of the day."

I looked from one to the other of them. "Is something wrong with the rental car? Why don't you just call the rental company and ask for a new car?"

For a second nobody spoke. Then Noel said, "It's not that simple."

Mom nodded. "We had a little accident on the way here."

I felt myself turn pale. "An accident? You didn't say anything about an accident. What happened? Are you OK? You're not hurt, are you?"

"We're fine, darling." She transferred her grip from Derek's arm to mine, with a comforting smile. "Nothing to worry about. We got a little too close to the side of the road at one point, and . . . um . . . a branch took some of the paint off the side of the car."

"Won't the insurance take care of it?"

Another beat passed, then . . . "It's not that simple," Noel said again.

"What isn't?"

I looked at them. They looked at one another.

"I have a condition called . . . um . . . white-coat hypertension," Noel explained after a moment, a little embarrassedly. He wasn't looking at me, but down at his shoes, and his cheeks were flushed. I glanced up at Derek. The corners of his mouth were compressed, but he didn't object, so white coat hypertension must be a real condition, even if it sounded like a joke. "The medicine can cause dizziness and drowsiness, and if the condition isn't treated, I can start having strokes and heart attacks. It can even cause blindness."

"Wow." I looked at Derek again, for confirmation. He nodded. I turned back to Noel. "Sounds serious."

"Oh, it is," Noel nodded, oozing sincerity. "Terribly. And if I start having accidents, and start filing too many claims, our car insurance company may notify the California DMV, and then they'll take away my driver's license."

"And that would be bad?"

Must be a guy thing. If I could get away with never having to drive again, I'd be thrilled, but men's masculinity seems to be tied up in their cars. Just look at Derek and his truck, and Gerard and his sleek, gray Lexus, not to mention Brandon Thomas and his patrol car, with the flashing blue lights and the siren.

"It would be horrible," Mom said loyally, hooking her hand through Noel's arm and fixing me with big, sincere eyes. They're a pale, slightly chlorinated-looking blue, like mine. "It's impossible to get around in California without a car. And this had nothing to do with Noel's . . . um"—her eyes flickered—"condition. Another car drifted over the median and forced us out on the curb."

"So we decided it would be simpler and easier just to take care of the damage ourselves," Noel said. "It'll be done in a couple of hours, and it'll be well worth the money. No one need know it ever happened." He smiled contentedly.

"That's fine with me," I said with a shrug. "Whatever you want. Are we going to Cortino's, then?"

Derek nodded. "I'll call Jill, make sure Peter can get it done today. But as slow as business is this time of year, I don't think it'll be a problem."

"Even if they were stacked, Jill would fit you in. Old girlfriend," I added, for Mom and Noel's benefit.

"High school prom date," Derek corrected.

"Whatever. You ready, Mom?"

Mom was ready, and together we descended the two flights of stairs to the main floor. Kate was in the kitchen, cleaning up. Keeping her hands busy while her mind spun like a top, no doubt. I could see the stress lines around her eyes when she turned and smiled. "You heading out?"

"We're going to Cortino's," I explained, taking note of the look of relief in her eyes when she heard her boarders would be making themselves scarce for a while. "And then we'll go to lunch. And probably take a look at Waterfield. See how much it's changed since the last time Mom was here. And you'll want to see Aunt Inga's house, right, Mom?"

"Of course," my mother said. "We'll get it all done, Avery. No worries."

Derek smiled and put an arm around my shoulders. I was probably babbling.

The car Mom and Noel had driven up in was a Beetle. It looked like the one I'd rented to drive up to Waterfield the first time I came, except this one was spring green and mine had been baby blue. I walked around it.

"Where's the scratch?"

"Here," Noel said and put his finger on the side panel.

I squinted. "I don't see anything."

"It's there. You just have to look at it from the right angle."

I adjusted my angle, but I still couldn't see anything.

"You don't need glasses, do you, Avery?" Mom asked, sounding worried. Derek chuckled.

"Of course not." I flushed. "Fine. Let's go, then, if you're sure you want to spend money getting rid of this nonexistent scratch you say you made on the car."

"We'll follow you," Noel said, "since you know where you're going." He opened the passenger door of the Beetle for my mom, who got in.

"C'mon, Avery." Derek guided me over to the truck and handed me up into the passenger seat.

"Did you see a scratch?" I asked when he was sitting beside me and was backing the truck out of the driveway and into the street.

He glanced over. "Not much of one, no. But it's your stepfather's car. And your stepfather's money. And if he wants to have Peter run a buffer over a scratch he says he sees, and he can afford it, and Peter and Jill can use the work, then I don't see any reason to dissuade him. Do you?"

"When you put it like that," I admitted, "I guess I don't."

He smiled. "You don't have to try so hard, Avery. Your mom and I will find our way on our own. And your stepdad and I, too. It'll all work out."

He reached over to tuck my hair behind my ear before putting the truck in gear and rolling slowly down the street.

Behind us, Noel maneuvered the Beetle into position and followed.

· · ·

Cortino's Auto Shop is located on the other side of down-town from the Village, but since Waterfield is a very small town, we were there in just a couple of minutes. While Derek drove, I called to let Jill know we'd be coming, and she and Peter were waiting for us when we pulled up.

The first time I met Peter Cortino, I thought he was the handsomest man I had ever laid eyes on. Off a televi-sion screen, anyway. In a purely aesthetic way, naturally, since he was married and I was in a steady relationship. But I'm not blind, and Peter is definitely the kind of guy who gets noticed. As dark as Derek is fair, he looks like an old-fashioned matinee idol: Tyrone Power or Rudolph Valentino or one of those guys. Swarthy and smoldering. These days, maybe Antonio Banderas. That general type, anyway, although Peter doesn't really look much like any of them. More like a Michelangelo sculpture right off the plinth. He's a little shorter than Derek, and stockier, with black, curly hair, melting brown eyes, olive skin, and bone structure to die for.

Call me shallow, but when I first saw him, I wondered how Jill had managed to snare such a god. Not that she's ugly or anything, but she's nothing out of the ordinary, either. Plain and a little on the dumpy side, with dishwater blonde hair and too much junk in the trunk. Not the type you'd expect a gorgeous specimen like Peter to get involved with. Nor the type you'd expect a teenaged Derek to get involved with, either, for that matter.

What I didn't realize at the time is that in addition to being gorgeous, Peter, like Derek, is a genuinely nice guy, and smart enough to know that women who don't look like supermodels often have other, better qualities to rec-ommend them. The Cortinos seem very happy together, and Peter is clearly crazy about Jill. He touches her every chance he gets, and when he looks at her, it's with his heart in his eyes.

Like now. He came into the office and immediately went to stand behind his wife's chair, one hand on her shoulder. She tilted her head back to smile at him, and he smiled back, all gleaming white teeth and smoldering sex appeal. And warm affection.

"Can't keep their hands off each other," Derek muttered, putting an arm around my shoulders. Jill rolled her eyes.

"What exactly can we do for you two?" Peter asked, without removing the hand.

Peter is from Boston, and whenever I hear him talk, it reminds me of my dad. I smiled. "It isn't us, it's my mom and stepdad. They rented the Beetle in Boston this morning, and on the way here . . ." I went through the whole explanation.

Peter shrugged. "I'll go have a look. Shouldn't take long. If you want to take your parents somewhere for lunch, Avery, the car should be done when you come back."

"If it's all the same to you," Noel said from the doorway, where he was ushering my mother inside, "I think I'd just as soon wait."

I must have looked disappointed, because Derek said, "Why don't I stay here with Noel, while you take your mom into downtown and show her around. Get some lunch and catch up on things. We'll see you back at the B&B later."

I hesitated. It was tempting, I had to admit. And it would give me a chance to break the news of Gerard's murder to my mom while it was just the two of us, which I guessed was what Derek meant when he said to catch up on things.

"Noel and I will be fine," Derek added. "We won't starve. There's a pizza place right across the street. We'll order a pie and get to know each other. Talk about things."

Like Gerard's murder.

"Great idea," I said, beaming. "Mom?"

"Of course," Mom said, nodding. "It'll be nice. Just like the old days." She smiled.

"Excellent." If I hadn't known better, I'd say that Noel was happy to be rid of us, too. He rubbed his hands together. "Derek and I can get to know one another while you girls go have a good time."

Uh-oh. I tried to catch his eye to signal that I really, really didn't want him to have that conversation about Derek's intentions that we'd talked about, but he wasn't looking at me.

Outside on the road, a van from the medical examiner's office in Portland drove slowly by. All of us followed it with our eyes until it had passed.

"Wonder what's happened?" Jill said, a wrinkle between her eyes as she stood up to snuggle closer to her husband. He fitted his arm around her waist. "I hope it isn't another situation like Carolyn's."

Derek and I exchanged a glance. We shouldn't have, because she noticed and straightened. "What do you two know that we don't?"

"Don't tell me," Peter added jokingly, "Avery has stumbled over another dead body."

I grimaced. His face sobered. "Really?"

Mom turned to stare at me, her eyes huge.

"I'm afraid so," Derek said. "It was in the carriage house when we got there this morning. Upstairs, in what'll be the master bedroom."

"We thought he was sleeping," I added. "At first, I mean. Before we got a good look at him."

"Who?" Jill demanded, at the same time as Peter said, "A bum?"

"I wish. No, it was Kate's ex. He's been hanging around Waterfield for a couple of weeks, getting to know Shannon."

For a second, no one spoke. Then—

"Oh, dear!" Mom said faintly, clutching Noel's arm.

"Poor Kate," Jill muttered, shaking her head. "Poor Shannon."

Peter looked down at her, then dropped his hand from her waist. He had gone pale under his usual olive complexion.

"Sit down, honey. Here." He pulled out the desk chair and put her into it. "I'll go take care of the car."

Truth be told, he looked worse than she did, but Jill sank down on the chair again and smiled at him. He smiled back—it looked more like a grimace—before heading out the back door into the auto shop. I watched him, perplexed, until I couldn't see him anymore. It seemed rather an abrupt departure, if you asked me.

"Why don't you go on, too, Tink," Derek said and patted my shoulder. "You and your mom go have a good time. I'll see you back at the B&B in a couple hours."

I glanced up at him. "You sure?"

"Positive. Noel and I will still be fine."

"If you're sure," I said tentatively. "Mom?"

Mom nodded. She kissed Noel on the cheek and took my arm. We walked out of the garage and left the three of them together.

"He's lovely, Avery," Mom said warmly a minute later, as we walked toward downtown. Her voice was the only warm thing about the situation: The temperature was below freezing and there was icy slush all over the road and sidewalk.

"Who? Derek?" I smiled. "He *is* great, isn't he? So you two got along?"

"Oh, of course. That man could charm a stone." Mom added, "Much like Noel."

"Noel is lovely, too," I agreed. "I really like him. Although I'm a little concerned that he's back there right now, trying to guilt Derek into proposing to me."

"Why would he do that?" Mom wanted to know. "Do you want Derek to propose?"

I blinked. It's hard to credit, but I hadn't actually thought about it in those terms. I mean, I had thought about him proposing. I had pictured it, wondering if he would, and wondering how I'd respond if he did . . . but I hadn't ever considered whether I wanted him to. Our relationship was pretty perfect just the way it was. We saw each other every day, worked together most of the time, spent more time together than most married couples . . . but at the end of the day, if we wanted to, we could get away from one another. We had our own individual spaces. And down the line, if things didn't work out, we could separate a whole lot more easily if we weren't shackled together in bonds of holy matrimony.

"I don't think so," I said eventually. "At least for the time being, things are fine the way they are. I don't need a ring on my finger to know I'm in a relationship."

Mom nodded. "It's early days yet. Taking the time to make sure how you feel before you make any decisions seems wise."

I glanced over at her. "Is that what you did? When you met Noel?"

Mom smiled, her blue eyes sparkling. "I knew the moment I set eyes on him. There was no need to take any more time than that. I just had to wait for him to realize it, too."

"How could you know? I mean, isn't that kind of like falling in lust?"

Hard to imagine anyone lusting after my portly and past middle-age stepfather, but surely it isn't possible to love someone from the moment you set eyes on them? Anyone else I'd met, who claimed to have fallen in love at first sight, had gotten burned. Derek with Melissa, Kate with Gerard—me with Philippe. Then again, Jill had probably fallen in love, or at least in lust, with Peter at first sight, and they seemed to be doing OK.

"It isn't like that," Mom said. "When it's right, you just know."

"So if I don't just know, then it isn't right? Because I thought I knew with Philippe, and with Will, and with Ian, and with Gareth . . ."

Mom shrugged. "I don't know what to tell you, Avery. I knew as soon as I met Noel that I wanted to be with him, but of course I'd known him for a while by then. Online, you know. I knew he seemed to be a nice man and that we had a lot in common; I just hadn't actually met him yet. And with your father . . . I was twenty-one or twenty-two, he was handsome and charming, and I fell flat for him. And we had a good life. We had you. We'd still be married if he hadn't died."

"But if you and Dad were still married, what about Noel?"

"I don't know, Avery," Mom said. "These are some very big questions. But if life had taken a different turn, and Kenneth hadn't decided to go for a ride late at night, and that other driver hadn't hit him, and we were still married . . . then maybe Claudette—that's Noel's ex-wife—wouldn't have decided she needed to stretch her wings and find herself, either, and they'd still be together, too. Or he would have met someone else he liked, who made him happy."

"Different futures?"

"Something like that."

"So why didn't the two of you just live in sin?"

"At my age?" Mom chuckled. "We're old enough to like the convention of marriage, I guess. I was brought up to believe that you'd meet someone, get married, and settle down. And I've already had one good experience; I wasn't afraid to try again. There is safety in marriage. And I like the commitment. It's too easy to leave if you're not married."

"There's that," I admitted. The flip side of easily being able to dissolve the relationship is that it's too easy to dissolve the relationship. (Yes, I know it's the same thing. The difference is in how you look at it.) Would I want it to be easy to dissolve my relationship with Derek, I wondered. My instincts said no—I'd want to hold on to him for as long as I could—but if he wanted to leave, would I perhaps feel differently?

"Don't worry about it, Avery." Mom patted my arm. "When it happens, you'll know what to say."

"You think?"

"Of course, honey." She smiled and looked around. "Well, this hasn't changed much."

We had reached Main Street, and I looked around, too. No, I imagined it hadn't, not since the last time Mom was here, and not in the eighty years before that, either.

"That's Derek's apartment," I said, pointing to the windows above the True Value hardware store. "He has a loft on the second floor. It used to belong to Peter Cortino, but when Peter and Jill got married—and Melissa divorced Derek—he moved in there instead."

"Seems like a fair trade," Mom opined. "You know, Avery, when I was here before, I don't remember there being quite so many handsome men in Waterfield. Derek, Peter Cortino, and that chief of police isn't bad, either . . ."

"Well, Peter's new. He's only been here for five or six years. He moved from Boston, I think. Not too long after Kate and Shannon."

"An Eastie." Mom nodded. "I recognize the accent."

"Right. And no offense, but they're all younger than you are. By a few years. When we were here for Aunt Catherine's funeral, Derek was"—I counted on my fingers—"nine, and Wayne Rasmussen was probably twenty or so. It's not likely you would have noticed him."

"That's true," Mom admitted. "Still, I can see why you like it here, Avery." She grinned.

"So you're not disappointed? You don't wish I was in New York, working on Madison Avenue? After all the time and effort—and expense—of putting me through Parsons?"

"As long as you're happy," Mom said, "it's all that matters. If you're happy, I'm happy."

I smiled. We linked arms and continued up the sidewalk.

Since it was going on lunchtime, I took her by Derek's favorite deli and bought her a lobster roll. She agreed that it was excellent, and she even ordered a Moxie to go with it, while I stuck to Diet Coke. Afterward, we headed back out into the ice and snow toward Aunt Inga's house.

We had gone maybe a block or so, to just outside John Nickerson's store, when we came face-to-face with Cora Ellis and Beatrice.

Cora looked worried, her round face pinched and her eyes shadowed. When she saw me, she grabbed my arm. "What's going on over at Kate's B&B, Avery? Why are the police there?"

"There was a problem overnight," I explained. "When we got to work this morning, we found a body in the carriage house."

Her fingers tightened on my arm. "A body? Whose body?"

Cora has lived in Waterfield most of her adult life. She must be wondering which of her friends or acquaintances had met with an untimely demise.

I hastened to reassure her. "Nobody local. It was Kate's ex. Shannon's father. From Boston."

Beatrice gasped.

"Oh, no," Cora exclaimed. "How awful! Was he in town for the wedding?"

"We don't know why he was in town. Except that he's been hanging around with Shannon for the past couple of weeks."

"Oh, dear. She must be devastated, poor girl." Cora glanced at her own daughter, who seemed pretty devastated, too, considering that she didn't know—couldn't have known—Gerard.

"She's pretty upset," I said. "She hadn't known him long—apparently there was very little contact while she was growing up—but they'd seen each other pretty regularly the past few weeks, from what I understand."

"Oh, dear. What happened to him?"

I shrugged apologetically. "I don't really know. Wayne mentioned something about poison, but I'm not sure whether that means he was poisoned deliberately or if it could have been an accident. And then he couldn't breathe. Not sure whether that was accidental or on purpose, either. Maybe a side effect of whatever he took. As for what he was doing in the carriage house in the middle of the night, I have no idea. I guess Wayne and Brandon will have to figure that out."

"Oh, dear." Cora shook her head sadly.

I took the opportunity to make introductions. "Cora, this is my mom, Rosemary Carrick. Mom, this is Cora Ellis, Derek's stepmother, and Beatrice . . . um . . ."

"Gremilion," Bea murmured.

"Beatrice Gremilion, Cora's daughter."

"Nice to meet you." Mom shook hands with both of them. While she and Cora discovered that they had both grown up in Portland and set out to decide whether they had any old friends or experiences in common, I turned to Beatrice.

"How are things with you?"

"Fine." She smiled. It didn't reach all the way to her eyes, but I didn't think it was anything personal.

"Are the Stenhams treating you OK? You're still up there at the Clovercroft site, right?"

She nodded. "I hardly ever see them. Melissa stops in once in a while, but I rarely see anyone else. There's no construction going on, either."

I shook my head. "Sometime over the summer, a backhoe turned up human bones on the construction site. The archaeology department at Barnham excavated and decided that it was an old Indian burial ground. Penobscots or Micmacs or something. And now the various nations are arguing over who has jurisdiction and whether or not to re-inter the remains. Ray and Randy just want to dig 'em up and get rid of them, of course, but the tribes would prefer that their ancestors stay where they are. Understandably so. If they were my ancestors, I wouldn't want to dig 'em up, either."

"On the other hand," Beatrice murmured, "one can understand why the Stenhams just want to move forward with their project."

I nodded. "Oh, sure. They've paid for the land, paid for the survey, paid for materials, and paid to get things rolling . . . and now it's all just sitting there, and they can't do anything but wait it out. It could take years before some sort of decision is made, and it's an unholy mess."

I smiled, since the idea that the entire construction zone was lying barren, and that the Stenhams and Melissa were unable to cash out and get their investment back, brought me great pleasure. Small of me, no doubt, but that didn't stop me from reveling in the feeling. Maybe they'd even fall on hard times and have to stop buying up land and putting up cracker-box houses. It wasn't like they were hurting. Their other development, Devon Highlands, was going great guns, with parcels selling for more than a hundred grand each, and the houses topping out at five hundred thousand or so. So there'd be presents under the Stenhams' Christmas trees this year, too, I was sure.

"I'm sorry you have to sit there by yourself all day," I added. "It must be boring."

Beatrice shrugged. "I'm used to being alone," she said. "And I'm finding things to do. Straightening out the Stenhams' bookkeeping is a big job. There's been some very interesting balancing going on."

"Really? I guess maybe Carolyn Tate wasn't quite the treasure Melissa claimed. I should have known she was exaggerating."

Melissa had gone on TV after the accident and extolled Carolyn's virtues as a bookkeeper and member of the team; heck, practically a member of the family.

Beatrice didn't answer. Looking around for a distraction, she found it in John Nickerson's display window. "Wow. What a great dress."

"Isn't it?" I moved to stand next to her. "I was actually thinking about buying it. Letting John keep it until after Christmas, since I don't want to destroy his decorations before the Victorian weekend, but putting a deposit down so I can wear it on New Year's Eve. Wouldn't it look great with black stockings and black shoes, and with a big, black flower at the waist?"

Beatrice glanced down at me. Like most everyone, she has me beat by a few inches. "You could pull that off. I don't think I could."

"Of course you could. Although that style probably isn't the best choice for you. Too"—I hesitated—"girly."

I knew her to be under thirty, younger than me by a few years. But she was looking older than her real age at the moment. Her mouth was pinched and her features strained, and there were shadows under her eyes, like maybe she was missing Steve more than she'd thought she would.

I added, "What I meant was, this isn't your kind of dress. You need something more sophisticated. More elegant. With your figure, you can pull off high fashion. I can't. I'm too short, for one thing."

And not bony enough, for another. My face is round, my nose is pert, my hair is kinky; there is nothing elegant or sophisticated about me. While Beatrice had that clothes-hanger figure down pat and cheekbones for days.

"I had a part-time job in the accounting department at Filene's Basement on Boylston Street in Boston for a while," Beatrice said, her lips curving reminiscently.

"No kidding?" Filene's is an institution. Designer clothes at fifty to seventy-five percent off, and then there's the Brides' Run . . . "Why did you leave it?"

She glanced over at me. "Steve got this incredible job with an incredible salary, and I didn't have to work anymore. I could just go home all day and putter. He told me I should take advantage."

"How long ago was this?"

"Two years." She stared into John's plate glass window. "At first it was wonderful. We'd been struggling to make ends meet for long enough that I appreciated not having to worry about money. I'd been holding down two and sometimes three part-time jobs so Steve could finish school, and suddenly we had enough that not only did I not have to work anymore, we could hire someone to cook and clean. I didn't have to do anything but sleep in, go to lunch with my friends once in a while, work in the garden, go shopping, and not in the clearance racks. . . ."

"But?"

"But eventually I got bored. I had everything, but no one to share it with. Steve was always working. Weekdays and weekends, holidays and vacations. Thanksgiving, Christmas, our anniversary, and my birthday. He was just never home."

"That must have been hard," I said, sympathetically.

She shrugged. "Not compared to what some people have to deal with. My dad used to beat my mom black and blue. Steve never raised a hand to me. We never argued, never fought, never even disagreed; he just wasn't ever there."

"So you left."

She nodded. "Better to be alone by yourself, than alone with somebody, don't you think?"

"I guess," I admitted.

• • •

"Nice lady," Mom said after we'd said good-bye to Cora and Beatrice and were on our way up the hill toward the Village.

"Cora? Yeah, she's great, isn't she? I've been looking forward to introducing the two of you. I figured you'd get along."

"They invited us for dinner tomorrow night. Of course you and Derek are included."

I nodded. I had heard Cora extend the invitation and had assumed as much. "I'll tell him. Although you do realize it'll be much easier to discuss us if we're not there, right?"

"Now, why would we be talking about you behind your backs, Avery?" Mom wanted to know and slipped her hand through my arm again. "You're not sixteen. It isn't like Noel and I have to approve of your boyfriend before you can go out with him."

"It helps if you like him, though. Not so I can go out with him"—since we were a ways beyond that by now—

"but because it's just nice when you like my boyfriends. I don't think you ever have."

"You've dated some real duds," Mom said calmly. "Starting with that garage band musician in high school and ending with Philippe. Phil. Whatever. Not a decent human being among them."

"Derek's a decent human being."

"He seems to be. And I remember Ben Ellis from when I was growing up; he's always struck me as a nice guy. And I really like Cora. Although her daughter seemed . . ." Mom thought for a second before she said, judiciously, "Troubled."

I nodded. I had noticed the same thing. Gerard's death seemed to have upset her, for some reason. Maybe she was thinking of Steve and realizing that anything could happen to him in her absence. "She just left her husband. He's always working and never home, so she figured if she was going to be alone anyway, she might as well be alone by herself. Or with her family around her."

Mom nodded. "It's a good thing, living in a time and place where a woman can leave her husband without legal or moral repercussions."

I had honestly never thought about it. Being able to leave a dysfunctional relationship seems like it ought to be a right. It's a sad thing when marriages break up, but sometimes, it's the only choice. But Mom had a point: In other parts of the world, it was a right many women didn't have. Even in our part of the world, women hadn't always had it. As recently as a hundred years ago, women didn't have the right to vote in elections. And as Miss Barnes and Derek had told me, up until World War I, the navy hadn't been willing to accept women in its ranks. As soon as the war was over, it kicked back out the ones whom it had relied on.

And even now, there were women who wanted to leave their husbands and couldn't for fear of repercussions. I had a feeling Cora knew all about that. So did Bea, having grown up with an abusive father.

"Looking on the bright side," I said, "at least it doesn't sound as if Steve is the possessive sort. I don't think he'll be showing up in Waterfield with a shotgun."

"Be grateful for small favors," Mom said. "There have been too many murders in this quiet little town already."

—10—

The Waymouth Tavern is located a few miles outside town, overlooking the ocean and the small islands that dot the Maine coastline. Rowanberry Island, where Derek's Colonial house is located—the Colonial house that Derek wants to renovate—is one of them, and we pointed it out to Mom and Noel over dinner. Noel had the lobster, of course; you can't visit Maine for the first time and not have lobster. Mom had crab cakes, and so did I, to show solidarity and because I like them. And Derek, being Derek, had a burger and fries.

He's one of those supermetabolic people who'll never get fat because his body burns calories so fast, and usually, when there's food in front of him, he focuses on eating it. To the exclusion of anything else, including conversation. At first it bothered me, since I took it to mean that he wasn't interested in me or what I was talking about. Now I know that it doesn't mean anything at all, except that he's hungry. Once he gets some food into him, he'll pay me attention again. This evening, in an effort to impress Mom and Noel, he was on his best behavior. I even managed to get a couple of words out of him between bites. The rest of the time, Noel, Mom, and I held down the conversation. Mom told Noel how downtown had changed—or not—since she was last in Waterfield, and how we'd met Cora and Beatrice and been invited to supper tomorrow, and how nice Aunt Inga's house looked and what a marvelous job Derek and I had done on the renovations.

Aunt Inga's house—my house now—is an 1870s Second Empire Victorian with a square tower, a mansard roof laid in a flower pattern, and tall, thin windows. Derek had painted it a lovely robin's egg blue, with cornflower and ochre trim, back in August, and just last weekend, he had hung strings of blue Christmas lights along the porch and around the front door for the season. It looked like a fairy-tale cottage.

Mom and I had stopped by for a brief tour before heading back to the B&B this afternoon. She had admired the mosaic backsplash I had painstakingly put together out of the broken china someone had left all over Aunt Inga's floor, and the original kitchen cabinets that Derek had made me keep and that I had jazzed up with some antique lace panels cut from Aunt Inga's never-used wedding veil. And of course she had met the cats, Jemmy and Inky, two monstrously large Maine coons that I had inherited along with Aunt Inga's house back in June. Six months later, we were still tiptoeing around each other, trying to figure out our relationship. Or I was tiptoeing, anyway, while Jemmy and Inky were making it clear that I was there for their convenience, not the other way around.

I didn't have any pets growing up. The apartment in New York was small for Mom, Dad, and me, as are most apartments in New York; plus, it had a no-pets policy. And I lived in the same apartment until I moved to Waterfield, with just Mom after my dad died; alone after she moved to California. I had friends who had pets, though. Amy had three rabbits, which chewed the electrical cords and tried to bite me if I attempted to pick them up. And Laura Lee, Philippe's lawyer, had a dog: a small Yorkshire terrier named Muffin who ate better food and had more expensive accessories than I do. Laura carries Muffin around in a monogrammed bag so the dog's polished toenails never need touch the pavement, and she feeds it gourmet dog food from the Kanine Kafé. Reba was the only one with a cat, and it was a Siamese so ancient it practically creaked when it moved. Mostly, I'd see it in Reba's lap, being stroked, or curled into a ball on the sofa. So nothing had really prepared me for the responsibility of two fully grown, extremely healthy Maine coon cats who were used to coming and going as they pleased, and who had absolutely no use for a human.

Aunt Inga had bequeathed them to me, though, so I did my best, and we'd forged an uneasy sort of bond where we inhabited the same house—when the cats deigned to come home—and where I made sure their bowls were filled with food and water and that they got their checkups regularly to keep them healthy. Beyond that, we coexisted by pretending the other wasn't there. Imagine my surprise when they both walked right up to my mother and butted their heads against her legs and—when she bent down—her hands.

"They liked her," I told Derek at dinner. "They don't like anyone, but they liked my mom."

"Of course," Derek answered smoothly, with a wink across the table. "They have good taste. I like your mom, too."

I sniffed. "So if they have good taste, and they don't like me, what does that mean, exactly?"

"Nonsense, Avery," Mom said, "of course they like you. I'm just new and exciting, that's all. Or maybe I remind them of Aunt Inga."

"Hah," I answered and turned to Noel. "So how did it go at Cortino's earlier? Was Peter able to help you?"

"Oh, yes." Noel caught Mom's eye as he nodded. "Peter was very helpful. It's all taken care of."

"Excellent," Mom said, smiling at her crab cakes.

I looked from Noel to Derek. "Did he say anything about Gerard after we left? Or did Jill?"

Derek shook his head. "Why would he?"

I shrugged. "No reason, I guess. I just thought he looked shocked when he heard the news."

"We all looked shocked when we heard the news, Avery," Mom said.

I huffed, exasperated. "I know that. I just thought he looked more shocked than he ought to look, if he didn't know Gerard."

"I guess maybe he thought Waterfield would be safer than this," Derek said. "I think he moved here to get away from Boston and all the crime. And now we've had nothing but dead bodies ever since you moved here in June."

"Thanks ever so," I began, and then stopped when he caught sight of something—or someone—beyond me. Derek's eyes turned flat, and he straightened up, as if bracing himself. I turned to look over my shoulder and rolled my eyes. "Oh, great."

"What?" Mom said.

"Melissa."

Mom raised an eyebrow.

"Hi, Derek," a voice purred as a vision in creamy white cashmere and taupe suede stopped beside the table. An elegant hand with long, French-manicure-tipped talons landed on his shoulder. Another reason to dislike her: I've never been able to keep my nails long or to keep polish on them. "Hello, Avery," she added, a good deal less sweetly.

I smiled back, insincerely. Or maybe it would be more accurate to say that I showed teeth.

Melissa James brings out the worst in me. Not only the worst of my inferiority complexes, but the worst of my behavior, too. I don't like her. In addition to having been married to Derek for five years, while I've known him for only a few months, she's tall and elegant, with pale hair razor-cut in a sleek wedge, and huge violet blue eyes. Real, of course; not contacts. She's always dressed to the nines, in designer originals and tasteful—and, above all, genuine—jewelry, while I'm short and bouncy with kinky hair the color of Mello Yello. I gritted my teeth, wishing I wasn't wearing jeans and a fuzzy turtleneck, and that I was taller and my hair wasn't so frizzy and that I had bigger boobs and longer legs.

Melissa had already moved on. "And these must be your parents." She bathed Mom and Noel in the brilliance of her smile. I swear she has more teeth than a crocodile, and they're impossibly white. "I'm Melissa James." She took the hand off Derek's shoulder and offered it to my mother.

"Nice to meet you," Mom said, with—I was pleased to note—just about as much sincerity as I'd been able to muster. Mom must already be feeling proprietary toward Derek, and Melissa clearly didn't intimidate her. "I've heard a lot about you."

"Oh?" Melissa glanced at Derek, whose bland expression gave nothing away. Then she turned to Noel and turned the charm up another notch at the same time, until it was almost visibly oozing out of her (invisible) pores. "And you must be Avery's dad. So nice to meet you!"

"The pleasure is all mine," Noel said politely.

Melissa beamed at us all. "So you've come up to visit Avery. How do you like Waterfield?"

As the most successful Realtor in town, the one whose slogan is "Selling Waterfield one yard at a time," Melissa obviously feels a proprietary interest in the place. She has bought and sold enough of it, certainly.

"Fine, fine," Noel said with a glance at Mom.

Mom smiled brightly. "It's quite different from what it used to be, isn't it? A few years ago, Waterfield was such a lovely, quaint little place. Before all the building and development, and before all the flatlanders started moving in." She sighed and shook her head, sadly.

Melissa flushed, I'm happy to say. Not only is she a flatlander and a Southerner—she's from Maryland or West Virginia or some such place—but she's also responsible for selling Waterfield properties to many of the other

flatlanders, and, through her boyfriend, she's responsible
for quite a lot of the building and development, too.

"So how is my dear cousin Mary Elizabeth?" Mom
added. "Avery tells me you're seeing Randall now."

"Raymond," I said.

Mom glanced at me. "Raymond. Of course. My mistake. How are the Stenhams, Ms. James?"

Melissa recovered her poise and told Mom that Aunt
Mary Elizabeth was fine, except for her health. Apparently Mary Elizabeth is what used to be called delicate. I'd
be delicate, too, if I had brought Ray and Randy into the
world. They'd been thoroughly nasty little boys who had
tied me to a tree and left me there for hours the summer
I was five. And they had not improved with age. I hadn't
even been in Waterfield a week when Randy threatened me
with bodily harm if I didn't sign Aunt Inga's house over to
him and Ray and leave town.

For this and other reasons I had endeavored to avoid
Aunt Mary Elizabeth during the time I'd been here. I didn't
think I'd know her if I saw her on the street. Mom, on the
other hand, had met her many times growing up, while my
grandfather was still alive and the family came up to visit.
Naturally, Mom might like to see her cousin while she was
here. Or if she didn't precisely want to, she might feel an
obligation. She told Melissa that she and Noel were staying
at Kate's B&B, and she would call tomorrow to see if Mary
Elizabeth might be interested in getting together.

The mention of Kate's B&B got Melissa off on another
tangent. "I hear you've found another body, Avery." She
smiled at me with no warmth whatsoever. "Who was it this
time?"

"If you know about the body, how come you don't know
who it was?" I countered.

Melissa shrugged elegant shoulders under the cashmere.
"Tony didn't know. Just that the police were investigating.
Apparently Wayne's being stingy with the details."

"In that case," I said, "I'm not sure I should tell you,
either."

Tony, by the way, is Tony "the Tiger" Micelli, investigative reporter for Portland's channel eight news. I'd encountered him before, a couple of months ago, after Derek and I found that skeleton in the crawlspace of the house we were renovating on Becklea Drive. The fact that Tony is slick and slimy and calls Melissa "Missy" was enough to turn me against him, although the final nail in his coffin was when he said that he was keeping his fingers crossed for another John Wayne Gacy story, as in the serial killer. The fact that anyone—even an on-air reporter with the IQ of a turnip—would wish such a discovery on anyone was seriously disturbing.

"Be nice, Avery," Derek said. "Wayne will go out with a statement as soon as he can, I'm sure, Melissa. But in the meantime, I'll tell you. The deceased was Kate's ex. Shannon's father."

Melissa turned pale under the meticulously laid makeup. "Gerard? How terrible!"

"Did you know him?" I asked.

She turned to me. "Of course not. How would I know him? He wasn't from Waterfield."

I shrugged. "You knew his name. And you do seem to hook up with every good-looking man who comes through town sooner or later, so I thought maybe your paths had crossed."

"Why, thank you, Avery!" She smiled.

"You're welcome." I hadn't meant it as a compliment, but then she knew that.

"Be nice, Tinkerbell," Derek murmured and put a hand on my back. It was warm and hard through my sweater, and I leaned a little closer to him.

Melissa watched us. "Tinkerbell?" she repeated, an elegant eyebrow arched. "How sweet." She smiled condescendingly before focusing on Derek. "What was it you used to call me, again?"

"You didn't really lend yourself to nicknames, Melissa," Derek said, although there was a little extra color in his cheeks, I thought.

Melissa smiled, as at a private joke. Or a nice memory.

"I should get going. I have a client waiting. Nice to meet you both." She smiled at Mom and Noel, who grimaced back, politely. "Here's my card. Give me a call sometime. I have some lovely condos just getting ready to go on the market in the new year. Granite counters, stainless steel appliances, ocean view, and a very good price, considering. I'll be happy to give you a preview, if you'd like."

"We live in California," Mom said.

"Oh, of course." Melissa nodded. "But with your daughter settled here, at least for the time being, I thought you might consider purchasing a place to stay when you come to visit. Kate's bed and breakfast is lovely—I sold it to her; I should know—but it isn't like having your own space, is it? And since you're family, I'm sure Ray and Randy would give you a good deal. Just something to think about."

She bathed us all in another blindingly white smile before turning on her heel and slithering off, cashmere swinging around her calves.

"I hate that witch," I muttered as I watched her go.

"That's not very nice," Derek answered mildly.

I glanced up at him, still tucked in the crook of his arm. "Can you blame me?"

His eyes were level. "Actually, I can. Melissa and I have been divorced for almost six years. It's over between us. You have nothing to worry about."

"It's not that I'm worried, exactly," I said. Although worried was exactly what I was, of course. "What *did* you used to call her?"

"Like I said," Derek said, "she didn't lend herself to nicknames."

"I can think of a few." I straightened up, putting some distance between us.

"I'm sure you can," Derek said and dropped his arm from around my waist. "But there's no need."

"Because you don't want to hear anything against her?"

"Because you won't call her anything I haven't already called her myself. Let it go." He turned away to the view.

Mom looked from one to the other of us. "If she'd never

met the murdered man," she said, "how *did* she know his name? She never explained that."

"Kate told her?" Derek suggested, over his shoulder. "They talk sometimes."

"When Kate can't avoid it," I said. "I doubt she'd confide any secrets in Melissa."

"I don't know that Gerard's name would be a secret," Derek answered. "It's not like Kate's ever tried to pretend that Shannon was found under a cabbage leaf."

"That's true." I took a breath, a deep one, to pull myself together. I wasn't doing myself any favors by acting like a jealous teenager. "She might have mentioned it when she first came to town, while she and Melissa were looking at houses together. Before Kate bought the B&B and realized what a waste of oxygen Melissa is."

Derek rolled his eyes. "Don't hold back, Avery."

"I never do," I said.

• • •

When we knocked on Kate's kitchen door around eight A.M. the next morning, both McGillicutty women were up and about, if not exactly chipper. Shannon looked like death warmed over, huddled at the breakfast table wrapped in a blue robe, her hair a straggly mess and her face naked. She was ghostly pale, with dark circles under her swollen eyes and a sort of little-girl-lost look to her that was painful to see.

Kate wasn't in much better shape. I had called her the night before to make sure she was OK, and she had assured me that she was, but it looked like she had spent a rough night. She was pale like her daughter, her freckles standing out across the bridge of her nose and her cheeks, and with the same dark circles under her eyes. If she had cried for Gerard, after the first time yesterday morning, she showed no signs of it, though. Her hazel eyes were neither red nor swollen, and although she was pale, she was composed. She was standing at the stove when we walked in, cooking what smelled like French toast.

"Any news?" Derek asked.

Kate turned to him. "Not much. Brandon has gone through the carriage house from top to bottom looking for evidence, and he says they'll probably release it sometime today or tomorrow. It's sparkling clean. Not so much as a speck of sawdust anywhere."

"What did they come up with? Anything helpful?"

Derek pulled out a chair for me and took one himself, keeping his eyes on Kate.

"They're not telling me," Kate said, her voice brittle. "Apparently we're suspects."

Shannon closed her eyes, as if in pain. Or disgust.

"Oh, for God's sake," I said, "of course you're not suspects. Wayne can't possibly think you had anything to do with this."

"Wayne's not in charge anymore. He's a suspect, too." She flipped a piece of toast.

"You're kidding!"

Kate shook her head. "He was here the night Gerard was put in the carriage house."

"Put?"

She nodded. "Apparently he died somewhere else and was dumped here."

"Ugh." Who'd do something like that to us? Or to Kate and Shannon?

"What does that have to do with Wayne?" Derek asked.

"Nothing really," Kate answered, "except that he got here late, when I was already asleep. He could have put the body in the carriage house before coming inside."

"Why would he do that?" I asked.

"No idea. But when my ex-boyfriend shows up three weeks before my wedding and ends up dead, the police have to look at my fiancé. That's just the way it is."

"Even when your fiancé is the chief of police?"

Kate shrugged and put her spatula down on the stove to rub her eyes.

"So who's in charge, if not Wayne?" I asked. "Is Brandon handling the investigation on his own?"

At twenty-two, was he ready for such a big responsibility?

I mean, if there was ever a case we didn't want mishandled due to inexperience, it was this one.

Kate shook her head. "Reece Tolliver from the state police in Augusta was called in to help."

"So what's Wayne doing now?" Derek asked.

Kate grimaced. "Directing traffic."

"What a mess," I said.

Kate nodded, picking up the spatula once more and turning back to the French toast.

"How are you holding up?" Derek asked Shannon. "You hanging in there?"

"More or less. I couldn't sleep at all last night." Her voice was low, rusty. "I just can't imagine who would have done this, you know? He wasn't doing anything to anyone!"

"I think he must have been," Derek said gently, "for this to happen. Are you sure he didn't say anything to you? Mention anything he was doing or someone he had contact with? Other than you?"

She shook her head, fisting her hands in her hair as if to tear it out by the roots. "I've thought and thought about it. All night long. All day yesterday. I've gone over every word he ever said to me, twice, three times, and I don't know anything. He came up here to see me. And that's all I know!" Her voice rose.

"Sssh." Kate abandoned the stove to put an arm around her daughter's shaking shoulders. "Don't worry about it, honey. They'll find who did this. They'll catch him and put him away. I promise."

Derek motioned to the French toast. "This looks ready. Can you eat, Shannon?"

"I don't think so," Shannon said, her voice exhausted.

"Try a bite, OK?" He put a plate in front of her. "Get some food inside you."

Shannon lifted a fork and picked at her food. "I'm not hungry."

"I am," Derek said. "Here, Avery." He handed me my plate before sitting down next to Shannon with his own plate mounded with glistening slices of French toast.

My stomach rumbled. "Looks great."

"One of these days I'll teach you to cook, Avery," Kate promised. "When things aren't so crazy."

"One of these days, I might take you up on that. Until then, I'll just enjoy food someone else made." I smiled and put a piece of French toast in my mouth and chewed. Mmm, yummy!

Under the peer pressure, Shannon managed to choke down a few bites. Derek, of course, polished off two servings in less time than it took the rest of us to have one.

"So what are you and your parents planning to do today, Avery?" Kate wanted to know after a minute or two of keeping an eye on her daughter between bites of her own breakfast.

"I'm not sure," I admitted, chasing the last few pieces of toast through the syrup on my plate. "Are they still sleeping?" I hadn't heard any sounds from upstairs.

Kate glanced at the display on the stove. "Almost eight forty-five. Three hours earlier in California. That makes it almost six o'clock. They'll wake up in the next hour or so, most likely."

"Well, Mom mentioned something about trying to get in touch with her cousin Mary Elizabeth. You know, Ray and Randy Stenham's mother."

Kate nodded. "I keep forgetting that you guys are related. You haven't gone to visit her, have you? Mary Elizabeth?"

I shook my head. "I've endeavored to avoid that pleasure."

Derek snorted. "I can understand that," Kate nodded.

"You know her?" I looked from one to the other of them.

Kate shook her head. "Oh, no. Know of her. Know her to look at. But I've never had occasion to talk to her. Don't think I'd care to."

Derek added, "I know her. Or rather, she knows Dad. Old Waterfield families and all that."

"Really? Well, Mom knew Mary Elizabeth growing up, so she doesn't really have a choice in the matter. She told me they never had much in common, but Mom can't very well come back to Waterfield and not see her family. And Mary Elizabeth is all that's left. Plus the twins."

Kate nodded. "Are you planning to go with her?"

I shrugged. "Depends on what she wants. If she asks, I don't think I can refuse."

"It'd seem petty," Kate admitted. "So does your aunt know that your mom's in town?"

"If she doesn't yet, she will soon. We ran into Melissa last night, at the Tavern, and Mom told her to tell Mary Elizabeth that Mom would be in touch. So Melissa will tell Ray, and Ray will tell his mom. And Mary Elizabeth will expect a call."

Like magic, Derek's cell phone rang and he picked it up, heading for the door.

"How did your mom like Melissa?" Kate wanted to know with a faint smile.

"She didn't. I've talked about Melissa, so of course Mom knew who she was as soon as she set eyes on her. Then Melissa flirted with Derek right in front of us, and she was a little too friendly with Noel, too. And then she totally dissed me. So it's safe to say that Mom didn't care for her. By the way, did you ever happen to talk to her about Gerard? Melissa, I mean? Not about the . . . um . . ."

I glanced at Shannon, sitting there like a shadow, and amended my statement. "Not about what happened yesterday, but before? That he's Shannon's father, where you met him, what happened between you, anything like that?"

Kate drew her brows together. "Why would I tell Melissa that I became pregnant at eighteen and that my boyfriend didn't want anything to do with me or his daughter? No offense, Shannon, but he hasn't been a regular part of your life until just a few weeks ago."

"You never liked him," Shannon said, too tired even to work up any steam about it.

Kate rolled her eyes. "Of course I liked him. I was crazy about him. Until I had you and realized he wasn't ready to be a daddy."

When Shannon didn't respond, Kate turned back to me. "Why do you ask, Avery?"

"What? . . . Oh, because she knew his name. Melissa. Knew Gerard's name. She swore she didn't know him, but she knew his name. So I thought maybe you'd mentioned him sometime. When you first moved to Waterfield, or something. While she was showing you properties, maybe. Before you realized what a witch she is."

Kate thought about it. "I may have," she said eventually. "It's not impossible. I don't remember doing it, but it's not inconceivable that I could have, in passing. It would have been six years ago, if so. That's a long time to remember a throwaway remark."

I nodded. It was. Especially for someone as self-absorbed as Melissa. It was also interesting. Fraught with possibilities, one might even say. If Kate had mentioned Gerard, then the problem was solved. But what if she hadn't? Then Melissa must have known about Gerard from somewhere else. And if she did, maybe she'd had something going with him on the side. I wouldn't put it past her. Like I'd said last night, she seemed to hook up with all the good-looking men in Waterfield sooner or later. First Derek, then Ray; she hadn't been above flirting with Peter Cortino when he first came to town, and I'd seen her sweet-talk Tony "the Tiger" Micelli. And if Ray had realized it—and Ray, like his twin Randy, wasn't above making threats and maybe even making good on them—was it possible that the Stenhams might have had a hand in Gerard's death? I had suspected them of having had a hand in Aunt Inga's, so it didn't seem like too much of a stretch.

Or was I grasping at straws and trying to find a way to implicate Melissa and the Stenham twins in anything I could? I'd been wrong about Aunt Inga—they hadn't had anything to do with her death—so maybe I was just as wrong now.

Before I had the chance to articulate any of these thoughts, the door opened and Derek walked back in. Hard on his heels came Josh, whose eyes went to Shannon immediately upon entering, and whose mouth turned down at the corners when he saw how she looked. She managed a smile, but it wasn't up to her usual brilliant standard.

Derek looked from one to the other of them for a moment before he focused on Kate. "Dad's gonna stop by in a few minutes, on his way to the office. He'll give her something to help her sleep. She needs rest."

Shannon looked mutinous, but Josh smiled approvingly, and Kate nodded.

"We need to go." Derek turned to me and reached out a hand.

"Sure." I stood and took it. "Have my mom give me a call when she gets up, OK, Kate?"

Kate promised she would, and Derek and I headed back out into the cold.

—11—

"What's the matter?" I asked as we made our way, not toward the carriage house, but to the truck. "Has something happened? Something more?"

He glanced down at me. "When Dad called, he told me that Beatrice didn't come home last night."

He opened the truck door and handed me up into the passenger seat.

"OK," I said when he had walked around the truck and boosted himself up behind the wheel. "That's a little unusual, I guess, but it's not like she's a kid. She's almost thirty, and has a job and a car and a life. I'm sure it isn't the first time she's stayed out all night."

"I know that," Derek said.

"Well, are you sure your dad or Cora didn't just miss a phone call, or something?"

"Cora doesn't think so." He put the truck in gear and headed down the road. "I called her after I got off the phone with Dad. She's worried."

"So maybe Steve finally showed up, and he and Beatrice are shacked up in a motel somewhere, making amends."

Maybe calling her mom had slipped Beatrice's mind. Under those circumstances, I think it might have slipped mine.

"She would have called," Derek said, turning the corner and speeding up.

I looked around. "Where are we going?"

"Clovercroft. It's where she was going the last time Cora saw her, after lunch yesterday, and it's where she's supposed to be this morning, in"—he glanced at the dashboard display—"eight minutes. She's very conscientious; she won't miss work without calling in sick. If she can." He rolled through a stop sign and kept going.

"What about Cora?" I wanted to know.

"She'll meet us there. Dad would come, too, but he's scheduled to work. And until we know that something's wrong, there's no sense in him missing time at the office. When he doesn't come in, sick people's appointments have to be rescheduled and stuff like that."

"Oh, absolutely." I nodded. "Chances are everything is just fine. Steve finally showed up, and they're together somewhere. Or she got tired of waiting for him and decided to go back to Boston. Or maybe she met someone else and went out on a date with him, and then one thing led to another, and now she's scrambling out of bed and throwing on her clothes to get to work on time."

Derek shot me a look. "Does that sound like Beatrice to you?"

"I don't know her very well," I pointed out.

"That's true. But you can take my word for it, that doesn't sound like something Beatrice would do. Go to Boston because she got tired of waiting for Steve to come after her, maybe, but she would have told someone she was going; she wouldn't just have disappeared. And it's only a couple of weeks since she left Steve; she's not going to jump into bed with someone else."

"If you say so." I sat back.

Derek ignored the comment and pushed down on the gas pedal.

• • •

Clovercroft, the Stenhams' currently nondeveloping multi-
use development of condos, townhomes, commercial spaces,
and single-family residences, is situated on the north side of
Waterfield, off the Augusta Highway. As we left the town
and headed inland, the signs of human habitation became
more sporadic and the landscape changed to include groves
of tall pine trees and slender birches, leafless now in mid-
winter. After about ten minutes, Derek turned right, onto
a road that ran through one such stand of trees, and which
let out into the usual construction zone. The ground was
plowed and mounded, and sprinkled with snow and ice.
Large rocks and boulders were grouped to one side, near
the tree line. Skeletal houses stood here and there, in various stages of completion, and tiny, triangular flags whapped
in the breeze, delineating the end of one parcel and the
beginning of the next. But instead of hustle and bustle, the
sound of hammering and sawing and large machinery moving around, and the activity and life that usually accompany
a construction site, Clovercroft was eerily quiet. Nothing
moved across the frozen ground save for a small group of
birds pecking at a piece of exposed dirt.

Derek parked the truck in front of the only completely
finished construction in the development: a row of four
brick commercial buildings with, most likely, apartments
or condominiums on the second floor. They looked to
be modeled after downtown Waterfield and the Victorian buildings lining Main Street, but without the quirky
charm of the originals. Rather than authentic and solid,
these looked like inferior copies, tossed up over a couple
of days.

"Shoddy workmanship," Derek muttered, looking at
them.

"I know. Pitiful, isn't it? Is that Beatrice's car?"

I pointed to the white Toyota with Massachusetts plates
parked in front of the far building.

Derek nodded. "That must be the office." He indicated

the far door and the tattered banner that was flapping in
the breeze from a pole above it, the words Model Home
printed on it in faded gold letters.

"Well, what are we waiting for?" I asked, when he didn't
move toward it.

"Cora. She's not here yet."

"No offense, but if you're concerned that Beatrice may
be in there, with something really wrong with her, don't
you think it would be better if we checked it out before
Cora got here?"

"Good point," Derek said. After a couple of steps he
looked down at me again, where I trotted alongside, half
running to keep up. "You know, Avery, sometimes your
mind works in very disturbing ways."

"Sorry," I said. "It's just that we found a dead body
yesterday, so they're on my mind. I've seen more than my
share in the past six months."

"Let's hope you won't see another today." Derek grabbed
the door handle. He twisted it, but the door didn't open.
"Huh." He knocked, then stepped back and waited.

"The sign says 'Back at nine,'" I pointed out. One of
those little fake clocks with the movable hands sat in the
window

"And it's past that now." He knocked again. There was
no answer this time, either.

I stamped my feet on the cold concrete and wrapped
my arms around myself for warmth. Derek tried to peer
through the window, but the interior of the building was
dark, and he couldn't see much. While we stood there
with our noses pressed against the glass, like kids outside
a candy store, Cora's green Saturn came into the lot and
parked next to the truck.

"Isn't she here?" she called as soon as the car door was
open and before she'd even swung her legs out.

Derek gave the office door a last rat-a-tat; more for
emphasis than because he thought he'd get an answer now
when he hadn't before. "If she is, she isn't coming to the
door. But that's her car, right?"

Cora glanced at the Toyota and nodded. "That's it. She took it to work yesterday, after lunch. Have you checked inside?"

"Inside the car?"

We hadn't, but now we did. There was no sign of Beatrice in the interior, and no obvious clues, either. No note conveniently left on the seat saying, "Call me at the Pines Motel room six," signed, *Steve*, and no signs of a struggle. Everything looked just the way it should, as if Beatrice had parked, gotten out, and gone inside to work. She had left the car doors unlocked, unworried about anyone trying to steal her vehicle out here in the middle of nowhere, so we were able to go over it with a fine-tooth comb. We even lifted and replaced the floor mats but didn't find anything more exciting than a parking ticket from last month in Boston.

"What about the trunk?" Cora asked.

Derek and I exchanged an involuntary look, and for all that he thought my mind moved in mysterious and disturbing ways, his own obviously did the same. "I'll check," he said and walked around to the back of the car. "Avery?"

I popped the trunk and waited a breathless moment before he said, "Nothing. Just some blankets and a little spade and an open bag of kitty litter. The usual."

"Kitty litter is usual?"

I own cats, but I don't carry kitty litter in my trunk. Or wouldn't, if I had a trunk to carry it in. Jemmy and Inky don't use a litter box—they're outdoor cats and do their business in nature—but what good does kitty litter do in a trunk? There aren't any cats there.

"It's for icy conditions," Derek explained. "Everyone in New England carries kitty litter. I'd have been more surprised if I didn't find it."

Cora nodded.

"I've never noticed a bag of kitty litter in the truck," I said, glancing at it.

"I keep it behind the seat." He slammed Beatrice's trunk shut. "Nothing useful here. Other than the fact that she obviously made it back to work after lunch yesterday, or the car wouldn't be parked here."

"Right." Cora turned back to the buildings.

"Not to be obvious or anything," I said, moving to stand beside her, "but you've tried to call her, right?"

Cora glanced at me. "Of course. Half the night and all morning. She's not answering. But I'll try again now. It's been fifteen minutes since last time." She pulled her cell phone out of her purse.

Derek came up to stand on her other side, like a matching bookend, silently adding his support. Cora dialed the number and put the phone to her ear. After a moment, we could hear distant ringing.

"What the hell . . . ?" Derek muttered, looking around.

"It's coming from inside." I pointed through the window, where a tiny green light pulsed. "She must have left her cell phone on the desk."

"Damn."

I nodded. That didn't sound right. If she'd left of her own free will, she probably would have taken her phone. If she hadn't left of her own free will, all the more reason to take it, of course, but she might not have had the chance. "You know her better than me. If Steve showed up and apologized and begged her to run off with him, would she be so overcome with joy that she'd forget her phone?"

"I wouldn't think so," Cora said, her voice strained, "but that's certainly a happier explanation than anything else I've come up with."

Derek pulled his own phone off his belt and dialed.

"Who are you calling?" I wanted to know.

He glanced at me. "We have to get inside. It's either breaking a window or finding someone with a key. So I'm calling Melissa."

I blinked. "You know Melissa's number by heart?" Or did he have it stored in his phone's memory?

Derek rolled his eyes. "Everyone in Waterfield knows Melissa's number, Avery. She's got For Sale signs all over town. In this case, though, I got it off that."

He pointed to a fifteen-by-thirty-foot billboard riding above the pine trees. "Welcome to Clovercroft," it said. "Lots from $50,000. Call Melissa James for more information." It was accompanied by Melissa's face, a hundred times magnified, all gleaming white teeth and violet blue eyes, and her phone number.

"Oh." I bit my lip, blushing. "Sorry."

"You should be. Melissa and I are done. Over. Finished. I wouldn't take her back if she . . . Melissa? It's Derek."

I choked back a giggle, and even Cora's lips twitched. Derek sent us both a sour look while he talked into the phone, his tone soothing. "No, of course not. Would I be so rude?" He grimaced, so I guess Melissa must have told him that yes, he would. "Never mind that, OK? I need a favor. Are you out of bed yet?"

Melissa quacked in his ear.

"Yes, of course," Derek said patiently. "Listen. I'm at Clovercroft. My stepsister Beatrice works in the office out here. Yes, I'm sure you know that." He rolled his eyes again. "Thank you, Melissa. To continue, then. Bea didn't come home last night. Her car is in the lot and her phone is ringing inside the office, but she's not here. Or if she is, she's not answering the door. I can break a window or take the lock off the door and get in that way, but I thought you might prefer to come out with a key."

Melissa quacked again. Derek glanced at his watch. "Fine. We'll be here." He ended the call and tucked the phone back in its pouch. "She's on her way. Or will be, once she gets moving. Her makeup is already laid, so it shouldn't take her more than a half hour or so."

Cora nodded.

We spent the next thirty minutes looking around the construction site. Derek got in the truck, which had four-wheel drive, and went bumping across the frozen ground, on the lookout for any sign of life or—although he didn't say it—foul play. I checked out the row of buildings as best I could. The commercial spaces were all locked, and there was no sign of life inside any of them. But I tried all the doors and peeked through all accessible windows, seeing nothing but construction debris and trash. Or rubbish, as they say in Maine. Cora, meanwhile, was on the phone. She called Dr. Ben to update him on the search, and then she called her other daughter, Alice, to tell her Beatrice was missing and to ask if she had spoken to Bea recently. I listened to Cora's half of the conversation with half an ear while I peered through windows and peeked into corners.

"You haven't? Not since the weekend? Well, what did she say? Uh-huh. Uh-huh. No, I'm afraid not. Not a word. She just didn't come home last night. Yes, I know that, honey. But her car is still parked outside the place where she works, and her phone is ringing inside the building, the only problem is that she's not here. Or if she's here, she's not able to answer the door."

Her voice hitched a little on the last sentence, and I went over and patted her shoulder.

"I would appreciate that," Cora said into the phone. "You have a key? Thank you. Let me know if you find her. Or what Steve has to say when you talk to him."

She shut her phone off. "Alice hasn't heard from her for several days. When they last spoke, Beatrice didn't say anything about leaving Waterfield or going back to Boston. She said she hadn't had any contact with Steve—as far as I know, too, she hasn't—and she didn't tell Alice that she'd met anyone else, either."

"It'd be very soon for her to get involved with someone else," I agreed. "Unless she was doing it to show Steve that they were finished, but I didn't get the impression that she was at that point yet." Unless she had simply indulged in a one-night stand. She wouldn't be the first unappreciated wife trying for some validation that way.

Cora shook her head. "I think she just wanted him to come after her. To promise that things would be different, and actually make them so. She wasn't interested in anyone else. She and Steve have been together for seven years. You don't just throw something like that away in a couple of weeks."

I nodded. "So Alice is going to go to Bea's place in Boston? And talk to Steve?"

Cora nodded. "Just in case Beatrice is there. Just in case Steve came to Waterfield and got her, and she was so excited she forgot to call and tell me she was leaving."

Her soft, blue eyes were shadowed, so in spite of the firm tone, I don't think she believed that Alice would find Beatrice and Steve snuggled up in bed together. She added, "And if she's not there, Steve needs to know that she's gone. They're still married. He's her next of kin."

"Unless he did something to her," I said.

Cora looked at me. I floundered on. "Um . . . he's not the type to come after her with a shotgun, is he? If he can't have her, no one can?"

"I wouldn't think so," Cora said, "although I wouldn't have thought anything could happen to her in our quiet, little town, either. I worried about her living in Boston—I worried about both my girls living in Boston—but maybe we're no safer here."

She looked around, as if seeing the place for the first time. In the distance, the truck navigated the ruts of a staked-out parcel and stopped for a second, engine running, so Derek could peer into the half-finished skeleton of a house. After a few moments, he moved on.

"Have you tried calling Steve?" I asked.

Cora shook her head. "Don't have his cell phone number. I tried calling the house, but there's no answer there. So he's either gone to work, or they're both there, together, and they just don't want to answer the phone. But Alice will figure it out."

I nodded, turning as another car engine approached through the trees. After a second, Melissa's cream-colored Mercedes came into the parking lot and pulled to a stop next to Cora's Saturn. Derek's truck changed direction and started making its way back toward us. The Mercedes' engine cut off, and Melissa got out.

I had hoped that since it was so early—barely nine in the morning—Melissa might look less put together than usual. Having her show up in ratty sweats with her hair undone and her face naked might be too much to hope for, but couldn't she have had the decency to be at least a little disheveled?

She looked just as dewy fresh as always, of course. Hair perfectly groomed, sleek and shiny, cupping her elegant jaw, and with no hint of dark roots. She was dressed in cream slacks and a sapphire blue silk blouse under that same cashmere coat as yesterday. The stones in her earlobes were probably real diamonds, and another sparkled on her finger when she pulled the key chain out of her purse.

"I'm so sorry," she said to Cora, her voice sympathetic. "I have no idea what's happened. I was out here yesterday morning and saw Beatrice then, and as far as I could tell, nothing was wrong with her. Should we wait for Derek before we open the door?" She glanced at the truck making tracks across the frozen ground, the tires spitting up little pieces of ice and dirt.

"Please," I said. Beatrice might be inside, in need of medical attention, in which case we needed Derek. Or, a little voice reminded me, Beatrice might be inside, dead, and if so, I'd definitely want Derek next to me when we made the discovery.

"I saw her in the middle of the day yesterday," Cora said. "She drove into town so we could have lunch together. We walked down to Main Street and met Avery and her mother on the way. And afterward she got back in the car to go back to work."

"And here's her car," I added.

Melissa nodded. "Of course."

Derek pulled the truck to a stop and got out, and she turned to him. "Derek. I'm so sorry."

He nodded, face grim. "Got the key?"

"Right here." She lifted it. "We were waiting for you."

"I'm here now." He headed for the door. "Let's do it."

Melissa inserted the key in the door and turned it. I held my breath as Derek reached out and turned the knob. The door opened soundlessly, and I was grateful.

The atmosphere at Clovercroft was creepy enough without doors opening with an eerie shriek. And it wasn't just the knowledge that Bea was missing and might be inside. Whether it was the fact that I knew that this place was an old burial ground, hallowed to the Native Americans, or because there's just something depressing about a construction zone where no one is constructing anything, I'm not sure, but the truth is, I was spooked. The sky was bright blue and the air was crisp, but the sun was hidden behind the bulk of dark pines, and they cast a shadow over the storefront where we were standing. I shivered.

"Beatrice?" Derek stepped through the open door. "Are you here?"

−12−

"I think it's time we call Wayne," Derek said ten minutes later.

We had ascertained that Beatrice was not in the office, alive or dead, and that there were no obvious clues to where she'd gone. Everything looked normal. There was no sign of a struggle or anything to indicate that she hadn't left under her own steam, except for the fact that her cell phone was still on the desk. And as it was half hidden under a stack of financial statements, things she must have been working on in the afternoon yesterday, it was conceivable she might have forgotten to take it with her when she left, quite possibly of her own volition.

A locked door at the very back of the office led upstairs to what Melissa called the model home.

"There are doors that can be locked on either end of the stairway," Melissa explained, demonstrating. "This door down here would be locked from the office, while the one up there would be locked and bolted from the apartment. That way, if the owner of the storefront doesn't need an attached apartment, he or she can rent it to someone else but not have to worry about the tenant getting into the office space. There's a separate stairway to the apartment with an entrance from outside."

"And the tenant can lock the door upstairs and not worry about the landlord or anyone from the office or store coming upstairs." I nodded. It was smart.

"Exactly." Melissa beamed at me, as if I were a slow student unexpectedly coming up with the right answer to a tricky question.

"Can we look upstairs?" Cora asked.

Melissa hesitated. "I'm afraid I don't have the key to the apartment on me. I gave it to someone a few weeks . . . I mean, a few *days* ago, and I haven't gotten it back yet."

I looked at her. She sounded like she was hiding something. "It wasn't Steve, was it?"

"Who?" This time she sounded perfectly sincere, and sincerely baffled.

"Never mind," I said.

"Steve is Beatrice's husband," Cora added.

"Oh. No." Melissa shook her head. "This wasn't Steve. Just a . . . um . . . maintenance man. Someone from the crew at Devon Highlands. The apartment needed some upkeep."

She turned to Cora. "I'm sorry I can't oblige you, Cora. If I can get the key back today, I'll let you know, and you can come back out and look around all you want. Although Beatrice would have had no reason to go upstairs, you know. And she wouldn't have had a key to get through the door up there, either, for that matter. But we can go to the top of the stairs, if you'd like, and I'll show you that the door is locked and bolted on the other side."

She undid the bolt on the downstairs door. As the two of them headed up, Derek pulled out his phone. "I think it's time we call Wayne."

"It hasn't been twenty-four hours yet," I pointed out. "Don't you have to wait twenty-four hours before you can file a missing-person report?"

"Officially, maybe. But Wayne's been relegated to traffic duty, so I'm sure he'd like something more exciting to

do than waving cars around for old Mr. Mosley's funeral."
He dialed. I waited while he connected with Wayne and
relayed the information.

"He's on his way," he said a minute later, tucking the
phone in his pocket just as Cora and Melissa came back into
the office. "Wayne," he added, in explanation. "It shouldn't
take him more than fifteen minutes to get here. Anything
upstairs?"

Cora shook her head. "Just a locked door. We knocked,
and there was no answer."

"There wouldn't be," Melissa added. "It's unoccupied.
Clovercroft isn't zoned for occupation yet."

"I'll talk to Wayne about getting the door open when
he gets here. He'll probably have a universal key, or something. Or a battering ram." Derek turned to me. "Do you
want to take the truck back to town, Avery? Your mom and
Noel must be awake by now."

"I don't know . . ." I said, glancing at Cora. And, I must
admit, at Melissa. "Don't you want me to stay?"

"Of course I want you to stay. I always want you to stay.
But there's nothing you can do here. And I know you're
eager to see your mom."

I nodded, reluctantly.

"We'll keep you up to date," Cora assured me. "I understand. Your mother came all the way here from California;
you shouldn't miss out on the opportunity to spend time
with her. If we find Beatrice, or find anything to tell us
where she is, Derek will let you know."

I took a breath. "OK. You convinced me, plus there's
nothing I can do here anyway. I just don't want you to feel
like I'm abandoning you."

"Never," Derek said with a grin. Cora shook her head.
"C'mon, Tink. I'll walk you out to the truck."

He guided me toward the door to the outside, pausing
only long enough for me to peck Cora's cheek. Once we got
out into the crisp winter air, though, he stopped.

"What?" I said, missing the feeling of his arm around
my shoulders.

"Didn't Melissa say there was an outside entrance to the model home? Wonder where it is?"

"Probably there." I pointed to a door on the other side of the storefront. "It's locked, though. I checked earlier."

"Huh." He went over anyway and shook the knob. It didn't open for him, either.

"Guess we'll just have to wait until Melissa gets the key back from whoever she gave it to."

"Guess so. Unless Wayne can get it open." He turned toward the truck again, but before he got there, he stopped. "What's that?"

"What?" I examined the ground in front of his feet. There was a glimpse of something shiny among the snow and dirt.

Derek bent to pick it up. "Cufflink," he said after a brief inspection. "With *RS* engraved on it. Ray Stenham, I guess. Or Randy. Not a clue at all. They've probably been in and out of here a million times, at least. One of 'em must have lost it sometime."

He stuffed it in his pocket. "Let's get you back to town, so you can see your mom."

When we got to the truck, he turned to me, boxing me in on both sides with his arms, hands braced against the hood and eyes serious. "Avery."

I nodded, my heart in my throat, the way it always is when I'm close to him.

"You'll drive carefully, right?" His eyes were deep blue, looking into mine.

I swallowed and nodded. "How will you get home?"

"I'll get a ride with Cora. Or drive Beatrice's car back to town, if Wayne thinks it's OK."

"You have a key to that?"

He grinned. "No, but I have a screwdriver."

I rolled my eyes. "The fruits of a misspent youth."

"Something like that." He leaned in. I closed my eyes. And when his mouth closed over mine, I lifted my arms and wound them around his neck and returned the kiss for a moment.

"Here, let me help you in." He opened the truck door for me and boosted me inside, a hand lingering for a second on my hip. "Drive carefully, Tinkerbell."

"You, too," I said, turning in the seat to face him again. "Don't do anything I wouldn't do."

"Never." He grinned and leaned in for another quick kiss, a light brush of his lips over mine. "I'll see you later."

I nodded. My breath was gone.

Derek hotfooted it back into the building after closing my door, and I put the truck into reverse and backed out of the parking space. When I looked back at the windows of the storefront, I could see a shadow standing there looking out. Just in case it was Cora or Derek, I waved. The shadow didn't wave back, so it was probably just Melissa.

• • •

Mom and Noel were up and dressed and drinking coffee with Kate when I got to the Waterfield Inn. Mom's face was made up and her hair fluffed out, and Noel's bald head looked buffed and shiny. They both greeted me with big smiles.

"Morning, Avery!"

"Hi." I smiled back. "Did you sleep well?"

"Oh, yes. Wonderfully comfy beds." Mom grinned. "Sorry you had to wait for us."

"It's no problem. I got French toast when I was here earlier, and then Derek and I had something to do."

My voice or face must have changed on that last sentence, because Mom looked at me with concern.

"Where did you go?" Kate wanted to know, mirroring my mother's look.

"Out to Clovercroft. It's one of the Stenhams' construction sites," I explained for Mom and Noel's benefit. "The Stenhams hired Beatrice to handle things in the office for them after their other accountant was killed in a hit-and-run accident last month, and she's been working out there for the past few weeks. Crunching numbers."

"So you went to see Beatrice?"

I shook my head. "I wish. We went to look for Beatrice. She didn't come home last night. Her car is parked in the lot out there, and the office was locked up nice and tight with her cell phone inside, but Bea is nowhere to be found."

"Oh, no," Mom said, paling. "That's horrible."

"It's a little worrisome, yes. We're hoping that it's something simple, like Steve finally realized she was gone and drove up from Boston to beg her to come back to him, and now they're shacked up in a motel somewhere. Cora called Alice—that's Bea's sister—and Alice is going to go to Steve and Bea's house in Boston to see if she's there. If she isn't, I guess Alice will track down Steve. He has a right to know that his wife is missing, even if she left him. Maybe that'll finally make him sit up and take notice." I rolled my eyes.

A long moment followed while the mental lightbulb flickered on over my head.

"You don't think that's what's going on, do you?" Kate said. "She faked her own disappearance to see if that will bring him up here, when just leaving him didn't?"

Mom and Noel turned to me, too, waiting to hear what I'd say.

"I'm not sure," I admitted. "I didn't think about it until just now. But it makes sense, in a twisted sort of way."

The others nodded encouragement.

"You told me her husband's been ignoring her," Kate said, "ever since he got this fabulous job that keeps him away from home all the time, right? She probably tried to get him to stay home more. Cooked great meals, maybe offered sex, or said she wanted to get pregnant and needed to practice a lot . . ."

I nodded. "When that didn't work, she left him, hoping he'd come to his senses when he realized he missed her. But it's been weeks, and he hasn't taken the time to drive the two hours from Boston to talk to her, and in the meantime, she's been bunking in Cora and Dr. Ben's guest bedroom, when she was used to having her own nice house."

"And she's been here in sleepy Waterfield, when she's been used to the hustle and bustle of Boston," Kate reminded me. "She's been working for a pittance and having to deal with Melissa and the Stenhams on top of it, when she's been used to being a lady of leisure. I wouldn't blame her for getting a little desperate."

"And she wouldn't have told anyone what she was planning," Mom added, "because the whole idea is to get her husband so worked up that he'll finally realize he might have lost her. And to do that, no one else can be in on the deception. Everyone has to think she's really missing."

"So where would she be?" Kate asked.

I shrugged. "If that's really what happened, she could be anywhere. She grew up in Waterfield. I'm sure she has friends here she could stay with. And she has money. Lots of money. She could have taken a cab to Portland and be staying at the Harbor Hotel, watching HGTV and eating Cordon Bleu cuisine from room service."

"That's easy to check, anyway," Noel said. "Not for us, but for the police. Or her husband. All they have to do is monitor for activity on her credit and debit cards. I assume she took her purse with her?"

"I assume she did, too," I said, "since I didn't see it anywhere. Not in the office and not in her car. That doesn't mean anything, though. If someone took her, they could equally well have taken her purse. And left the cell phone, not realizing it was on the desk underneath the papers."

"That's true," Kate said. "But at least this is another possible avenue to explore. It'll give Cora something to do today, instead of just sitting at home wringing her hands. She can contact all of Beatrice's old friends and see if they know where she is, or whether she mentioned anything to any of them."

I nodded. "I'm going to call Derek and suggest it. And also see what Wayne had to say. He was on his way out to Clovercroft when I left. Derek decided to wait for him and get a ride back with Cora. They may still be there." I pulled out my phone.

"How did you get into the office?" Kate wanted to know. "Was it unlocked?"

I shook my head, listening to the ringing on the other end of the line. "Locked up nice and tight. Derek called Melissa. She came out and opened it up."

"That was nice of her," Kate said blandly.

I shrugged. "Hey, it's me," I said into the phone.

"Hi, Tink." Derek sounded tired.

"Nothing new?" I asked, sympathetically.

"Unfortunately not. We're back at the house. Wayne's here, too, but there's nothing he can do until tonight. He's going to put out an unofficial APB, but until Bea has been gone for twenty-four hours, we can't file a missing-person report. And he warned us that a twenty-eight-year-old woman who doesn't come home from work, after she has left her husband and is bunking with her parents two hours away from where she lives, isn't going to be a high priority. As we've talked about ourselves, there are a lot of things that could be going on, and none of them criminal."

"I've got another one for you," I said, running through the scenario I'd just discussed with Mom, Kate, and Noel. "You know her better than me. Does this sound like something she'd do?"

"I wouldn't have thought so," Derek said, "but we're not that close. I get along well with both her and Alice, but we've never spent much time together. We were all adults when Dad and Cora got married, and Beatrice was already away at college by then. It's more a question for Cora or Alice, I think."

"Can you ask?"

"Sure I can. But I don't want to right now. Cora is too upset. I'll broach the subject a little later."

"It'll be something for her to do," I said, "something to make her feel like she's not just sitting there waiting. She can contact everyone Beatrice knows, friends from school, anyone she's met since, and especially anyone she's had contact with since she got back to Waterfield, and see if they know anything."

"I'll suggest it. It's not a bad idea in any case, whether Beatrice left of her own free will or not. But I may wait to make that other suggestion. Maybe I'll talk to Alice first. See what she thinks."

"Do what you think is best. Is there anything we can do to help?"

He sighed. "I don't think so. Just have fun with your mom and Noel. I'll catch up with you later."

"OK," I said. "Um . . . Cora invited us to dinner tonight. Remember? Me and you, Mom and Noel. I guess that's not going to be happening, right? I mean, I don't expect it to—she has other things to worry about—but I just wanted to make sure. Just in case she'd like the distraction." If our company would make her feel better, I was only too happy to go, plus I hadn't yet had the opportunity to ask Dr. Ben about William Ellis. Although we had more important things to think about now, I was still curious about the cold case.

"Let me ask." He moved the phone away from his ear, and I heard his voice put the question to Cora. I could also hear her answer.

"They're like family. They're welcome to come over. But it won't be anything fancy."

"She says you're welcome to come," Derek told me.

"I know. I heard. My mom likes to cook, so maybe we can throw something together between all of us. Potluck."

"Sounds good," Derek agreed. "I'll be in touch, OK?"

"Me, too." I ended the call and turned to Mom and Noel. "We're on our own. He's sticking with Cora for now. And there's nothing we can do for them, for the time being. Anything we can do for you, Kate?"

"Nothing," Kate said. "Shannon's asleep; the pills Dr. Ellis prescribed worked. Josh went back to school. He would have been happy to sit here and watch her sleep, but I kicked him out. No sense in both of them missing class. If you're leaving, I think I might just go back to bed, too. I didn't get much sleep last night, either."

"Sounds good." I smiled encouragingly. "Don't worry.

I'm sure the police will figure out who killed Gerard and get off your back. And they'll release the carriage house, and then we can get back to work. We'll still be able to finish by the time you come back from Paris."

"If we go to Paris," Kate said.

"Why wouldn't you go to Paris?"

Her voice was brittle. "I'm afraid one of us will get arrested before we get that far. When my ex-boyfriend shows up three weeks before my wedding and is murdered on my property, with my fiancé on the premises, not to mention myself, I'm not sure anyone will let us leave the country. Not until the murder is solved and the case closed, and God knows when that'll be. Especially if they won't let Wayne work on it."

"I'm sure Reece Tolliver from the state police will figure it out," I said. "After all, he wouldn't be where he is if he didn't know what he was doing."

"We'll see." But she didn't sound hopeful. "I'm going to go lie down. Excuse me."

She wandered out, taking her apron off as she went.

"Great," I said after I'd heard her door close, "that's all we need. Kate falling apart."

"You can't blame her, Avery," Mom answered. "There's a lot going on. Her ex-boyfriend getting killed, her fiancé being a suspect, she and probably her daughter being suspects . . . and you two renovating the house where he died, so she and her new husband can move into it once they're married. It's a lot to process."

"That's true," I admitted. "She might not want to live in the carriage house now that Gerard's body has been there." And what the hell would we do then? Would we get paid for the work we'd done and reimbursed for the materials we'd bought, or would we be out of luck? And what was wrong with me to even be worrying about something like money at a time like this?

Mom lifted a shoulder. "There's no telling. You'll just have to ask her. Some people wouldn't care, but some people would. I'm sure there have been other deaths in this house already. But this was someone she knew, so it might be different."

I nodded. Might. Might not. For now, renovations seemed to be on hold, anyway, until the state police decided to release the carriage house to us.

"So what do you want to do now?" I asked.

"I wouldn't mind showing Noel Aunt Inga's house," Mom said. "If you don't mind, that is."

"Of course not. Why would I mind?"

It had been sort of a rhetorical question, but Mom answered it. "Well, it's really your house now, and we don't want to intrude on your privacy."

"Don't be silly," I said. "You're welcome to look at anything there. If you had wanted, you would have been welcome to stay with me while you're here, too."

"I know." Mom smiled and squeezed my arm as we walked out together. "But we didn't want to cramp your style. Didn't want you to feel that you couldn't have Derek sleep over if you wanted, or do what you normally do because we were in your house."

"And maybe you didn't want me to cramp your style, either?"

Mom had been celibate for seventeen years—at least to my knowledge—from when Daddy died until she met Noel, so I had no doubt she and Noel had had fun the year they'd been married, making up for lost time.

Mom blushed. "Maybe so."

I grinned. "That's fine. But I don't mind you coming over and seeing the place. I made the bed this morning, and unless the cats have made a mess in the past couple of hours, the house looks just like it did when you were there yesterday. I left Derek's truck in the lot behind his loft and walked over here, so I'm without wheels. Do you want to walk or drive your rental car?"

"Let's walk," Mom said. "Such a nice, crisp day."

She breathed deeply of the nice, crisp air, cold enough

to freeze the insides of my nostrils. Noel huddled inside his sheepskin-lined coat and pulled his hat farther down over his ears. He sneezed twice on the way.

"Brrr!" he said when we were standing inside the central hallway in what had been my aunt's house, stamping his feet to regain circulation and flapping his arms like a penguin. "Nice place." He sniffed.

"You should have seen it in June," I said. "The grass was a couple of feet high, the paint was flaking off in sheets, the porch floor was a death trap, and the wallpaper in here was the most god-awful pattern of orange and green plaid I've ever seen in my life. But it looks great now."

I looked around, proudly, at Derek's and my handiwork. The hardwood floors gleamed with three coats of high-gloss polyurethane, the walls were painted in dramatic jewel colors—appropriate for an 1870s Victorian—and at the end of the hallway, my pride and joy, Aunt Inga's kitchen, was visible through the open door.

When I'd first moved into the house, the kitchen had been a total disaster area. I was able to look past the ugly wallpaper everywhere—wallpaper comes off—and the scuffed and dull heart pine floors throughout the house—hardwood floors can be sanded—as well as the clutter littering every flat surface—clutter can be removed—but the kitchen, with its rusty, half-circular wall-mounted sink, its crooked cabinets that looked like they were made from driftwood, and its peeling vinyl floor exposing dry and blackened floorboards, had me in tears. I didn't feel any better when Derek refused to tear out the cabinets with the explanation that they were custom made and would cost a fortune if I were to order them today. I didn't want them, so what did I care?

He turned out to be right, though. He usually is, at least when it comes to repair and renovation. The cabinets were fine once we leveled them, and painted them, and punched out the center panels in the doors and replaced the wood with pieces of Aunt Inga's wedding veil, which I'd found in a box in the attic. The broken pieces of china that someone smashed all over the floor in an effort to scare me into leaving Waterfield had turned into a marvelous backsplash, perfectly complementing the bright blue resin countertop, and the floors, though weathered and full of character (Derek's word), had come out looking great. At this point, the kitchen was probably my favorite room in the house. Not because I like to cook so much—whenever I eat at home, it's usually canned tuna or microwavable macaroni and cheese—but because it just makes me happy to look at the results of all our hard work.

Plus, that kitchen was where I first set eyes on Derek. And where I first realized I was in love with Derek. And where Derek first . . . never mind.

Anyway, I like my kitchen a lot. I like my whole house a lot, but I like the kitchen the best.

"The attic is full of Aunt Inga's stuff," I told my mom. "I had Derek take anything too ugly to salvage to the dump and put all the 1970s stuff on consignment in John Nickerson's antique shop downtown—he specializes in midcentury modern—but of course I couldn't get rid of anything personal. I sent you all the photo albums and papers I came across, but the attic is still full of old tablecloths and vintage clothes and little porcelain tchotchkes and things like that. There are a couple of pairs of old ice skates up there, and several pairs of snowshoes, and a pair of old, wooden, cross-country skis that look like they might belong in a museum. They're at least fifty years old, if not a hundred. If there's anything you'd like to have, feel free to take it with you. Or I can ship it to California, if you don't want to take it on the plane."

"I'll have a look," Mom said happily and headed up the stairs to the treasure trove while I showed Noel around the rest of the house.

After the tour, we all settled down in the little parlor in the front of the house with a couple of boxes Mom had brought down from upstairs. It was too cold to sit in the attic, she said; she could see her breath in front of her face, and her fingers were turning numb. So I stoked up a fire in the fireplace—something else I'd learned how to do since moving to Waterfield—and we sat there and sorted through some of Aunt Inga's knickknacks while the cats were competing for Mom's attention and very pointedly ignoring Noel and me. Maybe she was right; maybe she did remind them of Aunt Inga. Or maybe it was just that she was sitting on the 1940s loveseat that had been their particular spot for as long as I'd owned the house. The worn gray velvet had been caked with cat hair when I first moved in. Now the loveseat was reupholstered in a midnight blue satin blend with stars—my own design—and the cat hair brushed right off. It was a trick I'd learned from Melissa James, of all people. I had put her on the gray loveseat once, hoping that copious amounts of cat hair would adhere to her elegant posterior, but unfortunately she was wearing a slippery sort of dress, and the hair just slid right off and onto the floor, leaving Melissa, as always, spotless, but me with a mess to clean up.

"So tell us more about the carriage house you and Derek are renovating," Mom said, after we had finished talking about Aunt Inga's house. "It's the one at the back of the B&B, right? Small yellow building with a cupola on top and a set of French doors?"

I nodded. "There used to be a big barn-type door there that we took out. For the carriages and cars to fit through back in the old days. The French doors and sidelights went in instead."

"It looks lovely," Mom said warmly. "Of course I haven't seen the inside, and with what's going on, I may not get to, but I peeked through the window yesterday, and from what I could see, it's really nice."

"Derek does good work. And he's been working hard."

"I'm sure you've worked hard, too, Avery," Noel said with a smile and another sneeze.

I smiled back. "Bless you. I have. But not as hard as Derek. The early part of the process—framing, roofing, stringing wire, and laying plumbing—that's something he has more experience with than me, and I'd only slow him down if I tried to help. Kate—or rather, Wayne—didn't give us much time to get the job done. I've been running around ordering cabinets and countertops, picking out paint colors, and making sure Derek has lunch. He's not much good if he doesn't eat. Oh, and tracking down this set of initials he found carved in one of the posts inside."

"Initials?" Mom said, looking up from her inspection of one of Aunt Inga's knickknacks. "What initials?"

"WE, ER, and a heart. Before everything got so crazy, I had just discovered that Lawrence Ritter Jr. was married to a woman named Emily."

"Really?" Mom said.

I nodded. "I found a picture of the Ritter family at the topping-out ceremony for the carriage house in April of 1918. I have it here somewhere; you can take a look."

I dug through the bills and papers on the desk until I found the printout, which had been sitting there unheeded for the past week at least, and handed it to her. She put down the figurine she'd been looking at—a hideous ceramic kitten with enormous eyes—and she and Noel put their heads together over the article and photograph. Meanwhile, I carried on with my story.

"I already knew that Lawrence Junior was married. Miss Barnes at the Historical Society told me. She didn't tell me what his wife's name was, though, and I didn't ask, since I didn't think it was important. I mean, why would someone's wife carve her initials in the carriage house wall, inside a heart with someone else's initials other than her husband's? So I don't know if it's just a coincidence. But if you read the caption under the picture . . ."

"I already am," Mom said.

"Then you'll see that there was a guy named William Ellis working on the carriage house. Some relative of Derek's. His grandfather's uncle, I think he said."

Mom nodded. "And you said the other set of initials was ER, didn't you? So even if Emily Ritter isn't ER, William Ellis is likely WE, since he was working there and had every opportunity to carve his initials in the post. Are you sure he didn't just do it to sign his work, so to speak? The way a painter signs a painting? Carve his initials in the post to show he'd been the one erecting it? There's a man here named Edvard Rasmussen; maybe he's ER."

"And the heart is just a blip in the wood? Or . . . wait! Maybe William Ellis was gay, and he and Ed Rasmussen—who's probably a great-grandfather or uncle or cousin a few times removed of Wayne's—maybe they were carrying on an illicit affair in the carriage house after hours. And because they couldn't shout their love to the world, they carved their initials in the post instead."

"Don't be facetious, Avery," Mom said sternly.

"I wasn't." Not entirely, anyway. I'd started out being facetious, but now that I thought about it, the explanation made as much sense as any other. As much sense as the idea of Lawrence Ritter's wife carrying on an affair with one of the carpenters, anyway. People were gay in 1918, too, just not as openly as they are now. Homosexuality might even have been a crime. Coming out of the closet is never easy. More difficult in a small town like Waterfield, where everyone knows everyone else. And still more difficult a century ago, I'd guess, when people weren't as open-minded about alternative lifestyles as they are these days.

"If we're going to Cora and Dr. Ellis's house for dinner tonight," Mom said, sharing an amused look with Noel, "you could ask if William Ellis by any chance was gay or known for having affairs. It's not really the kind of thing you pass down, but they might know."

I nodded. "I was planning to talk to Dr. Ben about William anyway. When I was at the newspaper archives, I discovered that he was murdered. Just a few months after this picture was taken. At the navy base in Elliott. He'd signed up for the navy, and less than three days later, someone poisoned him."

"You're kidding!"

I shook my head. "It's true. At least according to the *Clarion*. That article is there, too. You can look at it."

Mom turned pages until she found the article about William. It took no more than a minute for her to read it. "Fascinating. Although it doesn't say that he was murdered, Avery."

"It does say that he was done to death. Although Derek suggested that he might have committed suicide, maybe to avoid being shipped out. Accidentally, maybe. I guess I'll have to look for a follow-up story. Once all this hoopla with Gerard and Beatrice is over and I have time to concentrate on other things again." I held my hand out for the printouts and Mom handed them over.

I was just stuffing them into my bag, so I could show them to the Ellises at dinner, when my cell phone rang. The display showed Derek's number, and I hastened to answer, heart beating faster. Maybe Beatrice had come home!

"Derek?"

"Hi, Avery." He still sounded tired.

"Any news?"

"Unfortunately not. Or nothing good. Alice just called. She's been to Bea's house, and it's empty. Beatrice isn't there. Nor is Steve. Alice has a key, so she went through the place, top to bottom. There was no sign of either of them."

"That's . . ." I hesitated. It was good, in the sense that nothing overtly wrong had been discovered. But it was bad that Beatrice hadn't been found and was still missing. "Weird."

"I know. She's going to go to Steve's work now. It's almost an hour away, so it'll take a while."

"Can't she just call?"

"She's already called. His direct line went straight to voice mail. And he's not answering his cell phone. And the receptionist won't tell her whether he's there or not. Company policy. I guess they're afraid some of their clients will come after them with guns if they know where to find them. Alice wants to go there. It's something for her to do until the kids come home from school or daycare or wherever the hell they're going." His temper seemed to be fraying.

"OK," I said soothingly. "That makes sense. Let me know what she says when she calls back, all right?"

"Sure. What's going on with you?"

"Oh, we're just sitting here at Aunt Inga's house, looking through boxes of ceramic kittens and waxed flowers under glass. I've been telling Mom and Noel about the initials in the carriage house post."

"That's nice." Derek didn't sound like he cared one way or the other. Under the circumstances, I didn't know that I could blame him. Obviously Beatrice and whatever had happened to her would be foremost in his mind.

"Was Wayne able to get into the model apartment earlier?" I asked. "You said he might have a universal key."

"He did. And used it, much against Melissa's wishes. She didn't try to stop him, but you could tell she didn't want him to go inside."

"Why?"

"I have no idea. There wasn't anything there. No Beatrice, and nothing else, either. It's just a generic furnished apartment. It looked like someone had cleaned it recently, since there were fresh vacuum tracks all over the carpet."

"Melissa said she gave the spare key to someone for maintenance. Maybe they freshened the place up afterwards."

"Probably," Derek agreed tiredly.

It seemed to be time to change the subject. "When does your stepmother want us to be there tonight? If she hasn't changed her mind, that is?"

Derek consulted with Cora and came back on the line. "She says six o'clock would be good. She's making lasagna. You can bring the salad and the breadsticks. I'll pick up the dessert."

"Can it be whoopie pie? Please, Derek? Mom probably hasn't had one for ages, and I doubt Noel ever has. And you can't come to Maine without eating a whoopie pie. It's like coming to Maine and not eating lobster."

Derek chuckled. It was rusty, but a chuckle. "If that's what you'd like."

"Please."

"See you at six?"

"See you then." I smooched the phone and then flushed when Mom and Noel both grinned.

—13—

My refrigerator didn't yield anything resembling salad fixings, so Mom decreed a trip to Shaw's Supermarket was in order. We all put our winter coats back on and headed out into the frigid December air. By now it was starting to turn dark—the days are short up north, and we were nearing the winter solstice—and crisscrossing Main Street, holiday decorations were lit up. Stars and bells and greenery were strung from building to building, high above the street. One long strand of lights with a blinking snowflake six feet tall was fastened to the wall above Derek's window, and I could only imagine how light it must be inside the loft. Hopefully they turned the displays off at night, or sleep would be impossible during the month of December.

After getting the ingredients for a lovely Caesar salad, as well as a couple of packages of refrigerated breadsticks from Shaw's, we headed for the B&B with our bags, since Kate's kitchen was likely to yield the salad bowls and baking pans my kitchen lacked. Also, it was closer, and the temperature was dropping. We were well below freezing at this point; the average temperature in Maine in December being right around twenty degrees Fahrenheit. Noel, poor guy, was practically burrowing into his coat, his nose bright red and dripping.

When we got there, Kate was sitting at one of the dining room tables talking to an older man with thinning, gray hair and the face of a bulldog, jowly and droopy, with bags under his eyes and sagging skin. The eyes were sharp, though, and shrewd. He was wearing the blue uniform of the state police, with lots of bars and insignia on the chest and shoulders. I didn't need Kate's introduction to know who he was.

"This is Reece Tolliver. He's come down from Augusta to help with the investigation into Gerard's murder. Reece, this is Avery Baker, her mother Rosemary, and Noel Carrick. Rosemary and Noel are staying with me while they're in town."

"Nice to meet you all," Chief Tolliver said, assessing me with what I can only describe as a cop's eyes. Steady and penetrating, giving nothing away. "You're the one that's been working on the carriage house."

I nodded.

"And these are your folks." He moved his attention to Mom and Noel, who stepped closer together. It was hard not to. I bet Reece Tolliver got confessions out of a lot of people simply by fixing them with those steady gray eyes. There was something in them that just made you want to start babbling. "In from California, are you?"

Noel nodded. "Santa Barbara."

"And you got here yesterday."

"We got to Waterfield yesterday. We spent the night in Boston."

"So you never had occasion to meet the victim."

Noel and Mom both shook their heads.

"Not to our knowledge," Mom added. "At least I've never known anyone with that name."

Reece nodded. "We'll be checking your whereabouts," he

said. "And you . . ." He moved his attention back to me; I swallowed and stood up straighter. "You never met him, either."

I shook my head. "No, sir. I saw him twice, with Shannon. I never spoke to him, though. And I didn't know who he was until after we found the body."

"Huh," Reece grunted. "OK. I know where to find you if I have any more questions." He turned back to Kate, dismissing us.

"Sure." I made tracks for the butler door to the kitchen, throwing a question over my shoulder as I went. "Is it OK if we use your kitchen to make a salad, Kate?"

"Of course," Kate said, waving a hand. "Make yourselves at home. You know where everything is."

"Thanks." I shooed Mom and Noel in and let the door swing shut behind us. In the dining room, low-voiced conversation picked up again.

OK, so I'm thirty-one years old. Thirty-two in a couple of months. Too old to be listening at keyholes. My mom certainly thought so. When I set her up at the counter, with a cutting board, Kate's butcher block full of knives, and a Tupperware bowl for the finished salad, and then proceeded to lurk at the crack in the door, she arched her brows at me. "Avery Marie Baker! Haven't I told you that eavesdropping is wrong?"

"Sure, Mom." I pressed my ear to the door.

". . . record," Reece Tolliver said.

". . . know," Kate answered, her voice strained. ". . . when I took Shannon and moved."

". . . tell him where you went?"

"No, I didn't. He was . . ."

This was frustrating. I was missing at least half of what was said.

"What are you doing?" Noel asked, interestedly.

I glanced at him over my shoulder. "Isn't it obvious?"

"I guess it is, at that. Why?"

"I'm curious," I hissed. "Gerard was lying in our construction area. For all I know, we're suspects. And even if we aren't, our friends are."

"All right," Noel said, conceding the point, "but . . ."

"Wayne would tell me what was going on. I don't know Chief Tolliver. He may not."

"Kate will tell you, won't she?"

"You'd think. But Kate's involved, too. I can't be sure."

"So you're eavesdropping." Mom shook her head sadly, albeit not without a twinkle in her eyes as she shredded lettuce. "I know I taught you better than that, Avery."

"You did. But I don't have a choice. So please be quiet so I can hear." I put my ear back to the door again.

". . . Ludlow?" Reece Tolliver said.

"No, I didn't want Shannon to see her dad in a . . ."

". . . see. OK, then. I'll be . . ."

I bit my lip and strained my ears, desperately wishing I could push the door open just a crack, so maybe I could hear enough of what they were talking about to actually understand.

Unfortunately, the conversation seemed to be over. I heard steps coming toward the swinging butler door. I jumped out of the way just in time, and although I did my best to look innocent, like I just happened to be loitering next to the door, I don't think I succeeded very well. Reece Tolliver sent me a hard look on his way past. I blushed. Mom shook her head again, her attention on the salad.

After Chief Tolliver had passed through the back door and was out of range, I joined Kate in the dining room. She was still sitting in the same place at the table, her face pinched and her eyes dull. "What was he doing here?" I wanted to know, sitting down opposite. "Is there any news?"

She shook her head. Even the usually bright curls didn't dance the way they normally do. "Not really. The ME's office has confirmed cause of death. Gerard was poisoned and asphyxiated."

"On purpose?"

"It wasn't food poisoning, if that's what you mean. He didn't die from eating poisonous mushrooms or bad seafood." She got up and headed for the door to the kitchen, continuing to talk over her shoulder. "The ME studied the contents of his stomach and said that Gerard had fish for lunch, and eggs and bacon for breakfast, with coffee, but no dinner. There was also some alcohol, so I guess he had a drink in the afternoon. Maybe he met someone somewhere for happy hour. The poison wasn't what killed him, though; cause of death was asphyxiation."

"Strangulation?"

She shook her head. "More likely a pillow or blanket or something. The ME said something about fibers in the lungs."

"What kind of poison was it? Something he could have taken accidentally?"

"I'm not sure," Kate said, pushing open the door to the kitchen. "Reece called it digitalin."

She glanced at me as I passed through. I shrugged. It sounded somewhat familiar, but Derek would know for sure what it was.

Letting the door swing shut behind her, Kate looked around, from Mom's salad fixings on the chopping block to Noel separating refrigerated breadsticks and arranging them on a baking tray. The oven beeped its readiness just as he finished, and he opened the door and slid the tray in after sprinkling the breadsticks with some garlic salt and other spices.

"Thirteen minutes," Mom said, and Noel set the timer, then sneezed.

"Looks good," Kate remarked. "Bless you, Mr. Carrick."

"Noel. Please," Noel sniffed.

"We're going to dinner at Cora and Dr. Ben's," I explained. "She's making lasagna. We're in charge of the salad and the breadsticks, and Derek's buying dessert."

"Whoopie pies?" Kate said. I nodded. "Oh, yum!"

"Why don't you come with us? I'm sure they'd be happy to have you. And Cora always makes enough food for a crew."

"Tempting," Kate said, shaking her head, "but I don't want to intrude. Plus, I should probably spend the night with Wayne. He's feeling a little put out about being on traffic duty. Not to mention being suspected of murder."

"Are you expecting him anytime soon?"

Kate glanced at the clock. "Not for another hour, at least. Why?"

"I had a question I wanted to ask him. About a relative of his. Guy named Edvard Rasmussen. Lived in the early part of the century and worked on your carriage house in 1918."

"Did he really?" She smiled. "Wayne'll be tickled to know that. Edvard was his great-grandfather. It'll be kind of like coming full circle."

"Right," I said. "Do you know anything about him? Anyone with initials WE he might have carried a torch for? Derek's great-grandfather William Ellis, for example?" I raised my eyebrows.

She chuckled. "He had two wives and seven kids, at least one of them with a woman who wasn't either of his wives. I don't think he was carrying on an affair with William Ellis."

"And here I thought I had it all figured out."

"Sorry about that. I'll ask Wayne, see if maybe one of Edvard's girlfriends had the initials WE. He had several. I know it wasn't a wife: His first was named Louise and his second Clara. But I'll find out."

"I'd appreciate that," I said, dejected. I'd been so sure I had something. "Meanwhile, I guess I'll ask Dr. Ben about William and his love life. It'll give us something to talk about tonight other than kidnapping and murder. Or recent murder, anyway. William was poisoned, but at least it happened long ago."

"Never hurts to ask," Kate agreed.

"I'll find out from Derek about the digitalin, too, while I'm at it. He'll know what it is. And if he doesn't, Dr. Ben will."

"I'm not sure what good it'll do," Kate said, "but knock yourself out, if you want."

I nodded. "I will."

But when we got to Dr. Ben and Cora's house an hour later, Derek shot me down regarding information on William's paramours—straight or gay.

"Sorry, Tink." He dropped a kiss on my cheek and relieved Mom and Noel of their coats and directed them into the living room before he grabbed the salad bowl and walked toward the kitchen, continuing over his shoulder as he went. "I have no idea who he might have had a thing for and no way of finding out. World War I was a little before my time."

"I realize that," I said, trailing behind with the breadsticks, "but . . ."

"It was a little before everyone else's time, too. Paw-Paw Willie is my oldest living relative, and he was born after his Uncle William died. I can call and ask him, but I doubt he'll be able to tell me anything. Even if William did womanize or even pitch for the other team, it may not be the sort of information that would be passed down through the generations."

"That's true." Much as it irked me to admit it. "Can I still ask your dad? Even if he doesn't know that, he might know who poisoned William, and why."

Derek put the bowl on the counter in the kitchen and relieved me of the package of breadsticks, setting them next to the bowl. "As long as you do it after dinner. Things are grim enough right now without having this conversation across the table."

"I'll wait until an opportune moment," I promised. "Since we're on the subject, though . . . what can you tell me about digitalin?"

"Quite a lot. It's Medicine one-oh-one. Why do you ask?"

"Reece Tolliver told Kate it's what Gerard took. I wondered what it was."

"Really?" He looked pensive for a moment. "It's heart medicine."

"Is it poisonous?"

"It can be," Derek said. "It's used to control arrhythmia, largely. In people with atrial fibrillation, especially if they've been diagnosed with heart failure. To someone who doesn't have heart trouble, it wouldn't be beneficial. They'd get dizzy, their heart would start beating erratically, and they'd probably have to lie down. They may even pass out."

"A perfect position for someone to put a pillow over their face and keep it there. I guess we can take it Gerard didn't have heart trouble. Or maybe he did, and he took too much of his own medicine. And then someone happened along and decided it was a good opportunity to get rid of him."

"Or someone slipped a couple of foxglove leaves into his dinner salad," Derek said, glancing at the greens on the counter.

"Foxglove?" It sounded familiar, but I wasn't sure where I might have come across it before.

"It's a plant. Cora has a border of it in the backyard. Pretty, with purple or white flowers. It's where digitalis comes from."

"Digitalis." I nodded. "Right. I knew it sounded familiar. I've read about it. Agatha Christie, I think. Is the plant poisonous, too?"

"Very," Derek said. "I treated a kid once who'd eaten foxglove leaves. Thankfully, the mother was right there when he did it and brought him straight to the emergency room. We were able to save him. Everyone isn't always so lucky."

"Obviously. Or Gerard would still be with us."

"Right," Derek said.

My next question might have sounded like a non sequitur, but wasn't. Thankfully, Derek didn't seem to realize it.

"Is there any news of Beatrice?" Who had grown up with a mother who liked to garden, and who might know the deadly properties of the foxglove plant . . .

He shook his head. "Not really. Alice called back again.

She went to Steve's work. He wasn't there, and of course neither was Beatrice."

"That figures."

"Wayne has put out an official APB now, since she's been gone more than twenty-four hours. We'll see if anything comes of it."

I glanced up at him. "You don't think it will, do you?"

He hesitated. "Let's just say that I'll be really surprised if it turns out that Beatrice is shacked up in some hotel room somewhere, reconfirming her vows to Steve. I don't think she would just go off without letting her mom know. It isn't like her. She's a considerate sort of person, and she knows we'd worry if she just disappeared."

"So you think there's reason to worry? What do you think happened to her?"

"I don't know," Derek said, face somber, "but something did. Someone came to Clovercroft yesterday afternoon or was waiting for her when she came back from lunch, and he or she did something to her. If she was able, she would have called by now."

"She doesn't have her phone," I said. "It was at the office."

He nodded. "Wayne has it now. He took it as evidence. There's nothing on it. She didn't get any phone calls yesterday afternoon and didn't make any, either."

"What about the office phone?"

"Wayne got those records from the phone company. There's nothing interesting there, either. A call to Cora in the morning, to arrange to meet for lunch, Cora said. A couple of calls back and forth with the office at Devon Highlands, to check figures, and then a call from Mary Elizabeth Stenham in the afternoon."

I wrinkled my brows. "What did Mary Elizabeth want?"

"No idea," Derek said, "but I doubt it was anything sinister. All the Stenhams plus Melissa call Clovercroft all the time, sometimes more than once a day."

"Right." That made sense. "And no one has called with

a demand for ransom or anything like that, I take it. Steve's well off, right?"

"Steve *is* well off," Derek nodded. "Not sure he's *that* well off, though. He may be able to raise a couple hundred thousand in cash, but there are people who can come up with much more than that. In any case, we have no idea whether anyone's called, because we can't find Steve, either."

"Has Wayne put out an APB on him, too?"

Derek shook his head. "Not yet. We don't know if he's missing. Or how long he's been gone. He could just be on a business trip, or something."

"So do you think he came here and got Bea? Or did someone else get them both? Or what?"

"I don't know," Derek said, frustration edging his voice. "I don't know anything. We'll just have to wait and see."

I nodded, hooking my arm through his. "Let's go see the others. Try to forget about all of this for a while. I realize that probably isn't possible, but there's nothing we can do right now, and those are our families out there. Let's go make sure they're getting along."

"Good idea." He managed a smile as he looked down on me. "And tomorrow, if Beatrice isn't back, I'll start turning Clovercroft over, stone by stone, if I have to."

"I'll help you," I promised and squeezed his arm as we headed down the hallway toward the living room.

$-14-$

The lasagna was excellent, of course, and the company equally so, but Bea's disappearance did put a pall on the gathering. Cora did her best to seem normal, but it was obvious that she was deeply worried, and a few times I caught her staring off into space, ears almost visibly straining, as if she were listening to something just out of range. When the phone rang about halfway through dinner, she jumped like a scalded cat and dived for it.

"Yes?"

From the expression on her face, the caller wasn't Beatrice. Cora's face puckered, and she closed her eyes for a second. "Yes, Alice. No, no news."

Alice talked in her ear, and Cora's eyebrows rose. "You did? Really? That's interesting. All right. Yes, I'll let them know. Thanks for telling me. And for your sacrifice."

Alice spoke again, and then they both said good-bye and Cora turned back to the table, where we all sat staring at her like attentive children.

"Sacrifice?" Dr. Ben said.

"It was Alice." Cora went back to her seat at one end

of the rectangular dining table, flags of high color on her cheekbones now.

"And?"

"She's spent the evening in a bar near Steve's work, getting chummy with the receptionist. The woman wasn't willing to tell her anything earlier in the day, but Alice got the impression that she knew something, so she waited until the office closed at five o'clock and waited for the receptionist to come out at the end of the day, and then offered to buy her a drink. Long story short . . ."

"Too late for that," Derek said, but affectionately.

His stepmother sent him a look, equally affectionate, before she continued. "Once she was away from the office, and had a drink or two inside her, she told Alice that not only was Steve not at work today, he hasn't been there all week."

"Really?"

"That's right," Cora confirmed. "The woman said he called on Monday morning, just after she came to work, and said he was taking a few personal days. He's been working for them for two years without a vacation. Apparently whatever case he's been involved with is at a point where it's OK for him to be gone, and so he hasn't been there for several days."

"Interesting," Dr. Ben said. Cora nodded.

"So do you think he's here?" Mom asked, looking from one to the other of us. "In Waterfield?"

"It's possible," Derek allowed.

"It's likely," Cora corrected. "Where else would he go? He has no family, and he hasn't taken a vacation for two years. It's not likely he'd suddenly get a hankering for the beach. But if it finally sank in that Bea wasn't going to come back to him of her own accord, and that if he wanted her back, he'd have to go get her—then it makes perfect sense that he'd come here." She got to her feet again. "Excuse me. I should call Wayne Rasmussen."

She headed back to the telephone.

The conversation continued, with sober excitement,

but as I listened to the others make guesses as to where in Waterfield or down east Maine Steve might be holed up, and what they could do to find him, I found myself thinking that while this was certainly useful information, it didn't really change anything. Beatrice was still just as gone. But at least the news that Steve seemed to be gone, too, made it appear a little more likely that they were together, making us all more hopeful that nothing bad had happened to Beatrice.

After a few minutes, Dr. Ben must have had enough of the speculation, too, and turned to me. "I'm so sorry, Avery. Derek reminded me that you were interested in talking to me about my great-uncle William. He mentioned it a couple of weeks ago, and I plain forgot. Tell me again what's been going on?"

I went over the story of the initials once more, and this time added what Mom, Noel, and I had discussed earlier in the day. I even dug the paperwork out of my bag and handed it to him.

"I'm afraid I don't know anything about his matters of the heart," Dr. Ben said apologetically when he had finished looking at my—admittedly skimpy—research. "He lived and died long before my time, and I can't remember anyone ever talking much about him. I didn't even know that he had died from strychnine poisoning until Derek mentioned it."

"Derek said it could have been an accident, that they used strychnine as medicine back then?"

Dr. Ben nodded. "Along with a lot of other substances we've since realized are deadly. Like arsenic, which pretty ladies used to get clear skin and sleek hair. That's a possibility, but if the navy gave him something, surely they would have chalked it up to an accident instead of making it sound like this." He tapped the printout with a fingernail.

"The article does make it sound like something more sinister happened," I admitted. "What about suicide? Or not suicide exactly, but more of an accidental suicide:

Maybe William was trying to make himself sick to avoid being shipped out, and then he took too much . . . ?"

"That's also possible," Dr. Ben nodded. "Poisoning does usually include vomiting, chills, fever, and the like. He might have thought ingesting poison would make him just sick enough to get out of active duty."

"Or someone killed him."

Dr. Ben nodded.

"But you don't know who? No family stories about Uncle William? No rumors?"

The doctor shook his head. "Not a one, I'm afraid. Like I said, I didn't even know the cause of death until Derek mentioned it. I don't think he was married, for what that's worth, but then again, I don't think he was very old when he died."

"When was he born?" The newspaper article hadn't mentioned anything about that.

"I'm not sure, exactly. Around the turn of the century, I believe. My grandfather was his younger brother, and he was born just on this side of 1900. We have an old Bible somewhere with a family tree. It'd be in there."

"I'd love to see it," I said.

"I'll show it to you after dinner. And we have some old photographs sitting around, too. People weren't good about taking pictures back then, since it was costly, and regular people didn't have cameras, but there may be one of William."

"Great."

By now, the others had finished their conversation, too, and Dr. Ben raised his voice. "Let's talk about something that isn't depressing for a while. No murders, recent or old, and no missing persons, either. Noel, it's your first time in Waterfield, isn't it? How do you like it?"

Noel hesitated, searching for a safe subject. With murder and kidnapping off the table—our more immediate concerns—he settled for the default, the weather. He liked Waterfield, he said, but thought he'd have enjoyed it more in the summer. Now he was cold all the time, and he missed the consistency of the California weather, with its seventy-five-degree Fahrenheit temperatures whether it was summer or winter, spring or fall. From there, the conversation went on to how Mom liked living in California, with its lack of seasons, after spending her entire life on the east coast. I concentrated on eating my lasagna and salad and let the others talk, looking from one to the other and watching their interactions.

I wanted Derek's family to like mine, and I wanted mine to like his, and it seemed I was in luck and they did. I had thought they would, but you can't ever be entirely sure. I didn't know Noel that well myself, for one thing, and I'd really known the Ellises for only six months or so. But although Derek and I didn't have any kind of understanding—we'd never really discussed the future beyond deciding to go into business together, and that was supposed to be on a project-to-project basis—I felt like it was important that our families got along.

Derek had never really told me how he felt about me. I mean, I knew he liked me. I knew he enjoyed my company, and he enjoyed working with me, and he liked the kissing and all the rest of it, but I knew all that because he showed it, not because he said so. I don't think the word "love" had passed his lips. Then again, the word "love" hadn't passed mine, either. Every time it got as far as my tongue, I caught it and put it back. Partly because I didn't want to be the first to say it, but also because I wasn't sure of what I was feeling. I was crazy about him, yes. I was *in love* with him. I liked him a lot, besides that. And the kissing and all the rest of it were certainly nice. He could make my heart beat faster just by looking at me a certain way. But I'd thought it was true love before and found out I was wrong, and I didn't want to make that mistake again. Not with Derek.

Cora came back about halfway through the conversation and joined in. I let them talk, and Derek did the same thing, occasionally nudging my foot under the table and shooting a glance my way. I wondered if he had worried about our parents getting along, too, or whether he was just playing footsie because he enjoyed it.

After the food was eaten and the table cleared, Derek brought out the whoopie pies and distributed them, and we all got busy chowing down on chocolate cake with vanilla cream filling. Once those were devoured, too, Derek and I loaded the dishwasher—the mothers had done the cooking, so the children could clean up—and then I sought out Dr. Ben.

"Can I see those photographs now?"

"Sure." He nodded to Derek. "You know where they are, son."

"Bottom drawer of the buffet?" He headed for it.

Dr. Ben nodded. "The family Bible should be there, too. Why don't you bring it all over to the dining room table so you can spread out. The rest of us can go sit in the living room."

Derek came back carrying a big, thick, leather-bound book so old that the calfskin binding left residue on my fingers when I opened it. The paper was onionskin, so thin it crinkled.

"The family tree should be on the inside of the front cover," Dr. Ben said over his shoulder as he squired Cora out of the dining room. "Have fun."

"Thanks." I grinned after him.

Derek pulled up a chair and sat down next to me. "So what are we looking for?"

"Anything relating to William, I guess. Here he is." I pointed to the name. "Your dad was right."

William Aaron, the family tree said, eldest son of Mallessa, born Carter, and Malcolm Ellis. Missed being a New Year's baby by a few hours. Born January second, 1900, died June sixth, 1918. Never married. Survived by his mother, one brother, Benjamin—Dr. Ben's namesake— and two sisters, Elizabeth and Mary Jane, all of them younger than he was.

"Nothing else of interest there," Derek said and reached for the stack of photos. I shook my head and closed the Bible, pushing it to the side.

Most of the photos were much more recent, beginning with the last few years. Ben and Cora on their wedding day, with Derek as best man, handsome in a well-fitting suit, and Alice and Beatrice as bridesmaids in sea foam green dresses. It looked like the ceremony had taken place in the garden behind the house, with the Reverend Bartholomew Norton, Derek's friend from high school, officiating. There were pictures of Ben and Cora sitting around the house. Pictures of Ben painting and Cora gardening. Christmas dinner with everyone around the table: Ben and Cora, Alice and Lon, Beatrice and a nerdy-looking type with glasses who must be Steve. Derek and Melissa.

I put that one down without comment, but the next one I wasn't able to. "Your wedding day?"

Derek leaned closer. "Sorry."

"No problem. It's not like I was unaware you'd been married." It's something different to actually see it, though. "You didn't have a church wedding?"

Derek shook his head. "Too much in a hurry. We got married on a Thursday because that was the only day I didn't have a rotation. At the courthouse."

I nodded, unworthy jealousy rolling in my stomach. They were so young and clearly deliriously happy. He had the biggest, goofiest grin on his face, and both his arms around her, and Melissa . . .

My eyes narrowed. She looks expensive and elegant now, but ten or eleven years ago, when they met and got married, she was breathtakingly lovely. Her hair, much shorter these days, hung down below her shoulders back then, like a fall of pure moonlight, and she looked ethereal in a pale, creamy white dress with a tight bodice and flowing skirt. She was carrying a small bouquet of what looked like lily of the valley, instead of the ostentatious spray of roses and baby's breath I would have expected, and—much

as I hated to admit it, because I really wanted to believe
that she had no redeeming qualities whatsoever and that
she'd only married him because she wanted to be married
to a doctor and he was on his way to becoming one—she
looked happy. Her eyes shone, and her smile was relaxed.
She had one arm lifted, her hand caressing his cheek, and
she was looking up at him with what looked like genuine
emotion.

"Lovely," I said.

Derek nodded, eyes still on the picture. "She was. I
thought she was the most beautiful girl I'd ever seen."

"I know," I said. "You told me."

He glanced at me. And then kept looking. After the
silence had dragged on for long enough to become quite
uncomfortable, to a point where my cheeks were as bright
as Rudolph's nose, he leaned forward and kissed me. Softly.
And long enough to take all my breath away. Again.

"What was that for?" I asked, after he had straightened
up and I had gotten my voice back.

He smiled. "Just because I could. And because I want
you to realize that you don't have to worry about Melissa.
She may have been pretty, but so is foxglove. Until you try
to eat one, and then it kills you."

I giggled, it was so unexpected.

"I was twenty-three, Tink. Just a baby. She was gorgeous and knew what she wanted. I didn't have a chance."

"She looks happy," I pointed out.

Derek looked at the photograph and shrugged. "No reason why she wouldn't be. She'd gotten what she wanted.
She was married and to a future doctor. Why wouldn't she
be happy?"

"So you don't regret that it didn't work out between you
two?"

His eyebrows shot up. "Hell, no. That last year or two
were so miserable I would have paid her to leave."

"Good thing you didn't have any money." Since this
was when he had stopped being an MD and started being

a handyman, and that's why Melissa decided she'd had enough. "She would have taken you for everything you had."

"She was too thrilled to land Ray Stenham," Derek said with a shrug. "She was happy to see the back of me. Here"—he reached out—"I'll throw that away."

He plucked the photograph from my hand.

I took it back. "That's not necessary. She's part of your life. Always has been, or at least for as long as I've known you. It's not like tearing up the wedding picture will change the fact that I see her every day and she delights in rubbing it in."

I put the photograph facedown on the pile and continued looking. Pictures of Derek as a teenager gave way to pictures of Derek as a child, with a woman with fair hair and the same blue eyes as his.

"Your mom?"

He nodded, eyes soft. "She died seven years ago. I still miss her."

"So she died while you were married to Melissa. How did your mom like your wife?"

"They hated each other," Derek said cheerfully. "My mom always was an excellent judge of character."

I smiled involuntarily, and he added, "She would have liked you. She enjoyed sewing, and thrift shopping, and doing things with her hands. I'm sorry you didn't get to meet her."

I leaned my head against his shoulder for a second. "I'm sorry, too. Although I love Cora."

"Oh, yeah. Cora is great. I couldn't ask for a better stepmother. Same with you, right? Noel seems like a nice guy."

I nodded. "Very nice. And he makes my mom happy, which is the most important thing. I wish they lived closer, but that's life, I guess."

"Unfortunately," Derek agreed and turned over another photo.

Baby pictures of Derek gave way to pictures of Eleanor

and Ben when they were younger, and then random pictures of people we had no idea who were unless their names were noted on the back. A man in World War II uniform with a medic's bag. A woman in nurse's whites. Pictures of the house we were sitting in at various times, from colored to black and white, going through various stages of wallpaper and paint. We were almost all the way through the photos now. Derek picked up an old—very old, and quite faded— black-and-white photograph of two people, and I snatched at it. "Give me that!"

"Whoa!"

"Sorry. But I know her. This is Emily Ritter, Lawrence Junior's wife." I stabbed at her face with my finger. "I saw a picture of her in the newspaper archives. Although she looks a little younger in this picture. Or at least less stressed out."

Like the wedding day picture of Melissa, this younger Emily looked relaxed and radiant, not uptight and nervous as she had in the microfiche photo. She was dressed in a light dress, not too dissimilar to the one Melissa had gotten married in, although it was patched on both elbows and didn't fit as snugly, and she was hanging on the arm of a young man who bore a certain resemblance to Derek. Something in the smile, I think. Their coloring was probably similar, too, although it was hard to tell in black and white. As was the fashion at the time, the young man's hair was slicked straight back from his face, with a little curl falling just across the brow. Definitely kin to Derek, that curl.

"Turn it over," Derek said. "That has to be William, don't you think?"

"I think it would have to be. Yep, says so right here. William Ellis, June 1917."

He leaned closer. "What about her? Does it say who she is?"

"Sure does. Emily Thompson. Must have been taken before she married Lawrence."

"She was pretty," Derek said.

I nodded. She had been pretty. Long, fair hair, big eyes, finely drawn features . . . "Wonder if she was related to Paige. That's Paige's last name, isn't it? Thompson?"

"If she was a Thompson, I'm sure she was related to Paige," Derek said. "In a place like this, everyone with the same name is related if you go back a few generations. Hell, if you go back enough generations, we're all related, whether we have the same name or not. Paige and I probably have the same great-great-triple-great-aunt, or something."

"I wonder if Paige would know anything about Emily. I mean, it seems as if she and William Ellis were sort of friendly, doesn't it? In the summer of 1917? But by the next April, she was married to Lawrence Ritter."

Derek nodded. "Maybe William threw her over. He looks like a bit of a cad, doesn't he?"

"He looks like you," I said.

"Really?" He glanced at me. "OK, then. Paige's family isn't too well off now, and probably wasn't then. Maybe Emily wanted to be married to a doctor—if William was an Ellis, he would end up being a doctor sooner or later; we've always been doctors—but when he said he wanted to join the navy as soon as he turned eighteen, she figured he'd probably die young, so she married Lawrence instead. He must have been well-off, if he lived in Kate's house."

"The Ritters were rich," I nodded. "New money. German immigrants. Not like the Cabots, Anna Virginia's family. But if all Emily cared about was money, not where it came from, then yes, it might have gone down like that."

"I think we should talk to Paige. See if she knows anything." Seemingly Derek had gotten caught up in the mystery of the initials now, too. Well, it could be only to the good, I told myself. Might give him something to think about besides worrying about Beatrice. Take his mind off things for a few minutes at a time, maybe.

I nodded. "Do you think your father would mind if I

took this photograph and made a copy of it? Kate might like to have it. To frame and hang next to her initials. If the police ever release the carriage house and we're able to finish renovating it, that is."

"I'm sure Dad won't mind," Derek said, gathering the other photographs in his hands and carrying them back over to the buffet. "As long as he gets the original back. Lowry Photo on Main Street can do it for you."

"I'll take it there tomorrow."

"And I'm sure the police will release the carriage house soon. I mean, there's nothing there. He didn't even die there. Someone dumped him there because they wanted to be sure he was found in a timely manner. Or maybe they were trying to put the blame on Kate or Shannon. Or Wayne."

"Or us?"

"Why would we kill Gerard?" Derek said. "We didn't even know who he was until he turned up dead."

"Good point. Although the killer may not have known that. But it must have been someone who knew who he was, anyway. Who in Waterfield knew who Gerard was, other than Kate and Shannon?"

"If we knew that," Derek said, "we'd probably know who the murderer is. C'mon, Avery. Let's go join the action in the living room."

He helped me out of the chair and put his arm around my waist as we wandered toward the door to the hallway. His fingers slipped under the edge of my sweater, warm and hard against my skin, and I shot a glance up at him. "Speaking of action . . ."

He looked down into my face, startled, and then his lips curved up. "If I had known my wedding pictures would affect you this way, I'd have shown them to you a long time ago."

"It wasn't the picture."

"So what was it?"

It had been the reassurance that although Melissa was

as pretty—and poisonous—as a foxglove, he was glad to be rid of her.

"Never mind," I said, leaning into him. "Just know that you'll be rewarded later."

"I'll remember." He dropped a kiss on my forehead, and then we turned into the living room.

—15—

In the end, Derek chose to spend the night with Cora and Dr. Ben, just in case Beatrice came home or something happened overnight. I went home alone and booted up the computer once I got there. Not to research William Ellis this time; William and Emily and whatever happened to the two of them had happened almost a hundred years ago. Interesting though it was to speculate, I had more immediate concerns, namely Gerard's death and Bea's disappearance. Of the two, I must admit, Gerard's murder interested me more. I still clung stubbornly to the conviction that Bea was just off somewhere with Steve, living it up with room service and splendor, and I'd keep clinging to it until I was proven wrong.

Gerard, on the other hand, was dead, and someone had killed him. Until the police figured out who that someone was, we were all under suspicion. Or maybe not all, but enough of us as made very little difference. I didn't think Reece Tolliver suspected me, Mom, or Noel particularly, or even Derek, but I wasn't too sure about Kate, Shannon, or Josh. All three had access to the carriage house, and they all had a connection to Gerard. But because I didn't want to entertain the thought that any of them were guilty, the question was, who else in town might have known him? Had he really been here just to see Shannon, or had he had another purpose? And could he have upset someone so much in just a few weeks that they decided to kill him?

I hadn't heard much of the conversation between Reece Tolliver and Kate in the dining room earlier, but I had heard the word, or name, Ludlow. I started there.

My only personal connection to Ludlow was that it's the name of a street and a luxury rental apartment tower on the Lower East Side of Manhattan, as well as a fitness facility on Delancey Street. Back in Civil War times, the New York County Jail stood on Ludlow Street. Now I discovered that it was also the name of a town and a village in Vermont, a market town in Shropshire, England, near the Welsh-English border, and a town in Colorado, where the Ludlow Massacre took place in 1914, during the Southern Colorado Coal Strike. There was also a place called Port Ludlow, clear across the country in Washington State, and a town in Massachusetts. Since Gerard was from Boston, the latter Ludlow seemed to be the most promising.

I spent a few minutes trawling the Ludlow, Massachusetts site, and soon realized something very interesting: The town of Ludlow is home to the Hampden County medium security correctional facility. In other words, prison. That jibed rather nicely with what I'd overheard Kate tell Reece Tolliver: that she didn't want Shannon to see her dad in a . . . what? Jail cell? Orange jumpsuit? It also explained Reece's mention of a record—a prison record, obviously— and it explained why Kate had taken Shannon and moved from Boston to Waterfield.

Of course, it was all conjecture. Kate hadn't told me any of this, so she must not want the information to get around. Shannon might not know that her dad was a felon. I couldn't call Kate and ask her. I couldn't call Wayne; he might not know, he might not tell me if he did know, and he was with Kate, anyway. Reece Tolliver had no reason to tell me, and if Kate hadn't mentioned it to me, it wasn't likely that she'd told anyone else. Except maybe Derek; but if Derek knew, surely he would have told me. Especially after finding the body.

Frustrated with my lack of options, I resorted to doing Internet searches of Gerard's name. It's amazing what you can find on the Internet these days, and I figured it was worth a try.

Uncommon though the name Gerard Labadie was, there were a few people who carried it, and I spent thirty minutes or more clicking on links at random to see what I could find. Jemmy and Inky came home in the middle of it and let me know, loudly, that they needed sustenance. I filled their bowls with clean water and kitty kibble and left them to it. When they were finished, they deigned to curl up on Aunt Inga's newly reupholstered loveseat across from the desk, and I kept going. Unsuccessfully. I was just about to give up and go to bed when a name caught my attention.

No, it wasn't Gerard's. The name that had jumped out at me was Cortino.

. . .

"You can have the carriage house back," Brandon Thomas said the next morning.

Derek and I had mustered in Kate's kitchen as usual: Derek to see whether he'd be able to go to work today, and me to tell him what I'd discovered yesterday, and also to see my mom and Noel when they got around to dragging themselves out of bed. And of course to find out whether there had been any breaks in either the murder or the missing-person case overnight.

I walked into the kitchen to find Kate and Wayne at the table along with Derek, Shannon, and Josh, along with Brandon, in full uniform. Unlike yesterday morning, Shannon was ready to face the day, fully dressed and looking rested and more relaxed.

"I'm going back to school," she explained, between bites of Belgian waffles.

"I guess you must be feeling better, then."

She nodded and swallowed. "Much. Reece will figure out who killed my dad, and he and Wayne will arrest them, and then everything will go back to normal. I'm sorry I didn't get to know him better, but at least I got to spend a little time with him. It isn't like I didn't get to know him at all."

"That's nice," I said, sitting down. "I'm glad you were able to get to know your dad before he died. I'm sure he was very proud of you."

Shannon smiled. I turned to Derek. "Any news about Beatrice? Or Steve?"

He shook his head. "Afraid not. We're just waiting." And clearly the waiting was taking a toll. His eyes were shadowed, and he hadn't taken the time to shave today, so his cheeks and jaw were stubbled with blond. I gave him a sympathetic smile and turned to Josh.

"Do you expect to see Paige today?"

Josh looked surprised behind the glasses. "I'm sure I will. If not, I'll see Ricky in class, and I can tell him to give her a message."

"The two of them are definitely together, then?"

Josh grinned. "They're getting there. It's crazy watching them: You can tell he's just crazy about her, and you can tell she kind of likes him, too, but they don't talk about it, and when they're with other people—with us"—he glanced at Shannon—"they act like nothing's going on. Seriously weird."

"I've seen weirder," Brandon muttered, and Josh flushed. I glanced at Shannon, but she didn't seem to have noticed.

"What do you want with Paige?" she asked.

"Nothing urgent. When she has a minute, I want to ask her about a woman named Emily Thompson who was born around the turn of the century. The twentieth century. I'm wondering if they were related. Here's a picture." I dug it out of my purse and slipped it out of the envelope I'd put it in for safekeeping. "Be careful with it. It's Dr. Ben's. That's his great-uncle, William Ellis."

"Avery thinks it's their initials in the carriage house," Derek explained. "Emily's and William's."

"How can it be her initials?" Kate picked the picture up by the corners, with her fingertips. "I thought you said her name was Emily Thompson. The initials were WE and ER, weren't they?"

I nodded. "Thompson was her maiden name. Until she married Lawrence Ritter Jr. in February of 1918."

I had stopped and checked the church records on my way to Kate's this morning. The Reverend Bartholomew Norton is a friend of Derek's from high school, and he'd been happy to help. It had been no problem finding the banns for Emily and Lawrence back in the winter of 1918.

"Anna Virginia's oldest son?" Kate said.

I nodded.

"Why would she carve her initials in a heart with William's initials if she was married—and recently married, too—to Lawrence?"

"She may not have," Derek said. "Maybe William did it. She may not even have known."

"Maybe he was in love with her," Josh suggested, "but she didn't realize it. Or didn't reciprocate." He made damn sure not to look at Shannon when he said it.

"Or maybe William jilted her and she hooked up with Lawrence on the rebound," Shannon said. "But then William changed his mind and signed on to work on the carriage house to get close to her. She was someone else's wife by then; he couldn't just knock on the door. And they picked up where they left off, and he carved their initials in the post."

"Or it could have been a marriage of convenience," Kate suggested. "She wanted to marry William, but her family wanted her to marry Lawrence. No offense, Derek, but I'm sure the Ritters had more money than the Ellises. I'd like a copy of this, if you don't mind."

"I figured you would," I said. "When we take it to Lowry's, I'll make sure to get a couple extras."

"Thanks." Kate smiled and put the picture back down on the table.

Josh picked it up. "She was pretty," he said.

Shannon leaned over to take a look, close enough that her hair brushed his cheek. "Has a little bit of Paige in her, don't you think? Around the eyes, maybe?"

"Maybe a little. And the smile. Paige is pretty, too."

"Of course." Shannon leaned back into her own seat. Josh gave the photograph back to me.

"Are my mom and Noel not up yet?" I asked as I returned it to the envelope, slipping it into my bag.

Kate shook her head. "Not yet. Another hour or so, maybe. Do you two need to jet off again, like yesterday? Or can you start work on the house again?" Obviously, Kate had decided that the murder was in the past and that the carriage house would still make a good home for her and Wayne.

Derek shook his head. "No jetting today. If I could think of something useful to do, I'd be all over that, but I can't. Maybe we can get in a couple of hours' work before Rosemary and Noel wake up and want to get going. Avery?" He made for the door.

"Coming." I put the bag over my shoulder and followed. "Send my mom out when she wakes up, would you, Kate? She said she'd like to see the carriage house. Or call my cell phone and tell me they're awake, if she doesn't feel like going out in the cold."

Kate nodded.

"I need to talk to you," I told Derek as soon as we were inside the carriage house with the door closed behind us.

I had been a little concerned about going into the carriage house for the first time after finding Gerard's body, honestly, but in my excitement, I forgot all about what had happened last time we had been there.

"Sure," Derek said, unzipping his jacket and tossing it on top of the kitchen counter. "What's up?"

"I did some research last night. Trying to learn more about Gerard."

"And?" He was gathering tools as I was talking, paying

me half a mind, with the other half running ahead to what he'd be doing today and what sort of tools he'd need for the job.

"Did Kate ever tell you that Gerard was a felon?"

Derek turned to me, tools forgotten. "No," he said. "She never mentioned that."

"Don't feel bad. She never told me, either."

"How do you know, then?"

"I . . . um . . . happened to overhear a conversation between Kate and Reece Tolliver yesterday."

"Yeah?"

My cheeks flushed, I admitted, "Actually, I was listening at the butler door. Mom, Noel, and I were in the kitchen. Getting ready for dinner with you and your parents. Reece and Kate were in the dining room. I didn't hear very much, but at one point, Reece talked about someone, or somewhere, called Ludlow."

"Massachusetts?" Derek said.

I nodded. "You know it?"

"Not apart from the fact that it's there. What about it?"

I explained that the Hampden County Correctional Facility was in Ludlow.

"So what?" Derek said. "That doesn't prove anything. Lots of other things are there, too, I'm sure."

"I'm sure they are. So I searched for Gerard *and* Ludlow instead."

He folded his arms across his chest. "And what did you find?"

I smiled triumphantly. "I found a newspaper article from six years ago about a community-outreach program. Apparently nobody too dangerous gets sent to Ludlow, so their inmates get involved in the community from time to time. This had something to do with a housing development playground and with building and putting together and painting the equipment."

"And Gerard was involved?"

I nodded. "There was a picture. Of him and a couple of other guys."

"That's nice," Derek said. "Good for you, tracking down the information. I'm not sure what good it does us, though." He made a move toward his tools.

"Oh, that wasn't what I was going to tell you," I said. "I printed out the picture. Here." I dug it out of my handbag and unfolded it. "See? There's Gerard. A little less gray around the temples and not as old. And look there, in the background? Recognize him?"

Derek squinted. "Shit," he said. "Peter Cortino?"

"I'm afraid so. His name is in the caption underneath, so there's not much doubt."

"There wouldn't have been any doubt even without the name. I've known Peter for five years, and I see him almost every day. When was this published?"

I shrugged. "Six years ago? Give or take a couple of months."

"Peter's been here for five." He uttered an even worse word than the one he'd already employed before he snagged his jacket from the counter again and shrugged into it. "C'mon."

"Where?" I said, trotting after him toward the door.

He tossed me a glance over his shoulder. "Where do you think? If you could figure this out, surely the police will, especially if they already know about Ludlow. It won't take genius to come up with the idea of checking the background of everyone here in Waterfield. Or everyone not originally from Waterfield, anyway. They'll show up at Cortino's sooner or later, and if Jill doesn't know about this, I don't want her to find out that way. You coming?"

"Right behind you," I said.

• • •

We took off down the street like a bat out of hell.

"Looks like Brandon's still inside," Derek remarked, with a glance in the rearview mirror at the patrol car parked at the curb outside the B&B.

I nodded. "Unfortunately, that doesn't mean anything. Under the circumstances, it's more likely that Reece Tolliver would be going to Cortino's on his own, instead of sending Brandon. Just in case Peter is armed and dangerous."

"Peter Cortino isn't dangerous," Derek said.

"How do you know that?"

He glanced at me. "Because I know him. Because I'd have seen some sign of it if he were."

Maybe, maybe not. It didn't seem worth arguing about. We took a turn on two wheels, and I was tossed against him and breathed deeply of Ivory soap and paint thinner before I straightened up. "You know, if Peter knew Gerard from before, that explains why he was so upset when we told him about the murder the other day."

Derek nodded. "I didn't think a whole lot of it at the time, but now that you mention it . . . yeah, he did seem rather inordinately surprised."

"And . . ." I paused, thinking. "You know, I could be wrong about this, but I think Kate told me that the only person in Waterfield she told about Shannon's inheritance from Kate's grandmother was Jill Cortino. Jill does some financial planning on the side, and Kate wanted Jill's help with investing the money."

"So Jill could have told Peter—no real reason why she wouldn't; they're married, and she trusts him—and he could have told Gerard, and that's why Gerard came to Waterfield." Derek's hands tightened on the steering wheel. "They could have stayed in touch ever since Ludlow. Peter could have been the one who brought the bastard here."

"We don't know anything yet," I warned, "so when we get there, don't fly off the handle."

"When do I ever fly off the handle?"

"There was that time you punched the birch tree in Aunt Inga's yard."

He rolled his eyes. "Besides that."

"I can't remember. Just don't do anything you'll regret. It may all be one big misunderstanding."

"Sure," Derek said, but he didn't sound like he believed it.

A minute later, we pulled into the lot outside Cortino's

Auto and got out. Jill waved at us through the office window, and inside the nearest bay, Peter looked up from vacuuming out the back of a ratty ten-year-old Explorer with the Stenham logo on the side. If he had a guilty conscience, I couldn't see it on him. He did look a little the worse for wear, though. Pale under the olive skin, like he hadn't slept well, and with dark circles under his eyes.

"Looks like he's got something on his mind," Derek muttered. I nodded.

The car Peter was working on didn't look like one of the shiny, new vehicles the Stenhams usually drove, and I asked, hopefully, "Have the Stenhams fallen on hard times, so they have to buy used cars now?"

"I wish," Derek answered, glancing at it. "I've heard rumors that times are tough for them, just like for everyone else—especially with Clovercroft just sitting there—but that's probably just one of the beaters."

I nodded. "That whole concept is bizarre to me, how I don't even have one car, and some people have cars they use only in the winter."

"Some people have cars they use only in the summer, too," Derek said, opening the door to the office for me. "They're called convertibles."

Before I could formulate an answer to that, we were inside, in the warmth, and Jill was looking up at us, smiling.

—16—

"Hi, Derek. Avery. What brings you out? Something wrong with the truck?"

Derek shook his head. "Came to talk to you."

Her smile dropped off in the face of his serious expression. "What's wrong? Is it Bea?"

"How do you know about Bea?" I interjected.

Jill turned to me. "Derek called me yesterday. I'm so sorry she's missing."

"It's not Bea," Derek said. "Bea is still gone, and so, it seems, is Steve. Her husband. This isn't about either of them. It's about Peter."

"Peter?" She glanced over her shoulder into the shop, where Peter was still busy with the Stenham vehicle. "He's right out there."

"Yes, I saw him. Jill . . ." He looked down, cleared his throat, glanced up, then away again. Jill was starting to look alarmed when I stepped in.

"What Derek is trying to say is that the police will probably want to talk to Peter."

I waited for her reaction. As a bombshell, the announcement fell distinctly short. "All right," Jill said slowly, as if trying to figure out why this might be a big deal.

"About Gerard Labadie's murder."

"Peter doesn't know anything about that. Why would he?"

I glanced at Derek. "Apparently they knew each other before," he said.

"In Boston?" Jill shot another glance over her shoulder at her husband.

"In prison."

As bombshells go, this one had more oomph, if not as much as one might have expected. Jill turned as pale as a sheet for a moment, and then her cheeks flushed. "How did you hear about that?"

"Obviously you know."

Jill nodded, anger flashing in her eyes now when she looked at Derek. "Of course I know. Did you think I wouldn't? He told me before we got married. It's one of the reasons the business is in my name and not his. No bank would have lent Peter money, but my credit is excellent."

"So . . . ?"

"Peter came here to start over. He wasn't a criminal; it was just a misunderstanding. I mean, I know he broke the law, but he wasn't one of the main guys behind the operation, or anything."

"Operation?" I repeated.

Jill looked at me. "It happened about eight years ago, when he was in his mid-twenties. He got involved with a chop shop. You know, stolen cars?"

Derek nodded. "We know what a chop shop is. I guess that's where he got in the habit of working fast."

He must have meant it as a joke, but Jill wasn't in the mood. "It belonged to someone else, and all Peter did was work on the cars. But when the police came down on them, Peter got swept up with the rest of the people involved. Some of the others got much longer sentences, but since he was just the hired help, he spent a little less than two years in prison."

"And that's where he met Gerard?"

She shrugged. "If you say so. He's never mentioned meeting Gerard."

"Not even after Gerard was killed?"

Jill shook her head. "Are you sure there isn't some sort of mistake? I mean . . ."

"They were in prison at the same time. Some place called Ludlow, in Massachusetts. I saw a picture of them, together. Working on building the same playground. I don't know how close they were . . ."

"Close enough," Peter's voice said from just outside the door. I wondered how long he'd stood there. Now he came in and put a hand on Jill's shoulder. She glanced up, and then leaned back against him. Peter continued, "We all knew each other. It was a medium-security facility; no one really dangerous or violent. Dormitories instead of cells, that kind of thing. Lots of time spent together; very little fighting. Mostly, we were all in for nonviolent crimes. White-collar stuff. Check fraud, forgery, that kind of thing."

"What was Gerard's crime?" I asked.

Peter shrugged. "Blackmail of some kind, I think."

"So when you heard he'd died . . ." Derek prodded.

Peter hunched his shoulders. "I knew he was here. He stopped by about a month ago asking for a favor. Said he thought he could trust me to keep my mouth shut since I wouldn't want him to tell everyone about my past."

"Keep your mouth shut about what?" Derek wanted to know.

Peter sighed. "He'd gotten into an accident, and he wanted me to fix the damage to his car."

"Well," I said reasonably, "that's what you do, right?"

He turned to me. "Sure, it's what I do. And I wouldn't have thought much of it, if not for the timing."

"The timing?"

"It was the day after that hit-and-run near Barnham College."

"When Carolyn Tate died?"

Peter nodded, looking miserable.

My jaw dropped. "Gerard did that?"

"I figure maybe he did. He didn't say and I didn't ask, but I assumed that must be what it was."

"Why didn't you call Wayne?"

"How could I do that?" Peter's beautiful face twisted. "I couldn't be sure it was him, and if he'd told all of Waterfield that I'm a criminal, we'd lose all our business, and poor Jill and the kids . . . I couldn't let that happen."

"What about afterward?" Derek wanted to know. "When you found out he was dead?"

"I thought about it," Peter admitted. He looked from Derek to me and back. "But I was afraid, OK? When the police find out I've got a record, and that I knew Gerard from before, and that he'd threatened to tell all of Waterfield that I'm a felon . . . who d' you think's gonna top the list of suspects?"

Peter would. No doubt about it. "Do you have an alibi for the night he died? Or was put in the carriage house?"

The Cortinos exchanged a glance. "Not really," Peter admitted. "Jill went out Christmas shopping, and I stayed here in the afternoon. Then she wasn't feeling good and went to bed early, just after the kids went down, and I spent the rest of the night watching TV. Alone."

"So what happened?" I asked. "After you decided you couldn't tell the police about the damage to the car?"

Peter shrugged. "I did the work—it wasn't much; his Lexus was built like a tank. I didn't fill out a work order or anything; he just sat around and waited until I was done. It took a couple of hours one night, while Jill and the kids were in bed, and then he left and told me to forget I'd seen him."

"Did you talk?" Derek asked.

"While I was working on the car, you mean? Some, sure."

"Did you ask him what he was doing in Waterfield?"

"Sure. He said he was visiting his daughter."

"Did you know who his daughter was?" I interjected.

Peter nodded. "I knew that when I came here. He had talked about Kate and Shannon while we were inside. Said they'd left Boston and moved to this little town in Maine. We even looked it up online, at one of the computers in the prison library. It sounded like a nice place, so I thought I'd check it out. Didn't want to go back to Boston, you know?"

"Was he expecting you to keep an eye on them? And report back? Is that how he found out about Shannon's inheritance?"

Peter shook his head. "I swear. I hadn't spoken to him for more than five years when he showed up here. I didn't tell him to come, and I didn't want to deal with him when he did. If someone told him about Shannon's inheritance, and it wasn't Shannon, I have no idea who it was. We didn't talk about it."

"Did he say anything else?" I wanted to know. "Give you any idea who might have wanted him dead?"

Peter puffed out a breath that sounded more like a cynical laugh. "Other than me, you mean? Not really. He talked about Kate and Shannon. The B&B. The carriage house. And . . ."

"And what?" Derek said when Peter faltered.

"And . . . um . . . your sister."

"My sister? Beatrice?" Derek's fists clenched, and I took one of his arms, just to keep him in place. "What did you tell him about Bea?"

"How did he even know Beatrice existed?" I shot in. "Had he met her?"

Peter seemed relieved to be able to look away from Derek. "Must have. He knew her name. Knew that she had left her husband. Realized who her husband was; it's an unusual name. I guess he figured there might be money in it for him."

Derek muttered something. It wasn't complimentary,

and I wasn't entirely sure whether it was directed at Gerard, Peter, or both of them. It might even be Steve.

"Be nice," I said. "Gerard had nothing to do with what happened to Beatrice. If anything did. She was alive and well after we found Gerard's body."

Naturally I didn't say so, but it did cross my mind that the opposite might be true: that Beatrice had had something to do with what happened to Gerard. I had no idea why she'd want to kill him, but if they'd known each other, and she'd vanished the same day his body was discovered, there was at least that possibility. As Wayne had told me once, when two unusual things happen right after one another, chances are they're related, even if it isn't readily apparent. Until now, we hadn't realized there was a connection between Gerard and Beatrice. Now, we did.

A car drove up outside, and through the office window I saw Brandon's squad car in the lot. Pulling in next to it was a paler blue state police vehicle. As we watched, Brandon and Reece Tolliver got out of their respective cars and stood for a second, conferring. Jill's eyes widened. "What are we going to do?"

Peter shook his head, his face calm, and his eyes steady. "There's nothing we can do. I'm not going to make a run for it and get shot in the back. That kid out there looks trigger happy."

I snorted—Brandon is nothing if not enthusiastic—and Peter's dark eyes lit up with answering amusement for a second. "I didn't do anything to Gerard," he said, his face sobering. "I didn't touch him, and they can't prove I did."

"But everything will come out. Everyone will know. Everything you've done to start over will be for nothing. And what if they charge you with obstruction of justice in Carolyn's death?" Jill's voice was agonized.

He looked down at her. "As long as you don't care, I don't care. We'll figure out a way to feed the kids. Even if I have to go back to jail for a while."

"I'm not worried about that. I just don't want anything

to happen to you." She leaned into his side, closing her eyes, and his hand caressed her hair for a second.

When the door opened, we all turned toward it. Reece Tolliver was the first to come through. He looked at me and Derek—just looked, with those flat gray eyes, until we were both squirming—before he turned to the others. "Mrs. Cortino. Mr. Cortino." He looked at Peter. "I'm afraid we're going to have to ask you to come down to the station with us."

"Are you arresting him?" Jill asked, her voice higher pitched than usual.

Chief Tolliver fixed his eyes on her, exuding calm. "Not at this time. We've just got some questions we need to ask. And it's probably better if we're not parked outside your place of business for too long." He turned to Peter. "Anything you need to do before we go, son?"

Peter shook his head. "Just let me get out of these overalls and grab a jacket." He squeezed Jill's shoulder before heading back into the workshop. A meaningful glance from Reece Tolliver sent Brandon trotting after him.

Chief Tolliver turned to Derek and me. "Anything I should know?"

Derek shook his head.

"He said he didn't kill Gerard," I said, "but I guess you're probably used to hearing that."

He smiled, but it didn't reach those cool, gray eyes. "That's mostly what they all say, yeah. Doesn't mean some of 'em aren't telling the truth."

"Right. Well, for what it's worth, I don't think he did it. Not that you asked me." I turned to Derek. "I guess we should go."

"Guess so." He seemed no more eager than I was to tell the police about Peter's revelation regarding Carolyn Tate's accident and Gerard's hand in it. We'd leave that sobering duty to Peter himself. "If that's all right?"

The question was directed equally at Jill and at Reece Tolliver. Jill was the one who answered.

"Go ahead. I think I'm going to close the shop and go home. Spend the day with the kids." Her voice was distant.

"Chief Tolliver?" Derek turned to Reece Tolliver.

He waved a hand dismissively. "Go ahead, son. I know where to find you if I want you. And you, too, Miss Baker."

I nodded. "Let me know if there's anything I can do, Jill."

The door from the shop opened, and Peter came in, followed by Brandon. He had changed out of the greasy overalls and was wearing jeans and a blue sweater under a black coat. Jill's eyes followed him as he went around the counter and over to Reece Tolliver, Brandon dogging his heels like a faithful—and really big—puppy.

"Right this way." Tolliver gestured toward the door.

"I'll see you in a little bit, *cara*," Peter told his wife.

Jill nodded and blinked, swallowing.

The three of them passed through the door and out into the cold morning. None of us spoke as they got into their cars, Peter in the back seat of Brandon's Waterfield PD black-and-white. Like a common criminal.

"This didn't work out right," I said to Derek.

He shook his head. "Tell me about it."

"You don't think they'll keep him, do you?"

He glanced at Jill, still standing like a statue, watching the cars drive away. "Let's just hope for the best."

Jill sat down abruptly, giving the impression that her knees had given out. Derek walked over to the door and flipped the sign in the window from Open to Closed. "C'mon, Jill. We'll take you home."

"I've got my own car," Jill said, weakly, staring straight ahead into space.

"You probably shouldn't be driving it, though. Why don't I drive you home in your car, while Avery takes the truck?"

"I don't want to impose . . ." Jill said.

"Don't be an idiot." Derek's voice was gruff. "It's the least I can do. C'mon." He grabbed her under the arm and hoisted her out of the desk chair. She followed him around the desk, docilely. "Coat?"

"Here." I snagged a down-filled, blue coat from the coat tree by the door and helped her into it. "Take care, Jill."

Jill nodded and walked out with Derek. He passed me the keys to the truck and dropped a quick kiss on my cheek. "I'll see you later, Avery."

"Right." I got into the truck and got myself out of there. Hopefully spending some time with Derek would help Jill to feel better. He has a very comforting presence, my boyfriend. It's probably something they teach you in medical school. The last thing I saw before I disappeared down the street was Derek gently easing Jill into her ten-year-old minivan and making sure she was strapped in properly before loping around to the driver's side door.

Mom was dressed and fully coiffed, sitting in the kitchen when I got back to the B&B and talking to Kate. But she was alone. I looked around. "Where's Noel?"

"Morning, Avery," Mom said brightly. "He's not feeling well, I'm afraid. His nose is red and runny, and he's sniffing and sneezing."

"Oh, no," I exclaimed. "I'm so sorry. I guess the cold weather has been too much for him. Walking all through town yesterday . . ."

"He's going to stay in bed today," Mom explained, "and Kate is going to bring him some hot tea with honey in a little bit."

Kate nodded.

"Well, do you want to stay home with him, then? Read him stories and soothe his fevered brow? I can find things to do on my own. Like work on the carriage house. I have to put some thought into the bedroom . . ." I stopped, biting my tongue, when I remembered that that's where the dead body had been found. Maybe Kate didn't want to be reminded of that.

"Can I see it?" Mom asked.

"The carriage house? Sure. Now?"

"No time like the present," Mom said and got up. "Just

let me look in on Noel first." She headed out into the hallway.

"Where did you guys go?" Kate wanted to know. "I thought you said you didn't have to run off anywhere today."

"Oh. Um . . . right." Derek had said that, hadn't he? Of course, that was before I'd told him about Gerard and Peter and Ludlow.

"Did something happen?" Her eyes were candid.

"Nothing new. We went to see Jill and Peter Cortino."

Kate blinked. "Why?"

I hesitated. How much should I tell her? Did I, for instance, confess to having listened at the door during her conversation with Reece Tolliver yesterday? Was it any of her business that Peter Cortino had a criminal record? And what about the Carolyn Tate hit-and-run; did I tell her that Peter suspected Gerard of being involved in that?

"Reece showed up just a few minutes after you left," Kate said into my silence, "and he and Brandon headed out together. Also to Cortino's Auto Shop."

I sighed. If I didn't tell her now, Brandon would tell her later, and then she'd be mad at me for having known but not told. "They got there just after us. Turns out Peter knew Gerard from before. They were in prison together in Massachusetts."

Kate paled under the freckles. "How did you find out that Gerard had been in prison?"

"Looked him up on the Internet," I said, skipping lightly over the conversation I'd eavesdropped on. "I came across a picture from a Massachusetts paper, about inmates in the Hampden County Correctional Facility helping to build a playground for a housing development."

"And Gerard was one of them?"

I nodded. "So was Peter Cortino. I told Derek about it when we got into the carriage house this morning. He had no idea, and he didn't know if Jill did. He wanted to make sure he told her before the police stopped by. We figured it

was just a matter of time." Although I hadn't realized they
were just a few minutes behind us.

"What did he say?" Kate wanted to know, her voice
uneven. "Peter? Did he . . . was he the one who killed
Gerard?"

I hesitated. "He says no. Of course, that's what he'd say
anyway. But I don't think he did."

"Why?" Kate challenged.

"Well, Gerard threatened to tell all of Waterfield that
Peter had a criminal record, so Peter definitely had reason
to want to get rid of Gerard. But he also had a more convenient way to do it."

"And what was that?"

"Um . . ." Mental head thunk.

"What? You know if you don't tell me, I'll get it out of
Brandon!"

I sighed. "He thought Gerard had something to do with
that hit-and-run that killed Carolyn Tate. Gerard brought
his car to Peter just afterward and wanted him to repair
some body damage. Without telling anyone. Peter doesn't
know for sure—he said he didn't ask and Gerard didn't
tell—but if Peter really had wanted to get rid of Gerard,
calling in an anonymous tip about the hit-and-run would
have been a lot easier than murder."

"That's true," Kate admitted, just as Mom came back
down the hall and into the kitchen, holding her puffy blue
coat. She looked from one to the other of us.

"Ready, Avery?"

"Ready," I said, getting up from the table with an apologetic grimace. "Sorry, Kate."

"No problem." She waved a hand. "It was bound to
come out sooner or later. You guys have fun."

I made a face. Fat chance of that while all this was going
on all around us.

"What was that all about?" Mom wanted to know as
soon as we were outside in the cold. I explained what I'd discovered last night and what had taken place this morning.

Mom opened her eyes wide. "You don't think that beautiful man is a murderer, do you? Oh, what a waste!"

"I have no idea," I said. "I don't like to think so, but someone killed Gerard. Who else could it be? It had to be someone who knew Gerard, someone who felt threatened by him . . ."

"Peter Cortino does seem to fit the bill. Or his wife, if she knew what was going on."

I hadn't thought about that. Now I did, and I didn't like it.

"I have a hard time seeing either of them as cold-blooded murderers," I admitted. "I just don't know who else to suspect. Besides Kate and Shannon, and Peter, I don't think Gerard knew anyone else in Waterfield. Except for Beatrice, but I don't want it to be her, either."

"Beatrice?" Mom echoed.

I nodded. "Peter said he asked him—Gerard asked Peter—questions about Bea."

"That's interesting. Any connection between his death and her disappearance, do you think?"

"Like, she killed him and then made a bunk? I thought about it. I'd be more inclined to believe it if I hadn't seen her face when she heard the news that he was dead. She was shocked, wouldn't you say? If she'd killed him, she wouldn't be surprised that he was dead, and anyway, why would she wait until after the body was discovered to leave? Wouldn't it make more sense to go before anyone knew he was dead?"

Mom admitted that it would. "Maybe she didn't realize she'd killed him. Maybe it was an accident."

"She just happened to be baking a batch of cookies when Cora's heart medicine happened to fall into the dough, and rather than start over, Bea decided that a month's supply of digitalis in the cookies probably wouldn't hurt anyone, so when Gerard asked if he could have one, she didn't see any reason to refuse? Yeah, that makes perfect sense." We stopped outside the carriage house door, and I fumbled for the—new—key. The old key was still missing; whoever had dumped Gerard inside must have walked off with it. "And then I suppose he wandered over here on his own, lay down in the carriage house, and died? Or do you think that skinny Beatrice dragged his dead weight over here and up the stairs?"

Mom rolled her eyes. "Maybe he asked her out for a drink. He might have, if he was trying to shake her down, or get closer to her husband to shake him down. Or if he was trying to seduce her. Gerard may have dropped something in her drink—from what you've told me about him, it's not impossible—but she realized it, and switched glasses with him, and then he drank whatever it was and died."

"That'd make more sense if he died of an overdose of Rohypnol or GHB," I said, pushing the door open. "I don't think digitalin is used much for that purpose. Still, it's worth considering. If he had a heart condition and was taking digitalin, getting an overdose like that might kill him. You should mention it to Chief Tolliver the next time he stops by the B&B."

"Maybe I will," Mom said and stopped inside the door to look around the interior of the carriage house. "Oh, Avery . . . this is lovely."

I looked around, too. It was, rather. "It will be, once it's all finished. Derek does good work, doesn't he?"

"You both do," Mom said loyally. "So tell me what you envision down here, and then we'll go upstairs."

"OK." Not one to need a second invitation, I launched into my plans for the carriage house, including the Parisian-inspired decor. Mom nodded and made encouraging noises, approving absolutely every word I said. "And up here," I explained, once we'd navigated the stairs, "is the master bedroom. It'll have cream-colored carpet on the floor, very opulent, and maybe some toile or something on the walls. With black-and-white photographs from the honeymoon. Maybe some silhouettes. Upholstered wall behind the bed. Mirrors everywhere; very French . . ."

"No mirrors on the ceiling, I hope?" Mom interjected.

"Of course not. I'm going for Parisian chic, not French bordello."

The ceilings were too steeply pitched for mirrors, anyway. Wayne and Kate would look like something out of a fun house. When we added the loft, we had kept the original pitch of the roof rather than squaring it off to a normal, flat ceiling. It dipped down low on both sides, so Derek had added a couple of skylights to make up for the lack of windows. Other than the skylights, the only natural light came from a set of French doors cut into the wall opposite the bed, leading onto a tiny balcony. It had a wrought iron railing, of course, and just enough room for another little table and two chairs. In the distance, above the now bare trees, the Atlantic Ocean winked. Or would wink, when the sun came out again after the winter. There was a window in the wall opposite as well, but since that was in the master bath, it didn't do much to add light to the bedroom.

But we had the skylights. They opened to let the gentle breezes in during the warm months, and they had remote-controlled shutters that slid across them in the winter. Very high-tech, and extremely useful. From the inside, though, they were just dark rectangles in the ceiling right now. Maybe I could do something fun with them to make them look prettier. And more French. Something like . . .

"Shutters," I said.

Mom stuck her head out of the bathroom. "What's that, dear?"

"Shutters. Fake ones. On the inside of the ceiling. To make the skylights look more festive. Maybe we can attach some window baskets underneath. With fake flowers, of course; I wouldn't expect Kate to get up on a ladder every couple of days to water them. Plus, if they overflowed, it would ruin the white carpet. But they'd look cool, don't you think?"

"Oh, very," Mom nodded. "Remember those pretty paper flowers you used to make, Avery? From scrapbooking paper? We had vases full of them all over the apartment when you were in high school."

"Of course," I nodded. "They'd be perfect." And I could even make one in fabric, to pin to the waist of that blue dress in John Nickerson's shop window. "D' you want to come with me to the lumber yard to look for shutters? Derek took Jill Cortino home in her van and left me the truck."

"I wouldn't miss it," Mom said.

—17—

The lumber yard did have shutters, and I bought four sets, two for each of the four skylights, and loaded them into the back of the truck. We were just about to pull out of our parking space when another black truck zipped past the back of ours and pulled into the vacant space next to us. I glanced over, past Mom, and out the passenger-side window. The truck had the Stenham Construction logo on the side, and after a moment, the driver's-side door opened, and my cousin got out.

One of them, anyway. Ray and Randy Stenham are identical twins, and I don't know them well enough to tell them apart. They're both tallish—over six feet—and broad, with overdeveloped muscles and matching egos. Like me, they've inherited the kinky Morton hair, but theirs is dark and a lot shorter.

Mom rolled down her window. "Hello, Randall."

I glanced at her in surprise, while Randy—it must have been Randy, because he didn't correct her—looked startled. After a second, he smiled. His teeth were less oversized for his face than when he was a kid, but there were still a lot of them. "Why, if it isn't Aunt Rosemary! And Cousin Avery, too! How are you, coz?"

"Fine," I said repressively, knowing full well he was no more excited to see me than I was to see him.

"You buying materials for that carriage house you're renovating?" He glanced into the bed of the truck.

I nodded. "A few little things for the bedroom."

"Shutters for the skylights?" Randy suggested.

I nodded. "What are *you* working on these days? I hear Clovercroft is still at a standstill."

"Not for long," Randy said, with a snap of teeth. "Devon Highlands is going strong, the parcels are selling like hotcakes, and we just picked up a property on the west side of town that we're going to start developing over the summer."

"Good for you. Melissa must be very excited about all the sales."

Randy smiled. He knows just how little I like Melissa.

"How is your mother?" Mom asked. "I've been thinking about stopping by to say hello, but I don't want to intrude if she's not feeling well. Mary Elizabeth always was delicate." ·

"Ma's fine," Randy began, and then seemed to think better of it. "But she's always been delicate, like you said, Aunt Rosemary. So maybe it'd be better if you called first, if you want to see her, instead of just dropping in. Just in case she's lying down or something."

"Of course," Mom said.

"I should get going." Randy glanced toward the entrance to the lumber depot. "Nice to see you, Aunt Rosemary. You too, Avery."

"Always a pleasure," I murmured insincerely.

Randy grinned. "Tell your boyfriend to stop by the office if he wants a job. We can always use another carpenter."

"Thanks, but I think Derek"—*would rather starve than work for you*—"has enough of his own work to do. And if he gets tired of carpentry, he can always go back to medicine."

198   Jennie Bentley

I smiled. Randy flushed, annoyed. Turning on his heel, he stalked off to see to his own lumber needs.

"Tell me," I said to Mom, watching him turn through the gate of the lumber yard, "just how did you know that that was Randy and not Ray? I can't tell them apart."

"I can't, either," Mom answered calmly. "But I saw him watch that girl over there"—she nodded at a fresh young thing, perhaps one of the coeds from Barnham, bent over her trunk—"and I figured Ray wouldn't be doing that."

"Good catch. I wouldn't put it past Ray, actually, but it sounds like you nailed it. If he hadn't been Randy, I'm sure he would have delighted in telling you so."

I put the truck into gear and pulled out of the parking space. And then I pulled in again. "Wait a second. Isn't that Paige Thompson?"

The coed Ray had ogled straightened up and shook blond hair back over her shoulder.

"No idea," Mom said. "I don't know Paige."

"She's a friend of Josh Rasmussen's and Shannon McGillicutty's. Native Waterfielder. I've been wanting to talk to her about Emily Thompson."

"Right," Mom said, "the picture you found at the Ellises yesterday."

"Exactly. Excuse me a second, won't you?"

"Of course," Mom said, folding her hands in her lap. "I'll just sit here where it's warm."

"No problem." I left the truck in idle with the engine running and got back out into the cold. "Paige!"

The girl at the car turned toward me.

Paige Thompson is a tiny girl, no taller than me, and ethereal looking, with pale blonde hair, blue eyes, and translucent skin. Where I'm sturdy, Paige looks like a strong wind could knock her down. She fastened those big eyes on me. "Good morning, Avery."

"Hey," I answered. "What are you doing here? New car?"

"It's Ricky's." Paige's cheeks flushed. "He's inside picking out some wood for a wedding gift he wants to make for Josh's dad and Shannon's mom."

"That's nice of him," I said. "I didn't know Ricky did woodworking."

Paige shrugged her narrow shoulders inside the over-sized coat she was wearing. "It's his hobby. He says it relaxes him."

"Have you seen Josh or Shannon at all this morning? I told them to give you a message."

Paige shook her head. "What do you need?"

"I wanted to talk to you about a relative of yours," I said. "It wasn't anything urgent, but since we're both here at the same time . . ."

Paige wrinkled her almost invisible brows. "A relative of mine? Who?"

"Her name was Emily Thompson," I explained. "She lived about a hundred years ago. Back in 1917, she knew William Ellis, who was a great-great-uncle or something of Derek's. I think they may have been dating, although I don't know that for sure. Maybe they were just friends."

"OK," Paige said.

"By April of 1918, she had married Lawrence Ritter. The Ritters owned Kate's B&B, although of course it wasn't a B&B back then, just a house, and Lawrence was their son. He died in August 1918. Freak accident. War related."

"OK," Paige said again. If this meant anything to her, or if she had heard any of it before, she showed no sign of it.

"You know that Derek and I are renovating Kate's carriage house, right? A couple of weeks ago, Derek found these initials carved inside the carriage house: WE and ER. We think WE is William Ellis and ER is Emily Ritter."

"Emily Thompson Ritter," Paige said.

I nodded. "I figured, since you have the same last name, you might be related. All the Thompsons in Waterfield are probably related."

"Probably," Paige agreed. "I don't think I can help you, though, Avery. I don't remember ever hearing about Emily."

"Really?" This was disappointing. I had had such high hopes for Paige, especially because she was a history major. If anyone would know, or care, I'd thought it would be her.

"I can try to find out, though," she added. "I have to go home every once in a while anyway, just to make sure that everything's OK. My dad lives alone, and sometimes he drinks a little too much. So I can stop by. If he's not under the weather, he might remember something."

"That'd be great. Only if it's convenient, though. Like I said, it isn't urgent."

"I'll call you in the morning if I find out anything," Paige promised. "Um . . . have they found out who killed Shannon's dad?"

I shook my head. "Not yet. The police are still talking to people. Did you know him?"

"Not to say *know*," Paige answered judiciously, just as Ricky came out of the doors of the lumber depot and headed toward us. "She introduced us once. When he first came to Waterfield."

"What did you think?"

"I didn't like him," Paige said. "I didn't think it was right that he suddenly wanted to be all buddy-buddy with Shannon now, just after she inherited all this money, when he couldn't be bothered to get to know her before."

I nodded. "I don't suppose you have any idea where he lived while he was here? Shannon didn't know. Said he always picked her up at the college."

"I'm afraid not," Paige said, as Ricky reached us. He nodded to me and put his armful of wood into the trunk of the car before slamming the hatch shut.

"What're you talking about?"

"We started out talking about a relative of Paige's who lived a hundred years ago. Now we're talking about Shannon's dad."

"Oh." He tossed the too long, dark brown hair out of his bright blue eyes. "That's awful, what happened to him. I'm really sorry for Shannon."

Ricky had lost his own family at a young age, so he could relate to someone else's loss of a parent.

"Did you meet him?" I asked.

Ricky nodded. "Briefly. Saw him pick up Shannon a bunch of times. Saw him on his own once, too."

"Where?"

Ricky shrugged. "Someplace on the north side of town. One of those real estate developments."

On the north side of town? "It wouldn't happen to be Clovercroft, would it?"

"Not sure," Ricky said. "I was just driving by and I saw his car coming out of the entrance. It has one of those big billboards with Derek's ex-wife on it."

Definitely Clovercroft, then. "When was this?"

"A couple weeks ago," Ricky said vaguely. "Nine or ten in the morning, maybe."

"Thanks."

"No problem." He looked down at Paige. "We should get back to school. Classes this afternoon."

"Sure," I said. "Nice to see you both."

"Likewise." I wandered back toward Derek's truck and my mom, gnawing on my bottom lip.

• • •

"Home?" I said when we were pulling out of the parking lot and onto the road back to Waterfield.

Mom hesitated. "Don't the Stenhams live out this way?"

"I really have no idea." I have endeavored not to know anything I don't have to know about that side of my family. "Ray and Melissa live in a McMansion on the other side of town. Derek pointed it out to me once. I'm not sure about Randy or Mary Elizabeth."

"I was talking about Mary Elizabeth," Mom said. "I don't know where Randy lives, either. But although it's been a while, I'm pretty sure Mary Elizabeth's house is out this way. At least if she lives in what used to be Aunt Catherine's house. I just want to see if my memory is as good as I think it is. Take a left over here." She pointed.

I took the left, away from the main road between Water-field and Portland, and pretty soon we found ourselves navigating a neighborhood of older homes on huge lots. Not old like Waterfield Village, with its Victorian and even Colonial homes: This was a neighborhood built in the 1920s and '30s, full of Craftsman bungalows and repro-duction Tudors, with the occasional pseudo–Greek Revival thrown in for good measure.

"There." Mom pointed. "That Colonial Revival right there. Stuccoed brick, two and a half stories, with the pedi-ment over the door."

I stared at the house she indicated. "It's enormous!"

"The Stenhams are well off," Mom said. "And so were Aunt Catherine and Uncle Hamish."

I nodded. I knew a little bit about the ways in which Hamish Kendall and his wife had made money, and I also knew about Ray and Randy's work ethics, or lack thereof. I wasn't surprised to hear that they were doing well finan-cially. "Are we stopping?"

"We may as well," Mom said. "We're here."

I pulled the truck into the driveway—the football-field-length driveway—even as I said, "What about Aunt Mary Elizabeth's delicate health? And her nap? You said you'd call first."

"It's not going to hurt her to make nice for thirty min-utes," Mom said callously. "And there's nothing wrong with her health, other than that her husband and those little boys of hers ran roughshod over her for years. It'd be enough to make anyone delicate."

"I'm not sure a husband and two boys, even if they were Ray and Randy Stenham, would be enough to make *you* delicate," I pointed out, with a smile. For all her small size and sweet disposition, my mother doesn't let herself be pushed around; she pushes back.

She smiled back at me. "Fine. It'd be enough to make anyone, even me, wish for some peace and quiet. That's all she's doing. Making sure her life is nice and quiet and orderly." She twisted the old-fashioned brass doorbell fastened to the middle of the front door. Inside the house, a bell rang faintly.

"Do you think she'll come?" I asked after a minute, when no one had answered.

Mom nodded. "When she realizes we're not going away, she'll open the door. She's standing inside listening to us." She raised her voice. "Mary Elizabeth? It's Rosemary. Your cousin. And Avery."

Silence.

"Are you sure she's there?" I whispered, just in case she was there and could hear me.

"She's there." She knocked on the door. "C'mon, Mary Elizabeth. I just want to say hello. Open up."

Another silence followed. Just when I was about to give up and suggest we leave, we heard the security chain rattle and the locks tumble. Mary Elizabeth pulled the door open and looked out at us. I fell back a step.

It was the first time I'd laid eyes on my aunt. She obviously didn't go out much, so I'd never run across her by accident, and as I said, I'd never sought her out, either. I had expected her to look something like the twins, sturdy and dark, with curly hair and big teeth. She didn't. Instead she looked a lot like I imagine Aunt Inga must have looked at this age, early sixties. She was tall, taller than me or Mom by several inches, and so pale as to be almost colorless. Her white blond hair (whether blond by nature or nurture I wasn't entirely sure) was immaculately styled. Her skin was paper thin and almost transparent. She was dressed in an icy blue pantsuit, so light in color that it was practically white, and her only concession to makeup was a sweep of pale coral lipstick across her thin lips. Her jewelry was, I hardly need say, a string of pearls. It was like looking at Hans Christian Andersen's Snow Queen, all the more so because she was clearly not happy to see us.

"Rosemary." Her lips barely moved when she spoke. "And Avery." Those pale blue eyes stabbed like icicles.

Mom smiled, her voice warm. "Mary Elizabeth! It's so good to see you!" She stepped forward, arms outstretched.

Mary Elizabeth stepped back. I guess she was trying to avoid the embrace, but the result was that she appeared to be inviting us in. Mom zoomed across the threshold into the house. "Wow." She looked around. "It must be twenty-five years since I was here. It hasn't changed a bit."

I could well believe it. It probably hadn't changed in the twenty-five before that, either.

The foyer was marble tiled in squares of black and white. The walls were white, the banister on the stairs was white (although the stairs themselves were covered with a runner), and the console table standing against the wall was white. There was a vase of flowers on it. White, of course. The green leaves were a nice touch of color.

"This isn't a good time," Mary Elizabeth said, with a glance over her shoulder. From the depths of the house, upstairs somewhere, we could hear a sort of thumping and a squeaking or whining noise.

"What's that?" I asked, curiously.

"The dogs." Mary Elizabeth looked at me.

"You have dogs?" I wouldn't have thought she'd have risked upsetting her pristine house with something she couldn't control. "What kind?"

"Poodles," Mary Elizabeth said, without moving her lips.

White ones, no doubt. "Cool. I have cats. Aunt Inga's cats."

"You remember, Mary Elizabeth," Mom added helpfully, "the cats that Raymond and Randall shaved when they were younger."

Mary Elizabeth nodded, lips tight.

"They seem to be doing well," Mom said. "Your boys. We saw Randall at the lumber yard earlier. He said the development at Devon Highlands is selling well and that the company just procured another property for development."

Mary Elizabeth nodded, her lips relaxing for the first time. Not much, but enough to allow her to speak without having to squeeze the words out. "They're good boys.

Smart and knowledgeable. Not afraid of hard work. Like their grandfather."

"Their grandfather?" I repeated. "Hamish Kendall?" He who had married my Aunt Catherine after Aunt Inga threw him over after realizing he was not only a thief and a murderer, but a coward?

"Burton Stenham. My father-in-law. He founded the company."

"Right. My bad. You know, I came across a picture of one of the Stenhams in the newspaper archives recently. From 1918, the crew that built Kate McGillicutty's carriage house. One of them was a Stenham."

Mary Elizabeth nodded. "My grandfather-in-law, no doubt. His name was Calvin."

Another barrage of thumping came down the stairs, and Mary Elizabeth threw another glance over her shoulder. "Excuse me. I really should take care of this. Perhaps we could arrange to get together another time?" She herded us toward the door.

"I'm staying at the Waterfield Inn," Mom said, as she found herself ushered out. "You can call me there."

"I'll do that." Mary Elizabeth closed the door behind us. We heard the locks snick and the security chain rattle before we were even off the top step.

"Weird," I said.

Mom nodded. "She always was odd. I'm surprised she has dogs. There never used to be pets in the house."

"She had Ray and Randy," I reminded her. "They were animals in their own right."

"True. And with their track record, it's probably just as well. They would have shaved the poor things, just like they did Aunt Inga's Prissy."

I glanced at the house over my shoulder. "The poodles were causing quite a ruckus, weren't they? Must be king poodles, the big ones, to make so much noise. I'm surprised they weren't barking."

"She probably had their tongues cut out," Mom said callously.

I closed the truck door behind me and cranked the engine over. "Anywhere else you want to go? Or just back to the B&B?"

"I guess I've left Noel alone for long enough. I'm going to make him some homemade chicken soup tonight and spend some time nursing him back to health. And you need to drop off the shutters, don't you?"

I nodded. "Let me just call and ask Derek whether he wants me to bring him food or whether Jill fed him."

"You do that," Mom said, leaning back against the seat and looking out. "I'm going to enjoy the view, meanwhile."

Jill had fed Derek, so I drove straight to the B&B, where I requested Kate's help with unloading the shutters, since she was younger and stronger than my mom.

"Where's Derek?" Kate wanted to know, breathlessly, as we hauled big slabs of wood.

"He's still with Jill Cortino." I glanced over my shoulder to make sure I didn't trip over the threshold on my way in, backward. "I guess she's pretty upset about what happened this morning."

"I would be, too, if I suddenly found out that my husband was a felon." After a second she added, "Of course, my ex *was* a felon. I've just known about it for a while."

Jill had known about it for a while, too, if it came to that. It was the police taking her husband away that had upset her. "Did his time in prison have anything to do with why he was killed, do you think? Someone from his past caught up with him?"

"Can't imagine who," Kate said. "I mean, he served his time. More likely he was up to his old tricks, trying to extort money from someone new, and they weren't having it."

I nodded. Made sense.

Kate and I ended up in the kitchen after the shutters were safely leaned up against the wall inside the carriage house. "Have you eaten?" she asked, hanging her coat back on the hook by the door.

I shook my head. "Too much going on today. I haven't had time."

She got up and went to the refrigerator. "Ham and cheese? Turkey? Salami?"

"Whatever is convenient. Thank you. By the way, I ran into Paige Thompson and Ricky."

"Paige and Ricky?" Kate repeated.

I nodded. "I asked her about Emily. She says she never heard of her, but she's going to ask her dad. Meanwhile, Ricky said he'd seen Gerard come out of a real estate development north of town. One that has Melissa's picture on a billboard. I'm thinking it's Clovercroft."

"Most likely," Kate agreed, setting a sandwich down in front of me. It was beautiful, with a frilly edge of lettuce peeping out on one side of the crusty bread. I admired it for a second before I lifted it and took a bite. Roast beef. Yum. "Devon Highlands is on the west side, near Barnham, so it wouldn't be that. Ricky is probably familiar with it, anyway. And then they've got that little cul-de-sac of condos up the ocean road to the east, but that's not on the north side, either."

"Exactly. And Peter told us Gerard had asked him questions about Beatrice. That must be where he met her. At the Clovercroft office."

"What would he be doing at the Clovercroft office?" Kate wanted to know.

I shrugged. "No idea. Got lost and stopped in to ask directions?" I took another bite of sandwich and chewed.

"Wayne stopped by for lunch," Kate said. "He told me Reece has put in a call to Augusta to have Daphne and Hans come back to Waterfield to sniff around."

That might sound like a bad pun, but in fact wasn't.

Hans was the cadaver dog that had searched our yard on Becklea in the fall, and Daphne was his handler.

"Sniff around what?" I wanted to know. "The Cortinos' shop?"

Kate nodded. "Gerard died somewhere, and it wasn't in the carriage house. That means he was transported here somehow."

And Peter had access to a lot of cars. His own as well as the ones in the shop.

"So when will they be here?" I pulled a sliver of lettuce off the sandwich and put it in my mouth.

"Not until tomorrow morning," Kate said.

"I saw Peter vacuuming out the back of a Stenham Construction vehicle when we got there this morning. If you see Brandon or Reece in what's left of today, you may want to tell them that."

"I will. Any news on Beatrice?"

I shook my head. "Hopefully she and Steve are just off somewhere, kissing and making up and promising never to leave one another again."

"That'd be nice," Kate nodded. "Although she disappeared the day after Gerard died, do you think there's a connection? That she had something to do with it, or maybe someone thought she knew something?"

I hadn't thought about that last one. The first, yes, but not the possibility that someone else might have murdered Gerard, and then snatched Beatrice because she had met him and might know the murderer. "That's scary."

Kate agreed. "Here's a thought. Didn't you say that Melissa knew Gerard's name? Maybe he saw her billboard at Clovercroft and drove in to see if they had an apartment for rent? And then he ran across Beatrice in the office. She's the only person there, right? And maybe Beatrice told him to call Melissa, and he did. And that's how she knows his name."

I sat back on my chair. "That's not a bad idea, actually. It would explain a lot."

"Maybe we should give Melissa a call," Kate said.

"Wait a second. I just had another thought. When we were out there the other day—was it only yesterday?—to look for Beatrice, Melissa couldn't let us into the model home above the office. She said she'd given the key to someone."

Kate blinked. "You think she gave the key to the model home to Gerard? Why?"

"Could be any number of reasons. She was sleeping with him and wanted somewhere private they could meet. Or he needed a place to live and offered to pay her."

"That's true," Kate said. She was quiet while I finished the rest of my sandwich. Then she said, "Maybe we shouldn't call Melissa after all. Maybe we should just go out there and have a look around."

"Break and enter?"

"Extenuating circumstances," Kate said. She got up and reached for her winter coat again. "Beatrice could be inside, in need of medical attention."

"Wayne already looked. Although he was looking for Bea and not information about Gerard. Yesterday, we didn't know there was a connection. Wait for me." I hurried out the door behind her.

• • •

"I already checked the model home," Wayne said when I pulled the truck to a stop next to his patrol car, which was parked on the side of the Portland road just outside town. "Beatrice isn't there."

"You mean, she wasn't there when you checked," Kate retorted. "She could be there now. But that's not why I want to see it. Listen to this."

She went through our reasoning and our suspicion that Gerard had been living in the model home since he came to town. Wayne's eyebrows crept up as he listened. "Do you have any proof of this?" he asked eventually.

Kate and I looked at one another. "Not exactly."

"It makes sense, though," Kate argued.

"If you go back there and take us with you," I added,

"maybe we can find some proof. I'm sure you didn't make a very thorough search when you were there yesterday. You probably just made sure that Beatrice wasn't there, right?"

Wayne agreed. "I did look in the closets and under the bed, though. People hide in the strangest places sometimes."

"Was there anything in the closet?"

Wayne shook his head.

"Someone must have cleaned Gerard's clothes and things out after the murder, then, if he was staying there."

"And vacuumed and cleaned up," I added, remembering Derek's comment about vacuum tracks across the carpet. "He couldn't have done it himself."

"If he ever stayed there," Wayne admonished us both.

"Maybe it was Beatrice," I suggested, paying Wayne no heed. "Maybe she killed Gerard for some reason, and then she didn't want anyone to put two and two together and realize that she'd known him, so she decided to get rid of all his things. Maybe that's why she disappeared. So she could go to Canada and dump it all."

"Without her car?" Kate said.

"Maybe she took Gerard's car. I don't think the state police have found it. Have they?"

I looked at Wayne. He shook his head.

Kate thought for a moment. "I suppose that's possible," she admitted. "Or maybe it was . . . what's his name? Steve? What if Gerard and Beatrice had something going, and he found out? Maybe he came to Waterfield to talk Beatrice into coming back to Boston, and then he found them together, so he killed Gerard and took off with Bea so she couldn't call the police."

"Or Gerard was bothering her, and Steve was protecting her?" I suggested.

Wayne was shaking his head at both of us. "If Gerard had been hit over the head, maybe. But poison is always premeditated. It's not a crime of passion."

"Oops." I bit my lip.

Kate shrugged. "Whether it was Beatrice or some-one else who cleaned out Gerard's belongings—Melissa, maybe?—I doubt he or she would have known about Gerard's secret stash."

"Secret stash?"

"The hiding place where he put his extra cash and anything else he thought was important. He had one everywhere he lived."

"How many places did he live?" Wayne wanted to know. Kate turned to him.

"He moved a lot. During the four years I knew him well—one year before Shannon was born and three after—he lived in at least three different apartments. The next ten years I didn't keep up with him, but every time I heard from him, or ran into him accidentally, he had a new place to live. And in every place, he had this certain hidey-hole where he put his valuables."

"Where is it?" Wayne wanted to know. I guess he was thinking he could leave us behind and go to the model home alone.

"I'd have to see the place," Kate answered. When Wayne looked at her, she smiled sweetly.

He sighed. "All right. I'll meet you out there."

"Great." I put Derek's truck in gear and we glided off down the street. Behind us, Wayne pulled out into the roadway and followed.

• • •

Clovercroft looked no different from the last time I'd been there, with the only exception being that Beatrice's car was gone. Derek had driven it back to Waterfield and parked it outside Dr. Ben's house. For when she came back, as he put it.

Wayne took us up the stairs from the outside and opened the door to the model home with a universal key from his key ring. Pushing the door open, he nodded to Kate. "Knock yourself out."

Grimacing at his tone of voice, she slid past him and into the apartment. I followed.

It wasn't a big place; six hundred square feet, maybe,

with a living room and eat-in kitchen, a bedroom, and a bath. It was carpeted, so footsteps would be muffled in the commercial space below, and as Derek had mentioned, there were fresh tracks from a vacuum in all the corners. In the middle of the room, they had been obliterated by footsteps. I recognized the tiny, round indentations of Melissa's spike heels, as well as Derek's deeply grooved construction boots. The walls were a generic warm vanilla with pictures of ocean scenes in silver frames, and the furniture was serviceable but uninspired.

"Smells like Gerard," Kate muttered.

"Really?" I sniffed but couldn't smell anything other than air freshener.

"Trust me. He's been using the same cologne for twenty years. I still remember it."

I hadn't noticed the body smelling—of cologne or anything else—but maybe they don't when they've cooled. In any case, I was willing to take her word for it.

"As you can see," Wayne said, opening the coat closet next to the door, "there's nothing here. Same thing in the bedroom. But feel free to look for yourselves."

Kate shook her head. "I trust you. Whoever cleaned this place out would be careful not to leave anything behind. Anything visible."

Wayne put his hands on his hips, just south of the gun belt. "So where's this hidey-hole of his?"

"I'm looking." Kate turned in a slow circle, scanning the room. After a moment, she went into the bedroom and did the same thing there.

"Well?" Wayne prompted.

"Give me a minute. There." She pointed.

"The air return?"

"If you open it, you'll find an envelope or something. He tried using the vents, but the paper he put in would rattle, plus, he'd need a screwdriver to get the covers on and off. And he liked to have things easily accessible. It doesn't work to put paper in the toilet tank, although sometimes he'd put other things there. That was only if he didn't have a shower rod he could take off, though. Like, if it was a claw-foot with a shower ring, for instance. Otherwise, he'd take down the shower rod, take it apart, slip whatever he wanted to hide into it, and close it back up."

"Sounds like an interesting character," Wayne said dryly. "I'm not going to ask what he might have put in the shower rod or toilet tank back then, OK?"

"I appreciate it. Although the statute of limitations has probably run out on most of it. I'll check the bathroom." She headed for it, head held high and back straight, but her cheeks flushed.

I watched her go and turned to Wayne, who was removing the cover from the air vent return. "Anything?"

"Not so far. Let me take the filter out. And . . . yep, here we go."

"What?"

"Envelope." He turned it over in his hands. "Manila. Sealed."

"Are you going to open it?"

"As soon as Kate gets back. You can both watch me do it. If anything comes of this, I'll need a statement saying you saw me take it out of the return."

"No problem." We stood in silence a minute or two, listening to Kate rattle around in the bathroom.

"Nothing," she announced when she came back out. Wayne gave her a searching look but decided not to press the issue.

"We found this envelope in the air return. I want you both to watch me open it, please."

Kate went to stand on the other side of Wayne. We both leaned forward, holding our breath, when he slit the envelope open.

The first thing he slid out was a couple of bank statements. Kate's and Shannon's. Paper clipped to them was an obituary. "Patricia Kathleen Logan?" Wayne read.

"My grandmother." Kate's lips were tight. "Wonder who he bribed to get copies of my bank statements?"

"We can try to find out," Wayne promised, putting the

statements aside. Next came a couple of newspaper clippings about a police action against an organized ring of car thieves some eight or nine years ago in East Boston. A follow-up to the first story had a list of names and prison sentences. Peter Cortino was one of the people mentioned.

"Bastard," Kate muttered. I nodded.

The next thing Wayne pulled from the envelope was a photograph. It was dark and blurry but clearly showed a woman in a state of undress, half sitting and half lying on a sofa, and holding a glass of what looked like wine.

"Melissa?" I ventured.

Kate shook her head. "Darker haired. And younger."

I peered more closely. "That's the sofa in the office downstairs, isn't it? And the picture of the town square behind it?"

"Looks that way," Kate said grimly. "It's hard to tell, but it looks like Bea."

"Derek's Bea?" I grabbed Wayne's hand and adjusted the angle of the photo. "Dammit. Yes, it is."

"This doesn't look good," Wayne said. I shook my head. I wasn't looking forward to telling Derek that Gerard had a picture of an obviously tipsy Beatrice with her shoes kicked off and her blouse open a few buttons farther south than was strictly decent.

"What's that?" Kate pointed. Wayne turned the photograph over.

"Looks like a couple of phone numbers on the back. One local, one Boston."

"Steve?"

"Or Beatrice. Home and cell."

I shook my head. "She lives with Dr. Ben and Cora, and that's not their number. And she gave me her cell phone number when she'd been here a few days. That isn't it, either."

"Try it," Kate suggested.

Wayne was already dialing. The local number first. He put the call on speaker phone and we heard it ring a couple of times, and then a voice answered. "Captain Morgan Inn. Lisa speaking. How may I help you?"

"Hi, Lisa," Wayne said politely, "this is Police Chief Rasmussen in Waterfield."

"Yes, Chief," Lisa chirped happily.

"Do you by chance have a young woman by the name of Gremilion staying with you? Beatrice Gremilion? Twenty-eight years old, thin, with long brown hair? She would have checked in two days ago."

"No, Chief," Lisa returned immediately. I guess the Captain Morgan Inn was small enough that she knew all the names of all the guests without having to look anything up.

"You're sure?" Wayne pressed.

"Yes, Chief. I'm positive. Mr. Gremilion has been here since Monday, and he's been alone the whole time."

Wayne blinked. I did, too. "I beg your pardon?" he said. "Did you say that Mr. Gremilion is staying with you? Mr. Steve Gremilion?"

"Yes, Chief," Lisa chirped. "Mr. Gremilion has the honeymoon suite. He said he was waiting for his wife to join him, but I guess she never did. At least I haven't seen her. Would you like me to put you through to Mr. Gremilion's room?"

"No," Wayne said quickly, "please don't. I'll be coming down there myself within the hour to talk to Mr. Gremilion, and I'd just as soon he didn't know to expect me. I'll be leaving Waterfield in the next few minutes. If Mr. Gremilion leaves before I get there, would you be so kind as to call me? On this number?"

"Sure, Chief," Lisa said. "Anything else I can help you with?"

Wayne said there wasn't.

"Thank you for calling the Captain Morgan Inn! We look forward to seeing you." She hung up. Wayne rolled his eyes and did the same thing.

"I'll call Derek," I said.

Wayne opened his mouth, looked at my face, and closed it again. "I'll just be going," he said instead, shooing the two of us toward the door. I was already dialing.

Derek answered on the first ring. "Avery?"

I didn't see the sense in beating around the bush, so I gave it to him straight. "We've found Steve."

Silence. "What?" he said.

"Steve. He's in the honeymoon suite at the Captain Morgan Inn."

"In Brunswick?"

"I have no idea," I said, realizing I'd never actually heard of the Captain Morgan Inn before now. "Let me ask Wayne. Wayne, is it in Brunswick?"

Wayne sent me a look. I guess he really didn't want us going with him. However, if he thought he could keep Derek away, he had another think coming.

"He's not telling me," I told Derek, "but I think it is."

"Come get me." He gave me directions to Jill and Peter Cortino's house on the outskirts of the Village.

"It'll take me a few minutes. I'm at Clovercroft."

"Just get here as fast as you can." He hung up, presumably to explain the situation to Jill and prepare to leave.

"He wants me to pick him up," I said, tucking my phone away.

"Of course he does."

"Steve's his brother-in-law. Beatrice is his sister. You didn't really think you could keep him away?"

"I'll just be grateful if he doesn't call Cora," Wayne said and opened his own car door. "Kate?"

"I'll ride with Avery and Derek. Since you're being so official." She scooted into the cab of the truck before he could say anything else. Wayne made a face and got into the police cruiser.

• • •

In the summer, with leaves on the trees and flowers in bloom and all that nice stuff, I'm sure the Captain Morgan Inn is a lovely place. At the moment, it was just as dreary as everywhere else, blanketed with a layer of snow. And whatever excitement had gone on, if any, was over by the time we got there. Wayne had beat us to Brunswick by ten or fifteen minutes; it was only because Derek had kept the gas pedal floored most of the way that it wasn't more. When we pulled into the parking lot, the chief of police was inside the honeymoon suite. With Steve, who I recognized from the photographs in Dr. Ben and Cora's albums. He was shaking his head vehemently when we walked in.

"No. I haven't seen her." And then he looked up and recognized Derek, and his face twisted. "Derek? Where's Bea? They say she's missing."

"We don't know where she is," Derek said, his voice controlled. "We hoped she was with you."

Steve shook his head. "I haven't seen her. I've been waiting for Mr. Labadie to get in touch. For two days now. His phone just keeps ringing and ringing."

Wayne, Kate, and Derek exchanged a look. "About that . . ." Derek began.

"Mr. Labadie won't be calling," Wayne said. "He was murdered a few days ago. Just for the record, where were you Monday afternoon between the hours of three and seven?"

Steve blinked behind the glasses. "I was here. Waiting for him to call."

"Call about what?" Wayne wanted to know, jotting a note in his tiny notebook with his tinier stub of a pencil. "I assume the front desk can verify your whereabouts?"

Steve looked uncomfortable. "I hope they can. And he was going to call me about Bea. He sent me a picture of her, on a couch somewhere, with a glass of wine, the way she used to look before I started working all the time and everything got screwed up."

She looked happy, in other words.

"This picture?" Wayne produced it from his pocket. He had put it inside a Ziploc baggie. Steve looked at it, winced, and nodded. Derek looked at it and swore.

"He said he had others," Steve said miserably, taking off his glasses to rub his eyes. "More compromising. And that he'd go public with them if I didn't pay him."

"Bastard," Kate muttered.

Steve glanced at her. "She's still my wife, and it won't do my career any good if compromising pictures of her come out in the papers or online."

"And that's the only reason you came up here?" Derek asked, hands fisted on his hips.

Steve hesitated, eyeing him. "I want her back," he admitted. "Unless it's too late."

"That's why you rented the honeymoon suite?"

Steve looked around at the king-sized bed with red satin sheets, the heart-shaped whirlpool tub tucked away in the corner. "It was the only room available. I thought maybe it was a sign."

"Some sign." Derek's lips were tight. "Why didn't you just call her?"

"I did. Weeks ago. I asked her to come home. She said no. And then I saw that . . ." Steve shot another glance at the photograph, "and realized why."

"Why?"

Steve looked at Derek like he suspected his brother-in-law of having lost his mind. "She's gotten involved with someone else, obviously."

"She hasn't gotten involved with anyone else," Derek said between gritted teeth. Steve glanced at him.

I added my two cents. "She was sitting at home waiting for you to realize you missed her so you'd come find her and bring her back. We haven't met. I'm Avery."

"Nice to meet you." Steve stuck out a hand and we shook. "I don't understand. Why wouldn't she come back to Boston when I asked?"

Kate and I did a simultaneous eye roll. "She wanted things to change," I explained. "For you to work less and spend more time with her. Start a family, all that. I guess she thought by going back when you asked, she'd only go back to the same situation. But if you cared enough to leave work and come here, the two of you might be able to work things out."

Steve looked stricken. For a few seconds, at least. "But what about the pictures?"

"There are no pictures. At least none we've found. That's the only one, and it's from the sofa in her office," I explained. "Gerard lived in the apartment above. He probably stopped by at some point."

"Probably tried to seduce her," Kate grumbled. "Or tried to get her drunk enough that she wouldn't notice him rifling through the office files."

"That's all fine," Derek said, impatiently, "but if she's not here, where is she? Cora called all of Bea's friends in Waterfield yesterday. There weren't many, and the few people she was close to growing up have mostly all moved away. The ones that are left didn't know anything."

Steve nodded agreement. "There was no one in Waterfield she stayed in touch with, other than her mom."

"We've been calling you, too, by the way. You haven't been answering."

"I didn't want to tie up the line," Steve muttered, his thin cheeks flushed. "In case Mr. Labadie called. Or Beatrice."

Derek rolled his eyes. "Whatever. She obviously didn't talk to Alice, since Alice is just as worried as we are."

"We know she knew Gerard," I said, "since he was staying in the apartment above her office, and it's likely she met the Stenhams at some point, too."

"I spoke to Melissa," Wayne said, "and she says she has no idea where Beatrice is. She says they weren't friendly . . ."

I shook my head. Beatrice loathed Melissa.

". . . but she said she would have expected Beatrice to let her or the Stenhams know if the office was going to be unmanned."

"She's very conscientious," Steve whispered. "And responsible. She wouldn't just leave."

Wayne nodded. "And Melissa says that as far as she knows, Ray doesn't know where Beatrice is, either. She says he would have told her if he did."

"You'd better believe it," Derek muttered. "Melissa isn't the kind of woman it's easy to keep secrets from."

"You would know. And where I wouldn't put it past her

to lie"—Wayne glanced at Derek, who shook his head—"I don't think she'd be a party to kidnapping or murder."

Derek agreed. "Absolutely not," he said. "She may have somewhat elastic morals, but she's too self-serving to take part in anything really illegal. She wouldn't do something that could get her in real trouble."

Wayne nodded. "The Stenhams are both accounted for the whole afternoon when she went missing. I figured I might as well ask, just so I'd know. Ray had lunch with Melissa and then they went home for . . . um . . ."

He paused, seeking an acceptable euphemism.

"You can say it," Derek said, "I'm aware of what they're doing."

"Right. And while they were busy . . . um . . . at home, Randy was holding down the fort at Devon Highlands. There were workers and clients coming and going all afternoon. Neither of the brothers, assuming Melissa can be trusted, had the opportunity to go to Clovercroft and abduct Beatrice."

"I wouldn't trust Melissa any farther than I can throw her," Derek said, "but again, I don't think she'd be a party to kidnapping or murder. If she says she and Ray were spending the afternoon in bed, I'm sure that's exactly where they were."

"So where is she?" Steve asked, desperation in his voice.

Nobody answered.

"Why don't you pack up and come back to Waterfield with us?" Derek suggested after a moment. "I'm sure Dad and Cora would be happy to put you up, and if not, you can stay in the loft. I can spend a few days with Avery." He glanced at me. I nodded.

"Thanks," Steve said, "I'll do that, although I won't kick you out of your home. If Cora and Ben won't have me, I'll rent a room somewhere. At a B&B or something. There's a nice one right there, a block or so away, right?"

Kate smiled. Indeed there was.

Steve went to settle his bill and put his suitcase,

champagne, and Godiva in the car, and Derek and I, Kate and Wayne ended up facing each other in the parking lot.

"What now?" I asked.

Derek shrugged helplessly. "I don't know what to do. I was so sure this would be it. I thought we'd find them spooning under the comforter. I'm not sure what to do next."

I nodded sympathetically. His worry was contagious, heavy, and we all felt it. He was right—we'd held out some hope of finding Bea alive with Steve . . . and now? We both needed something to distract us, I thought, something to keep our minds from returning over and over to a worst-case scenario. Glancing at Kate, I suddenly thought of the perfect thing.

Not a good time to suggest that we do some spooning ourselves, I calculated. Usually it makes for a very effective distraction, but now wasn't the time. I had to come up with something else instead. Something to take his mind off Beatrice for a while.

"Isn't this where Helen Ritter lives? The woman you bought the B&B from? She went to an old folks' home somewhere. Wasn't it in Brunswick?"

"I think so," Kate said.

"Do you think we could stop and talk to her? Or ask if she'll talk to us? We're here anyway; it seems a shame not to try."

"Never hurts to ask," Derek agreed. "Assuming we can locate her." He turned away.

I looked at Kate. "Can you remember where she ended up going? The name of the place, the address, anything?"

"She did give me a forwarding address," Kate said. "Just in case the post office made a mistake and some of her mail was delivered to me. Let me think."

"I'm gonna call home," Derek said. "Tell Cora and Dad that Steve's on his way. Maybe they've heard something."

"Sure." I left them both to it and turned to Wayne. "Thanks for letting us crash your party."

"You're welcome. Don't get in the habit of ambulance chasing, though."

"I won't," I said, grinning. "If it was your sister and brother-in-law, you'd want to see for yourself though, wouldn't you?"

Wayne allowed that he would. I lowered my voice. "So do you think there's a connection between Gerard's death and Bea's disappearance? You don't think she killed him, do you?"

"I'd hate to think so," Wayne answered carefully, "but I can't rule it out. It's more likely that someone else did, though, and then realized that Beatrice might know something about it. So they took her, too."

I lowered my voice another notch. "So do you think she's dead, too?"

Wayne hesitated. "Like I told you just after you came to Waterfield, most people who disappear without a trace show up sooner or later. One way or the other. We'll just have to wait and see."

"Right." I grimaced and turned back to Kate. "Have you remembered something?"

Kate smiled triumphantly. "The place is called Green Acres. Like the old TV show. It's on Church."

"Great. Derek probably has a good idea where that is. Do you want to come?"

Kate shook her head. "I'll go back to Waterfield with Wayne. Let me know what she says tomorrow."

I promised I would. And then I addressed Wayne when I thought of something. "Apparently Reece Tolliver is bringing in the cadaver dog from Augusta tomorrow to see if it can smell anything in any of the Cortinos' cars. Or the shop. Do you think you could ask them to sniff around Clovercroft, too? Just in case?"

"Of course," Wayne nodded, just as Derek shut off his cell phone and came back to us.

"Any news?" Kate asked sympathetically.

He shook his head. "Dad and Cora will be happy to take care of Steve. There's no news other than that."

"We'll find her," I said, although I had no idea whether we would or not. But the alternative was really not acceptable, so I had to keep on believing Beatrice was safe and sound somewhere. Even if she had killed Gerard and would end up in jail, that would be preferable to having her be dead.

"I hope so, Tinkerbell." Voice strained, Derek pulled me into a tight embrace, resting his cheek against my hair. I could feel the tension radiating from him and knew he wouldn't be able to relax or know peace until we'd found Beatrice, one way or the other. Over his shoulder, I saw Wayne and Kate exchange a look and quietly remove themselves to the police cruiser parked a few spaces away.

—19—

The assisted-living facility where Mrs. Lawrence Ritter III lived was located on a couple of acres of snow-covered ground north of town. It took us about ten minutes to find it, and another few to talk our way past the front desk and into the room. A few minutes after walking into the building, we were knocking on the door of Helen Simmons Ritter's room.

"Come in." The voice was wavery and weak, and the woman it belonged to huddled in a wheelchair with a blanket over her legs and another across her shoulders, though the room was far from cold. Her eyes were sharp, though, and when I had explained who we were and what we doing there, she seemed to know exactly what I was talking about. "Of course."

"You remember her?"

Mrs. Ritter shook her head. "Oh, no. I never met my mother-in-law."

"You didn't?" That was disappointing.

"She died in childbirth. Larry was brought up by his grandmother."

"Really?"

"Oh, yes." Mrs. Ritter nodded vigorously. Or as vigorously as a frail ninety-year-old woman in a wheelchair can nod. "And of course his father died before Larry was born, so I never met either of my parents-in-law. Larry and I didn't meet until 1941. We got married in '42, and then he went to France." A shadow passed over her face.

"But he came back," Derek said gently.

She nodded. "Oh, yes. And we had many wonderful years together after that. The Lord did not see fit to bless us with any children, but we had a good life."

I smiled politely. I was happy for her, of course, but I wanted to know about Emily and Lawrence—mostly Emily.

Mrs. Ritter fumbled in her bedside drawer, among tissues, magazines, and other debris. "This is our wedding photograph." She handed me a framed photo, black and white. It seemed to be my week for looking at wedding pictures.

Derek and I put our heads together over it. Like every other bride I'd seen recently, the young Helen Simmons looked deliriously happy. She was wearing a smart little 1940s suit, with a neat little hat on her dark hair, and she was clinging to the arm of her tall husband. He was in uniform, so they must have gotten married just before—and I do mean *just* before—he shipped out.

Larry took after his mother in appearance. Fair hair, blue eyes—at least I assumed they were blue—and a sweet smile. There was nothing of Lawrence Ritter's pugnacious look about him, and also nothing of Anna Virginia's snootiness. He looked like a nice, friendly young man. He looked—I blinked—familiar.

"His father died at sea," Mrs. Ritter explained, and I listened with half an ear as she told us the same story I'd heard from Miss Barnes at the Historical Society, about the sinking of *SC-209* in August 1918.

Derek listened avidly. He must have heard the story before, too, but Mrs. Ritter had his full attention. I devoted mine to the photograph.

The Ritters must have gotten married at the courthouse; at least I thought I recognized the stairs they were standing on. Helen had been a sturdy, blooming kind of girl back then—nothing at all like the willowy Emily a generation earlier. I'd give a lot to take a look at *her* wedding photo. But in any case, it was amazing (and quite a little disconcerting) to see the difference time had wrought.

". . . to prison," Mrs. Ritter said, and I sat up with a start.

"Excuse me?"

"I said, if my mother-in-law hadn't died in childbirth, she would have been sent back to reformatory after Larry was born."

"Emily was in prison?"

Mrs. Ritter nodded. "For murder."

Derek and I exchanged a look. "Whose murder?" he asked.

"I have it here." She dug through the things in the bedside drawer. "Larry went back to look for it after he was grown. Wanted to know what happened to his mother, since no one would talk about her. And this is what he found."

She handed me a clipping—not a copy: an actual clipping, yellowed and brittle—from the *Waterfield Clarion*, from September 4, 1918. *Tragedy strikes local family again*, the heading said, and the article was about the sinking of the *SC-209*, with a list of the many dead and the few survivors. By then, almost a week later, they must have gotten an accurate tally of exactly what had happened, and to whom. Larry's father Lawrence was mentioned, of course, among the dead, and the article ended with the sentences *This devastating news comes just a month after the conviction of Emily Ritter for murder. Mrs. Ritter was found guilty of feeding William A. Ellis of 34 Chandler Street a concoction of strychnine, thus causing his death. She is serving her sentence in the Massachusetts Reformatory for Women in Framingham, Mass., the great state of Maine lacking a facility for the purpose of adequately caring for the female criminal.*

"Wow," I said. "Can I make a copy of this?"

"Of course," Mrs. Ritter said, flapping a blue-veined hand. "There's a copy machine at the reception desk. You know, young man, you remind me of my husband."

She smiled at Derek, her teeth too white and even to be her own. He smiled back and patted her hand. I left them to their mutual admiration and headed down the hall to make a copy of the article. For good measure, I brought the wedding picture, too. The grainy Xerox copy I got wasn't much to look at, but it was better than nothing. When I took the photograph of William and Emily to the photographer on Main Street tomorrow—since I'd forgotten to do it today in all the hoopla of finding out about Peter's criminal past and Steve's presence in Brunswick—I'd ask if they had a copy of the Ritters' wedding picture. Both sets of Ritters: Emily and Lawrence Junior and Helen and Larry. If Lowry's had taken it—and they'd been in business long enough—maybe they had a negative sitting around.

We left shortly after that, driving back to Waterfield mostly in silence. It had been a busy day, with a whole lot of things happening, and I think we both were a little overwhelmed.

"You want to come in?" I asked when Derek pulled to a stop outside Aunt Inga's house. Some closeness and togetherness might give us both comfort, but I doubted he was in the mood, and I wasn't sure I was, either. Derek looked exhausted, his face drawn, those pretty, blue eyes shadowed with worry. Over Beatrice—where she was and what was happening to her; over Cora, if Beatrice didn't come back; and over Jill, if the police decided to charge Peter with murder. And now, over the fact that his great-great-uncle had been murdered by Paige's aunt or cousin several times removed. It was in the past, mostly forgotten, but must still be a shock.

He gave me a tired smile. "I don't think so, Avery. Not tonight."

I nodded sympathetically. "You look like you could use a good night's sleep."

"I could, but that's not it. I want to head over to Dad and Cora's. See if there's any news. Make sure that Steve is getting settled in OK. See if there's anything I can do."

"I can come with you," I offered.

"Thanks, but it's not necessary. There's no need for you to spend another miserable few hours watching Cora turn herself inside out with worry. You've got your own family in town; you need to be bright-eyed and bushy-tailed for your mom in the morning."

"Not just for Mom. I want to be at Cortino's tomorrow, when Hans and Daphne do their sniffing."

"Damn. I'd forgotten about that." He closed his eyes for a second; I studied the dark circles under them and the sweep of long lashes against his cheeks. "Yeah, I need to be there, too. Just in case Jill needs me."

"You know," I said, "I know you're happy doing what you're doing, and I'm not saying you need to stop, but the medical profession lost a great doctor when you decided to drop out of medicine. Your bedside manner is excellent."

He flashed a tired grin. "Is that another attempt at getting me to come inside? Because if so, I think you're gonna be disappointed. My bedside manner's too tired tonight."

I shook my head. "I'm just saying that you're a nice guy. You care about people."

"Most people are easy to care about. Especially when there's so much bad news going around." He put the truck in gear. "I'll pick you up in the morning, OK? We'll go to Cortino's together."

I nodded, sliding out of the car. "Sleep well."

"Oh, once I get to lie down, I'll sleep like a baby. No worries."

"Right," I said. "See you."

He drove away, while I let myself in through the gate and walked up the path to the front door. Slowly. I was tired, too. I had done a whole lot of running around today, cramming a lot of new information into my head, and both my brain and my body were exhausted from all the effort. Up until this afternoon, I had been able to tell myself that

Bea was fine, she was with Steve, they were figuring out their differences and getting back together. I no longer had that luxury. Unless Steve was the greatest actor since Olivier, and somehow I doubted that, he truly hadn't seen Beatrice.

Where could she be? I wondered as I inserted the key in the lock. Had she left of her own free will because she had murdered Gerard and didn't want to get arrested? Was he blackmailing her, threatening to show Steve that picture we'd found? Did he have others? Had she packed up his things and gone somewhere to get rid of them, and something had happened to her? Had she fallen and broken her leg and died of hypothermia, or stumbled off the edge of the cliffs and been swept out to sea? Or had someone else helped her? Although Gerard had been no Mr. Universe, he would have outweighed her by at least fifty or sixty pounds. How had she managed to get his body up the stairs to the carriage house loft by herself? If he had died in the office, or in the apartment above, she might have managed to roll or drag him out to his car. I pictured the body rolling down the narrow stairs from the Clovercroft model home, and grimaced. She might even have managed to roll or drag him into the carriage house. But how had she gotten him up those steep steps to the loft on her own? And if it had happened this way, why hadn't the body shown some sign of it? I'd seen it, and Gerard's suit had been pristine.

So had she had an accomplice? Someone she had gone off with after the body was discovered?

But no, Beatrice had seemed genuinely shocked when I told her about Gerard's murder. Or maybe not; maybe what she had been shocked to hear was that the body had been found. Maybe she had an accomplice, and that accomplice had told her to sit tight; he or she would get rid of the body. Beatrice had thought Gerard would end up in the water or in a shallow grave somewhere, and instead, he'd ended up in our carriage house. And *that's* when she'd left.

Jemmy and Inky appeared and began winding themselves around my ankles, a sure sign that I'd forgotten to fill their food and water bowls this morning in my excitement to get out of the house to tell Derek my news. I padded down the hall toward the kitchen to remedy this oversight while I continued thinking.

What was the point of leaving Gerard in our carriage house in the first place? Why not just dump him in the ocean? Unless it was personal. Someone who knew who he was, that he was Kate's ex-boyfriend and Shannon's father, and that they, along with Wayne, were the logical suspects if something happened to him. Someone else with a can't-miss motive for wanting to get rid of him, then. Someone who'd have reason to worry that they'd end up on the police's radar, and who wanted to make sure there were even more obvious suspects for the authorities to focus on. Peter was an obvious suspect. He had to have known that the police would find his criminal record and link him to Gerard. And Peter was a muscular sort of guy; he'd be able to carry Gerard up the stairs to the loft. He had access to plenty of cars to transport the body in, too. But if he'd committed the murder, why admit that Gerard had been blackmailing him? Why admit having spoken to Gerard at all?

I scooped cat food and ran water while my thoughts skittered and jumped. And now, on top of Gerard's murder and Bea's disappearance, the puzzle of Emily Ritter and William Ellis had taken a nasty turn. They'd looked so happy together in that picture Dr. Ben had shown me. It was still in my bag, and now I pulled it out and looked at it. Maybe Emily was faking . . . ? No, they really did look happy. Both of them were smiling, with their eyes as well as their lips. So how had they gone from this, in the summer of 1917, to his death at her hands just a year later?

What would make a woman who was obviously in love with a man marry someone else less than a year later? I curled up on the love seat in the parlor, still staring at the two faces forever frozen in happy ignorance of what was to happen to them both. Had William jilted her just after this picture was taken? Did she fall in love with Lawrence on the rebound? But if so, why would she take up with William

again the next spring? There was nothing in this world that
would have made me agree to go back to Philippe, not after
the way he treated me. But of course things were different
ninety years ago. Women didn't have the options they do
now. And William might have been the love of Emily's
life, the one she never managed to say no to.

Her marriage to Lawrence couldn't have been very
happy, anyway. If she'd been in love with her husband,
surely she wouldn't have cheated on him, even with her
former love. No matter how handsome or charming he'd
been. Maybe it had been a marriage of convenience. Maybe
she hadn't loved Lawrence, ever. Maybe she'd always loved
William, but for one reason or another, she couldn't have
him. He was engaged to someone else? Or maybe her family had wanted her to marry Lawrence and she couldn't
really say no?

But if she loved William, why had she killed him? Why
not kill Lawrence, so she could marry William? Or had it
been a case of feeling that if she couldn't have him, then
no one could?

None of it made any sense, and on a whim, I pulled out the
Xerox copy of Helen Ritter's wedding picture, too, and put
the two side by side. The quality of the latter was poor, but I
could clearly see the resemblance between Lawrence III—
Larry—and his mother. The fair hair, the facial shape, the
nose. The smile, though, must be his father's, because it
wasn't Emily's. But familiar, for all of that . . .

Then I looked at the man standing next to Emily, and
the brick dropped.

• • •

"Look!" I told Derek the next morning, holding the pictures side by side. "Just look. The hairline, the eyebrows,
the dimple. The smile, for God's sake! No wonder old Mrs.
Ritter told you that you reminded her of her husband. He
was William's son. Not Lawrence Ritter's. William Ellis's.
Your . . . great-uncle?"

"Something like that." His voice was distracted, his

eyes on the photographs, the truck idling at the curb outside Aunt Inga's house while he processed this new information.

Derek himself was looking better today. The shadows
under his eyes were diminished, if not completely gone,
although his eyes still looked hollowed. But if nothing else,
he must have gotten at least a few hours' sleep last night.

"You can see the resemblance, can't you?"

He nodded. "Oh, yeah. Clearly."

"I wonder if people knew. Like your . . . what would she
be? Great-great-great-grandmother? Mallessa? William's
mother?"

"Who knows. I'd be more interested to know if the Ritters knew. He was brought up as a Ritter, so maybe not."

"Not something Emily would have wanted them to
know, I think. If she married Lawrence for his money, and
then had someone else's child, they would have kicked her
out on her fancy behind. And the baby, too."

Derek nodded. "I don't see Anna Virginia putting up
with raising her daughter-in-law's bastard, do you?"

"Not at all. Poor Emily."

"She got what she deserved," Derek said, a little callously, I thought. When he saw my expression, he added,
"She killed my great-uncle. Actually, she got off easy. She
died before they could execute her. Or before she could
spend the next fifty years behind bars."

"I guess that's true. Still, it can't be fun being married to
one man and in love with another."

"I'm sure you're right." He straightened up. "This is
interesting, but I think we have more immediate concerns,
don't we? Are you ready to head over to Cortino's? See if
the dog is there yet, and if it has found anything?"

I nodded. "The sooner they can prove that Peter didn't
kill Gerard, the sooner the police can get busy finding the
real murderer." And Beatrice.

"So you don't think Peter did it?" He glanced down at
me as we walked toward the front door.

"I'm hoping he didn't. For Jill and the kids' sake. And

also because I think the murderer is the one who has Beatrice, and I don't think Peter is a kidnapper."

Derek shook his head. "I've known him for more than five years. He's married to one of my best friends. And Jill's a decent judge of character. So am I, marrying Melissa to the contrary. Even if Peter killed Gerard in a fit of temporary insanity or rage because Gerard was blackmailing him, I don't think he would have hurt Beatrice. Not just because she's my sister, or stepsister, and Cora's daughter, but because Peter just wouldn't hurt a woman. That's not the way he is."

I nodded. "I agree. So let's get over there to see what happens."

"Right." He closed the truck door behind me and hoofed it around the hood to climb in on the driver's side.

• • •

By the time we got to Cortino's Auto Shop, everyone else was already there. Jill was in the office with a cup of coffee, watching what was going on in the shop through the back door. Reece Tolliver and Wayne were standing by, each with his own cup of coffee—courtesy of Jill—while Brandon was gazing raptly at Hans the German shepherd. Or maybe it was Daphne, Hans's handler, he was watching so intently: a pretty girl around his own age, tall and trim in the uniform of the state police, and with a light brown ponytail sticking out of the back of her cap. I guess with a hot suspect in custody, Wayne was allowed back on the case again.

"Anything yet?" Derek asked Jill, his voice low.

She shook her head, and when she turned and I got a good look at her face, I saw that she was another one who had spent a mostly sleepless night. She was pale and her eyes were sunken and shadowed, bloodshot from lack of sleep. When she spoke, her voice was raspy with fatigue. "They've only just started. The dog will smell the perimeter of the shop first, and then they'll look at the various cars afterward."

She glanced up at Derek, noted the signs of fatigue written on his face as well, and added, "There's coffee over there if you want some. You, too, Avery."

"I think I'll pass," I said, "but thanks. Excuse me a moment."

I ducked out of the shop and over to where Reece Tolliver and Wayne were standing.

". . . not admitted anything . . ." the latter was saying, and then he bit back the rest of the thought when he realized I was within hearing range. "Hello, Avery. What can we do for you?"

"I just wanted to know if the dog had found anything," I said. "Who hasn't admitted anything?"

Wayne sighed. "Peter Cortino. He maintains that he was with his wife during the time Gerard was killed."

"He probably was. I mean, can you really picture him murdering someone? In cold blood?"

"He has a motive," Reece Tolliver said, "which is more than anyone else does."

"So does Wayne. Kate may have decided to dump him after seeing Gerard again. Not that I think she did, but it's possible. And motive is secondary, anyway. Or so I've always been told. And if he has an alibi . . ."

Reece shook his head. "He doesn't have an alibi. There's a reason spouses can't testify for their significant others at trial."

"They lie."

He nodded, jowls shaking. "Exactly. The fact that Mrs. Cortino vouches for him doesn't mean squat."

"If he wanted to kill Gerard, though, isn't it more likely that he'd haul back and hit him? With his fist or a handy wrench or something? There are plenty of tools around here he could use."

"We have not been able to make a connection between Cortino and the digitalin," Reece Tolliver admitted. "He doesn't have a medical history that requires taking heart medicine, nor does his wife. Nor do his in-laws or his parents in Boston. We're looking into the possibility that he got hold of a prescription pad at some point—one of Dr. Ellis's, perhaps—and wrote himself a prescription for digitalin. He's visited Dr. Ellis's house, and also Dr. Ellis's office."

"So now he's a thief as well as a murderer?"

"He already was a thief," Chief Tolliver said. "The chop shop conviction, remember?"

"He was a mechanic. All he did was work on the cars. He didn't steal them."

Reece Tolliver tilted his head. "And how do you know that?"

"Jill told me," I said.

"And how did she know?"

"Peter told her."

"Exactly," Reece said.

I shook my head. "Sorry. I don't believe it. I don't think the dog is going to find anything, because I don't think anything happened here. I don't think Peter had anything to do with it. I think the dog is barking up the wrong tree, no pun intended. And while you're wasting your time here, Beatrice is somewhere, probably with the real murderer, in God knows what kind of condition. If she's even alive."

My voice was shaking. I hadn't known Bea long, but she was family—sort of—and her death would be absolutely devastating to her mother and sister and husband, and that in turn would devastate Derek and Dr. Ben. And Derek being devastated would devastate me, in addition to the fact that I liked Beatrice, too, and didn't want anything to happen to her. I fisted my hands in my pockets, nails digging into the skin of my palms.

"You have to find her. Please."

"We're doing everything we can, Avery," Wayne said, putting a comforting hand on my shoulder.

I would have answered, but before I could, a single short, sharp bark echoed under the high ceiling of the auto shop. All of us turned to look where it had come from.

Hans had moved from sniffing the perimeter of the shop and had started to move from car to car, smelling the trunks

and interiors. He was sitting at attention at the back of a
black vehicle parked in the farthest bay, rangy body quivering. The hatch was open, and he was staring fixedly into
the interior of the car. It was a ten-year-old Ford Explorer,
beat-up and worn, and the logo on the side identified it as
belonging to Stenham Construction, LLC.

$-20-$

"We didn't get the car until Tuesday morning," Jill insisted. "It was parked outside when we got to work that day. With the key under the mat."

The same morning Gerard's body turned up.

"And you don't know who dropped it off?"

She shook her head. "It was just here. Nobody had called to tell us to expect it. So we did what we always do: checked the car for any problems, changed the oil and checked the other fluid levels, fixed anything that needed fixing, and cleaned the car real good inside and out."

"On Tuesday."

Jill shook her head. "We already had a car here that needed attention—it belonged to Kent Williams, over on Clarke Street, and it had a hole in the muffler—so Peter worked on that on Tuesday morning. And then around lunch, Avery's mom and dad brought their car in."

She avoided looking at me when she said it.

"And what was wrong with that?" Wayne wanted to know. He and Reece Tolliver both had their little notebooks out and were writing down every word she said.

"Um . . ." Jill said. Her eyes flickered from face to face before they landed on Derek.

He shrugged. "You can tell them. She's gonna find out sooner or later."

"What?" I said. The car had had an invisible scratch on it from where Noel had brushed against a branch on the way here, when some other driver forced him onto the shoulder of the road.

Jill sighed. "There was nothing wrong with it. They bought it in Boston before they came up here. They needed help getting it registered, so they could get a set of Maine license plates put on it."

"What?" I said.

"Why?" Wayne added.

Jill glanced at me before she responded to Wayne. "It's supposed to be a surprise for Avery. Christmas gift."

My jaw dropped, and I turned to Derek. "My mom and Noel are giving me a car?"

"You don't have one," he answered with a shrug, "and Noel can afford it. Just don't let them know that you know. When they hand you the keys before they leave, act surprised."

"Wow." I nodded. "I will. Definitely. But . . . a car? Wow!"

Now that that was established, Wayne and Reece Tolliver turned back to Jill. "So Avery's new car was brought in Tuesday afternoon."

Jill nodded. "Avery and her mom left, while Derek and Mr. Carrick stayed. That's when they told us what they needed help with. Derek could probably have taken care of it himself, but he and Avery are together so much of the time that he thought it would be easier to ask Peter to do it. That way she wouldn't catch on. Plus, he knows we could use the money. Business is slow in the winter."

"And is that also when you heard that Mr. Labadie had been murdered?" Reece Tolliver kept his pencil stub poised over his notebook.

Her face pale, Jill agreed that it was. "We were shocked,

of course. That we'd had another murder in Waterfield in the first place—this used to be such a quiet place—and then that the victim was Kate's ex-husband. I know Kate. And Shannon."

None of us saw the need to correct her assumption that Kate and Gerard had been married. It wasn't like it mattered, after all. Especially now.

"So no work was done on the Ford Explorer on Tuesday?" Reece Tolliver wanted to know.

Jill shook her head. "It's just Peter working here in the winter. And he worked on Mr. Williams's car in the morning, and on getting Avery's car registered in the afternoon. The Explorer just sat here all day. Peter said he'd work on it the next morning."

"And he did?"

Jill nodded. "All day. It's been a long time since we've had this particular car in the shop—it's not one the Stenhams drive much; they have newer cars they prefer to drive—so it needed some attention."

"By Thursday morning, when we arrived to speak to your husband, he was vacuuming the interior."

Jill paled but agreed. "He had finished the work the night before, but since the Stenhams have other cars, we didn't think there was a hurry getting it to them that night. They hadn't even called to ask whether anything was wrong with it. So we kept it until the next morning. Peter was cleaning it, and then I was going to call and tell them they could pick it up."

"Did you ever find out who had dropped it off?" Wayne shot in.

Jill shook her head.

"I'm afraid we're going to have to hold on to it for a while longer," Reece Tolliver said and nodded to Brandon, who immediately stood at attention. "See if you can get some kind of evidence from it. If there's a vacuum with a vacuum bag somewhere, confiscate that, too, and go through the contents. What you're looking for is evidence that this car is what was used to transport Mr. Labadie's body to the carriage house."

Brandon nodded, quivering with excitement. If there's one thing he loves, it's forensic investigation. Nobody's better at picking through debris for hairs and fibers. Or more excited about doing it, for that matter.

"C'mon, Hans," Daphne said. "Good boy. Let's go get a treat."

Tail wagging, Hans followed her out of the workshop and over to the K-9 vehicle parked outside.

"Guess we'll have to go see the Stenham brothers," Reece said to Wayne. "Someone has to have dropped the car off. When we know who, we'll know when. Then we can go from there."

Wayne nodded. He took a moment to give Brandon some instructions regarding the evidence gathering, and Reece paused to say good-bye to his canine and canine handler, I turned to Derek.

"My mom and Noel bought me a car?"

He nodded. "They knew you needed one. And your mom knows you like Beetles. So they bought one in Boston—didn't you notice that it had a dealer's plate on it when they first arrived? Not a rental plate?—and they brought it up here. They'll use it while they're here, and then it'll be yours when they leave. But you're not to say anything. They want it to be a surprise."

I nodded. I wouldn't say a word. Although it would be hard. I was totally overwhelmed by the whole thing and near tears. My mom and stepdad had bought me a car!

Derek turned to Jill. "Do you want to stay here while Brandon works, or are you going home?"

Jill squared her shoulders. "I'm staying here. This is my business. And it's my husband they're thinking of arresting for murder. I'm not going anywhere."

"Call me if you need anything, OK?"

"Where are you going?" Her look included me.

"Back to the B&B," I said.

"To work," Derek added. "I haven't lifted a finger in the carriage house for too long. This situation with Beatrice is driving me crazy, and there's nothing I can *do* about it. If I don't find something else to keep me busy, I'll start tearing Waterfield apart."

"Let me know if you hear anything. About anything."

Derek promised he would, and they gave each other a hug, although Jill sent me a sheepishly apologetic glance when it was over. I rolled my eyes. My feelings regarding Melissa notwithstanding, and the fact that I knew that Derek and Jill had dated in high school . . . it had never crossed my mind to be jealous of their relationship. Jill was married to the handsomest man in Waterfield; she could hug my boyfriend as much as she wanted. I wasn't worried that there was anything going on there, beyond simple affection.

"C'mon, Tink." He put an arm around my shoulders. "Let's go."

We went. Leaving Jill with Brandon, and leaving the two chiefs of police to go talk to the Stenhams about who had dropped the Explorer off outside Cortino's, and when.

It wasn't difficult to figure out what they were thinking. If Jill was telling the truth and the Explorer had been parked outside the auto shop when she and Peter came to work on Tuesday morning—the morning Derek and I found Gerard's body—then Peter couldn't have used the truck to move the body the night before. Someone else would have had to have driven the Explorer with the body in it. One of the Stenhams? Someone associated with them? Like Melissa? Or Beatrice? Someone who had dropped the car off outside Cortino's to get it off their own hands and also to have the car cleaned and detailed inside and out, the way Peter always did.

Unless the corpse Hans had smelled wasn't Gerard's at all. Maybe it was Beatrice's. If Beatrice had known Gerard, and he had told her about Peter's past, maybe, if Peter killed Gerard, he'd realized he had to get rid of Beatrice, too. Peter could have run out to Clovercroft while working on getting Mom's and Noel's car—my car—registered on Tuesday afternoon. He could have killed her and left her there, and then gone back in the middle of the night, while Jill was sleeping, in the Explorer to get rid of her body. He had probably used Gerard's own car to move Gerard to the carriage house, and then he had done something to it afterward. Peter had experience from a chop shop; maybe he knew someone he could give it to, or maybe he had simply taken it apart.

"Excuse me a second," I told Derek.

"Sure." He dropped his arm from around my shoulders and headed for the truck. I walked over to the state police vehicle, where Reece Tolliver was still talking to Daphne, while Hans the German shepherd was taking it easy in his K-9 compartment.

"What can I do for you, Miss Baker?" Reece Tolliver asked politely when I approached.

I smiled at Daphne. "Hi. I'm Avery Baker. You and your friend sniffed my yard for bodies a couple of months ago."

She smiled back, a pretty girl with soft brown bangs and an upturned nose. "I remember. Skeleton in the crawlspace, multiple old murders in the house."

"That's right. I was wondering if I could ask a question." I divided a glance between her and Reece.

"Go right ahead," Reece said. Feeling magnanimous now that he'd found a lead, I guess.

"Wayne said he was going to ask you whether Hans could sniff around the Clovercroft office while he's in town. And Beatrice's car. We're kind of worried about her."

"Of course," Reece nodded. "Wayne already asked. Daphne will be taking Hans to have a look at the model home right now. Daphne, you'll make sure he gets a chance at the office as well? And after that the Toyota? It's parked somewhere on Chandler Street. Ask Brandon for the address."

Daphne promised she would, and I thanked them both

and headed for the truck. Derek had turned it around with the nose pointing out into the road, and as soon as I was inside, he zoomed off. "What was that about?"

I told him. "If Hans doesn't mark in the office at Clovercroft, then we'll know that at least Beatrice was alive when she left there."

"Good thinking." He glanced at me. "Thank you."

"No problem. I care about her, too." I sat back against the seat.

We drove in silence for a minute or so, then Derek said, "Maybe I should go out to Clovercroft. To be there while the dog is searching. That way I'll know right away if anything happens."

"That's fine with me. I'll just prime and distress the shutters I bought yesterday while I wait for Mom and Noel to wake up. Noel wasn't feeling good yesterday. He may still be sick. So maybe there'll be just me and Mom again today."

"I'll drop you off," Derek said.

• • •

I walked into Kate's kitchen just as she and Mom were sitting down to breakfast.

"Oh, no." I looked around. "No Noel?"

"He's feeling a little better," Mom said, buttering a piece of toast, "but he's spending the day in bed, even so."

"So it's just you and me again?" I sat down on the other side of the table. "D'you want to help me paint and distress the shutters we bought yesterday?"

"I wouldn't mind," Mom said between bites of buttered toast, while Kate wanted to know what the shutters were for.

"I know I helped you carry them, but I guess I wasn't thinking straight. They're too big for the windows, and there aren't enough doors."

I shook my head. "They're for the bedroom, to go on either side of the skylights in the ceiling. I figure it'll make them look less like black holes and more like windows. I'll be putting some flower boxes underneath, as well. It'll look good, I promise."

"Sounds great," Kate said with real enthusiasm. "I can't wait."

"You're sure you don't just feel obligated because of the work we've done so far? I mean . . ." I hesitated, wondering if maybe it would be better not to bring up painful subjects. Too late now, however.

She looked surprised. "Of course."

"I thought maybe, after Gerard . . ."

"He didn't die there," Kate said steadily. "Someone put him there after he was dead, to throw suspicion on us. You and Derek or me and Shannon. Or Wayne. If I refuse to move into the carriage house, that person will have won."

"Glad to hear it."

"Even if Wayne and I decide to stay in the main house, we can always rent out the carriage house. I won't allow families with small children in the house—too many antiques and breakables—so the carriage house would be somewhere a family could stay. Or a honeymooning couple, for some privacy. Or even Shannon, if she didn't want to share with me and Wayne."

"Has she decided what she wants to do when you guys get married? Is she still talking about moving in with Josh?"

"I'm not sure what she'll decide to do," Kate said. "If Wayne and I move out to the carriage house, I guess she could just stay right here, in her room. It'll be convenient, having someone actually in the house. Once in a while, one of the guests requires something in the middle of the night."

I nodded. Made sense.

"So tell me what happened last night," Kate added. "Did you get to talk to Helen Ritter? What did she say?"

"You'll never guess." I told her what Mrs. Ritter had told

us, about Emily's death in childbirth following her conviction for the murder of William Ellis, and had the satisfaction of seeing both Kate's and Mom's jaws drop.

"That's incredible!" Kate gasped.

I nodded. "That's not all, though. After I got home, I got to looking at the pictures. The one of William and Emily from 1917, and the one of Helen and Larry, from 1942. And Larry looked just like William."

Mom nodded; obviously she'd already seen that one coming. "When was the baby born again?"

"January second, 1919," I said.

"He would have been conceived nine months earlier, give or take a week or so. That would make it the end of March or beginning of April."

"While they were building the carriage house," Kate nodded. "During the time when William carved his and Emily's initials in the post."

"William was killed during the first few days of June," Mom said. "Two months later."

"So . . . right around the time Emily would have realized she was pregnant?"

Mom nodded. "She was married to Lawrence. She would want her child to be born in wedlock, to her husband; she'd want there to be no question about that. Illegitimacy was a big deal back then."

"So she had to get rid of William, so he couldn't make a fuss about the kid's parentage."

"That makes sense," Kate said. "It doesn't make Emily sound like a very nice person, though."

"Like most of us," Mom said, "she was probably human. Her marriage may have been bad, she tried to snatch some happiness where she could, but when the rubber met the road, she did what she did for her child. She was protecting his future."

We sat in silence for a moment and digested this.

"I guess that's true," Kate said eventually. "Mothers will do almost anything for their children."

Mom nodded. "Up to and including murder. Not that

I've ever had occasion to kill anyone, but I would have, had they been threatening Avery. I was tempted to push Philippe under a bus just because I knew he'd end up breaking her heart."

"Awww!" I said, touched. Mom grinned.

I sat for a few minutes and listened to them talk about motherly things, and then my cell phone rang. The number was unfamiliar but local. My heart jumped; maybe there was news about Beatrice?

"Hello?" The person on the other end of the line was breathless. "Avery?"

"Paige?" I said.

"Avery! Hi! You'll never guess what I found!"

Her voice was exuberant, something I'd never, ever heard from Paige before. She's usually so subdued and quiet as to be practically colorless, and now she was stumbling over her words in her hurry to get them out.

"What did you find? Where?"

"At home. In Dad's house. In the attic. A letter. From Emily to her baby."

I blinked. "Wow. That's . . . amazing."

Kate and Mom both looked up and over at me.

"Isn't it?" I could almost hear Paige beam. "She wrote it before he was born, so he'd know what had happened, and she left it with her sister, my great-great-great-grandmother, but I guess he never came to get it. So it's just been sitting there ever since."

"What does it say?"

"It says . . ." She hesitated, her voice slowing down. "It says a lot of things. I think you'd better have a look yourself. But it says that Larry wasn't Lawrence Ritter's son; he was William Ellis's."

"I thought he might be. There's a distinct family resemblance."

"OK, but did you know that she was in prison when her son was born? For murder?"

"Actually, I knew that, too. I spoke to Helen Ritter yesterday. She was married to Larry. She'd have been Emily's daughter-in-law, if Emily had survived childbirth. She told us the whole story."

"Well," Paige said, sounding just a little bit peeved, "that must have been interesting, I'm sure. Here's something that Helen Ritter may not have told you, though. Emily didn't kill William Ellis. She was framed."

That was all Paige was willing to say over the phone: She insisted that I had to read the letter for myself. I could come to Barnham to pick it up, she said, or wait until she could send it home with Shannon at the end of the day. She couldn't bring it to me, since she had classes and projects all day.

"That's OK," I said. "I'll get there. Thirty minutes."

"You can take my car," Kate offered when I'd hung up and was looking around frantically, remembering that the truck I'd counted on for the past few days was off at Clovercroft with Derek at the wheel.

"Or the Beetle," Mom added. She looked and sounded perfectly innocent. "It's just been sitting there for the past two days. It could probably use some exercise."

"Do you want to come?"

"Oh, I wouldn't miss it. Let me go get my coat." She headed up the stairs.

"What about you?" I asked Kate.

She shook her head. "Wish I could, but now that I've finished decorating the B&B for Christmas, I have to get ready for the wedding. We're putting together the seating charts today."

"I'll help you when I get back," I promised, getting to my feet. "The shutters can wait another day."

"No, they can't. I've got Shannon coming over later, with Josh. Between us, we'll get it done."

"You sure?"

"I'm positive. Just finish my romantic retreat. Wayne and Reece will take care of finding Beatrice and Gerard's killer, and Shannon, Josh, and I will handle the wedding."

"Nice to know you're confident," I said as Mom came back down the stairs, pulling on her coat. "Ready to ride?"

"Ready when you are. Here you go."

I smiled when she handed me the car keys.

· · ·

The Beetle was wonderful. Little and zippy and so much easier to maneuver than Derek's big truck. I was going to enjoy driving it when it was mine. Obviously I would prefer not to have to mess with a car at all, but if I had to have one—and in Maine, I did—I could do worse than the Beetle. Of course, I didn't say a word about any of that. I didn't want to jinx anything.

Paige was waiting for us in the cafeteria at Barnham, and when we walked in, she stood up. "I'm sorry, but I really have to run. I have class in, like, three minutes. Here's the letter. I'd like to have it back when you're finished with it, if you don't mind."

"Of course," I said, accepting the envelope she handed me. The paper was thicker and rougher than what you see these days, more natural, somehow. The words "To my child" were written across the front in faded fountain pen, the script rounded, almost girlish.

"May as well sit here and read it," Mom suggested as Paige hurried off. I nodded. We sank down on a couple of chairs and put our heads together. I opened the envelope and pulled out the pieces of paper inside.

To my beloved child,

the letter began, on letterhead supplied by the Massachusetts Reformatory for Women.

*You will never know me, and perhaps that is for the
best. But I cannot leave you without the knowledge that
I have done everything I can to tell you that I love you,
and that what I did, I did for you.*

"Told you so," Mom said.
"I never doubted you," I answered, going back to the
letter.

*I am your mother, Emily. My husband was Lawrence
Ritter, but he was not your father. Your father's name
was William Aaron Ellis, and he was the love of my
life.*

"Hah!" Mom crowed.
"What do you mean, hah?" I retorted. "I never doubted
that, either."

*William and I were sweethearts as children, but
as we grew older, things changed between us. The
war came, and William wanted nothing more than to
enlist, to serve his country. I wanted marriage and
children. We drifted apart. When Lawrence proposed,
my mother urged me to accept. Lawrence was wealthy
and my family was poor. And foolishly, I thought that
the threat of my marrying someone else might make
William propose marriage, as well. He didn't. Instead,
he told me to marry and be damned. So I did.*

"I think I would have liked Emily," Mom said. "She had
a sense of humor."
"If the choice of words was deliberate."
"Oh, I think it was. Go on."

Things went badly from the first. Lawrence had no fond feelings for me beyond possession and the knowledge that he had taken me away from William. There had always been competition between them. He wasn't unkind, just indifferent. I found myself regretting my choice. The following spring, when the family decided to have a carriage house built on the property, William signed on as carpenter and we sinfully resumed a sort of courtship.

"Good grief," I said, "what a way to describe it."
"Guilty conscience," Mom answered sagely.

When the carriage house was finished and William asked me to run away with him, I refused. I had made my bed, and felt I should lie in it. He left, and I returned to being a dutiful wife to my husband. Until I realized that the result of my behavior had been you.

"Here we go," Mom said.

Due to the coldness of my marriage, I knew William was without question your father. At that time, William had given up any hope of persuading me to leave with him, and had joined the navy at Elliott. I went to see him there.

"Good for Emily," I said.
"I don't know about that," Mom answered.

I told him I had changed my mind, that I was carrying his child and I wanted you to know your father and him to know you. But the United States Navy is not forgiving of deserters, and William was unable to leave their service. We agreed that I would go to Lawrence and tell him the truth—and that I would then pack the few belongings that were mine alone and go to Dr. Ellis's house—and that William would come to me when he was able to leave the service. He assured me that his family would welcome me as their own, and that his father would ensure that our child— you—would come into the world safely.

"William sounds nice," I said. "I think I would have liked him."
Mom nodded. "Caring *and* brave. Good for him."

By the time I got back to Waterfield that night, it was late. I told Lawrence the truth and prepared to leave. However, his mother persuaded me to tarry, in an effort to convince me of the error of my ways. Meanwhile, Lawrence left the house in a rage.

"I'm not surprised," Mom said.

The next day, I was informed that William had died. And although I cannot prove it, I know in my heart that Lawrence killed him. There was strychnine in the house; my mother-in-law had used it during the winter as an antidote for bronchorrhea. When the police came, my husband and his mother conspired to tell them that I had taken the medicine to do away with my lover, as he was planning to make things difficult for me and as I did not wish to leave my husband's household and go back to abject poverty. The police chose to take their word over mine. I was arrested, tried, and convicted of the murder of William Ellis.

"Wow."

I never saw Lawrence again, as he died two months later, when the USS SC-209 was sunk off the coast of Long Island. Thus the devil got his due.

"Nicely put," Mom remarked.
I nodded. "No love lost there, obviously."

Shortly after the accident, his mother came to see me in the penitentiary. She offered to strike a bargain. There was nothing anyone could do to help me, nor did she want to, but she offered to accept you as her own and bring you up as Lawrence's child, with every privilege and opportunity. My own family had turned their backs on me, with the exception of my cousin Annabelle, to whom I will entrust this letter. And William's family believed me guilty of murdering their son. I had nowhere else to turn, so I agreed. Thus, your birth certificate says that you are the child of Lawrence Ritter Jr. and his wife Emily, when you are, in fact, the child of William Aaron Ellis and Emily Ritter, errant wife of Lawrence.

"Hmmm," Mom said.
"Yep. Definitely guilty conscience."

I am doing my best to provide for you, my darling child, since I cannot be there myself. Your new grandmother will take good care of you. You are all she has left, and you are her only chance to carry the Ritter name forward. Lawrence has passed on, as has my brother-in-law Frederick, a victim of the influenza. As, indeed, has my father-in-law. Anna Virginia and Agnes are the only two left. The family and the fortune need an heir. You are their last hope. I trust they will take care of you and that you will be happy. And when you are grown, if you ever decide to look into the fate of your mother, I pray you will find this letter and know the truth.

> *Your loving mother,*
> *Emily Thompson Ritter*

• • •

"Wow," I said, leaning back.
Mom nodded. "That's quite a missive. I'm not surprised

she wanted to get it off her chest. Or that she wanted her child to know the truth."

"A pity he never came and asked for it."

"That's life," Mom said philosophically. "Sometimes, in spite of our best-laid plans, life intervenes. Larry either didn't know where to find Emily's family, or he believed the lie and just didn't care to. At this point, it's six of one, half a dozen of the other. They're all dust."

"That's true," I admitted. "Amazing that they'd convict her of a murder she didn't commit, though. Why didn't she just say that Lawrence did it? That way she could have kept her son and the Ritter name, and avoided going to prison."

"It was her word against Anna Virginia's," Mom said. "And of the two of them, Anna Virginia Cabot was the one who was believed. Emily had been at the navy base that day. She had spoken to William. People had probably seen her. While Lawrence may have avoided being seen."

I nodded. "Or maybe he was seen, but not really noticed among so many men."

"And then Anna Virginia cleaned up the mess," Mom said. "Emily was expendable; she was planning to leave Lawrence anyway; she had betrayed him. Anna Virginia probably didn't like her much, since she was probably the kind of mother who would have thought that no girl was good enough for her darling boy. But then Lawrence died, and Frederick died, and there was no one left to carry on the Ritter name. So Anna Virginia decided she needed Emily's child. If it was a boy, anyway; if it had turned out to be a girl, she might have reneged."

"What an evil witch. It's amazing what some parents will do for their children, isn't it? You wouldn't have helped me cover up a murder, would you?"

"If it was Philippe . . ." Mom said, and then shook her head. "No, of course not, Avery. I love you, but if you killed someone, even if it was Philippe, you'd need to take your punishment like a big girl. Just like when you were little.

Remember when you staged that walkout of Mademoiselle Gagnon's French class in eighth grade?"

"God, yes!" I shuddered. "I talked all of French one-oh-one into going with me, and then they ratted me out and I got detention every day for two weeks. And when I came crying to you, you told me . . ."

" 'If you do the crime, you gotta do the time.' "

I nodded. "You know, that's probably what's wrong with Ray and Randy Stenham. Mary Elizabeth was too wimpy to discipline them. They were allowed to run wild, until they started believing that nothing could touch them. And now they think they can get away with murder."

Silence reigned for a moment, and I realized what I'd said. "I didn't mean that literally," I began, and then I stopped.

"You know," Mom said thoughtfully, "you're making a good point. Gerard seemed like the type to check out his environment thoroughly, wouldn't you say? He liked knowing things about people. And he was staying in the model home at Clovercroft. What if he found something out there, something that proved that the Stenhams were doing something wrong? Financially, maybe? The fact that they can't go forward with the development, that it's just sitting there, and all the while they have to pay the mortgage, must be a strain. You and Derek are facing that issue right now, with that little ranch house you renovated this fall."

"Except our mortgage is under one hundred thousand dollars, and we've owned it for only four months. The Stenhams must have borrowed millions to develop Clovercroft, and it's been sitting barren for a year, at least."

"Exactly. So let's say they've done something not entirely legal to keep things going. Something that could get them into some trouble."

"Beatrice did mention something about interesting bookkeeping," I said, thinking back.

"Did she really? Well, let's say Gerard found out about it. Either because Beatrice told him or because he was snooping around after hours. What would happen?"

"From what I know about Gerard," I said slowly, "I'd say he'd try to figure out a way to take advantage of it."

"Blackmail?"

"That does seem to have been his habit. And if he blackmailed the Stenhams, they might have gotten mad enough to do away with him. Especially if they see themselves as being above the law."

"Exactly. And then there's Mary Elizabeth and her delicate constitution."

I blinked, not quite following the connection. "OK. But you know, if I knew I was responsible for bringing Ray and Randy into the world, I'd have a delicate constitution, too."

"I don't think Mary Elizabeth is anywhere as delicate as she pretends," Mom said dryly. "She adores those boys. Never did believe that they could do anything wrong."

"She's not delicate?"

"She's about as delicate as fishing wire. Thin, but incredibly strong. What she's got is a weak heart."

"No kidding? So she could be taking digitalin? Ray and Randy could have slipped Gerard some of their mother's medicine? Just like Lawrence did with Anna Virginia's?"

"Could be," Mom said. "You know, Avery, I think maybe we need to pay Mary Elizabeth another visit. Have a look at her medicine cabinet. And convince her that it's time she let her boys take their lumps on their own. They're grown; she can't shield them forever." She headed for the door, briskly.

"Shouldn't we call Wayne and Reece Tolliver and tell them what we think?" I asked, trotting after. I'd made this mistake once or twice before: going off on my own after a clue and ending up in trouble. I didn't want to do it again. The Stenham boys were probably safely tucked away at Clovercroft, under the watchful eye of the two chiefs of police, and they wouldn't be at their mother's house, but even so I wanted someone to know where we were going.

Mom waved a hand. "By all means. Tell them to come meet us at Mary Elizabeth's house after they've finished booking Ray and Randy. By then, maybe we'll have convinced her to talk."

"I'll call Derek," I said, as the cafeteria door slammed behind us and we narrowly avoided being reprimanded by a monitor for running in the halls. "That way I can find out if the dog found anything at Clovercroft, too." I pulled out my phone and dialed as we sped along.

"Hi, Avery," Derek's voice said, before I even had a chance to say hello. "There's nothing new."

"Are you still at Clovercroft?"

"We are. The dog didn't mark in the office, which was a relief. Now it's upstairs sniffing the apartment."

"That's good news. I have a lot to tell you about Emily and William, but that can wait. Listen to this." I went through Mom's reasoning regarding the twins and Mary Elizabeth.

"Makes sense," Derek agreed. "I'll call Wayne. He's probably at the police station by now. I hope he's grilling Ray and Randy over hot coals. Are you going to Mary Elizabeth's?"

"That seems to be the plan. I'm just following Mom."

"Don't you think you should wait? I'm sure Wayne plans to go there later, after he's finished with the twins."

"That's all right," I said. "I'm not worried. It's just Mary Elizabeth. But call me when the party breaks up, OK? Just so I know to get out of there because someone might be coming. I'd hate for Ray or Randy to walk in on me snooping through their mother's medicine cabinet."

Derek promised he would, since he'd hate that, too, and I turned to Mom, who was standing by the Beetle, tapping her foot impatiently. "Let's go, already!" she said.

"Yes, ma'am." I unlocked the doors and we climbed in.

· · ·

Mary Elizabeth's big, white house looked exactly the same as when we'd been there yesterday. So did Mary Elizabeth; the only difference being that today's pantsuit was a pale platinum gray instead of blue. And just like yesterday, she didn't seem thrilled to see us.

"Oh. It's you again."

Mom took it stride, with her best smile. "Hello, Mary Elizabeth. I hoped maybe today was a better day than yesterday to drop in for a chat. May we come in?"

She didn't wait for Mary Elizabeth's assent—or refusal— but walked across the threshold into the black-and-white hall. I scurried after.

Mary Elizabeth closed the front door—reluctantly, I don't doubt, but it was cold outside—and turned to Mom. She opened her mouth to speak, but Mom cut in. "This won't take long. Why don't we go sit down somewhere?" She looked around, spying a sofa in one of the rooms just off the hall. "That looks like a good place."

It was a front parlor, with two matching love seats and a window overlooking the front yard, so we'd have fair warning if someone arrived. Mom didn't wait to be invited, just hooked her arm through Mary Elizabeth's and pulled her cousin toward the seating area. Upstairs, I could hear the poodles scratching. Mary Elizabeth glanced up the stairs, her expression boding ill for the poor animals, but allowed herself to be dragged, almost literally, to the nearest sofa and deposited there.

"Isn't this nice?" Mom said, with a big smile, and sat down opposite.

I looked around. "Um . . . if you don't mind, I think I need . . ." I cast about for a delicate way of putting it, and came up with, "a lipstick break." Best I could do for a euphemism on short notice.

"You go ahead, Avery," Mom said genially, as if it was her house instead of Mary Elizabeth's. "If I remember correctly, there's a powder room just at the top of the stairs on the left. Is that right?"

Mary Elizabeth nodded, tight-lipped. Mom beamed. "We'll just sit here and chat until you get back."

"Sure," I said and headed up the staircase.

The scratching got steadily louder as I walked up the stairs, and I could well understand that it was driving Mary Elizabeth crazy, especially if she had to listen to it all day. Although I had to assume that the poodles were allowed out when no one was there. Maybe they were biters.

The powder room was right where Mom said it would be, at the top of the stairs and on the left. It was big and opulent and—of course—white. I closed and locked the door behind me, just to be safe, and then I looked around. There was a medicine cabinet above the sink; I started with that.

All I found there, however, were creams and tweezers and lotions and the like. And the linen closet in the corner was full, but only with towels and sheets and a stack of toilet paper and a plunger and things like that. Seemed I'd have to go looking for Mary Elizabeth's private bath, and her bedside table, for her medications.

I flushed the toilet before I left the room, just to give some verisimilitude to my trip upstairs. Then I unlocked the door and stepped into the hallway, looking around.

Reproduction Colonials are very symmetrical, usually four rooms over four, laid out around a central hallway. The downstairs had a couple of parlors, a dining room, and a kitchen, while the upstairs had four bedrooms. The scratching noises, now accompanied by some sort of squeaking and muffled thumps, came from the room at the end of the hallway. She must keep the poor things muzzled, too, or surely there'd be full-on barking.

What had to be Mary Elizabeth's bedroom was on the right, almost opposite the bathroom. It had plush off-white carpeting, I noted, similar to what Kate wanted in her bedroom in the carriage house, as well as a huge four-poster bed with white sheets and a fluffy white duvet and lots of white throw pillows. The whole thing looked cold as ice, and I made a mental note to be sure to add some warmth to the carriage house bedroom; some sort of unifying color that would go well with the black and white, that I could use in the pillows and maybe a quilted satin comforter or blanket across the foot of the bed. Pale pink came to mind—it looks wonderful with black and white—but Wayne might object. Pale blue might be nice; it's very French, or at least Gustavian, and in the summer, it's like bringing the sky and water inside.

While mulling this, I tiptoed over to the bedside table and pulled out the drawer. And hit pay dirt: a handful of little brown medicine bottles with screw caps. I scooped them up and read the names. Tenormin, Lanoxin, warfarin, just plain aspirin in a white bottle . . .

I'm not sure what I'd expected—something called digitalin, I guess—but if such a thing existed, Mary Elizabeth wasn't taking it. Or if she was, one of her sons had removed the entire bottle. One of those I was looking at might even hold digitalin; I don't know much about medications, but I know that the name of the drug itself is sometimes different from the name of the medication, which usually has a generic name, as well. For all I knew, I could be holding the murder weapon in my hand right now. Derek would know. I put the bottles down and pulled out my cell phone.

"I'm at Mary Elizabeth's house," I whispered into it when he'd answered. "If I give you a list of medications, can you tell me if any of them could have been what was in Gerard's bloodstream? Aspirin, warfarin, Tenormin, Lanoxin . . ."

"That one," Derek said.

"Lanoxin? That's digitalis?"

"Sure is. What's the dose?"

I told him what the bottle said.

"A handful of those would be enough to knock him out. Just put them back where you found them and get out of there. I'll let Wayne know where they are."

"Appreciate it. Anything new on your end?"

His voice was tightly controlled. "The dog marked for a body upstairs in the model. Wayne and Reece have already taken Ray and Randy in for questioning. Now they want

Melissa, too. Good thing, because I was ready to start beating some answers out of someone."

"Gosh," I said, and then stopped, hoping against hope that condolences were premature. Hopefully, Hans was marking for Gerard and not Beatrice. "What are you planning to do now?"

"I guess I'll head on down to the police station," Derek said. "Tell Wayne and Reece where you are and what you've found. Maybe they can use it to squeeze some information out of one of the boys."

"We may see you there. If Mom can convince Mary Elizabeth to come clean and rat on one of her darlings. And . . ." I hesitated, trying to hunt down a stray thought. "Tell them to lean on Randy. When I saw him at the lumber depot yesterday, he said something about the skylights in the bedroom at the carriage house. He might have seen them from the outside, before the snow covered the roof, but he might have noticed them while he was leaving the body, too. It's something to ask him, anyway."

"I'll do that. Later, Tink." He hung up. I did the same, and then, as quietly as I could, put the medicine bottles back in the drawer and eased it shut.

Outside in the hallway, I took an automatic left to go back down the stairs to the parlor and Mom and Aunt Mary Elizabeth, but then I hesitated. That pristine white bedroom was bothering me, and the pristine marble floors downstairs, and the two white love seats in the front parlor, not to mention the icy coldness that exuded from Mary Elizabeth. She didn't seem like the type to enjoy the companionship of dogs. Everything was too well ordered, too clean, too oppressively neat in this house. There was no dog hair in the corners, no paw prints, no leashes or dog toys or water bowls. No barking. Just that thumping and squeaking noise from the back bedroom. The one with the closed door. The *only* one with a closed door.

I tiptoed in that direction, moving as quickly and as quietly as I could on the Persian runner. By now, Mom and Mary Elizabeth must be wondering what was taking me so long, but surely I could spare another twenty seconds to see what was making the noise. Whether it really was dogs, or whether it was something else.

I put my hand on the doorknob and twisted. And then I pushed the door open.

—22—

I'm sure it won't come as a surprise to you that it wasn't dogs making the thumping and squeaking and muffled groaning sounds.

The squeaking was the sound of bedsprings, and the thumping was the noise the bed made banging against the wall. The figure on the bed—not a king poodle—was writhing and straining, and for a second I just gaped, shocked.

Beatrice's wrists were tied to the headboard and her mouth gagged with what looked like a Hermès print scarf. Trust Mary Elizabeth to gag a prisoner with four hundred dollars' worth of designer silk.

The material used to bind Beatrice's hands looked like more of the same, incidentally, so let's make that eight hundred dollars' worth of designer silk.

The curtains were drawn, so when I first opened the door, it took a moment for her to notice me. When she saw me, her eyes widened in recognition and she tried to speak against the scarf. "Mph-hmph! Aa—ee!"

"Beatrice!" I responded. "My God! What's happened to you?"

The next few minutes were chaotic. As soon as I removed the gag, words poured out of Beatrice's mouth while I did my best to untie the knots around her wrists, made ever tighter by her attempts to free herself.

"I had no idea," she babbled as I worked the knots with my fingers and, when that didn't work, with my teeth. "That morning, I had no idea that Gerard was dead. Not until you told me. I knew I hadn't seen him that day, but that wasn't unusual. Sometimes he was there, sometimes he wasn't. I did my work, and then I went into town to have lunch with Mom, and that's when we ran into you and your mom, and you told us that he was dead. Until then, I had no idea."

I stopped to take a breath and ask a question. "So you definitely didn't have anything to do with killing him?"

She looked mildly offended. "Of course not. Why would I kill him?"

I shrugged. I could think of a few reasons, but obviously I was wrong, so better not to say anything.

She was silent for a moment, then she started up again. "No, I had nothing to do with killing him. I had a couple of drinks with him once, when he brought a bottle of wine down to the office, but that's all."

I spat out a silk fiber. "Was he coming on to you?"

Beatrice hesitated. "Yes and no. He was, but I don't think it was because he was interested. It was more because that was the way he was, and maybe because he thought there'd be something in it for him. He was asking me lots of questions about myself, and also about the Stenhams."

I nodded. "So what happened after I saw you the other day?"

"I went back to the office and back to work," Beatrice said, "and in the late afternoon, Mrs. Stenham came by."

"You mean Mary Elizabeth?"

"The one who lives here," Beatrice said. "Older lady. White hair."

"Not Ray or Randy?"

She shook her head, then winced. "Ouch."

"Sorry. You did a good job tying yourself up tighter."

"I was trying to tear the scarf," Beatrice explained.

"I'm sure you were," I responded. "Hermès is good-quality stuff. Anyway, go on. Mary Elizabeth came to the office?"

She nodded. "She said she wanted to tell me about Gerard, since she thought I might not have heard, and since she figured I would have met him, since he was staying above the office. It all sounded very nice and solicitous. She brought me a cup of coffee from the coffeemaker . . ."

"Doctored with more of her medicine, no doubt," I muttered. "We think that's how Gerard was killed. Ray and Randy doped him."

Beatrice nodded. "It made me woozy and nauseous, so she offered to drive me home."

"And instead you ended up here." I thought I might be getting somewhere with the knots, finally. One of them was showing signs of loosening.

"She said she was starting to feel bad, too, and why didn't we both just lie down until we felt better."

"And by the time you woke up . . . ?"

"I was here," Beatrice said, looking around.

"We've been really worried." I tore at the knots. "Alice has been driving all over Boston looking for you and Steve."

"Steve? Steve's missing, too?" Fear flashed in her eyes, along with the discomfort.

I shook my head. "Not anymore. We found him last night. In a hotel in Brunswick. He was waiting for Gerard to call him . . . it's a long story. I'll let him tell you."

"Steve's here?" Her cheeks pinked.

"Not here in the house. But in Waterfield. Staying with your mom and Dr. Ben."

"Wow. That's . . ." She lapsed into silence. I had no difficulty deciphering what it was, though. Sweet. Wonderful. Awesome. Nice. Beatrice was happy.

"Here we go." I undid the last of the knots, and Bea shook out her hands. I did the same, flexing my fingers while Beatrice rubbed her wrists. "We'd better get going. Mom's downstairs, keeping Mary Elizabeth busy. Let's see my darling aunt talk her way out of this one."

I headed for the door while Beatrice swung her legs over the side of the bed.

"There's something I should mention . . ." she said, but I was already halfway down the hall and then I continued down the stairs. After lying bound for the best part of two days, Beatrice was considerably slower, her knees were likely wobbly, and it was taking her some time to get the circulation going. So I was by myself when I hit the bottom of the stairs and turned into the parlor.

"The jig's up, Auntie . . ." I tossed off flippantly. And then I stopped—dead. My mother was sitting on one of the love seats, hands folded primly in her lap, eyes agonized. Mary Elizabeth was pointing an enormous gun at her.

For a second, the world stood still. The only sound was that of Beatrice's labored steps on the stairs. I turned to her as she got to the bottom. "You didn't mention the gun."

"I was trying. You got going so fast I couldn't keep up. And I thought it was probably best not to yell it after you."

She came up to stand beside me. "Sorry," she added after taking in the tableau in the parlor, "guess I should have."

"It might have been better. Still, water under the bridge."

Mary Elizabeth smiled, a very cold little smile that came nowhere near her eyes. "Come in, girls. Have a seat. Next to your mother, Avery. You, too, Mrs. Gremilion."

The gun didn't swing toward us, but with it pointed directly at my mother, it wasn't like I could refuse. I walked in and sat down next to Mom, while Beatrice took her other side.

"Keep your hands where I can see them," Mary Elizabeth ordered. I took Mom's. Her palm was sweaty; she must be terrified. You couldn't hear it in her voice, though, when she turned to Beatrice with a smile, holding her other hand out.

"There you are, Bea. We've all been worried sick about you. Your mom will be relieved to hear you're all right."

Mary Elizabeth snorted. In a ladylike way, of course. She didn't have to say it: Beatrice might be all right now, but her chances of staying that way—our chances of getting out of this with our lives—were rapidly dwindling.

Mom and Bea linked hands as well, and then we sat there, all in a row, staring down the barrel of the gun.

"Is that thing loaded?" I asked after a moment.

Mary Elizabeth looked down her nose at me. "Naturally. I'm an older woman living alone; my children want me to be safe, and an empty gun wouldn't do me any good. However, I'd be happy to prove it."

"No," I said, a little sick at the idea of losing a toe or part of an ear; or worse, Mom or Beatrice, "that won't be necessary."

"Glad to hear it." Mary Elizabeth smiled, chillingly.

Silence descended again.

"What are you planning to do with us?" I asked after another long minute.

Mary Elizabeth hesitated. She didn't seem to have an immediate plan. Maybe we could turn that to our advantage.

No sooner had the thought crossed my mind than the sound of a car engine could be heard coming closer and then stopping. I craned my neck to see out the nearest window, but all I could see was an expanse of snow-covered lawn with a line of snowcapped ornamental bushes like squat Christmas elves in pointy hats.

"Expecting someone?" I asked Mary Elizabeth. She showed teeth but didn't answer. I turned to Mom. "Did she call anyone while the two of you were alone down here?"

Mom nodded. "Unfortunately so. She left messages for both her children."

Damn, I thought. What I said was "Well, I called Derek, too, while I was upstairs, and told him where we were and that there was a medicine bottle with Lanoxin in the bedside table drawer. He said that would be what killed Gerard. And he said he'd tell Wayne."

Outside, a car door slammed. Loudly. I looked at Mary Elizabeth. "What do you want to bet that's the chief of police? If he walks in here and finds you holding us all at gunpoint, you could be going to jail for the rest of your life. Wouldn't it be better to put the gun away and cooperate? Just because Ray and Randy are going down, doesn't mean you have to."

"Raymond and Randall are not 'going down,'" Mary Elizabeth said coldly. "I will not allow that to happen."

Outside the front door, someone stomped the snow off their feet before coming inside.

"What are you going to do to prevent it?" I wanted to know. "Even if you shoot all three of us, you won't help Ray and Randy. They're already in custody at the police station as we speak."

Out in the hallway, the doorknob rattled and someone pushed against the door, ineffectually. Mary Elizabeth must have locked it behind us when we came in.

"They will be released," Mary Elizabeth said calmly.

"What makes you think so?"

"Because," Mary Elizabeth said, "they did not kill Gerard Labadie."

Now a key was being inserted in the door.

Mary Elizabeth continued, calmly, "And because they did not kill him, the chief of police will not be able to prove that they did."

"Of course they killed Gerard! I mean, who else . . . ?"

My breath caught in my throat. Partly because the front door opened, letting in a draft of cold air, but more because it had just hit me that if Ray and Randy hadn't killed Gerard, then Mary Elizabeth had. We were sitting in the sights of a cold-blooded murderer. And if she'd killed Gerard, surely she'd have no qualms about killing us. It was a miracle she hadn't killed Beatrice already.

Out in the hallway, we heard the door close, and the

next moment, lightly clicking heels came down the hall to the parlor door. I suppressed a groan. Of all the people in Waterfield, Melissa James was the last I'd put my trust in to save my life.

She breezed around the corner with her trademark smile firmly in place. The sight of the gun, and of the three of us side by side like ducks in a shooting gallery, didn't discombobulate her for long. She simply stopped, glossy bob swinging smoothly into place, and looked around. "Oh, dear. Am I interrupting something?"

"No, no," I said politely, before Mary Elizabeth had a chance to open her mouth, "nothing you need concern yourself with, Melissa. Your future mother-in-law is simply tying up some loose ends."

"I see. And how are you, Avery? Good, I hope? Lovely to see you again, Rosemary. And Beatrice . . . we've all been *very* concerned about you."

It all sounded about as sincere as I had sounded a minute ago. Then she turned to Mary Elizabeth, her voice soothing, "Now, Mary dear, I'm not sure this is a good idea."

Mary Elizabeth spared her a glance. "I'm afraid, Melissa, that your scruples are a little belated. Something has to be done. You never should have allowed that lout Gerard Labadie to stay in the model home. There were too many things at Clovercroft for him to get his grubby hands on."

"I'm sorry, dear," Melissa said, without sounding the least bit like she meant it. "I was just trying to recoup some money. How was I to know he would go through our files? Or that there'd be anything in the files for him to find? *I* had no idea Carolyn Tate was cooking the books!"

I blurted, "Carolyn Tate was cooking the books?!"

She turned to me, apologetically. "I'm afraid so. With Ray and Randy's full cooperation, of course. Clovercroft was just sitting there, simply hemorrhaging money, and the mortgage had to be paid, and I suppose the best thing they could come up with was fudging the numbers to hold off the creditors for a while."

"And Gerard found out?"

"I imagine he must have," Melissa agreed. "As I said, I had no idea, when I offered him the use of the model home, that he'd do such a thing."

"Always expect the worst," Mary Elizabeth declared. "That way you won't be surprised. If you had just used some sense on the front end, I wouldn't have had to take care of the matter later." She looked disgusted.

"I understand that, Mary dear," Melissa said, "but this is a different situation. They"—she looked down at us—"don't know anything."

We all shook our heads, doing our best to look like we had no idea what we were even doing there. In spite of the fact that she had just told us everything.

"That one"—Mary Elizabeth gestured with the gun in Beatrice's direction; Beatrice flinched—"worked in the Clovercroft office for weeks. Gerard probably told her what he was doing."

"Gerard and I didn't really talk," Beatrice said, her voice low. "Not about anything important."

"And dear Avery"—Mary Elizabeth bared her teeth in my direction—"was snooping upstairs, in my medicines. She found the Lanoxin. And called her boyfriend, who told her it was what had killed Gerard."

Melissa glanced at me. I shrugged. No sense in denying it. "Derek said he'd tell Wayne all about it. I'm sure he has by now. They're probably on their way here."

A second passed while Melissa thought about this. Then she turned to Mary Elizabeth. "I think we should take them somewhere else. If the police are on their way—and if Derek told them what Avery told him, I think they must be—then it would be best for them not to be here when the police arrive."

Mary Elizabeth hesitated but seemed to agree that this suggestion made sense. "Where?"

Melissa shrugged elegantly. "Back to Clovercroft? The police are finished there. We could just leave them outside somewhere, let them freeze to death. Nice and neat. No bullet holes, no gunshot residue, no ballistics. Or we could load them into that cute little car outside and push it off the cliffs into the ocean. With the water temperature being what it is, they wouldn't last long, even if they could get out of the car." Her look at us was clinical, and her tone chillingly indifferent.

"You can't do that!" I blurted.

Melissa turned to me. "Why ever not?"

"Derek knows where we are. If we disappear, he'll know that you did something to us."

"Don't be silly, Avery," Melissa said lightly. "Derek knows I'm not capable of anything like that. And with Ray and Randy both down at the police station, clearly the culprit had to be someone else. Someone like"—her eyes swung around, and she smiled brightly—"poor Beatrice, so depressed after her husband left that she killed Gerard and then disappeared to avoid being arrested. And when the two of you found her, she had no choice but to kill you, too."

Beatrice paled.

"Derek will never believe that," I said, but I have to admit that my voice was a little less sure this time.

Melissa gave a lovely little laugh. "After five years of being married to him, I'm pretty well versed in exactly what Derek will believe and exactly what I'll have to do to make him believe it."

My face twisted. Melissa smiled sweetly—she'd been waiting for just that reaction—before she turned to Mary Elizabeth. "Now, Mary dear, if you'll just give me the gun . . ." She reached for it.

Mary Elizabeth pulled it back. "Why?"

Melissa's voice was reasonable, although a tiny wrinkle formed between her eyes. "Because you must be here, dear, when the police arrive. It won't do for you not to be home. You'll have to explain that Avery and Rosemary have already left. After telling you that they thought they knew where Beatrice was. If *you* have to stay here, *I'll* have to take them away. And for that, I need the gun."

Mary Elizabeth wavered. Melissa's argument made sense. It was just that Mary Elizabeth didn't want to relinquish it.

"Can't you use another firearm?"

Melissa did an eye roll. "I don't carry a gun, Mary Elizabeth. And there's no time to go home and get Ray's. Now don't be silly . . ."

She made a snatch for the gun. Mary Elizabeth yanked it back, her eyes narrowing. Out in the hallway, something scraped.

"I think that's our cue," Reece Tolliver's voice said. The next second, he and Wayne both appeared in the doorway. "Put the gun down, Mrs. Stenham."

Mary Elizabeth stared at them for a second. Then she turned to Melissa. "You sold me out? You little hussy! I never did think you were good enough for my Raymond!"

And then, whether by sheer rage or simply because she forgot she had it, she squeezed the trigger on the gun and pumped a bullet straight into Melissa.

•   •   •

Things went a little haywire after that. Melissa crumpled onto the floor. The recoil from the shot knocked Mary Elizabeth onto her elegant fanny, as well. She also dropped the gun, as if it had turned red-hot in her hands. Maybe it had; I've never had occasion to find out. Reece Tolliver swooped in and scooped it up while Wayne yanked Mary Elizabeth to her feet. She was keening like a banshee the whole time he handcuffed her wrists behind her. "You have the right to remain silent," he began.

While all this had been going on, footsteps had been thundering up the steps outside and through the front door into the hall. They sounded like a herd of buffalo, but when they skidded to a stop in the doorway, they resolved themselves into just Derek.

He took in the situation at a glance; when you spend a rotation in an ER you probably learn to triage well. Blue eyes glanced off me, off Mom, off Beatrice—he showed no surprise, so he must have expected to see her—and determined that we were all upright and unharmed, even if we were huddled together like three sheep, crying and shaking. Then he looked down at Melissa, and paled. For a second, I saw shock and horror in his eyes, before he bit it back. He fell to his knees beside her. "Melly? Can you hear me? You're gonna be fine. Just stay with me."

Melissa's eyes were glazed with pain and her lips pinched, but she managed to lift her eyes to his, and his presence seemed to calm her a little. "Guess I got hit," she muttered, glancing down at her left shoulder, where a bullet hole oozed blood. It made me a little woozy to look at it, honestly, although I told myself that oozing was probably good. Pulsing would be bad; that'd mean the bullet had nicked an artery. But oozing didn't seem like too big of a deal.

"I need a compress," Derek muttered. He had already shed his coat, but it wasn't suited for soaking up blood. I offered him my knitted scarf, but he shook his head. "Too fuzzy. This'll be better." Hurriedly, he yanked the plaid flannel shirt over his head, followed by the T-shirt he wore under it. The latter he wadded into a ball, and pressed it against the wound in Melissa's shoulder. She sucked in her breath and turned a shade paler, which was something of an accomplishment right then. Still, after a second her eyes fluttered open and the corners of her mouth turned up. "Am I dying?"

Derek's voice was rough. "You'll be fine. I just have to slow the bleeding until the paramedics get here."

Behind me, I could hear Reece Tolliver on the phone with the 911 operator, explaining the situation.

"Thought I must be," Melissa murmured, through colorless lips. "Never figured I'd see this again." She lifted her other hand, sluggishly, to brush over Derek's chest.

Derek choked back a laugh—I'm pretty sure it was a laugh—and Melissa's eyelids lowered. When she was no longer looking at him, Derek's lips compressed into a tight line. The white T-shirt was slowly becoming saturated with bright crimson blood, and I could see the muscles in his arms stand out as he concentrated on keeping the fabric pressing down on the wound.

"I'll go get some towels," I said, and forced my legs to move out of the room and up to the second floor, where I gathered up all of Mary Elizabeth's fluffy white towels and headed back downstairs again, arms full.

Downstairs in the parlor, everyone was now standing around Melissa, watching Derek. Mom and Beatrice were huddled together, still clutching one another, while Wayne had marched Mary Elizabeth out to the squad car. I could see them through the window. Her lips were moving, although I'm not sure whether she was reaming him out or making a full confession, or maybe just muttering to herself.

Melissa looked in bad shape: deathly pale, colorless all the way to her lips, and her lovely face didn't look so lovely now, pinched with pain. I fell to my knees next to Derek.

"Here. I emptied the linen closet."

He glanced at me, eyes warming for a second. "Thanks, Avery. You OK?"

"Fine. Just shaken up. Let me know what you need."

"I can handle this," Derek said, relieving me of the fear that I'd have to do something to save Melissa's life. Not that I wouldn't have done what I could if I had to—she had saved mine—but I felt inept. "Take a couple of the smaller towels and fold them into a pad. Quickly, please. This is soaking through."

I nodded, my hands shaking enough that it was no easy task. "Here."

"Thanks." Derek pushed the sodden T-shirt aside and slapped the towel on Melissa's shoulder in its place. I closed my eyes, but not quickly enough to avoid a rather more in-depth look at the bullet wound than I had wanted.

"Gack!"

"Sorry, Tink." He glanced over, with a faint smile. "It isn't bad, really. I've seen a whole lot worse. The bullet probably hit a bone inside and stopped, since she's not bleeding from the back. The paramedics will get the bullet out and then bind it and treat with some antibiotics, and she'll be fine. They'll probably keep her overnight and let her go home in the morning. She won't be able to lift her arm over her head for a while, but with time, she'll be just fine. Except for a battle scar." He lifted the pad and assessed the blood flow. "It's slowing. And here are the paramedics."

Outside, the sound of sirens was coming closer.

"I love you," I said, impulsively.

He looked over at me, startled, and then he smiled. "I love you, too. Let's talk more about that later, OK?"

"OK," I said and sat back as the ambulance pulled to a stop outside.

—Epilogue—

"I really like that dress," Derek said, for what was at least the third, if not the fourth, time.

It was a couple of weeks later, New Year's Eve to be precise, and we were celebrating the occasion, as well as Kate and Wayne's nuptials, which had taken place earlier in the day.

The ceremony had gone off without a problem, as such things should. Kate had looked radiant in an oyster white satin dress with a matching jacket. It bore very little resemblance to a wedding gown, but it made her look like something out of a Golden Age Hollywood movie. Marilyn Monroe in *Gentlemen Prefer Blondes*, or maybe Rita Hayworth in *Gilda*, considering Kate's flaming copper curls. Noel would have been impressed, anyway, but alas, he and Mom had gone back to California. Noel had still been sniffing into his handkerchief at that point, his nose red and sore, and I didn't think the chances of getting him back to Maine for a visit were very good. At least not in the winter. He had invited us to California any time we wanted, though, and we were thinking about making a trip.

Mom had had a good time while she was here, scary incident with Mary Elizabeth and Melissa notwithstanding, and she and I both cried when we said good-bye at the airport. I had driven her and Noel back to Boston in my new car, and I had managed to look suitably surprised when they gave it to me, as if I'd had no idea it was coming.

Melissa had survived her encounter with the gun, just as Derek had promised, and had come out on the other end still kicking. She was actually here tonight, looking almost like her usual self in a lovely silk dress in her signature creamy color. I guess no one ever told her that wearing white to a wedding—even a second wedding, and even if the bride is wearing oyster—isn't proper. Not that anyone could really upstage Kate tonight, but Melissa gave it her best shot. The dress fit her like a glove, with a gossamer sort of jacket over the shoulders, which managed to hide Melissa's war wound while simultaneously making her look like a million bucks. Of course it screamed money and exquisite taste, and Melissa, in true Melissa style, had looked down at me along her elegant nose, curling her lovely lip, and told me I looked "cute." I had curtsied and said, "Thank you, Miss Melly," and had had the satisfaction of seeing her blush.

I was wearing the blue 1950s gown from John Nickerson's shop window, with the half dozen necklaces I had envisioned, the stiff black petticoats, the oversized fabric flower pinned at the waist—while I'd been at it, I'd made several matching black, white, and pale blue flowers to use in Kate's window boxes and as tiebacks on Kate's curtains, too—and a pair of strappy, black heels I had picked up at Filene's Basement in Boston when I took Mom and Noel to the airport. The fact that Derek had been particularly complimentary about my fishnet stockings with the seam up the back had done quite a bit to offset Melissa's snide comment. Obviously he didn't think I looked "cute." And I hadn't yet told him the stockings were attached to a garter belt.

"I really like that dress," he said, for what was at least the third, if not the fourth time, pulling me closer.

We were on the dance floor, swaying to the dulcet tones of Rod Stewart.

"Thank you," I murmured demurely, snuggling in. "You don't look too bad yourself."

If you ask me, Derek looks his best in faded jeans and a T-shirt—that is, if he's going to wear clothes at all—but Derek in a gray suit with a blue shirt to bring out the forget-me-not color of his eyes wasn't exactly hard on the eyes, either. It was the first time I'd seen him all dressed up in suit and tie, and he looked scrumptious. Good enough to eat, and then some.

"Any chance you need help getting out of it?" he inquired.

"The dress? Now?"

He chuckled. "Of course not now. We should at least wait until Kate and Wayne leave before we sneak off."

"That's what I was thinking," I said, my cheeks pink.

"If it's any consolation, I don't think it'll be too much longer. I'm sure they're eager to get off to the carriage house and be alone, too."

That "too" was quite nice, actually. So was the way his arms tightened around my waist.

I had taken Kate and Wayne across to the mostly finished carriage house in the morning, while Derek was inside the main house, helping to set up for the wedding. It had taken a whole lot of hard work, including a couple of all-nighters, to get at least the carriage house bedroom and master bath ready for occupation by New Year's Eve, but we'd managed. The final touches on kitchen, laundry, and downstairs powder room were still to come and would have to be done while Kate and Wayne were in Paris for their honeymoon, but instead of spending their wedding night in Kate's old room in the B&B, or in Wayne's apartment, where they'd be sharing their space with Josh, they'd get to spend it in their new love nest.

Kate had gasped with delight when she walked into the bedroom.

"My God, Avery, it's gorgeous. We'll be so happy here."

I looked around, pleased. I thought it looked pretty good, too, if I did say so myself, but it's always nice to have a happy customer.

"What's with all the empty frames?" she had asked, looking around her new bedroom.

I'd looked around, too, at the eight or ten empty black picture frames adorning the toile wallpaper. "They're for photographs. Make sure you take lots of pictures in Paris. I'll have them blown up, in black and white, and frame and mat them when you get back. That way you'll always remember your honeymoon and how you felt when you were there."

"Aww!" Kate said and leaned on Wayne. He put an arm around her.

"That's nice," he said, nodding to the copy of the photograph of William Ellis and Emily Thompson that I'd found in Dr. Ben's album. Now it was framed and sitting on one of the bedside tables next to a picture of Shannon and one of Josh. Who had decided to keep separate residences, by the way. At least for the time being. Josh would stay in his dad's apartment, and Shannon in her room in the bed and breakfast.

"It's just until I get a wedding picture of the two of you," I explained. "I figure we'll take that one downstairs and hang it near the initials, since you figured out a way to keep them. That way, when people ask, you can show them the picture. I made a copy of Emily's letter to Larry, too."

"Aww," Kate said again. She was getting sentimental, her eyes wet and her smile unsteady.

"I'm sorry this place isn't completely finished. We did our best, but it isn't easy to build a whole house in just two months, especially with everything that was going on. It'll be done by the time you get back from Paris, I promise."

"It's beautiful," Kate said. "Everything I always wanted.

I love the fluffy carpet, and the toile wallpaper, and the bed. Did you make the bed?"

"I . . . um . . . embellished the bed. It was a plain Shaker-style oak headboard when I started."

And now, it was a vision in antique white, with finials and scrollwork and a crackle finish.

"Are those skylights?" Wayne wanted to know, looking up.

I nodded. "We thought the shutters and window boxes would make them look more like windows. Once the snow melts, you can pull the shutters back—there's some kind of tool in the closet, and it hooks up there to hold them back—and retract the outside shutters as well, and then you'll have sunshine coming in. Or stars at night."

"Lovely," Kate murmured. "I love the paper flowers. They *are* paper, right?"

I nodded. "Definitely paper. Scrapbooking stuff. You don't want anything up there you'll have to water. It's a pain to do, plus it might drip and ruin the carpet. I could have gone with silk plants, I guess, but I had fun making them."

"They're beautiful," Kate said. "If I didn't already have a wedding bouquet, I'd take them down and use them this afternoon."

"That's sweet of you, but they can't really compare to your bouquet. I'm glad you like them, though."

"I love them. I love everything!" She left Wayne's side to throw both arms around me. "Thank you so much, Avery!"

"You're welcome," I said, hugging her back. "But it is the job you hired us to do, you know."

"This is above and beyond just doing your job, though. This is *perfect*!" She burst into tears.

Thinking about it now, out on the dance floor, I smiled. It was nice to see her so happy. It was nice to see *everyone* so happy, if it came to that.

"It's good to see Bea and Steve together again," Derek

said, as if reading my mind. "Bea looks happy, doesn't she?"

I nodded. Beatrice did look happy. As well she should. She had survived being kidnapped and held at gunpoint, and she had her husband back, all repentant and lovey-dovey. Steve had even decided to quit his high-powered job in Boston to settle down here in Waterfield—in our house on Becklea Drive, as it turned out—and start a small law firm right here in town. He was paying full price for it— the house—in spite of Derek's efforts to give him a family discount, which worked out great for us. Cora was thrilled, of course. Bea was thrilled, too; the only one who wasn't thrilled was Alice, but she'd just have to lump it and come up on the weekends.

"I think they're going to be all right," Derek said, look-ing at them across the dance floor. "Nothing like a brush with death to get one's priorities straight."

"Definitely."

Bea and Steve were back to discussing starting a fam-ily again, and that went a long way toward making Cora happy, too. I added, "I'm glad you and I weren't the ones in harm's way this time."

He smiled down at me. "Nice change, isn't it? Although you did have a gun pointed at you for a while there."

"I didn't get shot, though. That was Melissa, thank God."

"Yeah, well, it's too bad it went down that way—it would have been so much better if she could have just gotten the gun away from Mary Elizabeth, the way we'd talked about—but everything turned out OK in the end." His voice was serene.

"I wonder if Miss Melly would agree with you," I mut-tered.

At the time when Melissa appeared in Mary Elizabeth's parlor, I'd totally bought into the illusion that she just hap-pened to stop by, and that she would be more than happy to help Mary Elizabeth dispose of Mom, Beatrice, and me. Of course, as soon as Wayne and Reece Tolliver made their presence known, and then Derek appeared, I had realized that it had all been a setup. Melissa is nothing if not self-serving: As soon as she realized that the Stenhams were implicated in Gerard's murder—and she swore she hadn't known before that afternoon—she told the police everything she knew, and then offered to do whatever they wanted in order to avoid being charged as an accessory. She remembered that Ray had gotten a phone call from Randy in the evening the day Gerard died that had ended with Ray telling Randy to call back if he needed help later. And then she remembered the phone ringing in the middle of the night, and Ray telling her he'd have to go pick up Randy, who needed a ride home. One of the Stenhams—I'm not sure which—told Wayne where they had left Gerard's Lexus (at the train station in Bath), and Wayne found it there, with all of Gerard's things in it.

As for the next afternoon, when Beatrice was drugged and taken from Clovercroft to Mary Elizabeth's house, Melissa insisted that she and Ray had been together. Since Randy also had an alibi for that afternoon, it jibed with what Beatrice had said—that Mary Elizabeth had come to get her on her own.

All three Stenhams were incarcerated at this point. Mary Elizabeth had guilty to one count of first-degree murder, four of attempted murder, and one count of aggravated kidnapping, and would be spending the next seventeen years, if she lived that long, in the Women's Correctional Facility in Windham. Where, I had learned, they participated in the Pathways to Hope Prison Dog Project. Maybe Mary Elizabeth would be responsible for a couple of poodles. It would be only fitting. If I got the chance, I might even suggest it.

Ray and Randy, meanwhile, were serving much shorter sentences in local jails. Ray hadn't done much wrong as far as Gerard went, so he got off easy on that score. Mary Elizabeth had killed Gerard, and Randy had maneuvered the body down the stairs from the apartment, losing one of his cufflinks along the way, and had left it in the carriage house, while Ray had simply given his brother a ride home from the train station in Bath. So Randy was in jail on the charge of interfering with a corpse, while both Stenham twins had been charged with failure to report a crime and with perverting the course of justice. Ray would be out in a few months. However, he'd be returning to Waterfield without a girlfriend. It seemed to be a mutual decision: Melissa had decided she was above being involved with a common criminal, while Ray—along with Randy and Mary Elizabeth—was none too happy about her attempts to save her own skin by sacrificing theirs. They seemed to think she should have just let Mary Elizabeth kill all three of us and kept her mouth shut instead of interfering.

In addition to the whole murder issue, there was also the small matter of some financial shenanigans at Stenham Construction. Those were what Gerard had tried to blackmail the Stenhams about. Beatrice knew exactly what they were, of course; not because Gerard had told her, but because her background was in finance, and because Carolyn Tate's amateurish attempts at creative bookkeeping had been no problem for someone of Beatrice's intelligence and background. It was all a very tangled web: Carolyn Tate's death had been an unfortunate accident and nothing more, and Gerard's presence at Clovercroft had been entirely fortuitous, but now Beatrice was in a position to help the authorities wind up a whole slew of financial peccadilloes involving Stenham Construction. With any luck, once Ray and Randy were released from county lockup, someone else would slap them in irons over the financial misappropriations, and they'd stay gone for a good, long time.

Derek glanced across the room to where Miss Melly was sitting at a table, long legs elegantly crossed, watching the dancing. When she saw him look at her, she smiled brilliantly. He said, looking down at me, "She'll find someone else."

"I have no doubt she will," I answered. "Just as long as that someone isn't you."

He grinned. "I don't think you have to worry about that.

She couldn't wait to get rid of me the first time. I don't think she's gonna be too eager to try again."

I wouldn't be so sure, I thought, but I refrained from actually speaking the words out loud. "Oh, look," I said instead, "looks like they're getting ready for the garter ceremony."

At the front of the room, Kate and Wayne were on their way up on the stage, where a single chair was waiting for Kate. She sat down, demurely crossing her legs. Derek glanced at me. "What do you think? Should I try to catch the garter? We could have some fun with it later."

I smiled. "Not necessary. I've got on garters of my own this evening."

For a second he just looked at me, then he smiled. "Guess I'll just stick close to you, then."

"Please do." I snuggled into his side as we watched the proceedings. Kate's legs, like everything else about her figure, are magnificent, and there was lots of hooting and whistling while Wayne fumbled for the lacy blue garter Shannon had helped her mother pick out.

"At least he's using his hands," Derek remarked.

"What else would he be using?"

"Traditionally, the groom removes the garter with his teeth."

"Oh." I blushed.

Up on the stage, Wayne held Kate's garter aloft, triumphantly. All the single men, gathered in a group in front of the stage, started clamoring for the toss, while Derek looked indulgently on from the sidelines. "My money is on Josh," he said. "He's taller than anyone else."

Wayne shot the garter into the room. It flew across the heads of all the men, brushed Josh's fingertips, and smacked Melissa in the face. I snorted.

"Ooops," Derek said softly, turning aside to hide his twitching lips.

The bachelors dispersed, while all the single women gathered, waiting for Kate to toss the bouquet. "Go on, Avery," Derek said, giving me a gentle push. "You may have your own garters, but you don't have a wedding bouquet."

I looked up at him. "Do I want a wedding bouquet?"

His eyes were steady. "I don't know. Do you?"

My heart started beating faster. "I wouldn't mind a wedding bouquet."

He grinned. "Then this is your chance. Go get it."

"OK," I said, stepping out of his arms and forward to join the throng of single women in front of the stage. There are always more single women than single men at these things, and they're always rabid to win the bouquet toss. I've been mauled several times at friends' weddings. This time, my mind wasn't on the bouquet, though. It was on Derek and that searching look in his eyes and that rather pointed question he'd asked. Had he meant what it had sounded like he meant? Or was it just wishful thinking on my part?

I had just turned my head to look at him when something hit me squarely on the side of the head.

For a second I just stood there, stunned and blinking—and then I snagged the bouquet before it could lose its tenuous grip on my hair and fall to the floor. If it did, the other women would descend on it like a pack of vultures, and I'd get trampled. On stage, Kate was grinning and giving me the thumbs-up; looked like she'd aimed the bouquet directly at me.

Shannon grinned and patted my shoulder. "Congratulations, Avery. Go get him."

When I turned to look at Derek, Melissa had gone over to him, and she was whispering something in his ear. She faded away when she saw me coming, my hair straggling from the close encounter with the bouquet and my expression no doubt murderous.

"Great job, Tink," Derek said when I got closer. "Good catch."

"Yeah. What did she want?"

"To give me this." He lifted his hand, Kate's lacy garter dangling from his index finger.

"Wasn't that nice of her." My voice was flat, even in my own ears.

"She's not such a bad person," Derek said.

"In your dreams," I answered. And then thought better of it. "Never mind."

He just smiled. "Are you ready?"

"Ready for what?"

"You know the routine, don't you? Guy with garter—that's me, it seems—puts garter on girl with bouquet. That's you."

"Oh. Right." I stopped scowling after Melissa. "Now?"

"Can you think of a better time?" He grinned up at me, as he sank to one knee. "Lift your foot."

I braced myself with one hand on his shoulder—there had been quite a few champagne toasts drunk earlier—while I lifted one foot and felt him slide the garter up over the strappy shoe and the fishnet stocking, all the way above my knee. His hand lingered there for a second before he looked up at me. "You ready?"

"For what?"

"To go take it off again, of course. Along with the dress."

"Will there be teeth involved?"

"I wouldn't be surprised," Derek said, and showed me all of his.

"In that case, what are we waiting for?"

"I have no idea," Derek answered. In one smooth move he stood and scooped me into his arms, and then he carried me across the dance floor, between groups of cheering and pointing people, across the threshold and out into the night. I tossed the bouquet over his shoulder and into the crowd just before the doors closed.